W9-BZI-485

The Mapmaker's Daughter

The Mapmaker's Daughter

THE CONFESSIONS OF NURBANU SULTAN, 1525–1583

{A NOVEL}

Katherine Nouri Hughes

DELPHINIUM BOOKS

THE MAPMAKER'S DAUGHTER

Copyright © 2017 by Katherine Nouri Hughes

Grateful acknowledgment is made for permission to reprint the following
artwork: map of Ottoman Empire from William R. Shepherd, The Historical
Atlas, 1923. p. xix; calligraphic rendering of the name of Allah © Noor Alvi/
Shutterstock. p. 30; square lattice multiplication drawing from Matrakçı
Nasuh, Umdet-ul Hisab. p. 55; engraving of Suleiman the Magnificent by
Agostino Veneziano, 1535 .p. 70

First Edition

Jacket and interior design by Jonathan Lippincott
Family tree by John McAusland

Library of Congress Catalogue-in-Publication Data
is available on request.

ISBN: 978-1-88-328570-8

17   18   19   20   RRD   10   9   8   7   6   5   4   3   2   1

To Robert

I have written this book so that the sufferings of those who apply its contents may be at an end, So that they will feel no need for any other pilot as they cross the sea and travel the distances. . . . Be sure that no good may be expected of anyone who is satisfied with what he knows. To investigate is the task of the knowledgeable. . . . The man who searches out his way has reached maturity while the one who fails to do so has reached the end of the road. . . . The experienced man must . . . see what is necessary before it becomes necessary and when the time comes to act, he must not ask how. A seaman is a seaman only if he works with the heart of the matter and follows its lead.

—Piri Re'is, *Book of the Sea*

Contents

Preface

I came to Nurbanu because a great scholar and friend brought me. He explained that Nurbanu had been the most powerful woman in the Ottoman Empire when the Empire was at its zenith, yet very little was known about her. That "very little" captured me—the period in which she lived (most of the sixteenth century), her parentage (noble and illegitimate), the circumstances of her death. I was taken, too, by her name, since it's my own: *Nur* means light in Turkish; my maiden name, Nouri, means light in Arabic. This seemed more kinship than coincidence. My father—Iraqi by birth, and Christian—grew up as part of a privileged, vulnerable minority. It was a boyhood he barely spoke of. Only when I began to write about the lands of his past did he confide the details of his father's murder and what it felt like to watch it, and to become the man of his family at twelve. Nurbanu, in her way, had drawn my father out and closer to me.

I was also interested by a fact about Nurbanu's son, Sultan Murad III, noted in the *Encyclopedia of Islam*: "He argued at length against having his younger brothers killed at the time of his accession." Whom did he argue with, I wondered, and why? How was it the sultan lost the argument, and what happened to the person who won?

This is a work of fiction, as it has to be, given the scant facts about Nurbanu's life. It's written as a memoir because Nurbanu was clearest to me when she was getting on in years and had what she likely thought were all the facts her life was going to yield up; when she and I stood in the same relation to that life and, in our different ways, set out to consider it.

A word about the truth: the narrative and letters are invented by me. The images, reports, and poems are real and from the time—one of those poems translated by the same scholar and friend who made it possible to write this book at all. Not even words can convey my gratitude to Bernard Lewis, one hundred and one years old this year.

KNH
March 2017

Historical Context

THE OTTOMAN EMPIRE

The Ottoman Empire began in 1299 as a small state of warriors when its leader, Osman (reigned 1299–1326), broke from the Seljuk Turks. Before Osman, tribal leadership had customarily passed to the family's eldest male. When Osman's father died, though, Osman successfully challenged his uncle's claim to the throne. Power thereafter would pass from father to son. *Which* son was not specified, and a system of "open succession" evolved. Prowess, cunning, charisma all figured in the survival of the most fit successor, and Osman was succeeded by an expansionist son, grandson, and great grandson—Orhan, Murad I, and Bayezid I—who by the turn of the century controlled most of the Byzantines' holdings in Asia, had secured the Ottomans' place in Europe, and had taken the Empire east to the Euphrates.

The Ottomans spent the first decade of the fifteenth century engaged in a civil war between Bayezid I's sons, Musa and Mehmed, in which Mehmed finally prevailed and had his brother strangled. The nature, length, and violence of that conflict made an impression on the next generations. Mehmed I's successor, Murad II, disqualified his brothers by blinding them—a Byzantine practice the Ottomans emulated—and his successor, Mehmed II, not only eliminated his only brother (an infant) but took the precaution against civil war a crucial step farther. Mehmed II (r. 1451–1481), the Conqueror, made fratricide the law. He also—two years into his reign—rode his horse into Hagia Sofia and declared the end of the Byzantine Empire. Over the next two decades he extended Ottoman power as far west as the Adriatic and north to the Don River in Russia.

Mehmed the Conqueror's son Bayezid II (r. 1481–1512) took the throne after defeating his brother Jem, who was supported militarily by the Mamluks in Egypt and later the Knights of St. John in Rhodes—all to no avail. Bayezid's enduring contribution to the Empire was the order, following the Alhambra Decree in 1492, to evacuate Jews from Spain and give them safe haven in Ottoman lands. Toward the end of his long reign, Bayezid's sons Selim and Ahmet first rose up against each other and then threatened their father. Backed by the Janissaries, Selim I (r. 1512–1520) compelled his father's abdication. Selim I's conquest of Syria, Egypt, and large chunks of the Arabian Peninsula made the Ottomans guardian of Islam's holiest cities. Selim conspicuously did not adhere to his grandfather's code of succession. He forced his father to abdicate and then had him poisoned. And he had all his brothers and all but one of his four sons executed. The one he spared was Suleiman.

Known as the Magnificent in Europe and as Lawgiver in the Empire, Suleiman (r. 1520–1566) was acclaimed for his military prowess, valor, vision, and erudition. He took the Empire to the height of its greatness—revising and settling the *Kanun*—the so-called sultanic laws that complemented the Shari'ah; and he took the Empire to its farthest borders— west to the shores of Algeria and east to Baghdad. His last campaign was to Hungary, where he died in 1566 at the age of seventy-two.

Suleiman was survived by only one son, Selim II (r. 1566– 1574), who was known as the Drunk. It was on his watch that most of the Ottoman fleet was lost at the Battle of Lepanto, and it was upon his death that the bodies of the five young sons who did not succeed him accompanied him to his grave—a spectacle up until then carried out individually and not in public.

Selim II's peaceable and erudite successor, Murad III (r. 1574–1595), never led a military campaign but presided over construction of the most sophisticated astronomical observatory in the world and, with the help of his mother, Nurbanu, was able to strengthen the Empire's tenuous peace with Venice. His son, Mehmed III (r. 1595–1603), was the last sultan to be trained as a provincial governor and the last to enforce the law of fratricide.

The system of succession that replaced fratricide was imperial incarceration. "The cage" was a sumptuous pound inside Topkapi Palace, whose residents were not trained for leadership and were permitted relations only with sterilized concubines. The cage did succeed in perpetuating the dynasty—indeed, for another three centuries—replacing the enlivening fear behind fratricide with the ravaging safety of confinement.

THE VENETIAN REPUBLIC

The separateness of Venice determined from the start the city's customs, governance, and success, which was challenged by warriors, emperors, sultans, and popes from the fifth century on. For nearly a millennium it was the axis of maritime trade between Europe and the East. This accounted for its diplomatic corps, tolerance of foreigners, peerless navy, and exotic taste.

Venice evolved into the republic par excellence: a city governed by men dedicated to preserving and enhancing its freedom, wealth, justice, and peculiar stability. By the thirteenth century Venice had a constitution, and the ruling nobility had established a "locked" governing council—*la Serrata*—to which they alone could belong.

Though Venice did not engage in the earliest Crusades, when the Byzantine emperor slaughtered ten thousand Venetians living in Constantinople, Venice became the launch point for the Fourth Crusade, which sacked Constantinople (1204) and gained for the Republic a relay of ports down the Dalmatian coast and across the Aegean archipelago. The League of Cambrai (1508), a military alliance of the Holy Roman Empire, Spain, France, and the Pope, was Europe's successful response to Venetian expansion, accounting for the loss of many of its Adriatic ports and, at the Battle of Agnadello, many of its northern holdings.

Doge Andrea Gritti (r. 1523–1538) undertook an urban renewal project designed to restore Venetian preeminence, which was additionally bolstered by a booming publishing industry and a long era of extraordinarily gifted painters, including Veronese, Titian, and three generations of Bellinis. When the Ottomans took Cyprus in the last part of the century, Venice joined the Holy Alliance with Rome and Spain, which triumphed at Lepanto. The victory was short-lived, though, as the Republic's allies had no will to secure the gain with another offensive, and so Venice signed a peace treaty it had no wish for.

List of Characters

(in order of appearance)

MAIN CHARACTERS

Nurbanu, born Cecilia Baffo Veniero; wife of Selim II; mother of Murad III

Esther Handali, agent to Nurbanu

Violante Baffo, mother of Nurbanu

Sylvana Zantani, scion of the oldest family on Paros

Archangelo Piero Baffo, the grandfather of Nurbanu

Suleiman I, tenth sultan of the Ottoman dynasty

Nasuh, also known as Matrakci, imperial mathematician and mapmaker to Suleiman, Selim II, and Murad III

Mehmed, first son of Suleiman and Hurrem

Selim II, son of Suleiman and Hurrem; successor to Suleiman; husband of Nurbanu

Ismihan, last-born daughter of Selim II and Nurbanu; wife of Grand Vizier Sokollu Mehmed Pasha

Murad III, son of Selim II and Nurbanu; successor to Selim II

Safiye, favorite of Murad III; mother of Mehmed III

Mehmed III ("Little Mehmed"), son of Murad III and Safiye; successor to Murad III

Sokollu Mehmed Pasha, Grand Vizier to Suleiman, Selim II, and Murad III

Joseph Nasi, banker and protégé of Selim II

SECONDARY CHARACTERS

Hamon, Imperial Physician to sultans Suleiman, Selim II, and Murad III

Nicolò Veniero, father of Nurbanu

Jean-Baptiste Egnatius, Paduan classicist, tutor of Nurbanu as a child

Hurrem, wife of Suleiman; mother of Mehmed, Jihangir, Bayezid, Selim II, and Mihrimah

Suna, Head Scribe, Nurbanu's first teacher in the harem

Barbarossa, Admiral of the Ottoman fleet

Mustafa, son of Suleiman; half brother of Mehmed, Bayezid, and Selim II

Bayezid, second son of Suleiman and Hurrem

Mihrimah, daughter of Suleiman and Hurrem

Shah and Gevherhan, first- and second-born daughters of Nurbanu and Selim II

Taqi al-Din, Imperial Astronomer to Murad III

MAP of OTTOMAN EMPIRE, SHOWING
EXPANSION from the 15th to 17th CENTURIES

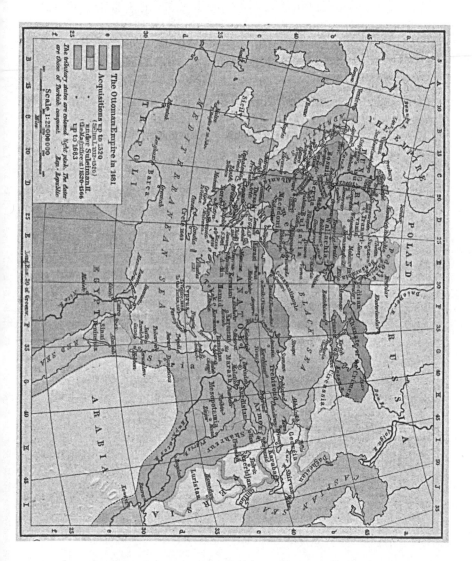

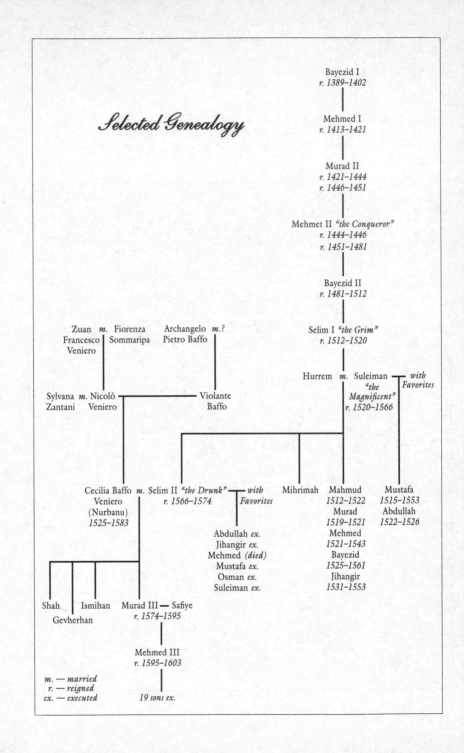

Selected Genealogy

Bayezid I
r. 1389–1402

Mehmed I
r. 1413–1421

Murad II
r. 1421–1444
r. 1446–1451

Mehmet II *"the Conqueror"*
r. 1444–1446
r. 1451–1481

Bayezid II
r. 1481–1512

Zuan   *m.* Fiorenza   Archangelo *m.?*   Selim I *"the Grim"*
Francesco   Sommaripa   Pietro Baffo   *r. 1512–1520*
Veniero

                                                    Hurrem *m.* Suleiman ——— *with*
                                                                  "the   *Favorites*
Sylvana *m.* Nicolò   Violante   *Magnificent"*
Zantani   Veniero   Baffo   *r. 1520–1566*

Cecilia Baffo *m.* Selim II *"the Drunk"* —— *with*   Mihrimah   Mahmud   Mustafa
Veniero   *r. 1566–1574*   *Favorites*   *1512–1522* *1515–1553*
(Nurbanu)   Murad   Abdullah
1525–1583   *1519–1521* *1522–1526*
                                   Abdullah *ex.*   Mehmed
                                   Jihangir *ex.*   *1521–1543*
                                   Mehmed *(died)*   Bayezid
                                   Mustafa *ex.*   *1525–1561*
                                   Osman *ex.*   Jihangir
                                   Suleiman *ex.*   *1531–1553*

Shah   Ismihan   Murad III — Safiye
Gevherhan   *r. 1574–1595*

                    Mehmed III
                    r. 1595–1603

m. — married
r. — reigned
ex. — executed   *19 sons ex.*

The Mapmaker's Daughter

Topkapi Palace

I have always been propelled by deaths. No matter how they've grieved and ground me down. Eleven of them were worst of all, and among those were the boys'. Those deaths are the heart of everything. The Empire's order, now and to come. The Sultan's power and prospect. Who I am, and who I thought I was.

It's time I weigh their cost and worth. That they had—or have, or might have—worth is the crux and the story. I will tell it as far as I can see. For this *is* about seeing, not remembering.

Let me see, then. Let me see.

In what's left of my mind's eye I see this: a terrace, two mutes, blue bowstrings laid out on a ledge. I see five pieces of death disguised as string, as silk, as blue—one for each boy according to custom and to reason and to law. Chaos is poison. Competition is chaos. Each is a source of civil war. Fatih Sultan Mehmed—the Conqueror—established the law to stem it. And the ulema gave him strong support, maintaining its accordance with the Shari'ah. *And to whomsoever of my sons the Sultanate shall pass, it is fitting that for the order of the world he shall kill his brothers.* That law has held us together; secured

3

our Empire; made us who we are—here in Topkapi, across the waters I look out upon, beyond Anatolia, beyond Baghdad, beyond Cairo, and Mecca, too. On warfields and peacefields, in harbors, tents, and caves, that law has kept order. It has lifted us up. And it has bowed us low, as well it might.

Let me see? I see I'm in bed burning with fever. I see my toes are beginning to turn black. I see blood under my fingernails. What is this? No mystery, I guess. I'm an aging woman back from a very long journey, and I've simply fallen ill. But just when I discover my son's wife has a heart! And my grandson has a son! Just when life opens wide as the world, I find myself sick from head to toe.

Hamon wanted to send for Murad the day it began. He's a worrier, Hamon. Who could blame him? He's a doctor, after all—Imperial Physician since before I was born. Plus, he's a Jew. Expelled with all the others from Cordoba in 1492. That's right—Hamon is *very* old. They got what they deserved, though—a safe haven *here*—because this dynasty is capable of wisdom. Very great wisdom. Imagine favoring Jews.

Still, I don't want to have Murad brought back from Edirne. He's hunting. He loves to hunt. He needs that time and entertainment. I just wish I'd seen him before he left. God, I do. I'm dying to thank him for his gift. It tells me so much that I didn't know—about him, about me, about what we have to look forward to. It's a whole universe, that gift. And I don't exaggerate—life is extreme enough. The journey I've just taken is quite a case in point. I encountered things I thought were gone from the world. I saw what I first laid eyes on and trusted and loved. I learned I should assume nothing about anyone—whether they're dead or alive, bad or good, wrong or right, someone else or me.

I know, too, that captivity *is* worse than death, as Esther always said, and as she's just troubled to remind me. She's like that. Not a qualm about rubbing things in. I told her about Murad's present and the joy it has released. And the turmoil.

Yes, I told Esther about that, too, this morning. Murad's gift has made apparent a whole new realm of regret. So much time has been lost to misunderstanding. To not knowing what has been true all along. And time is running out. Even if I'm less sick than Hamon thinks I might be, time is running out. I know it. I feel pressed. Very, very pressed.

I told Esther all of this and that I didn't know what to do about any of it, and her answer was, "Understand it." I raised my hand to give her a punch, but Esther is very fast. She grabbed it, held it to her chest, and daubed my blistering forehead with all the love in the world. "It's time you write," she said. "All of it." It was a command. And to see that it's carried out, she left, came back, and handed me a stack of parchments pungent as the calves they've come from. Damp as their little cadavers, too.

I'm not sure I can do this. See what I need to see in order to understand. Esther says I can. "You have nothing to lose," she said. I told her I did. I think those were our first lies to each other—ever. "Do it," Esther said. "Do it."

And so I shall. My mind and heart are stretched like the parchment itself, and, lying on my back, I see things as they're meant to be seen—sideways. The movement of the Bosporus. The passage of time. Space and hours, end to end. Not stacked but *stretched:* The length of time it *has* taken me to be where I am. The length of time it *will* take me to see. Day by day. I will.

I know this before I put down one more word, though: the living, not the dead, prescribe the order. And mothers are the key.

❧

There have been days of heaven and days of hell, and among them days that have changed life's course. I'll begin with the day I lost my mother. The day my grandfather showed his worth.

I am in Venice. It is 1537. I am eleven and sound asleep. My mother slips in, quiet as thread, and wakes me with her presence, her direction, her purpose and love. It is the Feast of the Ascension, and my mother has come to life. She says something about Paolo, our family's boatman, being ready since dawn. She opens the door to the balcony. There is the sound of wet rope slapping on stone. And a trumpet. My mother tells me her father's wish that we wear red—she and I. Blue outlines her slight frame as she comes close to kiss my forehead. Blue offers an account of her father's success with her and shows what she thinks of caprice. "You decide," she whispers. Then out she floats, and back I slide to dreaminess. Red, blue. Out, in. I listen to the covers' rhythmic hush and think about my breath making the world move, and a flutter augments the air. I believe an angel appears. Its wings are familiar, more flesh than feather, and on the banner floating above the angel, a message appears as if by virtue of my gaze. None of this surprises me. *Choose*, the rippling fabric says. I can see only that word. A feast day message, no doubt. It is the Ascension, after all. Christ is risen of His own accord. *Anything* could happen. That is the point. That He has done that unimaginable thing. And that we know that He has. I get up, and the day begins.

My mother shuns public displays of all kinds, but *this* one—the day that commemorates Byzantium's recognition of Venetian supremacy—is her one exception. The ceremony reenacts the marriage of Venice to the Sea, and she loves it—probably because this is a marriage that makes sense. My mother's blue dress is billowy as a bride's, and her look could have inspired Crivelli. Her almondine face set with acceptance. Her large-lidded, knowing eyes. Her exceptional fingers. I wear blue to mirror her. But I don't wish to resemble her, beautiful as she is. And I don't know why. Not then, I don't.

"There you are!" my grandmother gurgles, grabbing fistfuls of skirt. She holds out her arms like railings for the attendants to grab, and as she settles herself into our family's feast day gondola, my grandfather takes his own steps into thin air and, unaided, lowers himself into his favorite possession that isn't a book. Sparing myself a command from him, I speed across the slick stones while my mother advances in her own way, like a piece of silk or water.

"What do you think?" my grandfather is saying to his fingers. He is stroking the lynx that's all over his chest. I hop on the vessel.

"Very grand," I assure him. The voices of castrati fill the air. My attention is on the cloudy water we've begun to slice— we, the occupants of that lacquered hull. "Avanti," Nonno calls out. He's agitated. "Subito, Paolo. Subito!"

"Calm down," my grandmother says helpfully. She pats my grandfather's collar. "You will see him."

And he does—just as Doge Andrea Gritti is emerging from the basilica on his canopied litter. Scepter in hand, essentially regal, the Doge *is* God's intermediary, after all—though not so trusted he is allowed to even open a letter in private—ah no: checks on power in Venice are legion, warranted, effective. Still. If there is any doubt about the Doge's backing by God, one need only consult his retinue: the Ducal Sword Bearer, the Republic's Senate, the full diplomatic corps. Nonno stands in homage as we all process toward the baubled barge into which Andrea Gritti climbs. The Doge is clad entirely in gold: velvet puffy pants, dragon-scaled waistcoat, buckle set with a ruby the size of a clam. Gold, gold, and more gold. And on his head, atop the red linen cap that covers his ears and brow, is the curved golden camauro. He looks like a bird that's become a plant.

There he is that scorching festa noon, empowered and enthroned as boats amass by the thousands, waiting for him to lead the way. The barge's gold-painted bowsprit, *Justice*, juts her breasts eastward past the Lido to where the lagoon meets the sea. "This is our city at her best," my grandfather proclaims of the entire scene. The staves of his own jutting chest bend with pride.

From every parish, citizens are coming out, many of them, too, draped in marten, miniver, and lynx. Encumbered, expectant, they row in the Doge's wake. Then they form many circles around where he drops anchor to propitiate the sea with holy water, a ring, and a vow, renewed each year. *Desponsamus te mare, in signum veri perpetuique domini.* We espouse Thee, O sea, as a sign of true and perpetual dominion. I can see the tautening of the Doge's old neck as he lifts his voice above the slap and clatter of waves and oarlocks.

From one moment to the next, the wind changes direction. It scuds across the canal as the boats fan to right and left of the Doge's, and it catches one of the vessels, the Carusos', from starboard. It fills its thick sail and makes the boat jibe—always a huge motion and, in this case, a violent one owing to the sudden shift. The boom slams from left to right, and because all eyes but mine, it seems, are on the holy beaker, only I see Carlo Caruso, a boy my age, thrown over the stern. He goes over back first. Black velvet pooling where it was never meant to be.

"A boy's gone over," I call out, getting to my feet and lunging forth. My grandfather yells at me to sit down. "*Carlo.* Carlo Caruso has gone over," I yell back, scrambling ahead.

My grandfather's lion head snaps left and right to see what I've seen. Then Carlo's hand reaches out from the water to grab the rim of the boat. "He's *there.*" I am set to dive.

"Cecilia!" my mother cries out.

For one second, there is Carlo's pleated cap, soaked and askew. But then the boats on each side of him, his own and a larger one, clap together hard, about where his hand is. The last thing I see of it is a palm without fingers. My grandfather has covered his eyes for the collision, and he keeps them covered as though he is trying to understand a problem, as though there is nothing to see or do. "Hold on to her," my mother orders Paolo as she pushes on his shoulder for thrust.

"I'm going, too," I yell.

My mother's eyes are on the Carusos' boat. "You stay there, Cecilia," she commands. In an instant, she is on the boat next to ours, on the one next to that—they're rafted tight in solidarity and respect for the occasion—and then on the stern of Carlo's boat where his father, Jacopo Caruso, who once proposed marriage to her, is turning in circles like a dog trying to find where his son is. My mother dives in, blue and gold, skirt and sleeves.

My grandmother stands up, draws a breath from the bottom of the lagoon and shrieks, causing my grandfather to open his eyes and to finally watch and *see*.

Paolo holds me fiercely. My mother is down. And still down. And still. My grandfather looks on. No one says a word.

The first head to emerge is Carlo's—his eyes open and milky. Then my mother's breaks the surface. She is coughing and tangled in Carlo's clothes and holding him around the chest.

"Thank God," my grandmother cries out when she sees her. My grandfather closes his eyes again and bows his head. He makes the sign of the cross with his thumb on his lips.

Carlo's father needs help to haul in his dead boy. When he is in the boat the broken nobleman takes him in his velvet arms, falls to the floor and rocks him, screaming like a woman.

Then all eyes are on the water again to where my mother is, or should be.

"Where is she?" My grandmother is waving her arms wildly. "Violante!"

"*Mamma*," I scream and pray. "*Mamma!*"

"Get her," my grandfather commands Paolo, as he takes me by the upper arm—his hand encircling and crushing my arm—exactly as the only other person who would ever again hold me forcibly will do four months later. Never mind the different motives. The gesture is the same. A grip that announces death. "Go. Go!" my grandfather yells at Paolo. Paolo grabs

9

the cork belt stowed for emergency, leaps onto the boat next to ours, and dives in. My grandfather watches. He does nothing.

By that time, the Doge himself is aware there is trouble. His *bucintoro* is being rapidly oared clockwise, and he is moving toward the prow to see for himself what has happened. Others row close to the Caruso boat, which is rocking sharply in time with Jacopo Caruso's doubling grief. Beside it Paolo keeps coming up for air, again and again, each time without my mother. "Mamma," I am crying, my arm weakening in my grandfather's alarming grasp. Still, he does nothing.

"Find her," Doge Gritti calls out to nearby crew. They tear off finery and boots, they grab flotational gear—bundles of reeds, cow bladders pumped with air—and jump in the lagoon. Its just-quelled waters are chopped and foamed from all the arms and sputtering mouths. No one can swim. They're just doing their best.

My grandfather calls out, "*Look.*" He lets go of me to point to the Doge. Gritti has torn off his gold hat and is struggling to rid himself of his huge belt and is about to jump in when my mother's head, fanned with skirt, breaks the surface not far from Gritti's barge. One of his men catches hold of her. Strapping his arm across her chest, he frees her from her misplaced garments. Then he looks with horror upon her face.

Of my mother's funeral I remember only the ride out to Murano. We each go alone. My mother is first in our everyday gondola. She is in a box that appears to be part of the hull that carries it, but it's not. It's a coffin. Shiny, black, sealed without a seam. I wonder if my mother's eyes are open in that black place. They were open when they hauled her onto the deck of the Doge's barge. I wonder if she saw him even though she was dead. I wonder if she knew that the Doge was bowed in his glory over her, stunned, clasping her hand between his own. He had admired her. He'd had reason. I wonder if she can see me from inside her coffin. Can she see that I'm alone with Paolo? Does she know I refuse to ride with my grandfather? That her mother won't attend her funeral at all? Does she know what sort of parents she had? Can she help me understand what is happening? Make stop the uncomprehending panic of knowing she is dead? Not that I believe that she is dead. I do not. Her hand was on my forehead one day before. Her magic voice—always saying what was true—was alive. Now it is not. Now it is gone, and it is worse than gone. It is gone forever. I have no idea what that means. I had no time to understand any of this before it happened. No time to prepare. As though that were possible.

ॐ

And the second death. Nine weeks and three days after my mother's. I am back on Paros, and it is my birthday. Sylvana's—her fifty-fourth—was the week before. Birthdays have been dear to us all the years we've lived together. Sylvana, my mother, and I have celebrated them as though each belongs to the three of us. To this day, I feel I have three birthdays. While some, over the years, have been no cause for celebration, *that* one, my real, true twelfth, is the worst. My birthday without my mother.

"A day like this should not exist in the world," I tell Sylvana. "There should be no such thing as a child with a dead mother. My birthday is over."

"Certainly not," Sylvana says. "We will honor it, this evening—in Naoussa. I have something special for you. Furthermore, your birthday will be honored always. I will make sure. And you know what I think about *always*. Rare as an eclipse." Succinct by nature, Sylvana also knows her stars, the workings of the heavens.

The day I was born was the best day of my mother's life. That's what my mother told Sylvana while she watched Sylvana cut the cord that joined us. Sylvana says she'd never seen such an easy birth. No screaming. No agony. Just me slipping

11

into her ready hands—which placed me in my mother's happy arms. Sylvana tells me these things on the birthday I have no wish to celebrate. She doesn't want me going through life hating a day I've always loved.

The heat has closed in very tight this morning, and we've come down early from the little place Sylvana built up in the hills after my mother and I went to Venice years before. We take the plain slowly but still arrive before noon at my father's castle on the north coast's harbor. Naoussa harbor is a gift of nature. Paros's Golden Horn, you might say: a crocodile-shaped peninsula protecting it on one side; the shoulder of the island shielding it on the other. That is where my father's house is—in the lee of that shoulder. And that is why we don't see what is coming.

If we were at his other residence, the east-facing castle on the cliff at Kefalos, we would see from a distance what is on its way. If we were even at Marpissa or Pounta, we would see. But we aren't. We are at Naoussa in a howling hot wind, and we don't notice the thirty-six galleys, their decks mounted with guns, their prows fitted with rams. We don't hear the thousand oars grinding in their iron locks. We don't see a fleet of warships.

Sylvana and I are on the terrace mindful only of each other and of the surprise she is going to give me that evening and of the pleasure of being together—for we have been separated for a very long time. Seven years.

I have been back on Paros since June. I have found a way to think about my mother without feeling I am choking. I've told Sylvana exactly what happened. How my mother died; what my grandfather did and did not do. I've also told her what I studied and learned in Venice; the churches I went to, and why. I've told her about Egnatius.

Sylvana has told me about her life and about Paros since my mother and I left it. She's taken me to the house she has built on the hill. She's told me about the crops she's put in and about the siroccos that whipped across from the Levant this past spring and made the animals crazy for weeks. She has also spoken about her past—about her family and patrimony; about my father, whose family was close to hers; about his achievements and about the losses and confusions he sustained. "It is important, to the degree possible," she's said solemnly, "that children know their parents." She pronounced this as an expert not a seer. I have not told Sylvana what my grandfather revealed to me on this very subject the last day he and I were together. I intend to, though. Once I understand it. If I can understand it.

And so, Sylvana and I are done with questions. Our great happiness is to say nothing as we sit in the sun.

I have been reading and put my book aside. Sylvana is sewing, putting on a button. I am marveling, as I always do, at how it works: the needle's diving into the heel of a sock or a cuff and coming up, every time, in exactly the right, tiny spot, something so very subject to error always coming out right. It is as though she is allowing the needle to sew. To be a needle.

Sylvana is facing the water and the sun, and I am facing her. Salt spray has misted her old, beautiful face and gotten in her eyes. She closes them, but she doesn't stop sewing. "How do you do that?" I ask.

"Do what?" She is squinting. I point. "Oh. This." A faint harrumph acknowledges and dismisses her skill. "I don't do anything."

Inside the house something clatters. Sylvana blinks fast. "Probably the flowers." I picked her a vaseful that morning. More clatter, closer. Then a hand, immense and gloved, floats down on Sylvana's shoulder. The hand is all I can see. The rest is in the black shadow of the doorway. I know from how Sylvana lays down the mending and from the spell-like way she keeps her eyes on mine that she is gathering herself for something fierce, and when the "rest" steps into the light, Sylvana sees confirmed on my face the worst fear of every Christian man, woman, and child in the Mediterranean. That hand isn't a warning. It is confirmation. Our island is under siege.

"Do not move," Sylvana says to me, grasping the hand on her shoulder, pressing herself against it. She rises and turns. I stand, as though I'm tethered to her. "*Capritta*," she says, my pet name sounding the alarm. Sylvana is facing an oxlike marauder whose beard does not conceal a look of demonic pleasure. She thrusts her arm back and lands her fist against his groin. Without a pause he strikes her in the jaw and knocks her to the floor. Her head hits last, like the tail of a cracked whip, and it makes a thick, wet noise that takes a long time for me to stop hearing.

It is over.

"What have you done to her?" I scream, lurching toward Sylvana heaped in her purple skirt. Her eyes are open, and she cannot see me. I know it. Before I can throw myself on her to gather her up and make her be alive, the gloved fingers are inside my collar yanking me back, snapping me around, gagging and binding me—all one gesture. The attacker has done it a thousand times. I can tell.

He loads me on a cart, locks me in the chainlike clutch of a man whose lap is hard. Something bad, I know, is against me in his middle—something that connects to his mouth, open on my ear, and to his heaving breath, and to the sharp donkey sounds he makes as he clutches me and the cart pitches over rocks and ruts on the road to Kefalos. That I can't scream Sylvana's name is the worst part of all. Nor can I move, but I can see. Women being hauled from their houses. Churches being stripped bare—carts heaped with their contents—reliquaries, chalices, icons of Christ and His Mother. And I see the children. The ones coming down off Lefkes and Prodromos, the ones coming over the middle hills from Parikia, and the ones from Piso Livadi and Logaras on the coast. Boys and girls, little and big—children of fishermen, quarrymen, and farmers—hundreds of them, screaming in the wind as they stumble across the plain to the coast where the Ottoman standard can be seen flying atop the masts of three dozen warships.

I am handed over at the shore and swung into a tender by men wearing rings with huge colored stones. They have jewels on their ears, knives at their waists. They wear turbans. These are not sailors! They don't look able to love the sea or the wind or a ship. They are unctuous, heedless, haters of Christians, and especially Christian children.

I know who they are. I have heard from my grandfather when I lived in Venice. All my life, Turkish corsairs have been ravaging the Mediterranean coasts—off Spain, France, and Barbary, up the Adriatic and down the Aegean. They have a mighty leader. I have heard that, too. He is feared and famous everywhere for doing the unexpected every time—defying winds, tides, seasons; raiding coasts with unthinkable daring and force. Barbarossa, he is called—for his red beard. He has turned a collection of ships into a navy, and the Sultan has honored his effort by making him Admiral of the Fleet.

Their number is terrifying—twenty thousand, it turns out. They have come from Corfu, which, I'd learn many years later, they've nearly destroyed but failed to take. Enraged by their defeat, they've pressed down hard, around the Peloponnesus and up, taking Ios and Patmos, Skiros and Naxos, which is directly across the strait. They have washed across the islands like a tide, and now they are swarming on *our* hills, capturing the children of Paros, rowing us across water we know and love and swim in, out to the windowless holds of black and red warships gleaming in the sun.

The galley I am rowed out to looms like a cliff, and from a long row of fist-sized openings halfway up the hull come other voices of misery: those of the most unfortunate among men—captives from previous ventures of the Ottoman fleet, enslaved rowers sweltering below board, waiting for God knows what—maybe for the relief of rowing.

I don't even wish for a choice. With no one left to my name,

I wish only to be dead. But that is not my captors' plan. I am hauled up in a hemp sling that swings madly above the water, hitting the hull hard as the ship pitches on the whipped-up sea. "Veniero," my captor yells from the rowboat. "Veniero," he says again, making a horn of his hands, then pointing to my father's castle. I am throwing up before I reach the deck. I'm gagged, choking on vomit. The deck is blistering hot. I believe I am about to die. Suddenly it is no longer what I wish for.

An old man is there—waiting, apparently. His face is taut and warted, his orange beard is meager. His turban is darkened with sweat above his brow. He signals a minion to remove my gag. I cannot stop throwing up. Barbarossa's eyes water as he watches the spectacle of my sickness and, when it is done, he hands to the minion the rolled-up chart he has clamped under his armpit, slides the tip of his knife under the thick panes of hemp, and frees my hands and feet. Then he takes me under the arm and pulls me to my feet, not gently but definitely with care. This enrages me—the taking care with someone he's just stolen—as though one thing makes the other less wrong or as though there are rules of conduct for stealing people. It makes me so mad it pulls me back together and gives me a force I can feel even before I use it to crouch and, with the crown of my head, ram him in the crux of his body—right where Sylvana struck the raider she tried to fell. Then he *isn't* careful. Barbarossa's hands snap around my skull as though a trap has sprung. He holds my head there like a part of him, and I beat furiously against the back of his legs. With one motion, he curls his hands, solid callus, around the tops of my arms, presses me farther into him, and muscles my face up the front of him till we are eye to eye.

On the deck, men all around are shifting in their stinking boots muttering compliments about their commander's might. He puts me down. I take a step back. He looks as though he hasn't slept in a year, and he probably hasn't, with the kind of dreams he would have. He draws his knife and points it toward the cross on my chest. I lean forward to connect him with it, to make it easier. "Kill me," I yell at him, very surprised by what I've just said. He closes one eye and keeps the other on my chest. "Kill me, too!" I say, exaggerating with my mouth so he'll understand. But he doesn't understand. He narrows an eye and consults the others.

"Tchsk," they all say at once, tilting their chins up.

Barbarossa indicates a line around my neck with the tip of his knife, slips it under my necklace—just as he slipped it under the hemp—and jerks it hard. The gold holds firm. I yank free of his assistants and undo my necklace. "Keep it!" I say thrusting it toward him. He takes it with his knife. "What have you done with the other children?" I wave wildly toward the tenders returning to shore for second and third loads. "Where have you put them?" is the last thing I say before two men from behind bind my hands again, yank a rag around my mouth, and haul me to an unvented cabin on the main deck just short of the stern.

Of what happens in that hideous closet over the next four days at sea—I believe it is four—I can say only this for sure: I am alone in heat that should have killed me. I am fed horribly, but fed. And, with nothing but time to think, I reckon that if God would take my mother and Sylvana—the best people in the world and the ones I love the most—and take them one right after the other in the ways He has, then He cares nothing for me. I am cut from all that's ever held me in place. I don't have any reason to want to be alive.

This is how I endured the journey. And it is how I mourned Sylvana. By wishing and praying to be dead myself. And I see now, lying here—sick though hardly dying—that included in that wish was my grief for my mother. For being back in Sylvana's world and in her care that summer allowed me to put off that grief. To put it off until I was a mother myself. And to put it somewhere awfully deep. I wonder if this is how all children grieve—by harboring the death and wanting it to be their own.

Tuesday, November 8

Adjusting to the light hurt. I wasn't dragged into it, though. On the last leg of the journey, the door of the cabin was simply unlocked. I wondered if it was a trap and stayed crouched in my filthy corner. Then I considered the meaning of *trap* under the circumstance, got up, and ducked into the open. God had not stopped time to avenge my being captured. The day was bright, the sea dark, the waters calm. Barbarossa was at the helm, dagger in hand, looking at the ships behind us. He turned around, slapping the flat of the blade against his palm.

He was washed, clean, and he'd changed his turban. Around his neck was a long and thick chain of gold. Suspended from it was a gigantic red stone—far too big to be a ruby, I thought, but that is what it turned out to be.

"Recovered from your rampage?" I said, not caring if he understood my language.

"Tchsk," he hissed. The sound seemed to make his head jerk. He sheathed his knife. "Veniero," he said, as though my father's name were a command. He straightened the weapon on his waist.

"What's happened to the other children?" I said, pointing to the galleons in our wake. "Are there children on those ships, too?" I emphasized each word. But Barbarossa had shifted his attention. He was looking past me, interested by a slim wedge of gray beneath a low white cloud. Landfall.

Come here, he indicated with the snap of the chin that commanded both captives and crew. I followed him forward to where his men were moving into action, trimming sails and heading closer to the wind. From below began the clatter of oarlocks. Then the groans of the captives and the fiendish jingling of their shackles. At last, in a higher register, came the sounds of the children. Barbarossa made a gesture toward the bow, where we were heading. He was pointing to a black slash that was becoming visible through the humid haze. It was the wall of Byzantium.

I knew where I was. I was astonished.

We headed into the wind. Sails snapped and luffed. A hundred oars shot up, then down in a slicing thrust. We took the walls to port—first the sea wall, then the land wall that climbed a hill, on the top of which, coming into view, was a red mound. Something huge. "Yes. I *know* this place," I said. Of course I knew. I had read it in Virgil. "I know what's around this point. And I know where this waterway leads. To the clashing rocks. The ones defeated by Jason." There it was—Europe and Asia, edge to edge. And between them, the mightiest waterway on earth.

Where the sea joined the Bosporus, fish were everywhere—luminous arcs in the air, black blades in the water—mackerel, bonito, and bluefish so thick that men scooped them in their hands. Stags, boar, a giraffe roamed the shores; white-bottomed black birds streaked the air. On the finest harbor in the world the shadow of the wind was visible. And rising up on the Golden Horn's crown was a palace as irregular and excellent as the waterways it commanded. Topkapi. I had heard of that, too.

Barbarossa made his way to the bowsprit. He stood, gesturing landward like a lion rampant pawing the air as we rowed into the Golden Horn. Behind us in closing formation was a fleet of booty including—I realized only then from the unearthly howls—horses. We tacked into a harbor crammed with ships, slid into the Admiral's berth, and dropped anchor swiftly. An exit plank was swung up at a sickening angle. A slender, nimble person with shiny black skin clambered up the board. A woman dressed as a man? A man as a woman? I couldn't tell. Barbarossa called out something I couldn't understand except for one word—again, my father's name. He signaled for the unlading to begin. The black person put a finger to my back, and I was the first one off, leading the way deeper into an unrealness more vivid than even the ship's or the journey's.

Another indeterminate creature signaled for me to stand near and still. I looked down at my sandals and realized I was not connected with anywhere else. Those sandals should have stood for where I was from, but they didn't. They stood for nothing but what they were. It was the first inkling I had that my past was gone. I felt something trapped in my chest, something with a life of its own that wanted to get out. I was surprised that I didn't cry.

Barbarossa's most valuable booty began to stagger down the plank. Boys and girls who had already ceased to be children. Little ones who'd never been out of the sight of their mothers; older ones like me; all of them, staring like old people or people who couldn't cry anymore. There must have been a hundred of them, and no one would ever know how many had died at sea or were unable to walk off on their own that morning.

A party of Negroes, black as the stones on the shore, glided down a hill blanketed with flowers. They, too, were tall and slender, clad in white vests over blue tunics buttoned high under their baby-like chins. Recoiling at the smell of the children, their leader began the winnowing. Girls here, boys there. Older girls here, younger ones there. He snapped out his finger like a switch and directed me to his right. He directed a short girl to his left. One by one, the rest of the tall girls came with me. Then we were separated again. Those with missing teeth on one line; the rest of us on another. They assessed our profiles, noted the proportion of our features with a notched rule, gauged the clarity of our eyes, the quality of our hair. The efficiency of the dividing was alarming. "What are you *doing*?" I pushed a black and pink hand from my face. The eunuch put his finger to his lips and drew it across his own throat. It was advice.

Murmuring like fountains, shuffling, the eunuchs herded us in our groups up a hill thick with jasmine and heavy with the scent of jasmine past branches bent to the ground with apricots and lemons, and past the ramparts of the Sultan's palace and past the biggest holy place on earth—the red mound I'd seen from Barbarossa's deck: Hagia Sophia. *Ashadu an-la ilaha illa Allah, Ashadu unna Muhammadan rasulullah.* From over the hill before us and from across the Golden Horn behind, a voice cut the air. It was a crazy-sounding voice. A chant. *Ashadu an-la ilaha illa Allah, Ashadu anna Muhammadan rasulullah.*

The call to prayer continued as we stumbled past an arena with two obelisks—the Hippodrome—and made our way down a long cobbled road. As the Word echoed its last, we reached a vast and faceless structure—a prison. It had to have been. Muffled cries were seeping out.

A pair of black eunuchs took us in. They wore dresses and small turbans, and the creature with some life left in his eyes touched my shoulder and extended his chin in what seemed solidarity. He steered us through a maze of dim corridors, through a courtyard where more like them—long-legged, squinting, perched on hassocks—were eating sweets, and on to where the women were, and *there* was something to dread.

The Superintendent of the Old Palace and her deputies were waiting for us. They wore silver hats swirled with pearls and topped with scarves that made the women look like peaks of waves until they showed their faces. Blackened lips, blackened eyes, black lines drawn between their eyebrows. They looked like storms. They *were* storms.

The bejeweled and manly leader started with me, applying her hands to my not-large breasts. I pushed her away, she slapped the side of my head—not hard but with meaning—and resumed. I watched in disbelief as she cupped my breasts in her palms, assessed their weight, then took my nipples between her thumbs and fingers and rubbed them back and forth. Other women were doing the same thing with the other girls, and there was no doubt from their fluttering eyes that these warped monitors relished their assignment. All but three of them were led away then, and when the Superintendent ordered us to disrobe, while the other girls consulted each other with looks, I obeyed fast. I removed everything I had on—every visible vestige of Paros—where I'd awoken in my own bed five days before. I stood at attention before her.

I was handed over then to the Mistress of the Baths, who was not manly, not jeweled, and not clad, except for a wad of cloth looped around her haunches. This woman was a monument of fat. Thighs and throat rounded by it, nipples made smooth and extended from it; her age and origin encased in flesh, sumptuous and satisfied. She pointed me to an open spot among the girls who were stretched out naked on an octagonal plinth. I inserted myself facedown on the marble and listened to my heart thump against the steamy stone till it was my turn to be bathed. An attendant seated me in front of her, spanned me like Colossus, lodged my face between her breasts and began to scrub.

On the other side of a curtain examinations were underway. Girls were coming out crying, heaving. I was shown in. The examiner wore a white robe, wide open, and sat on a stool. She was naked underneath, her feet flat on the floor, her wet legs veed out, and I was positioned between them. She put a palm to my belly, a palm to my back, rose to her feet and slid her front hand down. I snapped away, but someone—I'd thought we were alone—grabbed my arms from behind and held me, hard. The examiner's face was very close to mine as she slid a finger into me, into a place I didn't know existed. Deep in her finger went. Then deeper. Then back and forth until she was on something in there—a nut, it seemed, with soft spikes that throbbed then ached then boiled and made my knees weak and made the examiner's eyes flutter and—crack—a hand was between her face and mine hitting her head so hard she fell backward, jerking her crooked finger from that depth so that it sliced its way into the open with me all over it. Sylvana had told me only a short time before to expect blood from somewhere in there one day. But nothing like that. The woman who caused it was hauled out of there fast. I never saw her again, ever. And the Superintendent—who had hit her—was holding me in her arms, calling out something, when everything went black.

꩜

It was a Nubian boy—the one with the not-dead eyes—who saved me. His name was Sumbul, and he knew a thing or two about bleeding. He was nine when he'd been castrated—taken from his home in the night and carted from Abyssinia to Alexandria. They'd laid him on a stone slab and pinioned him so tight he thought he'd die. It was the blade that nearly killed him, though—wielded by a Christian, according to custom: a little implement shaped like a sickle with which one of the men sliced off Sumbul's sex. All of it. They put a metal pipe in the opening left behind, bound it with paper soaked in water, and for two days kept Sumbul bound, blocked, and in agony. On the third day, since he wasn't dead, they took the linen off, removed the pipe and let the urine pour forth. They permitted Sumbul to rest for a day before they shipped him here for auction. All this, a few months before I lay on a plank in the Old Palace, nearly gone myself from bleeding—

which was what had caused the Superintendent to summon Sumbul.

I remember his face above mine as he stroked my cheek. I remember the white disks of his eyes against his black skin and his pink, soft lips and his saying something quietly to me. I didn't know the language, but I knew he was kind from the way he slid his hands under my back and the way he pushed the strips of linen underneath me and wrapped them up and over the ripped fork, tighter and tighter until I thought he might tighten me into something that wasn't a girl anymore.

The Bab-iHumayun is the imperial entrance to the Imperial Palace. Above the gate is an engraved invocation in Arabic script—letters that look like lovers and warriors until you can read them. They spell out Mehmed the Conqueror's prayer:

> With the aid and approval of God, the foundations of this auspicious castle were laid and its parts joined together solidly thereby strengthening peace and tranquility at the command of the Sultan of the Two Continents and the Emperor of the Two Seas, the Shadow of God in this World and the Next, the Favorite of God between the two Horizons, the Monarch of the Terrestrial Orb, the Conqueror of the Castle of Constantinople, the Author of the Conquest, Sultan Mehmed Khan son of Sultan Murad Khan son of Sultan Mehmed Khan. May God render eternal his empire and exalt his residence higher than the brightest stars of the firmament. . . .

Three days after I'd walked down Barbarossa's plank, I was packed into a very large stand of captured girls outside that gate. "You are entering a palace of order and tranquility," someone called out over our heads. It was possible to believe there might be order ahead. But tranquility? Never. The terror of the bleeding crowded out the greater terror of being where I was, which was in Constantinople, in Topkapi Palace on the verge of presentation as booty to the sultan himself. That was what the black eunuch was whispering as a phalanx of captured boys followed by what must have been a hundred Barbary horses followed by the captains of forty, fifty, sixty ships marched up the cobbled road from the sea—followed at a commanding distance by their leader. Mounted high on his gold saddle, his turban immaculate and huge, Barbarossa ignored the awed nods of guards as he surveyed the proof of his victory. And when he got to the gate, he leaned that knuckled face forward, adjusted the jeweled plate on his stallion's brow and, with a *tchsk* to the doorkeeper's tower, he caused the gate to grind open on iron tracks that were thick as legs.

All I did was cross a sill, and I was in a sphere without beginning or end. It was a world of paths and gates to more paths to more gates. A world of overhangs and symmetries off plumb. Space laid out like limbs of a rule. The yard was scored by stone walks that veered to a long portico, to a towered pavilion, and to a third gate that was in line neither with the gate we'd come through nor with the walk that connected them. The porticoes were the same yellow stone they are now, the columns the same white marble; the ochre pavilion had the same look of heavy sugar—its windows swirled in the gold that to this day makes the facade seem more word than wall. Gazelles in diamond anklets nibbled the grass, peacocks made noisy exhibitions of themselves, gold-fettered tigers disported modestly, and fountains on both sides of everything connected earth to sky. There was no need to understand. Seeing was enough.

Around the space, visible through slim black shadows, stood more people than I'd ever seen in one place. They were Janissaries, I'd learn. The Sultan's elite infantry—celibate, Christian-born captives—massed six deep on all sides and at the palace on that occasion to collect their salaries. There must have been a thousand of them, girdled in purple, coated in blue, their heads identically topped with hats that drooped like elbowed sleeves. Their boots alone told their rank—red in front, yellow behind them, all the rest black. All was order. Faces trained to numbness. Dead silence. What system—what leader, I wondered—exacted such vital obedience?

On the other side of the last gate was the answer.

We were paraded across a courtyard scored by lines of dignitaries—foreign, it was evident from their very different attire—fitted and furred. At the center were four commanders in white headdresses that looked like Doge Gritti's except for little satin banners on little red poles that stood a foot above their heads. Barbarossa swooped in front of us from I didn't know where and waved the girls' line forward; we were suddenly a quaking chevron leading the parade. The viziers were crabbing away. The air was whirling like paint.

And then it cleared. Straight ahead, very near to where I stood, cross-legged on an ebony throne raised not one bit off the ground on which the Ottoman Empire stretched and its subjects toiled and thrived, sat Suleiman. Bent nose, minnow eyes, sloped cheekbones—there he was before me. A man like no other. His titles alone told the story. I knew them from my grandfather. Sultan of the Two Continents, Servitor of the Two Sanctuaries, Warden of the Horizons. Suleiman the Magnificent—man and legend combined. His beard was black as pitch at forty-three; his crimson robe voluminous, wild, sleeved to the ground and woven with giant tulips. In his hand was a red rose. His turban was wound high with an aigrette fixed by an emerald big as my fist, and beneath the mountain of linen was a face dotted with light. Suleiman. Imperial, mirthless, deadly pale.

No one stirred. The stillness was an airless cage. The world itself was the command to not move. The world itself was death in a twitch. Then Barbarossa said *Paros* and *Serenissima*, meaning Venice. Then he said *Veniero*, my father's name, and something else I couldn't understand. The Sultan tipped the rose toward his narrow nose. The boys and girls were led away. I could feel the world firming around me. I was alone before Suleiman. And he was there and not there, and there was a space between the part of him that was present and the part that was not. I don't know if I sensed that that space would matter to me, but I knew that it mattered. And I knew this, too: I was being saved.

の

Picture a box with a lid. Something nearly sealed. Picture other boxes inside—close, hot; filings of light permitting a faint view of what's going on—the laundering, the coffeemaking, the complicated storing of jewels and robes. Smell the musk, the wet walls, and jasmine. Breathe the vapor and pervasive order. Smell the perspiration and the animal hide. You are in the harem as I found it.

Do not try to imagine what might have happened between the boxes where the girls who served the coffeemakers and jewel keepers toiled and faded. The empty eyes of the lowest-ranking girls could have cracked your heart, and the icy stares of their mistresses would have frozen you stiff. They might have had rank, a stipend, responsibility of one kind and another, but they'd been deformed by incarceration and absence of opportunity. They hadn't seen a sea or a horizon since the day they'd been dragged into that grim warren. They'd been passed over for sex with the Sultan—back when he was taking women other than his wife—and their submission had aged them horribly. Their pasty faces were identical, stamped with the repeat of spite.

I'd been assigned to the Head Scribe herself without question because I was educated. That was what Barbarossa had said at the presentation. *She can read.* And those women couldn't bear my good fortune. Lined up like trees, they were cawing like crows. Grown women. I despised them for thinking I was lucky when I wasn't. I was a slave, for God's sake, doing my best not to feel helpless. I hated them for hating me and also for making me hate them, because I'd always tried not to hate people, even if in the case of my grandfather and my father I had failed.

I was lucky, though. Copying the archetype of the Eternal Word was work held in highest esteem. More than that, the Head Scribe wanted me to succeed. She hadn't had a novice in her care in a long time, such was her topmost rank in the harem hierarchy. But Suleiman, whose personal calligrapher she was, had ordained the assignment. "*Fiat*," he'd said to her in Latin for emphasis. Fiat, indeed.

Suna was squatting on a bare floor when I first saw her. In the middle of a bright white room, she was the only color. Her puffed hair, pinkish in the light; her brilliant orange garment. She was setting out parchments to work on the way someone else might set out jewelry for a bride. "Here, now," she said emphasizing both words, fastening her eyes on mine. What was this? A warning? "Here, now," she said again, getting to her knees, reducing the moat of robe, welcoming me.

In the weeks since I'd been captured, I'd been able to see Sylvana only dead. I couldn't find her in my memory any other way, and I had tried. Then Suna was before me—down there on the floor, full of calm and industry—and I saw a flash of Sylvana alive. The limber, not young body, the in-difference to convention, the resignation turned to purpose, sympathy—these were all familiar to me. Suna held out her hand, welcoming me to the floor. She slid a vellum sheet my way, opened a volume in Arabic—script I recognized from books in my grandfather's library, though he couldn't read Arabic any more than I could—and she said in Italian, "I understand you can write." I nodded. "Write something, please." She handed me a stylus, weighted the parchment corners with shiny black stones, and I wrote my name. Suna said, "Something else, please." I wrote: *Many are called but few are chosen.* "Now why is that?" Suna said taking the pen and underscoring my words.

"Why are few chosen? Why do you write this?"

"My mother," I said.

"You are fortunate then. You had a mother who taught you."

I did not say—not then, anyway—that I'd had two mothers who had taught me everything from three languages and geometry to the names of every stone on the island and fish in the gulf. What I wanted to say was *Who are you? What happens here? What will happen to me?* But I didn't say those things either, or anything else—that day or for many weeks—that wasn't in answer to a question. I knew already that certain facts of my life could turn out to be keys, and I believed those keys might help me, though the gates they might unlock were hidden from view. Other facts of my life—I had learned from my grandfather only months before—could be explosives, and those were hidden, too—by me. I would hide them until I had a reason not to.

Carefully, Suna wrote a word in Arabic. She spoke it. Everything about her was kind, steady—her voice, her face—everything at ease. All the movement of which her body was capable was situated in her right wrist and palm and fingers.

"How do you do that?"

"It is what I love to do." Suna laid down the pen, fanned her hand out on a thigh and pressed her palm downward on her heavy silk robe. Not up and down. Just down and more down. Just the way Sylvana had. Old knobby hands fanning toward yellow stars on a purple hem. Toward dusty clogs. Dusty roads. "Writing makes sense," Suna said. "It reveals meaning."

In fact, Suna had been born to do this—not just because she was from Reggio Campagna, the calligraphy capital of Italy, but because she'd been born into a life she was better freed from. Her mother had died giving her birth, and her father, a quarryman, had had no time for her. A calligrapher with a heart, though—another Jew on the run from Spain—had taught Suna his art. He'd kept her as his apprentice till he came here. Suna, then, was already on her own when Ottoman corsairs swept the Mediterranean; and because her mentor had preceded her here—under the same circumstances as Hamon, our physician—she regarded her capture as a brutal blessing. She was certain it was going to be better here than there. This truth of hers made an impression on me.

I have no doubt that viziers, Janissaries, even princes had had Suna in their beds at some time long before. But pleasing men in that way was not part of the right path for her. Suna's path was foretold. She copied the Word a second time—to demonstrate the importance and possibility of my doing the same. "You, now," she said.

I copied the Word.

Allah.

"Good. Now. Allah"—she bowed her head—"delivered his Word to the Prophet." She pointed to the Word with the tip of her pen. "And the Prophet recited it to the people of his tribe. Do you know why?" I shook my head. "Because those were times of trouble. The Prophet's tribe had been tempted by mammon and power, and they were yielding to them. They were losing themselves. They were neglecting the poor and the weak. So for twenty-one years *Allah*," she wrote the Word again, "revealed His will to the Prophet, one command at a time." All this in the first moments of a first lesson.

What was I thinking in that unimagined moment when the faith I'd been born to started giving way to the faith that has been mine ever since? Did churches float by on lagoons and seas? Did I hear Sylvana teaching me the sacraments before I was even old enough to receive them? Did I see her thrusting her fingers into holy water, blessing herself and me—forehead, heart, shoulder, shoulder—as though we were one, while my mother watched in wonder? Did my tongue have its own recollection— of the Body of Christ against the roof of my mouth? Here is what I feel now, burning up in this bed, my feet killing me: I feel Sylvana next to me at the Communion rail. I feel her hope in my just-administered faith, her breath on my forehead. I feel her simple goodness, and it is not distinguishable from Suna's.

"And do you know what his people did?" Suna asked me. She was writing the word *Islam*.

I shook my head. No, I did not know. "Here. You try." Gently she pushed the ink toward me. "That is right. And his people *surrendered* to God. And to God's command that they live with justice and compassion. And this is why we pray as we do. It is why we fast and care for the poor and feed the hungry." It is how the sea of one faith flowed into the ocean of another. *God bears witness that there is no God but He,* Suna wrote, *and so too the angels, those who possess knowledge and stand firm in Justice.* (Qur'an 3:18–19) "It is why Islam respects the ways of others to whom God has revealed His Word. It is all a matter of living as God wishes us to."

Suna wrote something else. "*Ji-had*." She separated the syllables as she spoke and wrote them. "To strive." She drew a line under the word. "Do you understand?" She crooked a finger, lifted my chin up, looked at me. "You do. I can see you do. It is all a matter of striving to do the good and the right thing."

It never occurred to me that they might not be the same.

"What about the children from my island?" I asked.

Suna shut her eyes, opened them. "They are well cared for." She put her hand on my cheek as proof—which I needed. "Your concern is what I have said. To do the good and the right thing. Go quietly now and think about this."

All of this is why when I left Suna's quarters I didn't hate the hags I'd passed on the way in. Instead, I pitied them—as Suna had told me to. And Suna's compassion made me trust her, and trusting her allowed me to stop worrying about the children, and not worrying relieved me from a terrible burden, because there was nothing I could do for those boys and girls. The best I could do was find ways to not think about them. And, over the weeks and months that followed, I did. I believe it was the first time I managed something bad by not thinking about it—a skill that became a way of life.

Wednesday, November 9

I realize now that it is a credit to my first teachers that I didn't hate or resent my education, because it—or rather, the goal of my being educated—was the cause of my worst early misery—being taken from Paros to Venice when I was five. To be told it was the best thing for me by both my mother and Sylvana was a misery all its own. As far as I recall, it was my first experience of suspicion and the anger that comes with it. My mother's explanation was ridiculous. Thanks to her, I could read Virgil, do long division in my head, and identify half a dozen constellations per season.

"There are things we learn in cities that we don't learn on islands," my mother said. I pulled away from her embrace, petulant and not like myself, but she understood, and she fixed her attention on the sea as though she'd remembered to locate something on the horizon, and it was clear, like a change in weather, there was nothing I could do to affect this alarming decision. My father had died, and my mother was free. With that freedom she was going to reclaim her authority. In Venice. For both our sakes. My mother—the first to save me.

In those final days on Paros, I watched my life shrink toward the vanishing point. I tried to memorize it as it was fleeting away—the bougainvillea and gorse, the unloading of ambergris and glass, the fishermen and their boys sorting through the night's haul, mending nets, washing down the wharf. All of it was going, then more going, and then it was gone.

I cried for ten days—nearly the time it took us to go the length of the Adriatic. It was the choking crying that comes from knowing you have lost something forever, and it was sharpened by watching my mother change before my eyes. Always loving and protective, she had seemed more sister than mother, and now, all at once, she didn't. She seemed decisive. We were not out of Naoussa harbor before her bearing changed, her brow widened, and all the other parts of her that I hadn't realized were tight as little drums began to loosen and admit the fast-moving air and a future that she planned to affect. When my mother said on our first night at sea that I could do anything I wanted, I knew it was a declaration of fact, not permission. I could tell from the way her sadness was turning to excitement.

When we heard through the fog the muffled closeness of the Dalmatian coast, my mother called me to her. Squinting, remembering, she rolled out to its ragged extent the portolan chart given to me by my father, and with her arms around me my mother encircled me in map. I examined its swirling wind roses and the crosses that marked danger, I smelled the animal the parchment had come from, and I felt my mother becoming specific. I was feeling her become a mother. I believe I understood that could only be a good thing.

Then Venice came into view changing from bone to gold in the lifting mist. "There it is," my mother said. Her voice was full of promise. We sailed toward Venice's beauty as though it were a berth. Across the lagoon on the left, cypresses marked the outer edge of the Giudecca. Hard to our right, a little island, St. Helena, was so close I could smell the lemons on the trees. And straight ahead, forming itself, was a composition of shapes unlike anything I'd ever seen. One was a lace cliff;

one a spear; the largest a tabernacle—gold upon gold pointing to God: the Campanile, the Clock Tower, the domes of San Marco. I could make out the church's doorways, deep as caves; the jeweled pictures above them; every detail sharpening as we approached so swiftly I was sure we'd run aground. But the lagoon is deep, right up to the architecture. There was no wharf, no transition. We were just there, new points on the trapezoid.

A large, vividly turned-out crowd was waiting, or not waiting. Nearer the water than most of the others were two elderly people who I took to be a king and queen. An elegantly attired retinue protected them on one side from the gawking rabble and on the other from the sloshing of our ship. The royal pair were tall, she as tall as he. They weren't wearing crowns, but they stood erect as though they'd just removed them, and their posture, their dress, and the precisely maintained distance of the retinue added to their commanding air. The queen, my grandmother, was waving her arms, while the king had his hands over his eyes, for protection.

At once my mother changed again. Not back to vagueness, for sure. But she stiffened. An alarm. As though riveted to the deck, she stood shuddering while a sailor led me down the plank toward her father, whose outstretched arms had expanded his robe to the size of the basilica, who looked like a charcoaled lion—big gray beard, big gray curls, big mouth—and whose eyes were sad and red. "Oopla," he said, catching me under the arms.

"Oopla," I said back, not sure what language it was. I looked over his shoulder at my grandmother, who resembled a sunflower. "Oopla," I said in a show of politeness. She placed herself between my grandfather and me, clapped both her hands around mine as though I were a baby, and immediately started walking me away from the ship. "I will wait for my mother," I told her pulling back and knowing that was not the way I was supposed to act and not liking the way it felt. My mother and her father stood facing each other at the water's edge—he leaning back as if facing a hard wind; my mother leaning toward him at the same angle. Already my mother was talking to him. Not a small kind of talk—I could tell—but whole sentences with information in them that seemed to force my grandfather's head deeper within the incongruous fur rising up from his collar. All the while my grandmother was chattering about how happy she was to have me there and telling me my mother would join us shortly, and I was certain that was not the case when I saw my grandfather extend an arm toward my mother and I saw the way she stepped back from him, his elaborate garb, his way of being.

My grandmother directed me across the piazza, and we quickly reached a waterway where a boatman—Paolo—waited in a little vessel that looked to me like arms of a mad widow waving wheat. A gondola. Paolo's long, languid strokes moved us swiftly away from the lagoon. Past Calle Vallaresso, past Calle del Riodotto, he poled us to Campo Traghetto, where we disembarked before the water-level doors of Baffo Salt Works. *"Genio Urbis Augusto."* I read the words inscribed over the front doors.

"Goodness," my grandmother said.

"To the Glory of the City," I translated with a pride I hadn't known I had.

"What a clever girl," my grandmother quacked, as the coffered doors opened from within. I'd grown up in big houses on Paros—castles. But this was something different. This house had a staircase as wide as the canal. This house had ceilings painted with warriors—naked—and had chandeliers the size of goats and walls hung with the heads of antlered ruminants. And in the middle of it all, *this* house had in the place of honor a mesmerizing design penned on an oval cloth and framed in gilded wood. "It is a map," my grandmother said. I did not bother to contradict her even though I was sure the arrangement of ships, animals and bellow-cheeked faces overlaid on a cross hatch of straight, bent and jagged lines was assuredly not a map. "It is a *mappa mundi!*" she said triumphantly, summoning the term from memory or thin air. "It is your Nonna's favorite."

That my grandmother called my grandfather by what I understood would be my name for him not only told me she was capable of forethought, it announced a hierarchy of favor within our small family—an arrangement it took me the next seven years to get to the bottom of.

"It used to be more beautiful," Nonna said mildly of her opulent residence. "Sumptuary laws," she added over her shoulder, as though I knew about the Republic's legal restrictions on extravagance, a mechanism whose hypocrisy I appreciated only—and very soon—after coming here.

The entire house, from the public rooms of the piano nobile to the bedchambers above to the library on the top—a story of its own—supplied an intense idea of what it was to be a Baffo. My mother's room, a spare though velvet-walled space, contained a canopied bedstead, a small gilt credenza, and a writing table on which were laid out a half-open folding rule, a compass needle, and a ring dial. "They were hers," my grandmother said of the items, as though my mother were dead and as though I'd asked a question. "We moved her belongings here when we learned you were coming." I pointed out to Nonna that she'd just said it was my mother's room. "It is now," my grandmother commenced. "We thought you would enjoy having her old room since it is the nicest. Nonno thought so. Well, I did, too. Violante never talked much to us anyway," she noted with impenetrable preciseness.

Nor, over the next seven years, would my mother talk much to her parents, though for a reason very different from those she'd had before she went away. My mother was quiet as a youth because she was thinking. Indeed, her father's most ardent ambition—no, the *route* to it—was supporting his daughter's intellect and imagination, for it was very rare. It was why—and how—he had lured the greatest tutor in Christendom to 'Ca Baffo. My grandfather had sent Jean-Baptiste Egnatius the first map my mother ever drew. She'd done it when she was eleven. It was of Venice and based on coordinates she'd taken sailing around the lagoon in the small dhow my grandfather had had made for her. Her map was accurate and fanciful in equal parts, "a work of intelligence and heart," Egnatius wrote to my grandfather. "I will instruct your daughter in mathematics and astronomy. Monetary compensation will not be required."

Thrilled as he was by Egnatius's assessment, my grandfather saw my mother's gift in a different light, something I came to understand much later. This was a man defined by regret. And resentment and remorse. Venice herself had imposed the regret—especially after the defeat at Cambrai: her navy gone slack, monopolies lost, reputation gashed in so many ways. She imposed the resentment, too, for it didn't matter if Baffos were owners of the oldest continually operating business in Venice. According to a two-hundred-year-old law, they were *cittadini*, not *nobili*—meaning they were not patrician. Not eligible to hold office. Not authorized, not rightful. They were outside the *serrata*. The shame of these facts bowed my grandfather low. And unlike his daughter, he talked about it. He talked about nearly everything else he felt, too. All the time. He grumbled to me—when I was small—about the deceptions of the Salt Administration. He railed—in front of all of us—about the scourge of Jews in the Ghetto, especially those who had converted, and above all those loyal to the Ottomans, for they were the ones upon whom so much trade depended. The way my grandfather talked, you'd have thought the Republic was a form of perfection and its citizens and customs forms of failure. He was complicated, and still is. So was—and is—Venice.

All of this had made my mother sick. Certainly the agonizing about Venice and especially the pretensions about the city. To my grandfather, my mother's prodigiousness had been an endowment back before I was born. Something to be built upon, invested, deployed. Complementing her beauty and appended to the dowry he had established for her at birth and which far exceeded the legal cap—my mother's talent could not fail to attract a proposal of marriage, Nonno believed—and from the highest *nobili* reach of the Republic. Dowries could, if they were large enough, serve as battering rams. My grandfather's respect for the law was selective.

Children, however, are not conduits, emblems, or achievements. And they do not belong to their parents. Ask my mother. Ask Suleiman. Ask me.

Surveying this segment of my childhood, I'm struck by how quickly I got used to and close to my grandfather. I evidently wished to, and so did he. My special chair with the reindeer he'd had carved on the back was next to his desk—facing his own chair—in the warehouse. I can hear his medals jangling as he'd lower himself onto the leather and set about his work. I can smell the incense as I'd wait for him at mass in San Giovanni Evangelista, his redemption-seeking fraternity. Red-hooded penitents, white-lipped from flailing themselves, are something you remember, especially when you're alone in your family's pew waiting for your grandfather and he is one of the people in the hoods. *Kyrie eleison*, he would intone as he'd demote his hood to a cowl and pray. *Christe eleison*, he'd beg from the depth of his being, wherever that was.

It didn't happen immediately, but over the seasons the look, the rituals, the ominous scent—every detail the opposite of here in Islam—drew me in. And as these rites became part of my life, their allure only grew. They amounted to something I believed in. It wasn't until much later—when I was married—that I began to think about the sanctimony of so much of it. And it wasn't till I was a mother myself that I realized the degree to which my mother's childhood affected my own. Indeed, seemed my own.

And so, on that day of my mother's and my arrival, casting an eye toward the out-of-doors that, somewhere, contained my mother, I told my grandmother I wanted to find her.

"Oh, she's not lost," Nonna answered sincerely, prodding me toward the next room down the hall. Its centerpiece was the bed of a dream I hadn't even had. It was a magic cove, and on the underside of the baldachino were hundreds of gold-embroidered stars, and under the bed was a little door. "I'm sure you have brought some special belongings with you," my grandmother declared, tapping the cubby with her velvet-shod toe. I mentioned my portolan chart. "Ah. Yes. The chart." Her eyebrows bent toward each other. "Well, it will be safe here." She paused to gain access to a thought. "Why, it is where your mother kept the one given to her!"

"May I see my mother now, please?" I said this softly. I did not wish to upset my grandmother. For all my confusion and worry I felt smarter than her, and I did not think that was a good sign.

"What a good idea," she exclaimed, as though it were the only one she'd ever heard.

Paolo took me back to San Marco. "We will wait here," he said with reassuring authority. High above the piazza two metal shepherds banged twice on an iron instrument, tolling a bell and making appear a procession of iron kings telling the time. My grandfather had disappeared and my mother was out there on her own. Facing her, at a distance, was a man of medium height and understated taste, dressed all in black velvet—cloak, britches, big soft beret—except for a doublet of red buttoned tight over his barrel chest. He was looking at my mother, waiting for her. He straightened the index fingers of his clasped hands and, as I would see him do a thousand times over the next six years, he brought them up under his chin and nestled them knuckle-deep in his grey beard by way of saying *Yes*. My mother gathered the back of her dress and set out across the piazza toward her teacher, the only person in the world who could have gotten her to return to Venice. Egnatius was her savior, and mine.

Thursday, November 10

Hamon has just left. He has been in and out many times since yesterday. This fever has become hectic, and he's concerned that the pretty foul suffumigation he administered yesterday has done nothing to slow it. He's also saying things about my being up *all night*, and he says I should do this—he was waving his arms around as though writing were like any other way to pass the time—no more than one hour a day.

Hamon does not know what he is up against! I've embarked. The shore is well behind me, and I am *not* slowing down. This fever can melt me—and it probably will—right into this mattress. But Hamon is not going to stop me from writing.

I'll let Esther tell him. Apparently they think feigning calm will make me feel better. I would feel better if they didn't whisper in Hebrew. And if I weren't vomiting day and night, and if the fever were to go down. Hamon maintains the ailment's in my stomach. But Esther's attention is on my arms and legs. She is even more alert to what's strange than Hamon is—and that is saying a lot because he has had thirty more years of strangeness on this earth than she has. I'm referring to their being Jews. And because the toleration of Jews is essential to our story—the dynasty's, Esther's, mine—it is worth noting the routes by which Jews have gotten here and the nature of the welcome they've received, because it says important things about the quality of Jews' endurance and the nature of Ottoman enlightenment.

Hamon came from Iberia the very year the expulsion began—a baby in his mother's arms. Esther Handali was born a generation later—1520—in Lisbon, but matters were as bad in their own way. Esther's parents, like all Jews of that time and place, had been converted by force. "Dissimulation," is what she calls it. "It was permissible. A matter of intention." The intention was to survive *and* remain a Jew. For Esther's family that had meant becoming a "new Christian" and crossing all of Europe—Iberia, France, the Alps, Italy—to get to Venice. Not its gleaming piazzas, believe me, but into the ratty shadows of its Ghetto, where they were crammed like cattle, where the windows were sealed and opaque, where they could not make or sell their own goods and were forced to stay inside from dusk till dawn—except for the doctors. Oh yes. The doctors they let out—in their distinguishing garb—and that is because Jewish physicians were and are the best anywhere. This thumping fever has called to my mind more than once an image of my mother at my bedside. I am small and burning up, and she is standing near a bearded man in a yellow hat and a yellow armband and a yellow star sewn on his coat and she is listening closely becasuse he is whispering to her about what ails me, and because she trusts him.

Esther once had a husband. She married him the year she arrived in Venice. He was a rabbi, a widower. She did not tell me his name, nor did I ask. She just told me what he meant to her. He was a steady man and not young, but he had a young child. Moise. Esther said she and her husband wanted the same thing for different reasons. He wanted to be married for the sake of his son. She wanted to be married to affirm her faith. Esther had had enough of being considered a faithless dissembler, for that is how Marranos were viewed: as people who too readily switched from one religion to another and back again—as though lethal pressure hadn't *made* them do what they'd done. It was soon after she got married that Jews' conditions in Venice declined—sharply. Long-held suspicions that Marranos were usurers in disguise assumed the force of fact. Jews—converted, unconverted, reverted—were confined to the Ghetto in the ways I have mentioned—the appurtenances they were forced to wear being why Esther hates yellow to this day. As the Inquisition proceeded, Esther and her husband had choices: to stay or come here, to the Empire; to remain together or separate; to be Jews or not. Esther said she and her husband each knew what the other would do. They would continue to profess their faith and help their people. For the rabbi that meant staying. For Esther it meant leaving. There was barely any discussion, except that Esther's husband asked her to take Moise with her, which she did.

She and the little boy left before the sun set on the following day—on a merchant ship that would call on Valona and Salonika before it reached the capital, here, where they were taken in, and associates of the Nasi family quickly helped establish Esther as an agent. As for her husband, the moment, practically, that she and the boy left, he located all the Talmuds in the city—there were four in print by that time—and hid them in their house. He knew what was coming. He did not stand trial because the Inquisition concerned itself only with Marrano apostates. That didn't mean the authorities were comfortable with him in their midst, however. "They set fire to the house with my husband and the books inside." Esther was calm when she explained this. Nor was she interested in my sympathy.

Friday, November 11

I heard the money in his pockets before I saw his face. I heard the money even over the wind and over the snarling of the lank creature who goaded me. The fortune in gold ducats in the right pocket and the countless pieces of silver in the left were just as my grandfather had described—donatives the Sultan conferred in the course of a day on loved ones, supplicants, passersby. I heard the jangling coins over the frenzied waters where the Bosporus and Golden Horn churn each other down and hundreds of carracks and oared boats vie for right-of-way. On the far side of the Golden Horn hunched the stone berths of the shipyard. In the middle of the Golden Horn waited the imperial barge, its decks dotted with red-clad oarsmen moving in unison to keep the bow, upon which perched the waiting throne, clear of the swirling seas. The Sultan was going boating. He was taking a day on the Bosporus for the beauty of it. And I had been summoned to his presence along the way. In no one's memory—not Suna's, Sumbul's, or the Superintendent's—had such a thing happened. Sumbul was frozen with fear. The Superintendent was taut with jealousy. Only Suna and I imagined—for different reasons—that something better might be afoot. The Sultan did not waste time—ever.

He was a dot, then a spot, then the shape of a man, then

a man. How close do you have to get before perspective is gone and the size of the man is the man himself? He was standing in front of Tower Kiosk—a small, purple twist of tiny chambers that he had designed himself. The midday light looked like ice as it fell on the water behind him, and the part that fell on his robe made the mohair shimmer like a leaf. I slowed my step. He broadened his shoulders and straightened himself to a great height. This man was more than a tree or a mountain. He was an army, an education, a code of law. Suleiman was the dynasty itself. He was the Empire, too. He had fought and won in Baghdad and Tabriz, in Belgrade and Mohacs, on Rhodes and Paros and the islands all around. Tireless, he'd taken 100,000 soldiers, 20,000 horses, and 10,000 camels two thousand miles—eastward and back, westward and back. And he'd done it many, many times. Suleiman had shown the world what majesty looks like. He'd shown his own people, too—through the schools he founded, the buildings and bridges he commissioned, the arts he fostered, and discoveries he enabled. Life in the capital vibrated with Suleiman's advances. Across the continents of the Empire, his achievements inspired awe, admiration, and thanks. Beyond the House of Islam, they engendered envy and fear.

I had been aching to see him since the only moment I'd laid eyes on him a year before. Through hard work and obedience I'd been striving to find a way into his presence. I wanted—I needed—to test what I had felt that first day. An energy of some kind. I couldn't have said what. But I knew *he* had ignited it. And I knew he'd ignited it by saving my life.

And here is what I know now, lying here, still. What Suleiman awoke in me was an awareness of power—my own. And that power's source was my mother. Yes, my father's name had put me on the deck, not in the hold, of Barbarossa's ship. But my education was the ultimate term by which Barbarossa had identified me. And Suleiman saved me because of *that*. If neither he nor I knew that at the time, it doesn't matter. What I'm writing, now, is certain, and true.

What I sought and honed was practical. I directed my energy to learning the Celestial Word of the faith practiced by those in charge. I learned the Istanbul Turkish with which to get along. I put a lot of energy, too, into certain behaviors: avoiding the women who envied me, understanding what they envied, guarding against it, and guarding against strong affections, too. As Suna warned, attraction of that kind goes out of bounds before you know it. I could and would take no chances.

Framed by the purple kiosk, the Sultan surveyed the waters. An arm went up. Advance, said his inordinate sleeve. A eunuch from nowhere put a long-nailed finger to my back—a eunuch specialty—and kept it there till I was a boom's length from Suleiman's side, facing the direction he faced. From the edge of my eye I saw turban, a ruddy cheek, a bit of beard. Something stirred beside him. I looked down. A humpbacked boy was smiling up. The Sultan took the boy's hand and entered the kiosk. I followed.

He lowered himself on a green-carpeted platform, gathering his misshapen son near. His eel-like eunuch positioned me opposite, not close, and on my feet. The bare floor was painted purple. A pair of eunuch cadets glided in with tea and sweets. Suleiman folded his arms, his eunuch did the same, and the cadets stood, suspended, with their offering. Minutes passed. "You are Venetian," he said at last, which was not true, so I said nothing. He commanded me to answer. Thanking God and Suna for the language I'd absorbed, I said I was from Paros. "A Venetian possession. You are Venetian. A son of Gritti serves us. You know who Gritti is." Indeed I did. "Answer."

It hadn't seemed a question. I said, "My grandfather knows him."

"You are impertinent." The hunched boy drew closer

and nuzzled his father. "Your family is known to us." As my mother's father hated to know, Suleiman would not have been referring to the merchant Baffos. *Veniero* was how I'd been presented, and *Veniero* was what counted—on Paros, where they'd governed since before this Empire existed, and in Venice, where a Veniero had been doge a few generations before. Still, I wondered if the Sultan knew I had two families. I wondered what he would think of that. But he left my lineage for something more immediate. "Your teacher was who?"

"Jean-Baptiste Egnatius." Suleiman spat a pit of some sort into his hand. I had seen no fruit. "He is the teacher of all the Doge's sons."

"That is of no interest."

"And Violante Baffo."

Suleiman flicked the air with a very long-nailed finger. "Who has such a name?" He reached for more fruit.

"A mapmaker."

"We have said you are impertinent. You studied what in mathematics?" I considered why his syntax might be so tortured. I told him what in mathematics. He pronounced my answer impossible. Again, his eunuch snorted. "You are saying you have studied Regiomontanus's theorems." Suleiman clicked his jaw from side to side. His little leaf eyes were cold. Mine were sticking to my veil. I nodded. "Then say what their importance is." It was a crazy demand. Their importance was not reducible to words. I didn't know what he meant or what to say. "*Now*," he added.

"They permit measurements of the earth."

"And?"

"*And?*"

Slightly and decisively he turned his head toward me. "And *what?*"

"And . . . they allow for the curvature. The measurements do."

The accuracy—or more likely the correctness—of this answer seemed to set the Sultan in motion. He rose. "We brought that volume back from Buda. One of hundreds of books they stole. They knew—they *know*—which spoils have real worth." This was a gross thing for him to say. I was a spoil, after all. Not different from a plundered porphyry pillar. He stepped out of the kiosk. "Come." The eunuch, maintaining the space between us, hissed. "They have been carrying off our libraries and instruments since the time of the Conqueror," Suleiman said as he strode. "How do you think the king of Hungary came to have two thousand volumes? Because he had the foresight to collect them? No. Because he had the sense to steal them. Do you know the value of that library?" Suleiman turned around. "Do you?" I knew something about libraries, but, still, I had no idea what to say. He was talking to me as though we were arguing. "*Answer.*" He was still walking.

"In ducats?"

Suleiman came to a halt. "You dare mock our question." He turned around. "Their value is in expanding our reach." There was a not-small clot of something at the corner of his mouth. His eyes were watery. I imagined the tip of his mind, a fine instrument, tracing the perimeter of the Empire, depicting, valuing the might of its people. He dragged the back of his hand across his brow. Mohair is nothing against sweat, and the sweat kept coming. I wondered if going boating that day could do this man any good.

"Of course it is," I answered. "I would not mock anything. Ever, Padishahim. I could not. But I have a question." The eunuch, one eye closed, came toward me. "Did they steal all your books? Because I know someone who could help with this. Someone in Venice."

Suleiman signaled to the eunuch to stay put. "Outrageous," he said.

There are situations in life when the sum of parts—which sometimes can be people—is something completely different from the parts themselves. In this case the parts were qualities.

Suleiman's stature, temper, and loss. And the sum of them was permission to continue. I do not know how I knew this. But I was not wrong.

And so, swiftly, precisely, I told Suleiman the Magnificent about Egnatius's library. That it was the most important in Europe. That he owned not one but two volumes of *Geographia*—Ptolemy's treatise on mapmaking. That the first, hand-copied, included the instructions that had allowed my mother to lay out the projections, meridians, and parallels of her first map. And that from Regiomontanus she'd known to curve the lines. I told him the other *Geographia*—printed, from Padua—*had* maps, and this mattered because Jean-Baptiste Egnatius told my grandfather he was certain my mother could surpass those maps in accuracy. As a reward for that prediction, my grandfather had bought Egnatius the book. It cost a thousand ducats, I told Suleiman—the price of a galleon. My grandfather had also acquired a copy of the astronomical tables of Ulugh Bey. "Hence, Sultanimiz, the stupid thing I said a moment ago," I said to Suleiman, causing the eunuch, who had positioned himself behind him, to remove the little pipe all eunuchs carry in the folds of their turbans and to peer through it. The pipe is what allows them to urinate.

Suleiman scooped up a palm full of pebbles and shook them like dice. "Look at us." I looked. The space between his being there and not being there—that space was where I was. I was as sure of it as the ground beneath me.

And then he told me why I'd been summoned that day. "We have chosen you."

Suleiman was forty-four. I was fourteen. This was not what I'd meant by finding a space to slide into. *This* was what had happened to my mother—being claimed by a man three times her age—and it had nearly finished her.

ॐ

I made the mistake this morning of showing the last two entries of this account to Esther, who calls them embarrassing. I thank her with no sincerity for her opinion. Dismiss her. Call her back. "What do you mean?"

"Your subservience."

"Subservience? It was the Sultan."

"And pretense."

"I was thirteen, for God's sake."

"You were precocious, then. Why record it?"

"Why record it?"

"Are you going to repeat everything I say?"

Esther is honest to her core. Therein lies her expertise as agent. Her skill as negotiator. Her worth as everything she is to me. Everything. I remind her of how I'm feeling. The evacuations, the wretched, mossy mouth, the unslakable thirst. She gets up, turns away. The muscles in her neck are hard. I have seen this recently. She is scared of yielding to my illness. She dismisses Hamon's assistant, brings the basin of rose water next to me, and wrings out linens that she places on my forehead and across my chest. Then she kisses the cloth on my head, wrings another cloth, and goes to the end of the mattress. She lifts the covers to bathe my feet, and she lets out a cry.

☙

What Suleiman chose me for had nothing to do with him—or so I thought. The day after our meeting, Suna said I was to have a new teacher. *That* is what I'd been chosen for. To be whoever a person becomes when she has the best teacher there is.

Matrakci Nasuh was Suleiman's Leonardo. His master of the important and new. He was Imperial Mathematician, Imperial Historian, Imperial Mapmaker and Illustrator. Bosnian by birth, he'd been taken as a boy in the *devshirme*—the culling of particularly able Christian boys in Ottoman-conquered lands, although in Bosnia, uniquely, Muslim boys—including Matrakci—were recruited, too, and he'd risen like a rocket through the Janissary ranks during the reign of Suleiman's grandfather. He'd distinguished himself as a designer of war games—notably *matrak,* from which he took his name—then of weapons; then, during the reign of Suleiman's father, he gained eminence as a man of numbers. But it was as mapmaker that Matrakci captured the attention and, more important, the imagination of Suleiman.

Suna had set her heart on my studying with Matrakci, and as Suleiman's calligrapher she had been able to get that message across. It was astonishing to me that a woman in the harem—by definition a slave and in Suna's case not comely or young—could reach the Sultan of the Ottoman Empire with an idea. But she did.

Suna had been everything that was good for me up to that point. She'd taught me Arabic in a year's time. And she'd made me interested to know how the Word and the writing of the Word uphold the faith of Islam. In these ways she had given me the means to distinguish myself, and in these ways she had protected me. However different that protection was from my mother's or Sylvana's, it felt, at the time, like what I most needed. Suna helped me to be less afraid of my future. That *is* what a good mother gives her child.

Saturday, November 12

Go out in the sunshine. Close your eyes and look up. Do you see yellow swirling on top of black? And red and black along the sides? Do you see the faint image of what you'd been looking at before you closed your eyes? That is what I saw my first time inside a palanquin. Puffy golden silk lining the ceiling; black and red shrouding the window; the grim facade of the Old Palace as I left it for the Imperial Harem and Matrakci.

I was carried across the wide, weird spaces that separate the Old Palace and Topkapi, past Hagia Sophia, up the hill to the redoubtable gate, Bab-iHumayun, which I'd seen only once and through a fog of fear. Inside the First Courtyard I was toted past the Armory and the incongruous Church of Saint Irene on one side; past the Royal Mint on the other. It was a graceless space dripping with administrative dreariness—qualities I'd been blind to the day I was marched across it as loot. On this day, though, two years later, I was seeing with new eyes. We advanced into the dazzling Second Courtyard in whose farthest corner the Tower of Justice served— and still serves—as the true frontier between outside and in. It was by the base of this Tower, on the nonforbidden side, that Matrakci and I were to meet.

Silent and bleached, White Eunuchs dotted the paths and

bobbed like buoys. One—Josag, the Sultan's slithery pet—who I'd seen with him what seemed a long time before, was stationed by a small door to the left of the Tower's base. He offered no assistance as I determined how to step safely onto a teetering block meant to serve as a tread. The little door opened, and he led the way through a long maze of musty corridors to an interior terrace off which was a single room. The door was open. I paused, out of view. There was the sound of a stylus scratching on parchment and the scent of the parchment, rank in the heat. There was a voice. A foreign accent. I peered around. Crouching on a rug, a very large-headed man, bent like a branch, was poring over a proof, muttering to himself.

He glanced up at me, his eyes small and pink. "You are here. So. Be seated. And be quiet." I hadn't said a word.

I hated him the minute I laid my eyes on him. He was disheveled, pasty, morose, and small. And I could tell he hated me. This man a tutor? It was impossible. A tutor was proud and respectful, not shabby and queer. A tutor was like Egnatius—someone learned who wished to help someone else to learn. The self-absorbed bug on the floor in front of me could harbor nothing like the ambition Egnatius had had for my mother and for me. Besides, I figured, if Matrakci were so wonderful, Egnatius himself would have told me about him. He had made sure I knew about Piri Re'is, the Ottomans' greatest mapmaker. And about Ulugh Bey—the Timurid ruler and astronomer who had constructed the best observatory in the world. I felt my aggrieved assertions piling up as I waited for him to finish his calculation.

Thinking back on my original hostility to Matrakci, I believe it was nothing more, nor less, than fear, which is why the first weeks studying with him were among the hardest of my captivity. I see now that in having me study with Matrakci—in favoring me that way—Suleiman released me from the effort I'd been making, morning to night for more than a year, to win his favor—an exertion so great it had, evidently, staved off sorrow. In other words, my first seasons in captivity seem to have been a grace period. The consuming effort to win Suleiman's attention had allowed me not to be overtaken by loss and anger and fear. The assignment to Matrakci laid all of this bare. I was suddenly, crushingly afraid. I wonder if my fourteen-year-old self felt she owed that fear to the twelve-year-old who hadn't laid claim to it. I am certain that were I not lying here, awfully ill, I would not be wondering any such thing.

Following my first meeting with Matrakci—in which he had pushed toward me a parchment bearing what I am pasting in below and told me to come back when I could explain it—I was sick with dread.

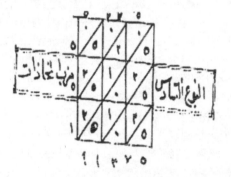

I hadn't cried the way I cried that day since Barbarossa's deck-jail. I ran, noticed by many, to Suna's quarters. I swore loudly that the purpose of the Sultan's teacher was for me to fail, and I waved as evidence the parchment on which Matrakci had sketched his miraculous ladder. I accused him of hating girls, of being deformed (which he was not), of missing many teeth (which he was), and of being crude, lofty, and foul, the last on account of his fingernails, so long that they curled.

Suna had been seated on her itchy hassock when I entered, and she got slowly and with effort to her feet. Flushed, disappointed, Suna told me I was welcome to visit her, indeed to continue my apprenticeship with her according to the command of the Sultan himself, but not until I had entirely regained control of my thoughts, feelings, and behavior. "You are not a credit to yourself at the time being," she said.

"But don't you understand?"

Of course she did. "Now you are fully here," she said, meaning here in the harem. Here in the order of things. "Before was an introduction." I told her I would fail with Matrakci. "You will succeed if you concentrate on what is before you. You *will* fail if you do not."

Then she told me a story. True, and about her. It was about a quarry, which was startling because there had been an important quarry on Paros, and I had never mentioned it to her. In any event, when Suna was eight, her father had walked her up to the limestone cave outside Bari—five hundred fathoms above the sea. Before they entered the cave, he explained that it was the source of the family's wealth and security. "I want you to understand this," he'd said. And then he put a torch in Suna's hand and told her to follow him, which she did, into a huge uneven space with water gurgling from places she couldn't see and with bats swooping. Loose rocks underfoot, inert debris, made the soles of her feet knot up as she descended because it is very steep inside those quarries. The space narrowed as Suna's father went ahead, and the light from outside narrowed behind her, too, until the cave in the torchlight looked like the inside of a throat. Then Suna's father turned to her and said he wanted her to reflect on where she was. She said she didn't understand. He said he wanted her to appreciate the source of the family's security. But she still didn't understand. And then her father told her to wait there until he returned. He didn't say when that would be. He was testing her mettle. Suna's father was gone for a very long time. Many hours. Suna prayed and prayed for him to come back. When she couldn't pray anymore she began to cry. Finally, long after she couldn't cry anymore, her father appeared. But the person she'd been praying for and crying for was someone she didn't want to look at again, ever. She didn't know that until he was there. And then she knew.

I was confused by this tale. It didn't make sense, and I didn't understand why she was telling it to me. "Because that is how lives are," she said. "I did not know why my father did this terrible and stupid thing to me. I do not know if *he* knew why. What I understood by the time he came back for me was that from then on I had to think for myself. Whatever had made him the way he was and made him do that to me was beyond the meaning of my own life, and I understood that I had better make myself separate from it or it would hurt me badly. You must think about the meaning of your own life *now*, Cecilia. Here, in this place. Do not compare what is here to what was before. Work hard. You will succeed."

She glanced at Matrakci's chart. "Do you understand this at all?" I nodded. "I thought so," she said, handing it back to me with care. Then I shook my head. "You will. You may go now."

Somehow I knew not to try to collect the embrace that had always concluded my meetings with Suna. A rush of sadness—contrition—filled me up. "Do not worry, Cecilia," Suna said. "Decide."

꙾

When I returned to Matrakci the following week—prepared at least to ask good questions about his algorithmic chart—he was again installed on the floor but this time surrounded by nothing. He was not busy. "Be seated." There were no cushions. I settled on the available patch of rug. He nodded toward the reptilian Josag I hadn't been aware of and from whom Matrakci took a very big green velvet box. The object inside was considerably smaller than the box—something rectangular, encrusted with jewels. A giant buckle perhaps? A fragment of breastplate? Matrakci inverted the box, angled the item out. It was most unlikely. A book.

"From the Imperial Library. For study." As I would learn, Matrakci said nothing unnecessary, starting with nearly all modifiers. What he might have added, though, was that the book had been sent by the Sultan. Turning it gem-side up he said, "The decoration is recently finished."

Matrakci handed me the volume.

I know the book.

࿇

I am nine and it is my birthday and I am sitting on the side of my mother's tall, tufted bed. My feet are dangling nearly to the floor, where my mother is kneeling like a tailor. "Come here," she says taking something from her bodice and getting close to a small compartment built beneath the place where she sleeps and dreams. She wiggles a key into the lock. It won't open. She sits back on her heels, centers her ivory pendant, tries again. I get down next to her; she smells of cinnamon. I bang the door and yank. "You're good at everything," she says as I peer into the hiding place. "See it?" I have my nose to an ill-smelling tube that evidently contains a parchment. "It's a book. There's only one."

"There's a tube with something inside," I say to her.

"Do you see the book?"

"Is it a map? It's yours, isn't it? Egnatius said you drew a map a long time ago."

"Well. Not exactly. Take out the book, Cecilia."

"May I see it?"

"Capritta. Take out the book. It is a surprise."

I rub my hands on my thighs and withdraw a faded red volume with two elaborate Es on the cover separated by letters nearly too rubbed to read. We get up on the bed and sit side by side. My mother rests her cheek on top of my head and says that it is time that the book she places in my lap is mine.

58

I opened the volume Matrakci placed in my hands. Its leather binding was a red gone to brown. I blew on the faint *Elements*, the rubbed *Euclid*, imagining they might disappear, or that the book might. I got burning hot. This book stood for everything that mattered to me. My education, the betrayal of my mother, my captivity and aspiration. I had worked hard since I'd been stolen from my old life. I'd been noticed and promoted to a high place. I had made myself be where I was by respecting the rules. And yet this book proclaimed to me that we'd both been stolen. I laid the book on the carpet as though it were an infant with not long to live. I said, "I believe it is mine."

Josag swept the floor with a pointed toe. "Ridiculous," he snarled.

Matrakci stiffened. His boxy jaw congealed. "You dare say that? This treasure belongs to the Sultan." He placed it decisively in the sling made by his robe between his knees.

The effort Matrakci had been making was about to be over, maybe. I had to save the moment—but how? Withdraw my claim? Press it?

"It used to be mine. I believe. If it is from Venice." It could *only* have been from Venice. "If it is printed by Tacuinus," I added. "1505." Matrakci looked at me—appalled, it seemed. "May I?" He said nothing. Carefully I took the book. I opened to the title page. There it was. The little stamp of John the Baptist at the bottom of the title page—the printer's colophon. And under it, the date: 1506. "I meant to say 1506." Matrakci's eyes batted one at a time. He was not accustomed to information that contradicted his own. "I haven't learned it yet," I said to the book.

A finger mark somewhere in Book I—in *Definitions*, to be exact—would have confirmed beyond a doubt that this was *my* Euclid, but I did not check. I kept the book closed, tracing the remains of the letters on the cover. Matrakci's voice was faint in the air. "Of course you haven't learned it," he was saying. I handed over *Elements* as if to a ghost, though I was the ghost.

Matrakci turned to Book III. "You have studied I and II," he said. "We start, then, here." *Theory of Circles*. It was illuminated. Exactly as I recalled it. Not with flora or fauna, or sages or putti, but with children. Merry, lucky learners playing up and down the margins, in and out of *Definitions*. Tacuinus alone printed such fantastical books. "Equal circles are those whose diameters are equal, or whose radii are equal," Matrakci read. Latin. His accent tripped on *r*s. The book was on the carpet between us. "You."

"Definition Two. A straight line is said to touch a circle which," I paused, unbundling the grammar in my mind, "meeting the circle and being produced, does not cut the circle."

Matrakci read the next. We went through them all. We reached *Propositions*. "Here." Matrakci handed me a small sheet of vellum. "Write them."

I sat on my heels, refolded myself. Josag snorted. I had written nothing but Arabic, big and leftward, for more than a year. The Latin felt cramped and weird. I needed a second sheet.

"You will illustrate the first five for tomorrow." Matrakci took what I'd written, waved it dry, tapped it into a tube he'd had in a pocket. "You may leave." He said this not emphatically or dismissively but with a kind of relief. Then, holding out the tube, he added, "You are not *that* special."

And I said to him, "I know."

The complicated promise of the encounter had, I think, peeled away my pretense. And it changed everything. In exchange for admission of my fear of being not special, Matrakci ceded his suspicion. He smiled. At least, it seemed like a smile.

This is how for the next four years foundations were laid one on top of another. Matrakci's on Suna's and both of those on Egnatius's and my mother's. Perhaps because he came last in the order of my teachers, it was Matrakci who secured for me the connections among numbers, letters, proportion, and beauty. And that was but the beginning of what he did for me.

Sunday, November 13

Days of heaven, of hell. Days that change everything. I call to my mind a certain summer morning in 1539, and it feels now exactly as it felt that day. I had been here for nearly three years, under Matrakci's care for half that time, meeting three times a week in the plain, happy room near the Tower of Justice. On that day I was ferried, as usual, to Topkapi by palanquin, and as we passed through the Bab-iHumayun I counted, as I always did, the bearers' footsteps. Across the First Courtyard, one hundred and twelve. Across the Second, a hundred and two. Suddenly, an upward jolt. I cracked the curtain. I was clearing the threshold of the Gate of Felicity. Beyond it—the Forbidden Abode. No one goes past that plinth without approval from the Sultan himself. My conveyance didn't pause. I was heading inward. I closed the curtain. When the palanquin came to rest there was no instruction. No one peered in. I climbed out and into the semi-dark. I was in the harem.

A quick-tempoed clicking, the high-heeled step of short legs, announced her arrival down the corridor. Red announced Hurrem, too, emerging from the shadows. Yards of it trailing from the silk-covered cone that peaked a foot above her head. The color was all around her as she entered.

A bloody tangle was my first impression of her. The second was of night—a face shaded and slivered like the moon's. Slim arcs of brows, of the upper lip, of the hairline that met in a black point on her forehead. Her shoulders had the same shape, sloping into short arms that curved into hands and fingers pressed tip-to-tip to form a pointed basket that seemed to contain something alive that she might make appear at any time. She had a strange quality of smoothness, as though she were made not of flesh and hair but of a single thing—water or stone. A single smoothness, except for the lower lip, which in the slanted rooftop light I saw was gnawed to a purplish pulp. This was the Sultan's wife.

The aura of the hyena is said to be aphrodisiac, and the head of the hyena is attached directly to the spine so the animal has to turn completely around in order to look back: Hurrem was said to have kept a pair of them. She was also said to be a witch—though that was not true. Hers was the power of an astrolabe, not a sorcerer. Hurrem didn't make things what they were not. She supplied bearings and determined direction. As far as Suleiman was concerned, she determined the length of the day.

Few, including me, could imagine what he saw in her. Yet here is what Suleiman wrote:

I Am the Sultan of Love

I am the Sultan of Love:
a glass of wine will do
for a crown on my head,
and the brigade of my sighs
might well serve as the dragon's
fire-breathing troops.
The bedroom that's best
for you, my love,
is a bed of roses,
for me, a bed and a pillow

carved out of rock
will do.
My love, take a golden cup
in your hand and drink wine
in the rose garden,
as for me, to sip blood from my heart,
it is enough
to have the goblets of your eyes.
If, my beloved, you ride
the horse of coyness
and trot in the polo grounds,
this head of mine
will do
as a ball for your mallet.
Come, don't let
the army of sorrow
crush the heart's soldiers,
if it is my life you demand
just send those looks of yours
that should be enough.
The heart can no longer
reach the district where you live,
but it yearns for a reunion with you:
don't think Paradise and its rivers
can satisfy
the lover of the adorable face.
Lover, I have enough tears
to sprinkle
over the ground you walk on
and my own pallid face
will do for me
as silver or gold.

The horse of coyness, indeed. In the seventeen years she had been with him, Hurrem had not once been to the Old

Palace. She had not seen, managed, or presided over the concubine corps for which she, as wife of the Sultan, was responsible. She had been too busy mesmerizing her husband and producing children. Flouting the one-son-per-mother rule—the purpose of which was to spare full brothers the requirement to eliminate each other—she had given birth to five boys—Mehmed, Abdullah, Selim, Bayezid, and Jihangir, though Abdullah died at three. And she'd had a daughter, Mihrimah.

She quivered in the hallway conveying haste and harm. Around her scurried an entourage of abasing concubines. Behind her oozed Gazanfer, the Chief White Eunuch—his presence a conspicuous symbol of the favor Hurrem enjoyed.

An attendant reached over to dab her sweaty upper lip. Hurrem pushed her away and straightened up to a height one had to wonder how—and why—she concealed. Come to where I am, her flicking finger ordered. *Now.* "Veniero." Her accent clamped onto the word as though it were cargo. Turkish hoisting Italian, lugging Ukrainian. *Forward,* she motioned, like a man—with a jerk of the chin.

"You think you know very much. You don't know anything. This studying, this is nothing." Hurrem's and Gazanfer's disdain reshaped their faces identically, as lizards. Whatever I knew from books—or teachers, apparently—counted for nothing, Hurrem said. *She* and she alone knew what counted as far as her sons were concerned.

Her sons? I had heard nothing about the disposition of her sons. I could not guess what had her so riled. She troubled to name them. Mehmed. Selim. Bayezid. She didn't bother with Jihangir, as his deformity rendered him ineligible for succession. Mehmed was known to be his parents' favorite, Selim the least favored, and Bayezid the most bold. Selim's and Bayezid's rite of circumcision had taken place not long before—the celebration having been appended to their sister Mihrimah's wedding to Rustem Pasha, the Grand Vizier.

Those few, not-simple facts were what was known to the concubine ranks about the children of Hurrem and Suleiman.

It must be said that not everything Hurrem claimed about her dominion was untrue. She was a force without equal. Suleiman had had many women before Hurrem; ambassadors had regularly reported on his lustful ways. When Hurrem was presented to him, though, it stopped. Not only was she his, he seemed to be hers. It concerned everyone.

It had been only a few years since she'd had herself moved from the Old Palace into Topkapi. Since the first rooms of the Imperial Palace had been built by Mehmed the Conqueror, no female—not a mother, sister, or daughter of the Sultan, let alone a concubine—had ever lived there. The Imperial Harem had been the residence of the Sultan and the seat of government—nothing else. Those lush and creepy courtyards had defined an order of spheres, from inner to innermost. Power steeped at the center. For Hurrem to have bypassed the network of liminal characters—the eunuchs, the dwarves, the mutes—with which Suleiman shielded himself was not only to lap at the hem of the Shadow of God on Earth but to have penetrated the machinery of government.

Everything about her—the feral alertness, the roiling will, the reason for the chewed lip—intrigued me. Hurrem seemed to have gotten very far, and without an education. She couldn't even read. I wanted to know how she'd done it.

"You have gone around me," she brayed. "Do not think it goes unnoticed." I told her I didn't understand. That I'd done no such thing. That, in fact, I wouldn't know how to go around her. "And you contradict me," she said, missing my point. Her unbending frame turned. "Do not imagine that any of this means more than it does. Learning counts for nothing here." Her backbone was pronounced through her tunic. She was thinner than she seemed. "And do not imagine it is my wish—or that this assignment won't be changed. I am watching you," she said directly to the wall.

What assignment? There was no chance to ask. Hurrem had turned herself around. "Go ahead," she said loudly as she headed back where she'd come from. "Take her there then."

Hurrem believed that what she said was believable by virtue of having said it. But learning had gotten me where I was. Using my head was freeing me from the customs of concubines, and I was interested that Hurrem would take a position so provably false.

"Take me where?" I said, irked and wishing she'd hear me.

"The Prince's school," my escort—a White Eunuch I'd never laid eyes on—answered. "You *don't* know anything," he added proudly.

Matrakci was waiting for me. And cross-legged on a rug beside him was a youth I'd never seen. His face was familiar, though. The face I had been hoping for—big, square, and open, with wide-set eyes that were gray and kind and a mouth that was full and turned down at the corners, not in petulance—that was clear from the eyes. But it was turned down from *something*. He wore a wide-wound turban, a purple tunic, yellow trousers, and a red sash. The tunic was dark from wetness under his arms although it wasn't hot in that room, nor was he exerting himself. Not apparently. His feet were bare, his simple sandals kicked off to the side, and he was squinting and leaning forward as though to better hear Matrakci, who was saying nothing. The only sound was the nib of Matrakci's pen on the hide. Matrakci sat back on his heels and consulted the youth with a propitious look. *Do you understand what I've written here?* it said. The youth pushed back his turban to confirm he understood, and framing the top of his head was hair like mine—black and curly—and his mother's widow's peak.

Matrakci blew on the ink, waved the sheet in the air. He tapped on the parchment, and glanced my way. *That's right,* the small gesture indicated. Tap, tap. Then the boy looked up, the corners of his mouth straightening into a smile. He looks like hope, I thought. Not my hope. Hope. "Prince Mehmed," Matrakci said to me.

Mehmed bowed his head, lined up his sandals, and said, "We were expecting you."

I took my seat beside Matrakci. Before us was a stack of books. In my own lessons there was never more than one volume at a time. But there in front of me was what my grandfather would have called "all of" Regiomontanus. *Algorithmus Demonstratus, De Triangulis omnimodus, Epytoma in almagesti Ptolemei,* and *Theorica novae Planetarum.* Matrakci took the second one—*On Triangles of All Kinds*—from the stack. "You will understand this," Matrakci claimed. I thought of the very sharp contrast between my shaky grasp of Regiomontanus's concepts and my mother's facility with them, especially as applied to maps, and it occurred to me only then—on a rug between Matrakci and Mehmed—that while Egnatius and my mother had given me every conceivable encouragement, neither of them had ever suggested I try my hand at a map. That I had not felt disappointed by that was just one more of their gifts to me. My mother and tutor wanted me to succeed in the ways that came best to me.

"I hope so."

Mehmed leaned in front of our teacher to see me. "You will. Nurbanu."

I looked to Matrakci for the meaning of this word. "Your new name."

"Nurbanu," Mehmed said again. I said it myself. *Nur.* Light. *Banu.* Lady. Matrakci reached for a pen. Mehmed did the same—the two of them signaling that the lesson and getting back to it was more important than a name and even than the reason I'd been given a new name, and that was true. But I certainly didn't think so at the time. What I understood was why I was on that patch of floor between those two people. I was being favored by means of learning. And I didn't need the reflection in the windows—which opened to the Golden Horn and Empire and all the world—in order to know what my face looked like—lit by a star shower of pride. I was the arrow enduring the string no more. I was released.

෫෨

In the effort to create order, we sometimes look for symmetry and even see it where it doesn't exist. When it does exist, it's often strange. The decision by Suleiman to have me tutored alongside a boy of high status, for instance, and my grandfather's decision four years earlier to do the same thing. How differently conceived and spurred those decisions were—Suleiman's aim being to make my education a bulwark for his successor; my grandfather's being to impress people in positions he could never attain—yet how similar their effect. My grandfather's occasioned one of the few real exchanges I ever witnessed between him and my mother. It made me thank God there weren't more. Given where I'm lying at this moment it seems eerie that the House of Osman and this Empire were the dinner topic, though they often were—which is how I knew about Janissaries, the *devshirme*, viziers, and Ottoman tolerance long before I came here.

My grandfather was opining on the personal relations of the Sultan with certain others, including Doge Gritti, and his communications via the Bailo—the Republic's ambassador—and my grandmother happened to have in her head the exact cost an elaborate helmet Suleiman had had made for himself in Venice.

I was surprised to learn it had been paid for in ducats—my first lesson in trade between countries—to which my grandfather's response was that the Ottomans prized order as much as the Republic did. "Suleiman may be a Turk," he said, "but he's

SVLIMAN·OTOMAN·REX·TVRC· X·

called the Lawgiver for a reason." My grandmother chimed in with intelligence that the Sultan had given the Grand Vizier a bedroom adjoining his own. "They are that close," she reported. My grandfather countered that that was better than what went on with the Borgias; he noted incest, murder; my grandmother specified cantarella, an arsenic mix concocted by the Moors. And that was when my mother, the Crivelli Madonna, blew up, just like a bomb. She slammed down her spoon and demanded silence. I had never, ever seen her act that way.

My grandfather instructed her with insincere gentleness to calm down, and while engaging in vigorous tooth-picking he launched into a report on the Aldine Press; an encomium on its founder Manutius; and an announcement that Manutius's nephew, a boy my age, would share my lessons with Egnatius. When my mother pushed back her chair—hard—my grandfather did the same, and it was clear the two gestures were one and that their common ground was mined. My mother bored her gaze into the side of her father's head and, in a voice that was raw as blood, she said, "My daughter's education is not a dowry." And then she left the room. My grandfather stayed where he was, raking his fingernails through his hair right down to what was on his mind—that my mother had a very great gift and "did nothing with it." What frightened me most was when he stood up and then dropped back down in his chair. He seemed, and as it turned out he was, less strong than me—a bad thing for a child to suspect. "Your mother can draw a map," he said out of nowhere."She knows how to translate Ptolemy's projections onto paper, and she refuses to."

"Well, why?" I shouted at him.

He hooked a finger—there was a little glob of liver on it—inside his collar, yanked to free a suite of warts, and told me that the most valuable thing he had ever bought he'd bought for her. "The most important astronomical tables in the world." Ulugh Bey's. When he started to say what an astronomical chart was for, I cut him off. And I did it rudely. I told him him I knew "exactly" what such a chart was for—and that scared me, too: having reason to speak to my grandfather that way and getting away with it. When I asked him why my mother stopped making maps, he swallowed hard. He wanted to tell his story without answering the question on which the story turned. He said I didn't know how much he'd done for my mother. He spoke to me as though he were speaking to someone who wasn't me. To someone he didn't like. To himself. Nor did he look at me when he asserted that

I would distinguish myself and not, like my mother, "abandon everything"—a charge that was false, I was absolutely sure. I told my grandfather to not talk about my mother that way. And then I told him he loved her, and that was what seemed to cause him to stand and turn around. It was as though he was unacquainted with the room. This was a man with no imagination whatever. He said to me, "I don't understand." It was as true a declaration as he ever made.

∽

Nurbanu, I murmured as the Mistress of the Baths pierced one ear, then the other, suspending from each diamonds big as teeth. Nurbanu, I repeated as the Mistress decorated the palms of my hands with henna, perfumed my nape and shoulders with musk and amber. I had been chosen by the Sultan himself. "Cecilia," I said getting my bearings. The henna woman clocked her eyes up. "My old name," I said.

Before the day was over, I was awarded an apartment facing the Golden Horn, given fifteen hundred aspers, measured for shoes—high ones—with soles the shape and size of okra. I was also allowed to choose my own Black Eunuch, and I was given a girl to wait on me day and night. My life kept being marked by sudden shifts of huge consequence. When this one occurred, I was fifteen.

In recalling that long-ago time when Mehmed was alive and Suleiman not yet old, my thoughts about the two of them are in many ways entwined. Suleiman brought Mehmed and me together, after all, and he joined us under the ordinance of Matrakci's imagination. In doing that he equipped us equally, and on purpose, and this makes me wonder. Did Suleiman know Mehmed would not feel diminished by having his lessons invaded this way? Did he know I would not abuse the privilege? This was not, after all, a man who trusted. Whatever Suleiman's intention might have been, it allowed Mehmed and me to find each other by observing each other's will. At no point did the very difficult material Matrakci put before me fail to make sense, and I am certain that was because Mehmed believed I could understand it. I knew he wanted me to succeed, and so I did. Suleiman wanted me to succeed, too. But Mehmed wanted it because he cared about me. What tugged down the corners of Mehmed's mouth was sympathy. A lifetime of it. Worry, too, but that's one of its features. And his sympathy for me took away what remained of my fear. There is no fear in loving someone who has no fear. I learned that first from Mehmed.

Mehmed and I studied Matrakci's algorithms for lattice multiplication—the table Matrakci had thrust in my hand the day I first met him. We read Taqi al-Din's *Sublime Methods of Spiritual Machines*, which taught me whatever I know about such unsunderable things as time-telling and Islam, clocks and astronomical observation, beauty and truth. Only Matrakci's *Beauty of Scribes and Perfection of Accountants*—which today is taught in every school in the Empire preparing students for government—proved too steep a climb. The first inkling I had that Matrakci had a heart—a big one—was his putting that book aside without comment. It wasn't till many years later, when Matrakci was teaching Murad trigonometry, that I learned that he and Mehmed had studied *Scribes* on their own. Matrakci said Mehmed didn't want anything to take the wind from my sail—much as my mother and Egnatius had felt about my drawing maps.

It was a heady struggle to gain mastery of these subjects and disciplines, and the unguarded interest Mehmed took in my progress, the excitement he seeded with the idea that order was knowable, imitable, and located in the heavens—all this got me thinking about my father, and this disconcerted me, because he was both a spectral stranger and the cause of horrible things that had happened in my life. It was with an awkward, unidentified disgust that I wanted to get to the bottom of something about which I had facts but no understanding. I wanted to know the circumstances of my birth. And I wanted someone with me as I made the descent. A second heart for the apprehending. I was coming to realize that that heart was right next to me, and it was Mehmed's. Matrakci had known this all along. When I petitioned him for time alone with Mehmed—a very irregular request—he said nothing, which I knew was an answer. When I arrived for my next lesson one person was on the floor with *Elements*, and it was not my teacher.

෨෨

I began with my father's patrimony on Paros, his naval prowess, his inventive streak and merchant spirit, and how those and other things brought him here, to Anatolia, where he learned Turkish, then Arabic, then Islamic commercial law. I told Mehmed about the shifting board—the device my father invented for separating cargo for maximum capacity—which changed the economy of merchant shipping, earned my father a fortune, and won him a seat on the Republic's Mercantile Administration representing its interest in alum, a mordant that fixes color in cloth. I told him that by 1512 my father was managing the trade of luxury goods between Venice and Asia—all of Asia. Silk, porcelain, dyes—cinnabar, madder root, licorice. "My father knew every inlet, marker, and shoal in the Adriatic," I said to Mehmed, bragging—about a person I hadn't known and didn't like. And when I realized this—which I quickly did—I stopped. I stopped my story as though I'd been ordered to. Calmly, immediately, Mehmed reached inside his robe and took out a small flask. It was made of goatskin, and the nozzle was made of gold, and a jade amulet hung from a little chain around the nozzle. Offering it to me, he said, "It was a gift from my mother. On the occasion of my circumcision." The confusing modesty and specificity of such a gift from such a person, combined with my own strange boasting about my father, ended whatever intention I might have had to resume my narrative. I handed the flask back. Gave Mehmed a wan smile of thanks. Instead of telling the rest of what I had to say about my father, or the rest of what I was acquainted with about my father at the time, I wrapped my story up fast. I said that in the autumn of 1524 the man who would be my father visited my grandfather's house, and that was when he met the girl who would be my mother, and I was born the next year.

When I was done, Mehmed held out his flask again. I shook my head. He took a long sip, and he said to me, "You are fortunate, then. And so am I—having parents who love—loved—each other." As though his parents were the same as mine, and as though our parents and their relation to each other were not, in fact, opposite. "Flaws and all."

Monday, November 14

Suleiman was said to be the perfect number. The tenth sultan in the tenth century of the Hegira. He was a glory foretold and fulfilled. He led the Empire to the height of the power it still enjoys; he grabbed the gullet of Europe and brought the House of War into the House of Islam, and in doing this Suleiman did right by the Empire. He adapted the law of Islam to accommodate the reasonable ways of *all* his people—including vanquished foes whose needs he served and welfare he protected, whose religions he respected, too. This was a man who looked into the lives of his people and supported them; who dispensed justice himself—on horseback; who inspired its warriors, lawmakers, and holy men; its men of science and letters; its architects and mapmakers; its boys and its girls. Suleiman was a man of vision and heart.

It was the same afternoon—when I'd told Mehmed about my father—that he told me about his.

"He was said to be the perfect number," Mehmed continued, "not a perfect person. No one is." Then he told me what he meant.

&

Many years—decades—earlier in Amasya, Suleiman and his half brothers had been summoned by their father, Selim the Grim. It was the eve of a campaign to Persia, and the Grim demanded to see his sons before battle. Suleiman's mother, Hafsa, knew what the summons meant. She told him his father was testing his loyalty, and that he should disavow his every ambition. When Suleiman and his brothers were in the circle of light before the imperial tent, a eunuch pulled back the embroidered door. Suleiman's father, jowly, soot-eyed, sat cross-legged on the campaign throne positioned in the center of the campaign rug, which happened to be Mehmed the Conqueror's most prized symbol of identity—the rug, not the throne. One by one the brothers removed their boots and took their places at their father's feet. The Grim reviewed the day's events. He reported news from the frontier. He solicited his sons' reports. Then Suleiman's father asked his sons—just as Suleiman's mother had warned—about their aims. "Who among you will succeed me when Persia is ours? Who will take the royal standard to the eastern edge of our Empire? Who will carry it beyond the edge of imagination?" The first son said it would be his highest honor to succeed his father. The second assured the Grim he would not disappoint him when he became Sultan. The third said the Grim's memory would live on in that son's every deed. Then it was Suleiman's turn. "I am your slave, unfit to step in your footprint. May God find another way for me to serve the House of Osman." It was the only right answer for a sultan such as the Grim, whose greatest fear was being murdered by a son. The next day broke with the first son's eunuch peeling around Suleiman's tent, streaked in mud and shrieking: "The Prince's eyes are all over his cheeks." A moment later came the second son's servant—ashen, ill, unable even to say what he'd seen. That was when Suleiman ran like a hart to the tent of his youngest brother, whose name was Murad, and he threw open the flap and there was the boy—the bowstring cinched deep in his neck, his eyes exploded, his body twisted around in its own filth. "And so was set this unfading image," Mehmed said to me, "right before my father's eyes."

Right behind them, too, where the image doesn't die.

✺

The sun is sharp this morning and slanting like a spear. The windows frame nothing but sky, but I know what's out there—out where I can't see. My Marmara and Golden Horn. My Scutari. Murad is having Sinan build me a mosque over there, in Asia. It was, when he told me about it, the first hint that he might put our trouble behind us. Esther went to the site yesterday with Sinan—who, by the way, is exactly the age of Hamon. The two of them—ninety-two. For years, Esther's been Sinan's source for decorative materials, and this time she has outdone herself—abalone, ebony, an entire elephant tusk procured through a middleman in Antwerp. No one has access to the materials Esther does. If I did not know her as I do, I would say she was born to be an agent. But she was not. She was born to save people. One more thing she has in common with Hamon. Both of them were put on earth to save lives in the land that saved theirs. They have this in common, too: they refuse to say—to me, at least—how worried they are about this illness. It's clear to me they are, though. Their faces tell the truth. It is part of their worth.

✺

The story Mehmed told me about his father and grandfather explained the blood that ran in Suleiman's veins. And it explains what happened next in our lives.

It had to do with a son of Suleiman I haven't mentioned. Mehmed's half brother Mustafa. Suleiman's very first son, born of a woman who was not Hurrem. A good woman

78

and an outstanding mother. Mahidevran. It means Moon of Fortune.

Mustafa was a dazzler. A horseman without peer, a great fletcher, a master of war games, and a reflective person, too. Suleiman enjoyed Mustafa's company. He liked hunting with him, and he liked having him along as he meted out justice. Mustafa had a sense of right and wrong. He'd been raised—by his mother—to have it, and his father loved that in him, and so did the people. Mustafa was much admired by all who saw and knew about him.

When he came of age, years before Mehmed did, Suleiman sent Mustafa to Manisa, the plum provincial post. Mahidevran not only accompanied her son, she protected his interest with talent and care. She created a court termed glorious by ambassadors and administrators who passed through that province. The Janissaries under Mustafa's command protected him as well, because they loved Mustafa. They loved his talent and his fairness. None of this was lost on his father.

Hurrem tolerated all of this attention to Mustafa barely, and when Mehmed came of age, ending Suleiman's support for Mustafa became her life's mission. Paternal pride, filial trust, honor—none of it meant anything to Hurrem. She decided to have Mustafa demoted and Mehmed elevated. To be precise, she wanted Mustafa moved to Amasya—a very distant and lowly post—and Mehmed installed in Manisa. And what brothers are supposed to settle, by law, between themselves, Hurrem would seduce Suleiman into settling himself. Hurrem intended to take no chances.

Hurrem had badgered Suleiman about this for years. Always he demurred. He had every reason to. But that didn't keep her from gaining ground. Suleiman probably didn't even know it. That's what being in thrall can do. I know.

The day of Hurrem's victory, so to speak, was the day she strolled into an audience Suleiman was holding with the Papal Nuncio. Suleiman suggested with a look that she attend him elsewhere, but Hurrem declined. She wouldn't move. Matrakci was there and saw everything. Rather than entertain *no* for an answer from his wife, Suleiman adjourned the session with the Romans, dismissed everyone but his confidant—for that is what Matrakci was to him—and touched his thigh to show his wife how close she could come. Hurrem knelt beside her husband and told him this: that his firstborn son was agitating against him. She had spies. Her assertion was backed by first-person accounts. Suleiman made no objection to her surveillance scheme. Matrakci guessed he must have admired it. "It is time my son have Manisa," Hurrem said to the sultan.

"Ours," Suleiman corrected her, gently.

"Yes, our son, of course." And batting her antelope eyes, she took Suleiman's hand, held it between her breasts, on her bare skin—in front of Matrakci—and uttered Mehmed's name.

"Mustafa has done well in Manisa," Suleiman told his wife calmly. "I do not see that this change is warranted."

Hurrem persisted. "Mustafa can have Amasya." The post of far less prestige.

"He merits his present post. He is well loved. He will stay there," Suleiman said.

"I understand," she said.

Hurrem then molded Suleiman's fingers around her breast and drew her tongue from side to side along her teeth. It makes me feel sicker than I do already mouldering in this bed to think about this display. She told Matrakci to leave the Sultan's chamber and return at an appointed time with their favorite son. Suleiman, Matrakci said, was too aroused to object. It was a weak link in the chain of his character. When Matrakci and Mehmed returned, far from being released or satisfied, the Sultan was on a hassock, agitated, pursed. He was alone. He nodded for the two of them to sit. Then he ordered an elaborate meal, including chicken pudding, Mehmed's favorite dessert. He sat before the food in silence, ate nothing, pushed the trays away, turned to Mehmed, and said that he had news.

"You have distinguished yourself in all you have undertaken. You deserve a post of your own, my lion. A change is in order. I am awarding you the governate of Manisa." The knot in Mehmed's throat bulged as he stretched and swallowed. His father saw it. Matrakci saw it.

"But that is Mustafa's post. Has he not earned it? My brother is respected in Manisa," Mehmed objected with his own respect. He admired his half brother. Mustafa had taught Mehmed how to hold a bow. In fact, he'd made him one. And he'd sent Mehmed his own prize falcon as a present when Mehmed had passed to manhood.

"Mustafa will govern Amasya. It is a worthy assignment."

"But it is so distant," Mehmed pressed on—referring to the disadvantage its governor—by custom a pretender to the throne—had in reaching the capital to claim that throne, when the time came. "Won't this change cause trouble?"

Matrakci whispered, "Indeed."

Mehmed observed his father's distance, and he backed away, slightly, to appeal to it. That's how well he knew his father. "It is you, Sultanimiz, who has impressed on me the imperatives of order. Over many years you have done this. And my part in upholding it." The awkwardness was terrific. "And understanding it. And I will. By many means." Mehmed looked right at Matrakci to make clear what he meant—numbers, their meanings, their applications. "My work with Matrakci. Correcting the Tables of Ulugh Bey—and what that entails."

"An observatory," Matrakci indicated, this time so the Sultan could hear.

These were direct challenges to the Sultan, and they got him to his feet. It wasn't anger, we'd learn a long time after. It was interest, and Suleiman declined to express it. Immediately Mehmed tried another tack. Suleiman was towering over him, his serpentine sleeves all over the floor. "Could the new arrangement be postponed?" meaning until Mustafa possibly had done something construed as so heinous as to deserve it. Possibly. Mehmed was trying to correct his father, because he loved him.

"I took his elbow," Matrakci said afterward. "Prince Mehmed—the mildest of all people—was shaking from the inside of his bones." Did his father see this? The dynasty, the future, were shaking through his favorite son. Then, an astonishing thing happened. Suleiman got on his knee. He was not imploring, of course. But there he was, on one knee. "Those are reasonable questions," he conceded. "I have considered them myself." As he got up and smoothed his robe, Mehmed did, too. "Nevertheless, it is decided that you will go now." *Nevertheless* said it all. And that is when Suleiman took Mehmed in his arms and held him, awkwardly, owing to the turbans. They both kept their eyes open, Matrakci said, each staring over the other's shoulder. And I hope I do not give too much away when I say that it was not only the first but also the last time that Suleiman embraced a son.

I believe two weeks passed before I saw Mehmed after that exchange. Maybe more. It was a very long time. I had no idea, until he vanished that way, that our lessons had become my life, and I don't mean the life of my mind. They were my energy and purpose. When Mehmed didn't come I had neither, and there was a dread that even the deaths in my life hadn't brought on. All Matrakci would say was that the Prince was indisposed, and he was testy when he said it. "What did I do wrong?" I kept asking him.

Finally Mehmed appeared. He strode in specifically unlike himself, his expression both blank and imperial—and, without acknowledging either Matrakci or me, he made a speech, every word of it spiked with distress. It was about everything that mattered to him. He started with the importance of order and order's beauty and the proof of each being in the numbers with which we measure space and measure time. He moved to the order of the Empire and the dynasty and the imperative to protect it by propagation—many princes to protect the throne—and preventing civil war. He spoke of the order of the governate system. Of his brothers one by one. Of his half brother Mustafa and his love for him. Yes. He loved him. He then got to the news—about Mustafa's transfer, his own assignment to replace him, the trouble it was going to cause; the disruption. Order, order, order. He untied his collar. He was saying things that were very obvious to him. That they needed saying was shortening his breath. He ventured a guess about his mother's role and said she meant well, which was when Matrakci gathered his parchments and pens to leave, and Mehmed told him to stay. "The Sultan's intention is to support—and to honor—me. He has ordered you to accompany me to Manisa. Both of you."

I realized I was not taking in the scope of what Mehmed was saying. "But this is *good* news," was all I could manage. My instinct was to fall at his feet, take his hands, kiss them, hold them, put my head in his lap like the darling I wished and was being told I was about to be. But I didn't. I sat beside him, faced the direction he faced and assumed the position he was in, leaning forward, elbows to knees, like a man or a friend. Mehmed's fingers were laced and white from clutching. He pressed the heels of his hands to the sides of his head, his fingers cragged up like antlers. His long lashes fluttered, and his body shuddered, head to feet. It is a fit, I thought. He has whatever ailment his poor brother Jihangir has. It was no fit, though. It was the key rattling in the lock. And Mehmed's eyes, glazed like stoneware, began to fade. His face was a sketch getting paler. He was the representation of erasing. And in the voice not of a ghost but of a real, sure person, he said to me,

"You are in this now. And there is a certain custom, a law. And it is important that you know about it."

"What do you mean? I am in what? Where's your little pouch, your flask, Mehmed? You need some water." He took a sip, offered me his flask. I put my lips where his had just been. There was no scent of goat, no taste of gold.

"The problem is not Mustafa," Mehmed said, both answering and not answering. "The problem is that the sons of the sultan who do not succeed him are not permitted to survive." I pulled back. Mehmed put up a hand: listen to the rest, it signaled. Now that I've embarked on this. Listen. "Usually they are half brothers. Often they have resolved the matter themselves before their father has died. Sometimes they have not. The Conqueror's father made his brothers ineligible to succeed. Blinded them. My mother's special attention—it is a burden. It puts me where I should not be." Mehmed was swooping like a hawk from one ledge to the next. All he wanted was a decent solution. He is all heart, I thought. Everything in him beats with that force. He took my hands flat between his—the way Christians pray. Hands steepled and closed. "She intends for me to succeed my father. For *me* to keep the order. Effect the law." He paused. "And I will not."

"*Mehmed.*"

"What I mean is that you will be my wife."

"What law?"

His forehead was raveled and dripping. He put up his hand as though I were aiming a weapon or he were taking an oath. Sure of at least one thing, he said, "My older brother merits his post. I intend to help my mother understand that."

"What law, Mehmed?"

"You help me," he added.

It was a strange thing for him to say. And with what I recognize now as the first gesture of grown-up love, I did not ask him to explain. He was getting up to leave, and it was time to let him go. I did not ask or hear about the law again—not until many years later, when nearly everything about life was different.

"A battle, a campaign, these are manageable," Matrakci said to me the next day, "compared to rivalry between princes. Especially when stirred by the Sultan." Mustafa had more than his pride. He had his men. The prospect of Mehmed's going alone to Manisa flanked Matrakci with fear.

Moments later, as Matrakci walked me to my palanquin, he and I saw Mehmed and his mother in the Second Courtyard. They were on horseback—she was riding pillion behind him, holding his waist as they circled. Mehmed, his head cocked back, was talking to her. Matrakci sighed. He recalled Mehmed's having said he intended to teach his mother to ride. She feared horses, and Mehmed wanted her not to.

"Someday, I will help her with that," Mehmed had said. Unlike most people who say *someday*, Mehmed had meant *soon*. That Hurrem was receptive to being taught anything was as surprising as the little flask she'd given him.

"Mehmed is her darling," Matrakci said. "Perhaps I am wrong in thinking he cannot sway her." Around and around Mehmed and his mother went, at a walking gait. Past the Imperial Kitchens, the Dormitories of the Halberdiers, the Treasury. Hurrem speaking, Mehmed turning his ear toward her to hear. Mehmed answering, his mother fastening her chin to the shoulder of her favorite son, who was trying to talk sense into her even as the horse, perhaps on its own, was picking up speed and making of Hurrem's veil a slight scarlet wake in the air.

Tuesday, November 15

Suleiman's favorite flower was the hyacinth. He had a hundred thousand of them planted around the Old Palace for the residents' sake and another hundred thousand on the bank below Topkapi, for his own. A myth surrounds the flower—about the gorgeous god Hyacinth dying in the arms of Apollo, and Apollo wailing over the loss of his beloved boy. I wonder if Suleiman knew that something wondrous had issued from Apollo's grief—for a flower then sprang from Hyacinth's brow, and the marks on the petals' tips mean "wailing" in Greek. There is no path through the hyacinths from Topkapi to the Golden Horn. When Mehmed called me to the Conqueror's Kiosk, I had to trample them by the hundreds to get there. By the thousands.

The key to Suleiman's command was Hurrem's will. Mehmed believed he could bend it—helping her fathom the governate system, the loyalties of Janissaries, the severe consequences of doing things out of order. I chose to believe he could, too. If you are lucky enough to love, I told myself, it is better to trust. And so, as the days had mounted without seeing him, I had tallied each as a good sign.

I made my way over the flower slick toward an opulent little octagon whose canvas curtains were flapping like mad red arms. Mehmed was holding on to a post as though the floor were heaving. He had arranged for no eunuchs. It was oppressively hot, the air warped and waving, colors seeping from their sources and running toward the sea. Red alone stayed put as the curtains flapped. What you see is true, red affirmed. My heart began to sink.

Mehmed said, "My mother's mind is set. There is nothing I can do about it. I will go to Manisa. Your presence, though, is *my* prerogative, and I welcome this hard office if only for that. You will come when I know it is safe. My wish—my interest—is to protect you. I will sort through this matter with my brother. Then you will come."

Even if he hadn't sounded like a foreign ambassador delivering his monarch's message, I knew I was standing before a different Mehmed. This was someone who had determined a right thing to do and was on his way to doing it. I could no more change his mind than he could change his mother's, and the finality of his *You will come only when I know it is safe* felt freezing and no different from another time I was powerless to change a decision that had huge consequences for me—when my mother took me from Paros. "I'm afraid to lose you."

"You cannot," Mehmed answered.

સ⁀

I saw my father once. I was five. The Doge had asked him to accompany him to Bologna for the coronation of Charles V, who, of course, was Suleiman's arch-nemesis—though that doesn't bear on this story. My father was so proud of this invitation that he came to Paros to make it known. He wanted us to know about it. My mother, Sylvana, and me. He was vain, and people who are vain do unlikely things. He arrived clothed in velvet and fur. It was summer. He was like a thick dream—a mix of things that didn't belong together—including the attire. I remember thinking he wasn't dressed like a woman, but

87

not as a man should have been either. The hat with a black feather, the gold chains around his neck, the short, shiny boots that would have been good for nothing anywhere I had ever walked. He stood before my mother and Sylvana and me as though he had been expected or invited, and he wasn't, and he hadn't been, and his appearing so suddenly after five years of not a word just about turned my mother to bone. She said, "This is your father." That's all she could say. I remember looking up at her and saying, *It is?* And turning to Sylvana. *Is it?* And Sylvana saying, *It is.*

The Doge was sending him on a mission, he informed us, and he reached into a pocket of his big coat, kept his hand there, and said to me, "You are . . . "; he paused. He was trying to reckon my age. "I am five years old," I told him. My mother held my hand as though I were being pulled away. "Well then, look what I have," he said. He withdrew a small tube from his pocket, tapped out the contents—two parchments—and unrolled the smaller one, which was the invitation, in Latin, which he read, starting with the Holy Roman Emperor's titles—King of the Balearic Islands, Duke of Carniola, Count of Swabia, Lord of Asia. Not unlike Suleiman's titles. Not at all. My mother asked him a second time why he had come, and my father's answer was to give me the other parchment, which I unrolled. My mother let out a short, sharp sound. She had the back of one hand up against her mouth. I looked at the thing he'd given. Considered its design of lines and markings, then rotated it a quarter turn. "That's right! You recognize North!" my father said, very pleased. My mother straightened herself to a startling degree. Her face was taut. Sylvana took her arm. "Of course she recognizes North," my mother said. "This," my father said emphatically, "is a portolan chart. An excellent one. It was drawn by your mother." He glanced at her, very quickly. I did, too. She still seemed taller than usual, but it also seemed Sylvana was holding her up. My father said, "I will try to come more often, Cecilia." Even more than seeing my mother act so suddenly strange, it was the ease with which my father said my name that made me feel suddenly and completely lost, cut loose. Hearing my name in his voice made it seem he'd known me all my life, and he hadn't.

Two months later a letter came from my grandfather—about whom I'd never heard a thing. On the day of Charles V's coronation, he wrote, the imperial suite had been crossing a wooden bridge when it collapsed and hurtled sixty people into the freezing river. Despite the Emperor's girth, he was ballooned to safety by the volume of his cape and, it was said, his odd minimum of decoration. The others, though, weighted by arms and family jewels, "went down like anchors." I have dreamt about what my father might have been wearing that day. About the meaningless medals that wound up taking him to the bottom.

My grandfather's letter was also a summons. After nearly six years of silence, he was telling my mother to return to Venice. Also to "bring the child." The one means by which he evidently knew he could effect this command was to promise my mother that I could study with the only person in Venice she trusted. My grandfather had the wits to include a message from Egnatius with his own letter. When my mother read these letters, she broke into a kind of crying I have come to know by heart—convulsive, confused, horribly endurable. Sylvana held her till it stopped. And when my mother collected herself she really did seem different. Maybe she envisioned what she was about to do for me. She said I'd be happy again. I did not believe this, though—especially seeing Sylvana's sadness. I clung to Sylvana's waist, wailing that I'd never see her again, and my mother got her arms around us both and said that I would. In fact, as I recall, she promised.

I had seen ships all my life but never with an eye to becoming part of one's journey. Roped to the wharf, the Baffo carrack that came for us looked like a prison with masts. The ascent, over water I had learned to swim in, to a deck from which my mother and I would watch our lives disappear, made me sick. Only when we were out of the harbor and looking back at land did my mother loosen her hold on my hand. Sylvana had one arm raised in a salute. My mother was saying "I love you."

❧

I told these things to Mehmed just before he left for Manisa. "It was just like now," I said. As he often did, he opened the top of his tunic. Then he took the garment by the shoulders and shook it as though he weren't inside. He put his hands around my waist and slid them up and under my arms and lifted me off my feet and held me there, breathing into me. He didn't kiss me, at least I didn't think he did. I had never been kissed in such a way. He just breathed. We never took our eyes off each other. When he put me down he said, "We will be together as soon as it is safe. And then we will be together always." He took my hands, kissed the palms, and folded them tight, to keep the promise in.

I fell into this assurance of Mehmed's from a great height. Taking terror with him, he let me fall through layers of air suffused with his goodness, honor, and love—including love of his family, of which he, along with his father, was making me a part. This was when my greatest wish changed from a wish to belong—which I was assured I did—to the wish to be happy. This was when I fell in love.

Wednesday, November 16

It was never part of Hurrem's plan to accompany her son to the post she achieved for him by upending the lives of everyone around her. But the household of four hundred she had assembled for Mehmed, and through which she would have established her authority, didn't go either. Mehmed went to Manisa practically alone. Just with the skeleton staff he had insisted on so as not to further rile Mustafa. That compromise was the product of pensive strolls and the riding lessons.

Three weeks after Mehmed left, a letter arrived. Holding the parchment packet, I felt the weather it had traveled in, the vistas it had passed. It had been stitched closed with green cord. I felt the fingers that had threaded it, placed it in the hands of a messenger who had been instructed to return with my reply.

Inside was not a letter but a very small picture. A continuous narrative that told a story of place. It was green top to bottom—the Prophet's color, with a mosque in the middle, a single minaret and a low enclosure in front of the mosque, four cypresses inside the enclosure, a row of houses with red roofs, a carnation in the green sky, and half of a black aloe tree on the right side of the parchment where it ended. Near the carnation the sun and moon were side by side. "Soon, you, too, will pass through these towns," Mehmed had written on the bottom. There was no other message. Nothing about Mustafa.

I wrote Mehmed that his painting enchanted me and that it lay open by my bed and was held down by compasses lent by Matrakci, who praised the painting and showed it to the Sultan. I asked about Mustafa.

Mehmed sent back a design for the clock he planned to construct for his younger brother Selim. He described its escapement and enclosed a copy of a poem Selim had written for him. It was called "Love What Is Before Me." Mehmed said he "took comfort in Selim's nature." Again, the courier waited for my reply.

I wrote of the state—shaky—of Suleiman's alliance with France, and that there was talk of Barbarossa joining the Bourbon forces led by François I in Marseille. I mentioned Barbarossa's coarseness and eminence. I asked about Mustafa.

Back and forth our letters went, not the way letters normally go, crossing each other on the route, putting questions and answers dangerously out of sequence, but in calming, good order, assured by couriers of uncommon stamina and kindness. Mehmed and I were speaking to each other. In his last letter, Mehmed wrote that Mustafa had departed, and that he was bitter, but toward his father's wife. Mustafa knew that Suleiman had his interest at heart, and that he loved him. "No harm will befall you here," Mehmed said to me in closing. "It is safe for you to come now. I await you, my Nurbanu, with love."

I wrote back that I would leave for Manisa three days hence—as soon as an entourage was assembled. I did not mention that Suna, whose duties encompassed no such matters, was intervening with the Superintendent, who revered her, Suna, and who'd grown ever more hostile to me. I told Mehmed that I had never known what happiness was until then, that day, reading his words. I told him that I loved him.

I included a picture I'd painted of the view from the harem to Scutari. Suleiman's own courier left with the parcel that same day. The day after, I wrote Mehmed again. I wanted him to know about *Elements*. I had gone into a panic about it—about telling him—during the night. I should have told him in the letter I'd written the day before. In fact, I should have told him before he left for Manisa. I meant to, but I hadn't wanted anything to dilute the sweetness of our parting. I wanted Mehmed's promise to be the last thing that was said. And it was. But now—then—on the verge of becoming Mehmed's wife and the mother of his children, I wanted him to know what *Elements* was about, because of all the things *Elements* defined, betrayal came first. Betrayal was what it stood for. I wanted Mehmed to know the route that book had traveled, and what it had led to. He had to know this right away. I omitted nothing essential to his full understanding, but I made the letter very brief because I was sending it by pigeon—Suna's idea. It would reach him the very next day.

I wrote to Mehmed that the year before I was born, 1524, my grandfather had added a long-sought feather to his cap when he lured the "great Veniero"—my father—to 'Ca Baffo. The meeting was to be about navigational devices, and the lure my grandfather had held out was Egnatius. My mother was also present for this meeting—which is the crux of the matter. At the insistence of her father she talked about the map of Europe she was working on and about those she'd completed, of Venice and the Adriatic. My grandfather noted my father's surprise. Egnatius nodded confirmation that every thing my mother described was true. Her future was sealed. The authority of her originality plus that of her beauty brought my father back with a gift for her. He was forty-five. She was sixteen. He'd acquired *Elements* from the printer himself, Tacuinus. My mother, because she was candid, and perhaps because she was confused, showed the book to her father, and all I can conclude is that the quality of his pride in the attention his daughter commanded from the man—the nobleman—who would become my father was such that he yielded the concern a parent might normally have, or that a normal parent might have had, about the pursuit of a girl by a man three times her age. I am certain my grandfather believed something important would accrue to him. I don't know if he considered the cost. If he did, it only makes the transaction more awful.

This was my message to Mehmed, though in fewer words. I know he read that letter. When I arrived in Manisa a few weeks later, his eunuch told me he'd found it, open, by his bed the day he went hunting for quail by the Gediz. The letter I'd written the day before was not found.

৯৩

I have never done this. Thought this. Gone where I am heading. I have never let myself see what I had better see now.

It is a day in late summer. It is morning. Mehmed has taken his favorite bow, the one Mustafa made him, and gone down to the river to hunt quail. The ground is wet from the night, and it is layered with mulching leaves. Poking through a heap of them at the bottom of the embankment is a grayish object. It is the size and shape of a head. Mehmed is alarmed and intends to inspect. His Chief White Eunuch calls out, points up the river, says he thinks he sees the rest of the body. Mehmed signals to him and the others—there are several on the outing—to stay where they are. He wants to protect them. He starts down the hill. Agile though he is, Mehmed loses his footing on the leaves, then on the roots. He slides down the bank, which is long and steep at that part of the river. With the force of the steepness, Mehmed hits the object, which is not a head but a nest of wasps. He lands on it with both feet and crushes it. Mehmed's eunuchs shoot down the hill after him. They try to free his feet from the hive, but the scarlet killers are filling the air, making it dark and harrowing, and

94

they can't get near Mehmed. In a moment his face is covered with wasps. At no time does Mehmed make a sound. The eunuchs call out his name. They fear he can't see them. They use their sleeves as bats and when they're able to get close they use the edges of their quivers as blades to scrape the wasps off him, but Mehmed is paved with them—face, neck, hands, inside his tunic, too. He is swatting at his chest limply, trying to make them stop stinging him. He rolls from side to side on the bank, his feet buried in the sticky hive, and his eyes sealed with what is killing him, and then he comes to rest. His feet jerk up, hive and all, then back, and then he stops moving. The eunuchs stare while Mehmed continues to not move. Then they withdraw to their haunches and repeat his name in a frantic chant until Mehmed's body begins to inflate—his eyes, lips, hands, all of him— and before he bursts the eunuchs fall silent.

When I watched my mother die, sinking into the hem of her Ascension Day dress, I thought there could be no worse thing to see or know. There had still been a breath left in her when they hauled her onto Gritti's barge; her bosom still was heaving, but unevenly. I heard them say that she was drowning inside herself. That she was trying to breathe but the water wouldn't let her. She knew what was happening. I could see the pain. She turned her head from side to side. Someone said they heard her say *Now*. And the moment she went—the moment her life became her death—I believe she knew that, too. One would know such a thing. One would feel the about-to-be difference and know when it arrived. One might feel relieved at that moment—if one had been thrust there by pain. Or one might feel terror. I am beginning to understand. Lying in this bed, not getting better, I understand. I believe my mother felt sorrow. She was leaving me. Watching her beautiful face change so quickly from rosy to gray to green, from soft and full to stony and sunk, that was the worst. Not for her. Just for me.

Then I watched Sylvana go—struck like a beast. And I was dragged away from her by my wrists.

I believed—and I gave thought to this—that I could experience and could endure no worse things than these deaths and these *kinds* of deaths. And then there was the death of Mehmed. And it had no equal. Not because he was attacked by a million poison needles launched by fate and nature. Not because it was needless and perverse and hideous. Not because I didn't see it, wasn't there, couldn't hold him in my arms or have him hear my voice as he let go of his life. Mehmed's death was worse because he had become my hope. And my love for him and his for me would have put me on a path that would have been happy and good and sane.

⁂

Suleiman returned at once from his campaign in Europe, two weeks at full gallop to reach the capital before his favorite son arrived, brought the hundreds of miles from Manisa in a cortege half a mile long. They laid Mehmed out in the Hall of the Divan, and his father sat by his body for three days and three nights, and in that time everything with life in it drained out of Suleiman, which may be why, on the fourth day, he did not deny the request of Matrakci, who had been cast into complete silence and solitude, to mourn at the Sultan's side. Suleiman was battleless with his army of sorrow. On the fifth day he summoned Sinan, the Empire's architect, and ordered a mosque built for his beloved Mehmed, the first prince ever to be laid to rest in the capital.

When his mourning was officially over, Suleiman summoned me to the Conqueror's Kiosk. The hyacinths had died on their own by then, and the spot smelled only of sea, which was a relief. Suleiman was seated on a carpet, his hands on his knees, his palms up. The sun through a lattice made small squares on his hands and on his turban and on the side of his

96

shriveled face, which had no expression at all. He looked like a painting of someone who had never been alive.

"I am here, Sultanimiz," I said of the spot I'd last been with Mehmed.

Suleiman moved a forefinger, but he didn't turn around. Tips of branches clicked on the kiosk roof like little claws. He was looking out toward the Princes' Isles. "When he was a boy, I took my son there many times," he said, as though he had had but one son. "Come here."

He was a wreck, a dried-out knot of grief and other things I didn't yet know by name. "What has happened to you?" he asked. *To me? What about to you?* I said nothing. *You do not take care of yourself. You do not eat.* My head was heavy. I felt it tipping. I didn't answer. "Sit." I knelt. "No. Like this." He showed me, palms down on his knees. He blinked so slowly he seemed almost to be asleep, and I saw that his eyelashes were gone. They had not been gone the last time I saw him. "You do not yield to this," he said. "Death." He meant grief. "It is right here." He held up a finger to show me where it was. "We live with it." He ran the tip of his tongue across his lip—a gesture intimate and needy. His mouth was white, outside and in. "You will go to Manisa."

"*Manisa?*"

"You will accompany my son, Selim. You will be his favorite."

Did Suleiman have no idea what Mehmed had meant to me? Having put us together as he had as students, having promised me to him as his wife. Did he have no idea what fruit that would have borne? Did he care? I knew it was irregular, even forbidden, but I asked—I begged—him not to send me. With awful effort, Suleiman's eyes opened as wide as they could. "We are telling you where you will go. *We* are telling *you.*"

"But I was to be there with Mehmed. I was *his,* Efendimiz."

Suddenly and fully alive, Suleiman barked, "Yes. And he

was mine. And that is the end of it." It had started to rain over the sea. It was coming toward us in striped shadows across Marmara, and Suleiman was trying to console us both. It was hopeless. "You will go to Manisa. We have chosen you for our son." Again, but so differently, as though he had only one. Suleiman moved my hands from my face. "You have a part in this. You know much and you will know much more. Do you understand?" No, I did not. I felt myself recede into a familiar place of unfamiliarity. He leaned closer. He looked at my ear. I had on my pearls. "We have given those to you."

I hadn't known that. "You have?" I said vaguely.

"Now, collect yourself. We have chosen you for a reason. And we are sending Matrakci as well. It will help him. That should tell you enough."

Enough? What was enough? What did any measure mean? Mehmed was dead, and according to Suleiman I was not going to think about any "of that" again. That was his decision. We—Suleiman and I—were not going to grieve for Mehmed more than we had because it would consume us. In his case, it would gut him in a way that no battle or campaign had or would. In my case, it would keep me from advancing beyond whatever I'd attained in a room with a book and a prince and a teacher, and Suleiman wasn't going to allow it. From then on, according to his command, I would do what was required, however repellent I might find it. I didn't argue. Either I didn't have it in me or I thought he might be right. Maybe both. I was sixteen. "We are not giving you to Selim," Suleiman added. "We have given Selim to you. Now, help us up." He was only in his forties then, and strong. I wonder why he needed help.

I stood and took him under the arm. His robe was flecked with things that had blown into the kiosk—spurs of weeds, germinating specks. He put his weight on me as we took the kiosk's small steps. I didn't have a choice, it was true. But I had Suleiman the Magnificent leaning on my arm, and he walked me through the flowers called Solomon's Seals up to the woods where there was a little reflecting pool that's gone now, and we stood there a long time on the crumbling apron of that pool and watched the oily edges of its surface suck themselves into new shapes.

Thursday, November 17

The day he knew Mehmed was dead, Suleiman sent Selim to Manisa. He left the capital barely equipped, traveled two hundred miles, and reached his destination in six days. Selim and Mehmed passed each other on the route. I imagine Selim, a sharp angle against his flaming steed, looking up and there, coming at him, the conveyance of Mehmed, shrouded, riding parallel to the plain.

Matrakci and I left the capital one month later. It took that long to appoint, assemble, and pack Selim's household. Suleiman made the assignments himself—chose the Janissary guards, the eunuchs black and white, the senior administrative staff—Treasurer, Falconer, Gunner, Keeper of the Standards, Clerk of Secrets—all of them. The Superintendent culled her ranks for the household servants. Hurrem had no part in the effort. She was nowhere to be seen. Had Suleiman not enjoined *her* to resist giving in to grief? She without whose influence Mehmed never would have left Topkapi? Did Suleiman have a say at all in what his wife did or thought? I wondered what grief was doing to her looks. How purple she might have become. How abraded and reduced. I wondered if Suleiman saw Hurrem in those weeks, or cared to. I wondered if he blamed her.

Matrakci vanished, too. The door was locked, from the outside, when I went for my lesson. I placed a little stone on the bolt. Twice more I went. The stone was always undisturbed, the lock untouched.

I called on Suna. Needing her—for the first time in years—made me aware of how much I had needed her before. "What you might seek from me you will find in yourself," she said proudly. Her cheeks had grown pendulous, her eyes bright. She was telling me I didn't need a teacher. She was mistaken, but I understand her saying it. Now, anyway.

As our convoy, more than a hundred carriages long, clattered away from Topkapi and from the capital, I saw us as a small city breaking off from a larger one; the severed arm of a starfish that would become whole on its own. We were a regeneration. Miserable but poised; fresh and able.

I had never experienced travel over land. The pace of it, in just the first hours, appalled me. I wondered how men going to war could stand it. I thought about the difference between armies and navies. I wondered about war as a place and about the elaborate slowness of reaching war before war can be waged and about the madness of that. I sought Matrakci's permission to ride with him because I feared I might go mad from the journey. At the end of the third day I received an answer. The first word from Matrakci since Mehmed died. *Of course you may not ride with me. We shall meet at the next stop. There are materials for you.*

As tent pitchers were pounding together our small city I called on him. He likely heard the scuffle my presence was stirring among his attendants. There are even fewer secrets in a convoy than in the Old Palace. Without much need for bending, Matrakci emerged from the tent's low opening. His face was shadowed, grimed from the grief. His turban was partly undone and a length of muslin hung over a shoulder. Clamped under his arm was a parchment, in his hand a bunch of pens bound together. "Ink," he said to a eunuch who ducked into the tent. "Here." He handed me the pens. There was a wet crescent on the top of the parchment—from being under his arm, apparently for a while. "Here," he said again holding it out. He wasn't being terse. He was simply boiled down. Only his essence was left. His sunken eyes were shiny with what he couldn't shed. I took the sticky, pounded hide. "We draw the journey." Matrakci mustered a nod toward the town on whose outskirt our small city had paused. "Gebze. Show me tomorrow." His square, stacked body turned toward the tent as the eunuch came out with the ink.

"Matrakci?"

"What."

"How?"

"Draw what you see. There is no rule. Start with what is closest."

"That sounds like a rule." I smiled.

"It is." He went inside.

I showed him my rendition of Gebze before we rolled away the next day. He said, "Start closer."

I wish to make this clear: Matrakci was saving me—from drowning in sadness and for a discipline that could, and would, be my own. That I was there to be saved helped him as well, it is true. But saving is to aiding what succeeding is to trying. I nudged Matrakci back into daylight. He reminded—and taught—me how to see.

On the road between one life and another, Matrakci turned my attention to proportion, to mass, and to light; to colors and structure; to the parts of things, large and small: domes, stems, pebbles. Not to perspective. Not to people.

As our little city plodded around Marmara I drew Izmit, then I drew Ikizce. But it was only when snow-capped Mount Olympus bulked into view, and the golden minarets of Bursa appeared on her hilltop in front of the mountain, and a silver lizard—a caravan—crept across the emerald plain, and a single nomad in his dingy robe strode out from a grove of woolly-twigged loquat trees—it was only then that I understood what Matrakci was instructing me in. The imperative to start with what was closest was my first step toward learning to draw a map. And it was Matrakci's way, incongruous but complete. It says a lot about Suleiman that Matrakci's maps appealed to him as they did.

From having aspired to create accurate maps like my mother's to learning to draw revealing maps like Matrakci's was a bridge between ways of seeing. On the road from one life to another, my worlds were joined.

I handed Bursa to Matrakci as we breached the city wall. He said, "You are improving."

The ancient Ottoman capital was the only city we stopped in. Matrakci wanted me to see the colors. The stalls stacked with brocades, velvets, organdies. The silk cords made for beauty and strength. Awful, awful strength. As our convoy left Bursa behind, from across the valley its looms gave the air a clack and a thrum I could feel. It was a good and gathered sensation, and I could not bear it, for it suggested the possibility of relief—from dreading a future without Mehmed. Matrakci didn't save me overnight.

⁂

I was given a day.

On the night of the day after arriving in Manisa, I was summoned.

The air was thick with incense and amber, lanterned light. The room was large and wrong for its purpose. The mattress was adrift in the middle, and on it was something very big. A fat boy covered by a blue sheet. He was still and shapeless, and I was on my way to him. There was no going back. Not to anything. "I can't," I said to the attendant when she lifted the sheet off the boy's feet, which were turned inward. Selim groaned like a big, old dog.

103

My robe was somewhere behind me then. I had walked out of it, I knew the rule. The floor was cold, my breasts were hard, my hair undone. "Now," said the attendant. And *now* was the only possibility.

"Now," the attendant said again, turning Selim's feet outward in preparation.

Then she lifted the sheet higher, and I was inside the tent, unable to see over the mound of Selim's hairy middle, able to see, in fact, nothing but the problem, and, because I had stalled, he lifted the sheet from his end and peered around his stomach, and he said, "I beg you." Our introduction. His face was wet and sad. Even at that foreshortened angle, it seemed the face of an old person.

Before I began I said, "Shhhhh." I imagined a river rushing over its volcanic bed. I imagined its cold water around me, its bank holding the shape of Mehmed's body. Then I did what I had been taught. With my mouth, with my hand. It did not take long. And then. The thunder of him was in me. A sickening, tidal pumping. Salt seeped from Selim's scalp and brow, sluiced around the family nose, and dripped through hair and spit into my mouth. "Thank you," he whispered and kept going.

When it was over, Sumbul accompanied me to my chamber. In the flickering light the mattress looked like a yellow silk sea, and I ruined it with what was in me when I sank down. I held Sumbul's hand as I said Mehmed's name. I never did that again.

Before I woke, I was summoned again, and again that night, and again the night after, each time introduced to Selim from the foot of the bed as instructed by the attendant, approaching him on my stomach. I was a snake, a tongue, a throat. I had neither weight nor force. I was an end of motion, mortified flesh. I was an inlet for someone else's frenzy, and I was drowning in what he was doing. I could not separate Selim from what was happening to me.

Night after night, it went on, all in silence, until I bled. It resumed, in silence, when the bleeding stopped. Week after week, regular as time, it went on. I was a timepiece, an escapement transferring Selim's effort to the balance.

One night there was a voice. *I am yours,* I said.

Night after night I told him that. And then, in the spring, there was no bleeding at all, and I said, *I have news for you, Selim.*

In response Selim wrote me this:

Taken my sense and soul have those thy Leyli locks, thy glance's spell, Me, their Mejnun, 'midst of love's wild dreary desert they impel, Since mine eyes have seen the beauty of the Joseph of thy grace, Sense and heart have fall'n and lingered in thy chin's sweet dimple-well. Heart and soul of mine are broken through my passion for thy lips; From the hand of patience struck they honor's glass, to earth The mirage, thy lips, O sweetheart, that doth like to water show; For, through longing, making thirsty, vainly they my life dispel. Since Selimi hath the pearls, thy teeth, been praising, sense and heart Have his head and soul abandoned, plunging 'neath love's ocean-swell.

He had his eunuch bring it to me. I asked if I might call on the prince. "That is his wish," the eunuch said dryly.

I had not tried to imagine the details of Selim's face in our encounters. I had tried to imagine nothing. I suppose I had assumed his features would somehow accord with his large middle and stubby limbs, but they didn't. His face was long and wider at the bottom, like an eggplant. An old face, as I've said. His eyes squinted from overuse, and small lines radiated from them toward his turban. His nose, long and notched at the crest, was not possible to imagine on someone who had ever been a baby. His lips, like his mother's, were very dark—but not gnawed—the one feature I could have guessed, for sometimes when he was done in bed, he would put them to my forehead.

I thanked him for his poem. "It is I who thank you," Selim said.

"It is bold to write verse." My mother had told me that.

"The Sultan has instructed me."

"The gift is yours, Selim."

"The gift is you," he said.

I had thought that whenever we finally spoke we might speak of Mehmed, for Selim loved him too. But when we were together, in daylight, with all that we knew, we did not speak about Mehmed. Nor did I go down to the Gediz. Not ever. Until a month ago.

On a warm night, ten and a half months after we arrived in Manisa, I was awakened by a blinding flurry of pain—worse than even now—and so different from my own coming into the world. They made me crouch on the mattress, my head down, the rest of me up. They rubbed me with oils of lily, iris, and dill. They said I screamed for my mother, and they swabbed my throat with almond oil for the screaming. Long after night fell, through a steely haze I heard the midwife counting the nodes on the umbilicus—the number of children I would have before dying. "Six," she said. And at that moment Shah appeared.

The awareness that I could be disappointed by a daughter—and I was—was a sickening shock. As she drew her first breath I wished that my child were not who she was. Of my own birth my mother had once said, "You cannot imagine how I thanked God for you." Yet when I looked at my own child I was aware of only a void and the imperative to start the awful process over.

Quickly the nurse put not Shah but some other baby to my breast to suck out whatever impurities there might be, and then she handed me Shah. *Mamma*, I said to myself. As Shah's little gums clamped down, I said it out loud. And I kept saying it until the huge, unvoiced missing of my mother filled the sphere of my daughter's birth. Through my mother's funeral, through returning to Paros, through being captured and brought here and educated like a prince because of what she herself had had me learn—through all of it I had contained the sorrow of losing my mother. Until I gave birth to a girl. And then I couldn't contain it anymore. I missed my mother so much I thought I'd die. I missed everything about her. Her calm and modesty and interests. Her beauty on which she did not rely. Her wide-apart eyes, the flushed hollows in her cheeks, her thick tangled hair. I missed having a mother who had things hidden in her and imagining that those things would help me. I missed my mother in my future, a grandmother. I missed her being with me as I lay there, with Shah in my arms. And I knew this: my mother would have been happy about my daughter. And she would have told me to be happy about her too, and knowing that helped me to try.

"It is yellow," Selim said of Shah's curls as he stroked them with the back of his finger.

"I wonder what the Sultan will think."

I assumed Selim was not referring to Shah's hair. "He will be charmed," I lied.

"As I am," Selim said, looking me in the eye.

Whatever Suleiman thought about the baby, he didn't let us know.

I had to have a boy.

"Try peony seed tea," Matrakci counseled. "And no fruit that is green. And no fish."

When I asked him how he knew such things. Matrakci blinked left, then right. "Because I had a wife once, and a child who was hard to come by and died when she was born, along with her mother. Here," he added, as though the folio he was taking from inside his robe were the last part of the answer to my question—which I suppose it was. Among so many other things, Matrakci showed me the power of dignity and conciseness. Never once did I cry in his presence.

Inside Matrakci's parcel was our journey. Sheets on which were drawn Gebze, Ikizce, Bursa, but also Karacabey, Karesi, and Saruhan. Every town we had passed.

Words are not up to conveying the marvel of these pictures. Matrakci put indoors above and outdoors below. He put the sea in the sky and ships on the air. When he anchored the corner of a map with a tree with cornelian cherries or cardamom, it was so you would smell what you were looking at. When he painted a mosque Iznik-red, it was so your mind saw the tiles inside. When he cast a path in brown, it meant desert nearby. A carnation meant a garden. A citron tree, a grove. I had drawn four towns as best I could in thirty days. Matrakci had depicted all of life at every stop.

It was only then that I realized what Mehmed had drawn me years before was a map.

"It is to celebrate," Matrakci said. He put his hand on my head and rubbed the way my grandmother used to rub the head of her awful dog. Matrakci didn't know how to pat, and I reckoned he did not know how to embrace, either.

In the weeks that followed I drank the tea, gave up the fruits and fish. I let the physician insert inside of me a piece of pork wound in wool, and I allowed him to tape a wad of oakum to my navel, too. And still I kept bleeding. Selim didn't mind. "I wish only to be with you," he said a month after Shah's birth. I remember how gently he lowered himself onto my mattress.

"Can you wait? Please?" I asked him. He got on the floor and waited. "That's not what I mean, Selim."

He bent over and put his head against me, and for a long time he didn't move. I thought about his knees bearing all that weight on the stone floor, about the weight of his face on my breast, about his skin taking on the imprint of my garment. He slid his hand beneath the silk and took hold of me. I watched as my skin filled the vees between his fingers, and the weight below my waist began to shift as the million filaments that carry arousal from one place to another came alive with their own understanding of the difference between arousal and desire.

For all of the months between the birth of Shah and her sister I was sick, unable even to read. I was also absolutely certain the next child would be a boy, though, certain God wouldn't give me two girls in a row. Still, when Gevherhan arrived I was less distressed. For one thing, I didn't think I'd die giving her birth. Gevherhan's birth was not easier for Selim, though. This time it took almost a week for him to visit. He stood by the cradle and looked down over his stomach. He arched back so as not to see her—or maybe so she wouldn't see him. His eyes rolled in the direction he was arching. Whites topped with black slivers. He looked as though he was drowning in shallow water.

"Are you upset?" I asked.

"I have a name for her," he said, patient, worried. Gevherhan was his idea.

I wrote to Suleiman. I told him that Shah and Gevherhan were blessed preludes. I promised that Selim would provide the Sultan with a grandson within the year, and that the child's mother would be me. I stopped eating yogurt, vinegar, every last herb, and, because Matrakci insisted on it, my chamber was sprayed with musk of civet, aloe, and amber. I lay on my side, as the midwife instructed, while Selim—to whom had been applied a mixture of ground quail, oil from the inner bark of storax, and a paste of musk, amber, and crushed ant wings—entered me and seized my breast as though it were food. He put his mouth to my ear. "This is the one," he said.

The third pregnancy was easier, and it was not a coincidence that this was when Matrakci had me try my hand with Ptolemy's coordinates. With his very concerted help, I—I—was able to translate the sides of triangles into the curves of the earth. I drew a map of the world on a little goatskin shaped like a vestment. I was very proud of it and did not try to repeat the exercise. I remember those as especially peaceful months, except that I still heard nothing from the Sultan. That I continued to believe he would send word makes me now look back on myself with some tenderness. I feel as though I am my mother looking at me—somewhat sad that I could be so hopeful.

The following summer I gave birth again, only differently this time. Ismihan came early, and she was born blue. Her body was as knotty as the cord that attached her to me. They said she would die—*they*, the faceless voices I heard when they wiped my forehead with hellebore. They said I would die as well. I had bled too much to live. There was not enough left of me, they said; the labor had lasted too long for me to survive. At the time, I agreed. Selim did, too. He was terrified, and he said so. Not once did he visit the baby.

Precise, elusive pain. I think about it nearly all the time now. The churning and burning up inside that has kept me on my back for all these days now. The strangling on water that killed my mother. But what about the pain my mother suffered while she was alive? Is there a life-slicing difference between torture and humiliation? Between labor and despair? No, there is not.

༒

After Ismihan, Selim did not come to my bed. Nor did he hunt or mount a horse. All he did was eat. He ate when he rose, he ate all afternoon, and he ate through much of the night. He ate delicacies and humble foods. He ate as though it were a way to be dead. He had failed his father, and I had failed *him*, and he didn't know what to do. And neither did I, because the physician said Ismihan was my last child. One more would kill me. He did not need to add that my chance to succeed—by giving Selim an heir—was over. Selim knew it as well as I did. I decided to write one more time to Suleiman—begging for his patience. Before the letter could have reached him, Hurrem arrived in Manisa.

Hyena neck, worn mouth, bullet eyes—Hurrem's distinctive features should have given her away. But as the bullets pierced Selim, her expression betrayed nothing. Certainly not affection or pity, not even anger or disgust. She refused to recognize him. Her own son.

Selim had decided to greet his mother outside the palace. He'd waited a good hour in the heat for her. His mother's response to his respectful gesture was to look at his mossy eyes and his swaying, round body and pretend she didn't know him. She teetered from her palanquin to the front steps—a slender woman with no grace at all—and she snarled at the Chief White Eunuch to take her to her quarters immediately. She didn't come out for two days.

Her people occupied the palace like an enemy force. They took over the kitchen, the hammam, and the gardens, and the trouble they caused was great. My daughters, small as they were, stopped eating. And Selim would *not* stop eating. He gagged his distress with food. Just like a child. No. Just not like a child.

On the fourth day, Hurrem summoned him. Selim came straight to me. I was feeding Ismihan, just finishing. She was extraordinarily small, and still not quite pink. He stood beside us for a moment, then reached down, cupped her head, her black curls, with his big hand—a perfect fit—I could see him feeling it—and he lifted Ismihan to his chest. It was the first time Selim held one of his children. He did it with assurance, perfection. She was his favorite. "We will go together," he said.

Hurrem sat draped in displeasure, picking at her cuticles while a pair of girls plaited her hair. "What is all of this?" she said to Selim. "I called for *you*." Ismihan was asleep in Selim's arms. Hurrem bit something from the edge of her fingernail and spat it on the floor. She acknowledged neither me nor her granddaughter. Her field of vision was the size of a piece of dead skin. I wondered how Mehmed had ever tolerated her.

"I am here," Selim said.

Two of the girls she'd brought were playing music—terrible tunes produced by tiny cymbals and sticks tied to their fingers. A click of her tongue made the little percussionists stop. "In what condition?" she said through her teeth. "You are fat. You have no control." No reference to the infant in his arms. Then to me she said, "Nor do you," meaning something altogether different. She continued to address me. "You destroyed one of my sons. You will not destroy another." And then to Selim, "And you will produce a boy. It is the Sultan's command." She thought she could extort a result.

Selim said, "Yes. I will. I am producing daughters first." He was patting Ismihan's back. *Good for you, Selim!* I said under my breath.

"Why do you think I chose the concubines in this household!" Hurrem brayed, pointing to a blank wall. I wondered if she knew how accurately she illustrated her words. "You will take those women *now*. This is a foolish errand. I am taxed."

"You will rest, then," Selim said helpfully.

Hurrem placed herself in the middle of the room, her fingers making their habitual basket. In doing this she brought herself to full attention. "I will leave here presently," she answered. "I have come only to convey the Sultan's order." Then, with her eyes dead on me she added, "You will take other women, and you will have a son."

"I *will* have a son," Selim said. "I do not wish to have other women. You can understand that. I do nothing more than what my father does."

No wonder Mehmed loved Selim as he had. His nerve and reserve went hand in hand.

Hurrem bared her teeth and grew. She was like a giant wave, steepening and advancing at the same time. "I have no interest in your excuse."

Selim went to his mother and, adjusting Ismihan in his arms, put his hand on her shoulder. He aimed his eyes toward hers. "I did not offer an excuse," he said. Honest to a fault.

Hurrem took a large step back—a daring move in the high

shoes she favored. She was changing her relation to Selim, so she wouldn't have to look up. Then she said, "You do not offer anything." She meant it.

I could not fathom the feeling of such a knife in one's heart—so sudden, aimed, and thrust there by one's mother. Flaunting nothing, including the daughter in his arms, Selim said, "Yes I do." He meant it, too.

Hurrem did not leave immediately, however. The following day she called for me. The exchange did not last long. "You are an impediment to the Sultan's order," she pronounced. *No one is an impediment but you*, I said, only to myself. "You have failed to produce a boy three times." *Three times you have borne boys—and the law is one son per mother*, I said under my breath. "You displease the Sultan. You interfere with the Sultan's command. You will *not*." *I please the Sultan very much. He chose me. That's why I am here in your son's bed. That is why Matrakci is here. I know what pleases the Sultan. I know you are lying. And I hope you can hear what I am thinking.*

I said, "I will not, ever." It was a promise.

"Nor with mine. The Sultan commands that our son take other concubines. Now." She emitted a wet, equine snort. The arcs and bows of her face flattened into straight lines. Her gaze locked on mine. I hated her as much as I had ever hated anyone. "Take . . . her . . . away," she directed the Superintendent. All of this in my own house.

That was when it occurred to me that I might have been wrong about Suleiman's will. That if I didn't fulfill it, he would find someone else who would. The space in which I belonged could be readily occupied by another who *was* able to produce a son. It suggested to me suddenly and clearly that what mattered to Suleiman was the *purpose* of a favorite, not that *I* be the one to carry out that purpose. It scared me to my core.

"I am not afraid of her," Selim whispered that evening. His face was twisted with distress—the assurance of that morning was gone. "No matter what she says to me."

"Come. Come sit here." I lay there, torn and still bleeding from delivering Ismihan. I reached up and swept my thumb back and forth, as he so often did to me, on the back of his neck. He did understand his mother. He understood that she had no use for him. I wondered if anything could dull the pain and sadness of such awareness.

"I wish to be only with you," he said. I told him I believed him. "But I believe I have no choice." I told him he did. He insisted he was right, and he wasn't talking about his mother's visit or his father's command. "The physician has left no doubt," he said. "Another birth will kill you."

"I will do it. I *will*." I pushed hard on my stomach to make it—I didn't even know what—ready, I suppose. He pulled back, astonished. I was burning. Dripping from the nape, between my swollen breasts, between my legs. Very much like now. The swallowing heat. "You will see," I panted, sitting up.

"You are not well," Selim said. He put his palm to my forehead quickly. "You are very hot."

The room spun around. I took his face in my hands, steadied myself, and began to stroke his cheeks. As I drew his face to mine, he seemed to want to ask a question: Why hadn't I been that tender before, perhaps. Or why had I concealed my affection? But he closed his eyes and said nothing.

"There is nothing to fear," I told us both.

Selim stayed still and let his arms be limp. He, too, wanted my words to be true. Slowly he moved his head up and down, back and forth, yes and no. When I slid my hand inside his robe and took him, he gasped into my mouth a word I didn't understand, and I dipped more into the sourness that caught at the back of my throat. I held harder. I realized that Selim's strength *was* in his sex. "Come to me," I said, moving him with my hand. "Come," I said in another voice, moving him hard. He opened his eyes, and there we were, on an edge we'd never approached.

"The blood," he whispered. It had always been my concern, not his.

"It's all right," I said, my mouth on his ear.

Together we entered the darkness, smooth and joined—he on me on him in a place we'd never been, where there *was* no pain, where every move doubled his force as he continued to grow and engross me and to put in my mouth the words for what he was doing, hard, even as he slid his palm, to protect me, under my head. Then, at the bottom of his thrusting, I felt something—a part of him that matched a part of me I'd nearly forgotten or had made recede.

"There," I said as he was finding it. He was listening. "*There*," I said again. The match was exact. We were bringing each other forth.

It was no surprise to me when, on the fourth day of July 1546, on the bright side of the still snowy Bozdag, the child who came into our world was a son. Murad required no effort, and his birth took no time at all. One warning pang, and he was there in the broad daylight. I never took my eyes off him. Not while they cut the cord or purified him with rose water or wrapped him in linens the color of cream. I loved him as I had never loved anyone. I *was* love. I was also gentle. I think I might not ever have been gentle before. The effort to pretend I wasn't disappointed by the births of my daughters had steeled me. With Murad in the world, I could yield. In that respect, Murad brought his sisters to life for me—though Ismihan had been enlivened by her father's devotion. In all respects, Murad brought me to life. He joined me to his father in purpose and affection. He saved me from sonless failure. He brought me into the family that has been mine ever since. He vindicated and freed me. And as my love for the child who could do such things began to enlighten and fill me, I could feel that there was not enough room in my heart for both the love of this boy and the bitterness I harbored toward the men who'd betrayed my mother and me. Sylvana had tried to help me understand this just before I was taken from her. Murad's coming into the world was the heart of the lesson. Love can displace rage.

I took Murad, severed and swaddled. I pressed a grain of salt on his forehead to protect him, and a little tune gurgled forth—music I'd long before made up to charm him into the world. I unfolded his fingers till his hands were tiny stars. I understood that who he would become was there in my arms. What was not there were the things that would challenge his goodness. He would struggle with them, I knew, and prevail.

Friday, November 18

Word came from the capital. The Sultan would see his grandson. Suleiman had come back from Hungary—again—victorious but spent. He believed, apparently, that seeing the child would do him good. I believed the same thing, of course, and that seeing the rest of his grandson's family would do him good as well.

Selim absented himself from the weeks of preparation. He went hunting in the mountains beyond the Gediz. I thought, *He will celebrate in his own way.* I thought, *I know how he feels.* Except I didn't know how he felt. Selim didn't come back from Bozdag until the day before we were to set out. He'd never gone off on his own that way; he had never not done what was expected. I found him kneeling near a window, his hands and forehead pressed against the glass. A large amount of food was nearby. His pose was that of a dejected child waiting for something worse. I said nothing about the panic I'd been thrown into by his tardiness. I said, "There's someone here who wishes to see you." Selim didn't move. "Look who's here," I tried again, patting Murad closer to my chest.

Selim turned around. His eyes were blank and bulged, his robe wet and soiled. He said, "My father has asked to see only my son."

It was an apology, and I was not going to accept it. "Your father is pleased with *you*, Selim, for producing him. Why do you do this to yourself?" I gestured at the smell of garlic, cheese, and wine that filled the air. I was swaying to keep Murad asleep.

"Why not?" He extended a finger tentatively toward Murad, as though testing for heat. I understood the corresponding shape of Selim's vulnerability and his parents' hardness—the pit in the fruit.

I got behind him—he was jammed among cushions damp from his meal—and saw for the first time that his hair, black though it was, was getting thin. Selim was twenty-two years old, and he had many of the features of someone who had lived a long, bad life. I cupped his shoulders in my palms and began to knead his fleshy neck with my thumbs. "I have an idea," I whispered close to his ear, signaling to his eunuch to prepare his bath. Selim's hand drifted up and took mine. He didn't resist when I helped him to his feet, or question when I walked him down the hall, or close his eyes when he sat before me as I washed his hair and pail after pail of rose water coursed over his sad and then less sad face. When he was powdered and dressed and Murad was brought back in, I arranged him on Selim's lap. "I feel as though he belongs to the Sultan," Selim said.

"Of course he doesn't. He is yours, Selim."

A look of unmistakable surprise caused his face—every feature—to loosen. "Isn't he tiny for such a trip?"

"He will have the best care on earth," I said, and it was true.

Selim looked over the bridge of his long nose at Murad. "Do you think he sees me?"

"Of course he sees you. He knows you."

Selim wiggled a finger close to Murad's eyes and then patted the soft top of his head. "He couldn't," Selim said.

Daggers of light flashed off the River Gediz. Poplar, juniper, and pepper trees lined the route. Gilt finials bobbed above our golden standards as scouts fanned out east and west. Armed Janissaries flanked us; a military band played alongside. There were three divisions of cavalry, five-score footmen, five-score houndsmen, stablemen and tent pitchers, a dozen cooks, a wet nurse for Ismihan, two physicians, Sumbul, and Matrakci. Everyone necessary, in other words, to attend a family with four children under the age of three—though no one fed Murad but me, ever.

I held Murad facing out so he could see the forests of ash and oak, smell the miles of tobacco and thyme, and with my lips to his ear I said a little something about the accretion of will that had made all this his family's. I felt the roots beneath the land stir under our passing weight, and I did not question Suleiman's silence following the birth of my daughters or dwell on the hard-hearted ultimatum he had delivered by his vicious wife. I questioned nothing, doubted nothing, feared nothing. We were a force on the landscape. The force of a family with a son.

We rolled into a capital whose streets and midans thumped with life and its upkeep, the city alive with prosperity and attainment. Merchants lugged goods on carts; madrassas buzzed with boys' recitations; women of all means tripped from hammams giddy from pleasure with each other. Captive that I'd been, I had not been alert to this vivacity before. Nor had I seen the souk that gave rise and life to so much of it. Mehmed the Conqueror had established it—a market near the Golden Horn—but it was Suleiman himself who'd made it great and vast. The morning we arrived from Manisa I saw it for the first time as we passed the very long side of a bazaar that has no equal—eleven gates, sixty-two streets, and four thousand stalls in which are bartered and sold brass, bronze, silver, gold, gems, glass, silks, saddles, stirrups, tulips, bales of saffron, screens of schist, rugs of pashmina, covers for Qur'ans, lamps for mosques, amulets for protection, and talismanic garb for guidance.

We climbed the hill to Topkapi. Without fanfare the gates ground open. We passed through two courtyards brilliant with flowers, paused for ablutions in the third. Beneath the noonday sun there wasn't a shadow. Buildings, grounds, animals—everything was bathed in the same vertical light. Everything was evenly spaced. Everything was right.

At the entrance to the Privy Chamber, Gazanfer, the Chief White Eunuch, pressed his back to the wall, as a symbol, to let us pass, Selim with Shah and Gevherhan, the wet nurse with Ismihan, me with Murad. The eunuch thrust out his arm and rapped on the deep-carved door. I whispered to Selim to come close to me. He'd been raking his teeth over the hair beneath his lip. I scraped with a fingernail the yellow matter at the corner of his mouth. "There," I whispered.

The door opened. Straight ahead was a low platform—the base of Suleiman's throne was but an elevation of floor, and upon it was a large, unmemorable chair. He reigns where he sleeps, I thought. The light that fell across the dark carpets made them appear more silver than the red they were, and it made Suleiman, who was sitting cross-legged upon his bed, squint. He was in ceremonial attire, something with very large tulips on it, and wild. "Move where we can see you," was the first thing he said.

We went to the foot of the bed and faced him. He looked awful. No wonder we hadn't heard from him. No wonder he was thinking about heirs. His eyes had sunk deep into his face and were heavy from what they had seen and knew was still to come. Suleiman was fifty years old. He looked older than Egnatius.

A click from somewhere inside Suleiman's beard made the servants vanish. He sat up straight as a wall, his hands free of his sleeves, one fingering the ropy scar that covered the other. One eye closing, he looked at his son as though he were reading and trying to understand what he read. "Come here."

Selim squeezed Ismihan's hand and let go. He knelt beside the bed, took the hem of Suleiman's raiment, and brought it to his lips. Suleiman leaned so their turbans touched. I wanted to say *Do you feel that, Selim? Your father is glad to see you.* Suleiman said something I couldn't hear. Selim let the hem go, but his hands stayed where they were, clenched close to his mouth in the little sanctuary beneath the turbans. His father sat up, and Selim sat back on his calves; even with the girls' restlessness, Suleiman was attentive only to Selim. Music began to play in the hall, something ancient with bells. I held Murad out for his father. Selim's fingers were layered across Murad's little back, and he clutched him to his chest, putting his nose to his head and taking in his scent as he turned him around to face Suleiman. Then the scent, the tune, the throne, the breeze from Odessa, the stars and the moon that hide in daylight, all became things with names and futures as Suleiman reached toward his grandson, brushing his thumb across his forehead in a gesture that looked for all the world like a blessing. He nodded toward Shah and Gevherhan and then toward the wet nurse, indicating that she hand Ismihan over to me. The girls and I drew close, and one after the other Suleiman touched the girls' foreheads, too, and when he turned to me and smiled, I saw that his teeth were white and small.

⟞⟝

The morning after we met with the Sultan, Matrakci called on me early. "You look well," he said.

I had been up with Murad all night. "Of course I look well. Look at this little sparkler." I swept Murad's curls to one side. He was in his cradle, a moonstoned monstrosity offered by his grandmother. As Matrakci and I looked down at the slumbering cause of what even Matrakci believed was responsible for a favorable change in Suleiman, I imagined that our gaze was borne on golden rays—as blessed intention is shown in so many paintings I grew up with. Depictions of annunciations, stigmatizations.

Matrakci withdrew a sheet of folded paper from a pouch slung around his middle. "This is for you. I have been keeping it. For the good time." Every once in a while he still mistranslated from his language. Something was strange.

"Anything would be good from you."

"When it would only please you," he said. "You will see." He held it out. "It is not from me."

I unfolded the sheet. Drawn in each quadrant were meticulous mechanical designs. Gears. An escapement. Underneath were words, terms, all in a hand I knew. I kept my eyes on the drawing so it would stay real.

"Selim found it. When he first went to Manisa. It was drawn by Mehmed."

"I know."

"Selim insisted that I give it to you . . . when . . . " Matrakci stopped.

"When what?"

"When it would not make you unhappy."

I looked to Murad, thinking the sight of him might hold me together, and it did not. "It was for Selim, Matrakci. Mehmed was making a clock for Selim." Matrakci's chin dropped to his chest. He fell back on his heels then forward till he was folded in three. A raw, battling sound was coming out in gasps. He was trying to cry.

I slid to the floor beside him, Murad's awful cradle a fortress beside us. I put my arm, like a stave, across Matrakci's bony back. "When will we not feel this?" I said, close to his ear. We were down there a long time, on the bedrock of our loss, Mehmed joining us like a dovetailed corner.

Esther once told me that in her faith there are levels of misfortune. The least of them is death, she said, and that is because it is in the order of things. Worse is war because it maims body and soul. And worse than war is famine because it does the same but even more extremely. But worst of all misfortunes, because it joins the others, is captivity. Those— we—who have been captive and become free know as others cannot what it is to be fortunate. Mehmed had been dead for four years when Murad was born. For not one moment of that thousand and more days had I been free to think of Mehmed as he had been when he was alive. His aliveness had been so far-reaching, so composing, so promising and various that I could not—no, I would not—reproduce it in my mind.

Any death dictates the end of someone, and forever. Not until Mehmed's, though, did I know that the end part of death is comprehensible, and the forever part is not. When Matrakci gave me Mehmed's drawing for the clock, I stopped—or I began to free myself from—needing to understand *ever*, and Mehmed returned to my imagination as himself, as I knew him. He came home to my heart. Murad was the barest infant when this occurred, and I believe firmly that is why he has the nature he has.

かー

At exactly noon the next day, as the call to prayer became the air, Matrakci returned with an announcement. The Sultan was ordering my freedom.

I didn't know what it meant—my freedom. I didn't imagine it mattered. I had done what I most wanted without it—given birth to a son. It did matter, though, very much. Although I'd borne Selim four children, I was still a Christian slave. Suleiman had a plan for me, and it was predicated on being neither. "You will become Selim's wife," Matrakci told me. In a swift and single act of reordering, I was to be manu-mitted, married, and made Muslim—by fiat, ceremony, and a self-administered oath, respectively.

I think I didn't know until that ceremony how precise had been my girlhood assumptions about the wedding I'd one day have. There must have been a wedding a week outside my window on the Grand Canal—gaudy, validating celebrations in which citizens—the public—joined hands while whoever that man was and whoever that woman was proclaimed the banns of their marriage for all to know. Weddings in Venice were triumphal mergers. Tons were at stake as gifts were exchanged, dowries accorded, brides themselves handed over from father to husband. At my wedding to Selim, I was married by proxy, feted in seclusion, and presented with a hundred sacks containing a thousand ducats each—Suleiman's gift. It was a dowry in reverse, and it made me the second-richest woman in the land—the very richest asserting herself by being absent. The parade to our secret ceremonies wound through glittered streets lined with stalls serving citrus sherbets, rose-water rice, caviar from Caspian coves. Selim led on horseback; I followed in a garish red conveyance; between us, the customary and scarcely relevant fertility procession: fifty black eunuchs bearing carved ivory fronds topped with phallic finials. When Selim entered an emerald silk pavilion for his marriage feast, I repaired to another for mine, accompanied, ceremonially, by Selim's sister Mihrimah, whose presence would have comforted any woman since, with respect, she had the misfortune of resembling her father.

As for my conversion, it could not have been more natural, or surprising. I had grown up in an elaborate faith whose rites and what they stood for had themselves stood for who I was. That was my condition when I was taken into captivity. In my first seasons in that captive state, especially those with Suna, writing the Word of God had had its effect, though. The beauty of the letters and the truth they spelled had concentrated my heart in a way I hadn't known before. And so when, on a winter day in 1547, I uttered the *shahada*—"I believe that there is one God, and Muhammad is His prophet"—

and let go of Original Sin, the True Cross, the promise of the Resurrection, and so much else, it was with neither regret nor pride. It was simply with faith. The promise of my former religion had proved an effaceable dot.

When I returned to Topkapi that evening, a strange thing happened. Home came to mind. Manisa. Home filled the air like an answer.

Saturday, November 19

The fog is so thick I can hear it, and I've opened a window to let it in. I do not feel better. There was sun earlier but not anymore. Maybe it's night. I can't tell. I think I am worse. I am cold and hot at once. I am evacuated and famished and can't stand the sight of food. I can't tell the time of day but remember everything that ever happened to me. Or that ever mattered. Or so it seems. That is why I'm pressing on. To say the rest of what I know, especially about Suleiman, for he was the architect of just about everything.

The birth of Murad not only vindicated Selim, it turned the circumstance of my own birth on its head. I had learned what that circumstance was the day after my mother died— when my grandfather felt he couldn't not tell me anymore; when he insisted on telling me why my mother and I had come to Venice from Paros, and why I wasn't born in Venice in the first place, and that my mother and I had lived on Paros because there was a rule that made it not possible for us to live in Venice. I was out on the balcony of my room with a fishline in the side canal when he bleated all this out—as though I had asked him a question and as though he'd had no choice about any of it. My mother's death had evidently raised the anchor on his life. He didn't know where he was going. His face was a mess of folds and lines, and he made no sense. "Your mother had rejected many proposals of marriage," he said. "All she wanted to do was draw maps"—as though her gift for drawing them were not something he'd prized and furthered and profited from. "And then your father appeared." That is how my grandfather described it. You would have thought it was the end of the story. Apparently he didn't know Egnatius had told me my grandfather had arranged for that "appearance," as well as for Egnatius and my mother to be part of the visit.

"You planned it," I said.

To which my grandfather's response was, "How could it occur to me that that would happen?"

I said, "That *what* would happen?"

He answered, "Your mother was truthful. She came to me directly. Once she knew what condition she was in."

I was twelve. My mother had died the day before. I wanted to push her father off the balcony. "Me, you mean?"

He lowered his head. His insincerity was sickening. Speaking solemnly and fast, he then recounted that my mother had told him that, under the circumstances, she was willing to marry my father. My grandfather had been relieved by that. That she'd have a husband at last "And such a fine one." He'd begun to weep. He said he never—oh not *ever*—would have imagined my father might do such a thing to my mother. And I told him—I, who was twelve—told *him* that imagination was to be used for exactly that sort of thing. I told him he had no heart in his mind.

"You wanted it to happen," I yelled. My voice bounced off the wall across the canal. I knew very well that in Venice, if *cittadini* married *nobili* their children gained the higher rank. That was just the sort of thing discussed over dinner when I was growing up. My grandfather wanted a grandchild who was a Veniero.

"So I reported your mother's condition to your father.

Also her willingness to marry him. You will not imagine what his answer to me was."

I was furious that he was dragging this horrible story out. "Then tell me!"

"Your father said he could not marry your mother because he was already married."

My grandfather wanted a Veniero, and what he got was a bastard.

"Why are you *telling* me this? *Married?* To *whom?*"

He didn't know. But what he did know—and what he wanted me to know—was that my father was "very concerned. He assured me he would take care of your mother—and of you." My father told my grandfather that he'd have my mother and me "seen to" on Paros.

Without a choice to her name, my mother was shipped to an island in the Cyclades. And all my grandfather could say about it was, "There were rules."

Screaming, crying, I told him he didn't have to have follow them. And then, without a pause or thought, I told him *I* was going back to Paros. On the next ship. I remember turning to leave the balcony and my room and that house, and stopping, turning around, and saying, "I'm taking her maps. Any map she drew I'm taking with me."

My grandfather's shoulders shot up, the fur on his collar got all meshed with his beard, he became wild. "No!" he bellowed. It was his Salt Works voice.

"Yes," I said in the same voice as his.

My grandfather took a step toward me. "No," he said softly. "They are all I have." His shoulders had fallen back and his whole body had shrunk inside his robe and kept on shrinking, and I didn't say anything. And then he said, "Won't you open your heart. Cecilia. Just a little. For your old Nonno."

"It is open," I told him. "But before I go, you tell me this, Nonno: What happened to all the rules that made you send us away in the first place? Why were we allowed to come back?"

I really think, now, at the age I've attained, that my grandfather did not know how awful what he next said was. He was too distraught even to dissemble. "It wasn't about your mother anymore, Cecilia. There was no chance she could ever marry. It was only about you. You were not legitimate, but you were still the daughter of a nobleman." And the nobility prevailed.

It shocked me—it is shocking—that love can end in an instant. Mine for what was left of my family did, right then. And I did go to Paros the very next week.

᪣

I told all this to Selim shortly after we were married—on the journey back to Manisa. I don't know where we were. Near Bursa, maybe. It was on a plain. I remember Selim was, unusually, holding Murad. He had him up against his chest. He was being the best father he could. The awful distance between what I had just told Selim and the sweet, precise present of his holding his son made me worry I might have harmed the one with the other. But his response not only removed the concern, it illuminated the mind and heart of the man whose wife I had just become. "Why don't you see if your old teacher can visit. The one from Venice. It would be good for you."

᪣

Soon after I wrote to my grandparents:

Dear Nonna and Nonno,

I expect you have known from the Bailo where I have been all this while. I imagine you have known that Paros was seized by Ottoman forces, and that I was captured.

I write to tell you that I am free now. I am married to a prince, Selim—a son of the Sultan Suleiman, called Magnifi-

129

cent, as you know, although here he is called the Giver of Law. I wish you to know that according to that law I am a member of the dynasty. The House of Osman. I wish you to know, too, that I have given birth to a son. The Sultan has chosen his name, which is Murad. I call him Aslanim—My Lion. The Sultan has also given to me a book of maps. They are drawn by Piri Re'is. I mention these shows of interest because they are not common and you are not acquainted with our customs.

I am Muslim now. I have been treated well and my education is being furthered by a great teacher. I should add that I have earlier given birth to three daughters and have received a considerable dowry. Dowries function differently here.

I understand there has been an Inquisition in Rome. I would be grateful for word of Egnatius.

There are other things to say, but that is all for now, except that I have been given a new name.

Nurbanu

My Dear Cecilia,

Married to the son of Suleiman the Magnificent! Imagine my happiness for you! To know you have attained a high position and that you are content and favored. I am very pleased that you have found a teacher for yourself. Is it the "custom" for girls to study as you do?

You are correct that the Bailo informed us of your ordeal. It has pained me to think of it. The Sultan's geniture, which Cardano, the astrologer, has circulated, indicates that your Sultan is a man of honor, however. In that, I take heart. Cardano has written, "He is better than all his predecessors, having kept faith absolutely with his enemies and showing less barbarousness and cruelty."

As for Inquisitions—do not imagine that they will stop in Rome. The Church here is agitating for one. It has some reason. Jews are subversive! Marranos in particular. New Christians— there is nothing new about them. They are Jews.

As for Egnatius, regrettably, he returned to Padua the week you left Venice.

Now, my dear girl. I have sad news for you. Our Nonna is gone. She is at rest, God knows. She was sitting on your very own balcony when she took leave of herself, and I believe she was ready to go.

Write again when you can, my dear, and concern yourself with nothing here. As ever,

Your devoted,

Nonno

જી

I have to get to the bottom of this. How it happened: the boys, the observatory, the library. All of it. Are these memories eyes? Can they tell the truth when they see it? Will they see me to the bottom?

I'm concerned about time. I'm concerned that Hamon's remedies are doing nothing. I'm concerned about what this illness might be. I'm having difficulty walking now even in my new slippers—the only ones I've ever had that don't hurt at *all*. For the first time in my life, my feet hurt on the inside, not the outside.

જી

One night —four years after Murad was born, perhaps a little more—Selim crept into my chambers. He hadn't been to my rooms or I to his bed since Murad's birth. There'd been no reason since—I have said this, but it is worth repeating—the mother of a prince is allowed only one son. Keep in mind that Hurrem, with Suleiman, had had four. Selim stood swaying next to the mattress. "What is it?" I gagged. He smelled like sulfur. Vomit and sulfur. He seemed to have been drinking. "What's happened, Selim?"

"The Sultan is heading to Persia," he reported. It was Suleiman's second campaign there—the first having taken him as far as Baghdad, which he'd seized. But the Safavid Shah, Tamasp, was still in place. Suleiman meant to topple him once and for all. "He has called me to Kutahya," Selim said, hoarse and miserable. "To meet him. He is displeased. He favors my brother Bayezid. He will change my assignment." Out and out it poured. "What have I done? This is not good news for me. I am governor of Manisa. What shall I do?" Selim's arms were hanging like mallets.

I sat up. Made myself alert. "This is not bad news, Selim. Sit down here." I patted the covers. He stayed where he was, belching like a furnace. "Your father favors you. No one else. That's why he's given you the most important post. You need to think clearly about this. It is you the Sultan trusts. Only you."

In fact, Bayezid *was* favored—but by Hurrem, not Suleiman. It was well known. But bad facts about his mother or brother were not what Selim needed right then. He needed the other part of the truth: that he alone was his father's favored son. Selim's eyes were glazed, his lips cracked; the effects of night were all over him. "That your father wishes to speak with you is a good sign," I told him. "You just need to understand what's on your father's mind. Then, there's nothing to fear."

Now it starts, I thought. The testing. Suleiman would try his sons, one by one—just as his father, the Grim, had done with him. I was not going to let Selim take that test alone—for his sake, and for Murad's. Selim was rubbing his face back and forth inside his palms, which weren't catching much of what was coming from his nose and mouth. "I will come with you."

"You will?"

"Of course I will."

Selim went limp, and the weight of the mallets reduced his shoulders to nearly nothing. He looked like a post with a head.

Then he made the most revealing statement I would ever hear him utter. "I am not afraid. I just don't know what to do."

"All you have to do is show your father he can trust you. You will tell him that you wish for nothing more than what you have. Say it twice. It is all he needs to hear."

"But that is true. I *don't* wish for anything more than what I have," he said miserably.

"I know you don't. I know. Your father has a weakness, though, and some kinds of weakness threaten the ones who are closest—in this case, his sons. It's not the Sultan's fault. He just needs to be assured."

Then I told Selim how Suleiman's mother had warned him, and of the circumstances in which that warning had saved him. Selim slumped down beside me, evidently collapsed by pity for his father. It confused Selim—pitying someone who was powerful.

We left Manisa in a hailstorm that cost us a day and forced, for the next six, a harrowing pace across the most desolate landscape I have ever seen—barren, carcass-strewn, a ghoulish grisaille. Then, as though one world were ending in another, black cliffs gathered in the distance, stretched north and south, and terminated the journey. On top of one of them loomed a windowless fort. Among its crenellations stood a figure. He was by himself, and he was waiting.

Janissaries led us up flights of small unprotected outside stairs designed, it seemed, for brave children. Around and up we climbed, and the peril of that ascent, combined with Suleiman's bellowing about Selim's tardiness before he'd even reached the top, jarred Selim. Even though he hadn't drunk for days he lost his balance and breath. "I've forgotten what to say," he wheezed.

"You don't need to remember, Selim. Just tell the truth, and your father will have his answer."

I gave him a push up the last step. He cleared the embrasure. Many moments passed without a word.

Finally, there was a low and tired voice—Suleiman telling Selim to rise. "We have said rise," Suleiman said louder. There was a quick clank of a halberd on the stone, the involuntary groan of a weary rider, and Selim was upright before his father.

"While we are away, one of our sons will take charge," Suleiman called out over the very wind that blew my veil into plain sight. "Who is there!" he called out. "Who is there!"

I gathered up my cloak and took the last step. Selim bowed his head fearfully. I placed my hand on my heart as I tried to gauge the consequence of having come uninvited. The Sultan before whom Selim and I stood was rigid with anger. The wild mistrust that was clawing its way out of him—clawing out of his eyes and the corners of his mouth and out from under his black fingernails—brought me face to face with the end of favor. This is it, I thought. This is the end of everything.

But surely he knows I'm trying to help. I thought that, too. But what if he doesn't? Should I explain? Should I beg his pardon?

Suleiman took a large, ungainly step. Behind him crouched his hunchbacked son. Then Suleiman yelled. He howled like a dog. "This is no place for women!" Jihangir did not flinch, which is part of why he was there.

I thought, *This is how you think of me? A speck in the whole of women? Well then, I am not sorry I've come.*

There was nothing to say, though. That was for sure. I bowed my head.

"Come here," Suleiman yelled. The command was to Selim. "While we are away, one of our sons will take charge of the western front." Suleiman turned toward the plain. "Tell us your thoughts."

"I am at your service," Selim said steadily.

"Tell us your thoughts before we meet our other sons." As though Jihangir were not a son.

Selim did not falter. "To serve as you like is my only wish.

You have honored me with a fine governate. I seek no other command."

With the pace of a timepiece, Suleiman turned around. His head and neck were in a tortured position that could not hide the look of release, then of exhaustion, then of pent-up thanks. It was pitiful. And I thought, *He cannot help his past—and he can't forget it either.* I thought, *That is captivity.*

Suleiman came close to Selim and put his hand on the back of his neck. "The way you do," Selim said to me later that night. Then Suleiman reached his thumb under Selim's chin and, lifting his face toward his own, said, "You are most fortunate," by which he meant *fortunate to know and follow the rules,* and probably *fortunate to lack ambition,* and certainly *fortunate I intend to spare you.* It was difficult to check the excitement that ran through me when I heard those words. They signaled good things to come for Selim. It was so difficult, in fact, that I believe I didn't resist.

Sunday, November 20

One year and a half later, Suleiman abandoned that second campaign to Persia. He gained some ground, yes, but he left with the Shah still in place. And so, four years after he and his hundred thousand men returned, he turned them around and set out again. Suleiman's third campaign against the Safavid Empire—with campaigns to Corfu, Moldavia, and Hungary in between.

Fear is a garden, fertile as Eden before the Fall. It's the garden Suleiman was raised in. This is why he sought order, and why he crushed it, too. It's why Suleiman did many of the things he did. It wasn't his fault. He learned it as a youth. Fear is a garden. But how could the germ have flourished in the particular ways it did in a man such as Suleiman, who had loved Mehmed with such tenderness; who'd shown me such kindness; who revered justice and order and learning as he did?

I will tell you. The garden of fear thrived because it was tended—by Suleiman's wife. And there the image of garden and gardener dissolves. For an image of Hurrem, you had better consider a cauldron, or a pyre. That woman could have melted iron. And when Suleiman went to Persia in the spring of 1548, she proved it. She began by persuading Suleiman not to lead the campaign himself. It sickened me to think of the methods she must have employed to sway him. She then got Suleiman to deputize the Grand Vizier, Rustem Pasha—who happened to be married to their daughter Mihrimah—to lead the campaign for him. The appointment thrilled the trammeled Mihrimah, and it furiously riled the Janissaries, because if Suleiman wasn't going to lead them, they wanted a deputy they trusted. And there was only one. Mustafa. The very son— Suleiman's firstborn—whom Hurrem had gotten Suleiman to expel from Manisa ten years before. Mustafa who, far from having made trouble for his father when he'd been demoted, had made a thundering success of his post in Amasya. There, too, the help of his mother, Mahidevran had been essential. Even in that remote and lowly post, she'd created a household of merit and grandeur. The Venetian ambassador thought this worth reporting on. "He has with him his mother who exercises great diligence to guard him from poisoning." I learned this from my grandfather. "She reminds him every day that he has nothing else but this to avoid, and it is said that he has boundless respect and reverence for her." The single goal of Mustafa's mother was to have her son succeed his father.

You can imagine Hurrem's response to all of this. Or maybe not. She was as brazen as she was cunning. The shuffling of governates she'd engineered to demote Mustafa was but a prelude to what she instigated this time. She instructed the Grand Vizier to foment a revolt in order to trap him. Busbecq, the Holy Roman Emperor's ambassador, wrote of it at length. Among the papers I had the sense to gather is a copy of his report:

From a Report of Ogier Ghiselin de Busbecq, the Holy Roman Emperor's envoy

The Grand Vizier was approaching the Persian frontier when he suddenly halted and sent a dispatch to Suleiman saying that he was in a critical position, that treachery was rife, and that the soldiers had been bribed and were zealous for no one except Mustafa. The Sultan, he added, alone possessed the necessary authority. He himself could not cope with the situation, which required the Sultan's presence and prestige. If he wished to save his throne, he must come at once.

This was a lie, and it was invented by Hurrem. But what did Suleiman know?

Nothing of this. He responded to Rustem Pasha's invidious call—Rustem was called "the Cunning" for a reason—with a letter to his son. Suleiman still had hope for Mustafa. Of course he did. He had never stopped loving him.

"God forbid that my Mustafa should dare such insolence and should commit such an unwise move during my lifetime," Suleiman wrote to him.

God *was* forbidding it. Mustafa had no such intention. But that didn't keep Hurrem from saying otherwise. Remember the fate of your own brothers, she was saying to her husband. Do not be gulled by hope, my precious. Words to that effect. And so Suleiman, weary as he was, commanded his troops to mobilize on the edge of Persia—the farthest edge, near Ararat. He would see for himself if there was treachery; battle for himself, if need be. Along the way Suleiman ordered Selim to join him.

Selim had no wish to attend what was coming, nor did I wish him to. Among other reasons, he had become huge. Once so adroit on horseback he'd been able to hit a mark behind him at full gallop, now he could barely mount his steed. But he did as his father told him—as he had to do. No question.

Suleiman wrote again to Mustafa. Busbecq reported on this as well.

From a Report of Ogier Ghiselin de Busbecq
(The Sultan urged his son to) clear himself of the

138

crimes of which he was suspected and now openly accused by Rustem Pasha (the Grand Vizier). If he could do so, no danger threatened him. Mustafa was confronted by a difficult choice: If he entered the presence of his angry and offended father, he ran an undoubted risk. If he refused, he clearly admitted that he had contemplated an act of treason. He chose the braver and more dangerous course. Leaving . . . the seat of his government, he sought his father's camp, which lay not far off. Either he relied on his innocence, or else he was confident that no harm could come to him in the presence of the army.

Mustafa did not fear his father. He knew Suleiman loved him. He knew, too, it hadn't been the Sultan's idea, so long before, to remove him from Manisa. Mehmed had written to Mustafa to assure him of that; Mehmed had written to *me* about writing to Mustafa. It was an astonishing thing for Mehmed to do—to separate himself from the positions of both his parents that way—and do it openly and with respect and, surely, with love. Mustafa trusted Suleiman, and he believed that when he told him the truth, face-to-face, it would root out the mistrust Hurrem had planted in Suleiman's heart. Root out the fear the Grim had planted there before that. I will put it this way: there is a line around each of us, continuous and key. Mustafa was trying to change the line around Suleiman. He was trying to make him better. Even the letter Mustafa got from his mother—warning him of the plan afoot—even that didn't change Mustafa's mind or heart.

It was late morning when Mustafa arrived at the camp. As prescribed by Suleiman, Selim's tent had been pitched next to the Sultan's. Also, as prescribed, there was a corridor connecting those tents. It was in that embroidered tunnel that Suleiman stationed Selim.

Janissaries, thousands of them, stood at attention. They

didn't make a sound until their favorite, Mustafa, was there before them, tall and hopeful in his gold saddle, and then they began to murmur their words of praise. Mustafa was encouraged. He entered Suleiman's soaring red pavilion. Jihangir was seated on the carpet, his head resting on his father's lap. Suleiman signaled to have the boy taken away. Mustafa knelt before his father, took his hand and put the old veined extremity to his lips. The Sultan seemed to be waiting for something, Selim said later, by letting Mustafa honor him that way and by letting him show his affection. But Suleiman wasn't waiting—not for honor or fondness or even proof of his son's guilt. Suleiman was—had been—convinced of Mustafa's treachery. He'd been talked into it by a person who, as the mother of his other sons, had a very great deal to lose if Mustafa succeeded. He looked past Mustafa to the executioners in the doorway. When Mustafa lifted his eyes to look at his father, the mutes turned to look at him, too, and that is when he grabbed his father's arm. "Have you not believed me?" he gasped. "Ever?"

Suleiman wrenched himself away. "You are out for yourself. It is known by all," he said in a low, mauled voice. In the time it took him to say those words, the three mutes surrounded Mustafa, holding the Sultan's verdict in their hands and tightening it around his son's neck. Mustafa's torso buckled first, as though it had taken a blow. Then his eyes bulged from their sockets and twisted—whatever holds an eye in place having been severed. The Chief Executioner shuddered, and Suleiman gave a second command lest the mutes lose their grip or nerve. Selim saw it all, as he had been meant to, for that is the reason Suleiman had wanted him there. To see. The executioners understood their Sultan's signal and understood that they would be next if they failed in this, and they doubled their efforts, pinning Mustafa's arms back and jerking the bowstring into a line so straight and with an edge so sharp it could have cut the world in two, which in a way it did, for the next moment Suleiman's firstborn son was dead.

Word reached us fast by riders—seven days. The messenger found Matrakci. Matrakci came to me. He pressed his bow-and-arrow calluses against my hand and told me, carefully, what he'd learned.

"But that's not right," I answered heatedly. "Suleiman could not do such a thing."

"Should not," Matrakci corrected. "The Conqueror's law applies between brothers, not fathers and sons. It's to maintain order after—not before—the Sultan's death." Just as Mehmed—my Mehmed—had said—though that had scarcely been Mehmed's point.

"Then he must have been forced," I protested.

"Suleiman? Forced?" Matrakci looked at me askance. "No."

Busbecq, wrote of what followed:

From a Report of Ogier Ghislin de Busbecq
For days there was general mourning throughout the camp, and it seemed as if there was no likelihood of any end to the grief and lamentations of the soldiers, had not Suleiman stripped (the Grand Vizier) . . . of his dignities and sent him back to Constantinople without any position. . . .

This change soothed the grief and calmed the feelings of the soldiers, who, with the usual credulity of the vulgar, were easily led to believe that Suleiman had discovered the crimes of Rustem and the sorceries of (Suleiman's) wife and (that Suleiman had) learnt wisdom. . . .

In fact it was Matrakci's idea to replace the reviled Grand Vizier. "Even the most loyal warriors can turn on their Sultan," Matrakci reminded and counseled Suleiman. If they feel betrayed. Or disrespected. Or duped.

In this matter, Matrakci alone had the agency to prevail

with Suleiman. Suleiman was wise to take his advice. He got rid of Rustem Pasha—furious though it made Hurrem, distraught as it made Mihrimah. Those vulgar people filling the streets of the capital and tilling the fields of the provinces weren't cornered by credulity, though. People believe what they need to believe. What is faith if not that? Suleiman's people *believed* him. And they quickly excused him. And I did, too—and that surprised Matrakci. He said so. But he left it at that.

As for Selim, bearing witness to his half brother's execution made just the impression on him that Suleiman had intended. It haunted Selim's soul. For many months, he came to me sobbing in the night, reciting what he had seen, begging for the picture in his mind to go away. He hoped there was an end to seeing it. That there might be a certain number of times he would torture himself with going over it, and then it would end. But there wasn't, and it didn't. This was when Selim began to drink in earnest.

かわ

On Paros and in Venice the Circumcision is a mystery of Christ. Here in the House of Islam, it is a revealing; a boy shorn—the welcome preciseness of our faith. For the issue of the Prophet, circumcision is pivotal. Preparations for it are concerted, delirious even. Something like provisioning the Sultan's troops or building a new navy. It was why tentmakers had been at work for half a year, why Shah and Gevherhan and Ismihan had spent even longer composing music, creating pantomimes, writing poems. They wished to please and honor Murad.

It was the spring of 1558. Murad was passing to manhood. In one respect it was not a passage at all, for Murad at twelve was the same person he'd been at eight and five and three. This was not so for my daughters. Accumulated traits changed them—Shah's patience turning to coolness, Gevherhan's gloom leading her to be fearful, Ismihan's wit making her clever and warm. What never changed in any of them, though, and the only trait they shared, was devotion to their brother who above all else was trusting. It not only animated and propelled Murad from the moment he took his first steps, it was exactly what drew the girls to him—their devotion (and their father's and mine) contributing further to Murad's store of trust. I was aware of this cause and effect of trust. In varying degrees, it made us all better. Until I lost sight of it.

Some weeks before the festivities were to begin, word came from the capital. The Sultan would attend his grandson's rite of passage. There are no words for the elation—and, I must acknowledge, the surprise—we all felt. We had not heard from Suleiman for a long time. He had been occupied, after all. After Selim and I met him in Kutahya, Suleiman had indeed pressed on to Persia, where he stayed for three years and reached an agreement with Shah Tamasp that would prepare the way for a horror that I'm about to come to. He had also been managing the consequences of Charles V's abdication, which included the rise of Philip in Spain. And he'd constructed a mosque—the greatest in the world. That he would make the journey to Manisa, then, was a great and telling gesture.

Not a week after the first missive, however, another one came. The imperial messenger galloped into the courtyard before dawn. You didn't have to sleep lightly, as I do, to know that something not good was about to be transmitted.

Suleiman would not be attending Murad's circumcision after all. The Sultan's wife was indisposed.

There was no doubt in my mind what was indisposing Hurrem. She was in a covetous, jealous spin and was not going to let her husband favor her least favorite son—and certainly not me—by attending our son's festivities. She wasn't even going to allow Selim the dignity of a serious substitute for his father. The Grand Vizier, say, or even the Chief Chamberlain or Chief Falconer. No. The Sultan was sending his cipher of a daughter, Mihrimah, who had been born with everything and turned it into nothing, in his place. Hurrem alone could have prevailed in imposing such a proxy.

If only we hadn't known Suleiman had planned to come! We would merely have wished him to be present. We wouldn't have been crushed by his absence. I had no doubt Hurrem had planned the sequence.

Selim did not leave his bed for two days. When he did, it was to eat far too much and drink far too much and to do it alone in his chamber. I understood his hurt and disappointment, and I told him that, trying to coax him out. But it was to no avail. I thought about asking Ismihan to try—there was nothing he wouldn't do for her—but that is just the sort of thing a parent should not ask of a child, and I was as aware of that then as I am now. So Selim sequestered himself.

In the days following the circumcision itself—at which horn players dressed as women did their utmost to add a note of joy or at any rate of distraction while four holy men held Murad in place for a procedure that, to this day, I find too awful to contemplate—a mournful mantle hung over the banquets and entertainments, and even over the fireworks. I suppose it required a great effort to keep on believing that Suleiman was not indifferent to Murad's achievements or feelings, or to Selim's or mine, though it was the kind of effort one doesn't recognize at the time.

On the last day of the festivities, because his father was indisposed, Murad took his formal leave from me. I received him in the small but elaborate tent I'd had made for the occasion—gold organdy with gold streamers and a black velvet floor embroidered with gold stars. I had them pitch it near an oleander grove between the palace and the palisade of Bozdag. Nowhere near the Gediz. The tent was a real fantasy, and the contrast with Murad's expression made me wonder if he would one day adopt Selim's and my grandmother's method for dulling disappointment. But Murad's dejection taught me something important. I realized that Selim was not—and poor Nonna had not been—out to destroy themselves. Had that been the case Selim would have stood up to Suleiman and Nonna to Nonno, and both of them would have been crushed. No. Those two took life as it came to them and managed the ache as best they could.

"I have seen my tughra only etched until now," Murad said joylessly, noting his initials on the banner waving over the entryway. It was my gift to him. Embroidering it. Sewing does not come readily. I had worked on it for months.

"Do you like it?"

Murad held out his answer—an oblong parcel wrapped in green silk. He settled beside me on the velvet floor. I shook it. Something rattled. "I wonder what this is." I held the item up to have a sniff.

Pleased, Murad said, "I made it. It's a . . ."

But I'd already untied it. "It is what I always wanted."

"Really?" His soft, darkening voice cracked with relief.

"Really."

"It is for your writing instruments."

I rubbed my thumb along the front of the shiny wood box, and then across the top where *Muhterem Valideme* was etched in the teak. I examined the sides and then the underneath—all of it burnished to a gleam, and I levered up the cover with a thumbnail. Inside were four reed pens.

"You like to write," Murad explained.

"I do."

"I made them, too."

I held the box tight to steady it against the force of what it stirred up in me. "I will always write with these, Murad." Which is true—I always have. And I am, this very moment.

Then it was my turn. I withdrew from under a cushion an unboxed, unwrapped, and unadorned volume. "It is from your grandfather." *The Book of the Sea*. Piri Re'is.

Murad looked at the volume glassy eyed, as though it

had both special meaning and no meaning at all. "But this is yours, Muhterem Validem."

Suleiman had given it to me when Murad was born. "Only for safekeeping," I said. "It was always meant for you." Which I always believed it was.

The book itself is a celebration. The navigable world rendered. The greatest work of the greatest navigator since Magellan and the greatest mapmaker ever. Matrakci was the first to say so. In the *Book of the Sea* Piri Re'is had combined the portolan chart with the *mappa mundi.* He'd described every shoal from Aden to Fez, every continent and coast, every wind and tide. He had taught sailors how to observe and to reckon. And he had done it as a lesson and a poem and a narrative. This is an important reason for drawing maps. It unites us with all the others who have ever understood time and space joined in a pinpoint, in a curve. Ptolemy. Piri Re'is. My mother.

Murad brought the book to his face. It was damp with newness, alive with all the things no one had known before it was written. "All for the glory of God, His Prophet and the Emperor of the Two Horizons." Murad read Piri Re'is's dedication of the book to Suleiman—for Piri had, indeed, written it for the Sultan. Then he turned the thick pages.

"Does Suleiman know?"

"He does," I said.

An eyebrow went up. Murad shook his head. "I wish he were here."

"I do, too."

"I don't understand why he isn't," Murad said, rapping his knuckles on the book. "Do you?"

There were two possible answers to that question, only one of which was apparent to me at the time. Either I didn't understand why Suleiman was absent or I didn't want to. I removed a mint leaf from the tea I'd been blowing on. Murad focused his attention on the amber glass in my hand. He said, "Efendimiz should have come."

"There is no *should* for the Sultan, Murad," I said gently.

He thought about that for a moment. Then he said, "I suppose he does many things he does not wish to do."

"That is absolutely right." I was relieved Murad was supplying his own logic.

"Still." Murad stood up. A tear, then another, streaked the purple tulips of his tunic. His hurt was turning to woe. I had forgotten how ardently Murad cried. Sadness was pouring from his whole face. I reached into my sleeve, handed him a cloth.

"It can be difficult to accept as they are the people who are closest to us, Murad. We should try, though. It is a freedom. If we can manage it. And it was you who helped me to understand this. When you came into the world you gave me the beginning of that freedom. An opening."

He blew his nose hard, wiped his eyes, handed the cloth back just as he did as a child. "I began to accept the people who had hurt my mother. I didn't decide to. It just began to happen."

Murad's eyes were on the kerchief as I folded it and put it back. Then he looked up. "Your mother? Who hurt your mother? You never mention her. What happened?"

I got up; went over to the tent's entry. My robe was sticking under my arms. Through the trees I could see the jugglers packing up their batons, a boa constrictor being coaxed into a cage. The remaining entertainments and festivities were not until evening. I did not need to change clothing. We had time. Murad observed my deliberation. He said, "Muhterem Validem, there is time. What happened?"

༄

I began with the Salt Works, 'Ca Baffo, my grandfather and his aspiration. I reminded Murad of certain facts about the Republic—things that have contributed to its character—

147

and the citizenry's. Recriminations over Cambrai, anger over the *serrata*—the locking out from opportunity of *cittadini* by *nobili*. I told him what my mother was like, her beauty and reserve, her place in Egnatius's esteem, and her genius, which was the right word. Murad noticed that I chose it carefully. And then I came to my father and who he was or was thought to be, and his appearance, so-called, at 'Ca Baffo. And, when I was close to saying what had happened, I said something else instead. I told Murad that my parents wished to marry and live on Paros, but as it happened only my mother went, and she stayed there with a woman—an angel, really—to whom my father had sent word. I didn't mention to Murad how the woman had spotted the small blue thing my mother was in the distance on the Vigla peninsula the day the Baffo carrack left her there. Something with slight wings, it seemed, owing to the wind's making her dress flap and fly around her. "A good woman will see to you. You will be well cared for." Those were the only words my father had offered my mother—for he'd written to her as well—the week before she had been put, by her father, on the Salt Works ship. I cannot imagine what Sylvana thought as she approached my mother. I know what she would have seen, though: a perfectly made face that had been tightened, skin to bone, from hurt. And a satchel by her side that had practically nothing in it.

I told Murad that on the second of October, the good woman, Sylvana, delivered me into the world. She placed me in my mother's arms and then sent word of my birth to my father, who was on the mainland. Word came back from him that my name would be Cecilia, which means blind in Latin. Maybe my father didn't know that, I said to Murad. He'd chosen his other child's name, too. A simpler name. Andrea. "I learned about him when I was just your age," I said to Murad, "and had returned to Paros after my mother died."

"You were my age when your mother died?" I didn't realize I'd never told him that. It upset him—and upset him even more when I told him the circumstance. "Were you there when it happened?" he said softly.

"I was. And my grandparents were there too, and no one . . . " I stood up. And then I addressed myself: No one *what*? Is there a reason to tell your son about your grandfather's inaction? You have told your husband. That was appropriate. And that is enough. Proportion matters in this life. There is none in telling Murad the worst—especially since your point is for him to accept his grandfather's behavior. It was quite a lecture I gave myself.

Murad, too, was on his feet and had taken my hands. "Muhterem Validem. You are very tired. You should stop now."

"I should. You are right."

"And I am grateful. You did not say, though, who hurt your mother."

Nor was I going to. "I meant only that she would have been happier—and I would have been, too—if my father had been with us more."

"He meant to be though. That's what you said. He would have been. If he had lived."

"That's right. That's exactly right."

Murad took a breath, got up. I looked toward the rolled-back triangle of a door and saw that the sun had moved from its high point to below the tops of the oleanders. At sunset we would attend the final entertainment, a piece of war theater Matrakci had created for the occasion.

"You changed my life, Murad. Backward and forward. Your birth made me a lawful part of this family. It was a gift beyond measure." I gestured to the world outside to show him what I meant.

Murad took my hands the way a priest would take those of a penitent. "Muhterem Validem, thank you for telling me this. I will go now."

"Your grandfather does not mean to hurt you," I said, certain that was true. And neither does your father, which was also true, but I didn't say it—the two kinds of hurt being so different, so unequivalent.

"I understand," Murad replied. "I will see you in a little while." He needed time. I could see it. He headed for the triangle, turned around. "I am glad you like the pens."

"And the box," I said.

಄

The evening celebration was extravagant with waterworks, fireworks, and animal displays. Selim, on his own I think, though Ismihan may have had a hand in it, collected himself and attended. I think I'd all along believed he would, because his presence made me feel not relief but admiration. And it pleased Murad very much. As did what he'd just discovered—that he could change someone by helping her. Murad had approached the imperial reviewing stand and noticed the dejected pose and wounded stare of his Aunt Mihrimah, who was next to Selim. Instead of taking his place next to her, Murad knelt before Mihrimah, spoke to her, gestured to the fireworks, called for refreshments for her, and talked and talked to his aunt until she smiled. Only then did Murad rise and take his seat. When, shortly after, I took my own next to him, Murad embraced me, and he, too, looked like a different person.

Monday, November 21

The signs of plague are well known—as a matter of fact, I have a few—but in the summer of that same year it was something different that seized the wife of the Shadow of God on Earth. A knife-like headache announced the illness, tearing her from the Sultan's arms in the dead of night. She vomited till she was limp, then hiccupped, hysterical, for hours. By the time the sun rose, half her face had slid toward her jaw. By noon one arm hung useless. By evening she could not speak her husband's name. Suleiman's life and revelry, his be-all and everything else, was dying.

My Very Own Queen, My Everything
By Suleiman

My very own queen, my everything,
my beloved, my bright moon,
My intimate companion, my one and all,
sovereign of all beauties, my sultan.

My life, the gift I own, my be all,
my elixir of Paradise, my Eden,

My spring, my joy, my glittering day,
my exquisite one who smiles on and on.

My sheer delight, my revelry, my feast,
my torch, my sunshine, my sun in heaven,
my orange, my pomegranate,
the flaming candle that lights up my pavilion.

My plant, my candy, my treasure who gives
no sorrow but the world's purest pleasure,
Dearest, my turtledove, my all,
the ruler of my heart's Egyptian dominion.

My Constantinople, my Karaman, and all the
*   Anatolian lands that are mine,*
My Bedakhshan and my Kipchak territories,
my Baghdad and my Khorasan.

My darling with that lovely hair, brows curved like a
*   bow,*
Eyes that ravish: I am ill.
If I die, yours is the guilt.
Help, I beg you,
my love from a different religion.

I am at your door to glorify you.
Singing your praises, I go on and on:
My heart is filled with sorrow, my eyes with tears.
I am the Lover—this joy is mine.

The word came by pigeon. Hurrem was failing fast. The relief of being in a world that Hurrem was about not to be in anymore was dizzying. Suleiman sent word that Selim was to go to the capital, and Murad was to stand in his place as governor of Manisa. Murad refused, though. It was the first time he had ever defied an order. Murad refused not to be present to share the grief—as though grief were finite and divisible. "Someone should have done that for you when your mother died," he explained, which meant—and it took me a moment to understand this—that it was his father's grief he wished to assuage, not his grandfather's. It surprises me, now, that I didn't try to keep Murad from going. His confidence in his own judgment had prevailed. Nor did I ask him to watch his father's drinking.

Before they entered the harem, Mihrimah intercepted them. Her father had been at her mother's side for eight days and eight nights, she warned them. "He is a shadow of himself." They found him exactly as she said—on his knees on the bare floor, back straight, head bent forward, watching his wife drift in and out of sleep. His eyes didn't leave her ruined face, not even when Selim and Murad were shown in and took their places at the foot of the bed, where they remained for a long time without a word or a sign. When one finally came, wouldn't you know it was from Hurrem herself. She opened the working eye and fixed what was left of her attention on Selim. "You have not been drinking," she said—the slurring not masking her usual precision. It was true. He hadn't. And it *was* thanks to Murad. She extended her good hand, which surprised Selim, and he was about to take it when it jerked past him and she grasped her husband's sleeve. Suleiman gasped, whispered her name, and Hurrem died—right then, with Selim between them. Suleiman rose and fell across his wife's corpse, and he stayed there.

So that the maximum number of mourners might honor his wife, Suleiman decreed that her funeral be in the mosque of Mehmed the Conqueror, which, at procession pace, is a half-day's walk from Topkapi. Selim was to lead the cortege and Murad to ride alongside him. When morning arrived, however, and the procession was about to begin, Mihrimah would not leave her quarters. She was lost without the person who made her feel worst. Selim tried to coax his sister out first. Full of pity for what she had suffered at the hands of their mother all those years, he wanted to show Mihrimah that he had noticed her and understood how she felt. But she refused to see him. Murad then sought her out, and Mihrimah received him. A procession of two thousand and a crowd of thirty times that waited while Hurrem's daughter and grandson explained things to each other. When they concluded, Mihrimah emerged, solaced. They proceeded to the terrace of Ibrahim Pasha's palace over by the old Hippodrome to watch Hurrem's cortege.

Suleiman was present for none of this. He shut himself off completely.

Once again, the people excused their Sultan. And I excused him, too. Why wouldn't I? I had excused him for worse things than loving such a woman.

&

For thirty-nine years Hurrem had held Suleiman's attention the way a cleat holds a line. Hard, twisted, not unwilling on the part of the line. When she died, the cleat was ripped right out of the deck. Suleiman's attention turned from what he was fond of to what he feared. It didn't take him long to go after his least favorite son.

Bayezid was the very embodiment of Suleiman's fear. He was a son prepared to inherit power—perhaps even to hasten that inheritance. As long as Hurrem had been alive she'd had the sense and force to check Bayezid's ambition, for he was her pet. After she died, though, he was free to act as he wished. When, a year after Hurrem's death, Suleiman learned that Bayezid was procuring strategic maps—from a Venetian cartographer—Suleiman acted, too. Suleiman demoted Bayezid. He assigned him to Amasya, the distant post to which he'd displaced Mustafa all those years before, and he counseled him with care—in writing. "In future you may leave all to God, for it is not man's pleasure, but God's will, that disposes of kingdoms and their government. If He has decreed that you shall have the kingdom after me, no man living will be able to prevent it."

And Bayezid refused to go.

Suleiman's response was swift. He immediately summoned his Grand Vizier, other top administrators, and, to make an impression, his fabulously successful banker, the dashing Joseph Nasi—a Sephardic Jew. Then he called up his troops—an army of more than five thousand mobilized overnight—and with his entourage he thundered east to teach Bayezid a thing or two. Along the way, he ordered Selim to meet him on the plains outside Bayezid's fort. He ordered Murad there, too.

Murad had been concerned since his grandmother's death about Suleiman's state of mind, and he believed the pursuit of Bayezid was about something newly unleashed in his grandfather. In any case, he knew it was a grave mission Suleiman was on, and he had no wish to be part of it—nor did I want him to be. I wanted to spare him what Selim had had to witness with Mustafa. I was unsure that I could.

"I haven't a choice," Murad said to me. He knew not to make this a question.

"The Sultan honors you," was all I could manage.

"I hope so," Murad answered.

They left Manisa at the break of a child's day. Warm, clear, budding blue. That's how I've always thought of days like that. Off they rode toward Suleiman's wrath—my husband, my son, and—because, with the possible exception of me he was the only person on earth trusted by Suleiman, Selim, and Murad—Matrakci. Matrakci also went because I asked him to.

The encounter began the day they arrived. Matrakci stood by Murad as Suleiman's men covered his body with iron—greave, codpiece, breastplate. They covered him until he could have been any knight of any age except for the voice that came from inside the helmet—a boy's voice, sweet as ever and steady. "I am ready," Murad told Matrakci, who led him toward the purple-and-green formations that were Suleiman's army.

"This day a son of mine is called to account," Suleiman called out once they were assembled. "He will meet the fate other sultans have visited upon other unwise sons: my brothers; my uncles; my great-great uncles and those before them who wrongly challenged their fathers instead of their brothers." He turned toward Selim, "Prepare yourself." He turned to his grandson. "Murad, you ride behind me." Murad's eyes welled up, Matrakci said, but he straightened up high in hope of doing the right thing. Visors clanked shut. Hooves scraped the dirt. Suleiman and Murad bowed to one another—as much as armored warriors can.

There was Suleiman at the head of his army of sorrow, swords and bows about to be drawn, the air itself sharp and taut. The Sultan had been betrayed. A son had risen up against him again, and order hung in the balance.

The encounter was over in less than a day. Bayezid's armaments were primitive and paltry, his troops outnumbered many times over. Before evening the force was decimated. Three thousand dead, strewn across the plain. For reasons I've never learned, Bayezid was allowed to lead the remainder east, aiming for Persia. Notwithstanding the accord Suleiman had earlier reached with the Shah, Bayezid believed he and the Shah had a common foe in Suleiman. Bayezid thought he had a refuge.

The Shah took Bayezid in, all right, and harbored him on the condition that Bayezid disband his troops. Bayezid—out of choices—complied, and before the week was done, his men were divided, disarmed, and dispersed. Then they were slaughtered. For complete peace of mind, the Shah locked Bayezid in a remote and putrid cell beneath the ground. Because he had a soul, I suppose, he allowed Bayezid to try to make peace with his father by means of a stream of messengers. Bayezid promised Suleiman silk carpets, elaborate tents, a rare genus of anteater. You can imagine the impact of the offerings. Bayezid had threatened his father. It was over.

Suleiman designated his Chief Falconer, Hasan Agha, who was a boyhood friend of Bayezid's, to negotiate Bayezid's fate. A boon companion would be this son's executioner. The party traveled twenty days across the killing winter landscape, losing dozens of men at every station, to the place where Bayezid was being held. They found him in a corner of a corner, barely recognizable, encrusted in himself, furred with neglect. Hasan Agha, who'd known Bayezid all his life, was not certain who was before him. He took Bayezid's face in his hands as the guard shaved his matted beard, scraping off scabs the size of thumbnails. Bayezid believed he had another chance, there, in the hands of his old friend, handpicked by his father to free him from the enemy in exchange for—never mind the price. But Hasan Agha wasn't there to free Bayezid. He had an order to follow. And Bayezid knew it when he saw the blue bowstring wound around the young man's right hand and saw the left hand came round out of the light to meet the right, and then Hasan Agha turned just enough for Bayezid to see him catch the loose end of the cord and ravel it up and make it perfectly ready.

By rapid relay and courier pigeon the Sultan received word that Bayezid had been strangled and that his pregnant concubines had been tied in sacks and thrown into Lake Urmia.

Most of us live in the space between what we do and what we *can* do. We guard the illusion that we might be anything we wish. Bayezid lived outside that space. He had nerve and a goal—which would have been admirable if his father had not been a person with every reason to fear the worst between fathers and sons.

Thinking about Bayezid's fate this way I was able to say to myself—and to Matrakci—that, perhaps, his death was comprehensible.

"Mehmed the Conqueror indicated fratricide," Matrakci said, riled by the suggestion. "It is between brothers. And it is a prescription for *after* the death of the Sultan." Just as Suleiman had said on the battlefield. The color went from Matrakci's face; the heat made him gray. "The duty is to preserve order, Nurbanu. Not to remake it."

Matrakci had never, in all the years I'd known him, called me by name. He was summoning my attention. Matrakci hadn't even cared for Bayezid. In fact, he too had mistrusted him. But that was not the point. That was exactly not the point.

Wrong. Right. Order. Good. Fratricide. Patricide. Filicide. What did anything mean? A clot of panic blocked my throat. Matrakci saw what was happening. He knew me. He sat me down.

Then, in a whisper, so as to not roil the future, he said, "You must think clearly." Just what I told Selim, more and more often.

"Am I not?" I answered sincerely. "Are you angry?"

"No," Matrakci said, "No, you are not. And no, I am not. I know you too well to be angry with you. I am concerned for you."

I was concerned for me, too. And I will close this awful chapter with an admission. While the death of Bayezid was horrible and cruel, there was relief—immense relief—in Selim's being uncontested. It also advanced the succession of Murad—the full implication of which I could not have imagined. And awful does not begin to describe it.

৵৩

I have good news. My problem isn't poison. I haven't wanted to record my alarm, but this illness *is* getting worse, and because it remains a mystery to Hamon, it's not unreasonable to have been considering the possibility of poison. And various justifications for it. And I have. But, as I said, poison has been ruled out. The proof is the porcellanous stoneware—celadon—that turns red on contact with nearly any bane in nature. And the proof is sound because it comes from a new set—just arrived from Longquan—upon which every morsel of food I have taken has been served. Murad commissioned the dishes three years ago. After the Observatory, to be exact—which I'll come to. The Observatory. I thought the commission excessive since there are more than thirty thousand pieces of celadon in the kitchen already—thanks to Suleiman, a big believer in poison detectors. But the pigment's potency weakens with time. I learned that today from Esther. That's where her mind is. Knowing I'm not poisoned does not, of course, cause the lesions on my feet to heal. It doesn't stanch the bleeding from my fingers or any of the rest. But one takes comfort where one finds it. For now I will content myself with looking at Esther. She is elsewhere as little as possible lately. At the moment, ten feet from where I am lying, she seems to be sleeping standing up. She is all vigilance and defiance of harm when it comes to me.

꓿

Suleiman was down to two children—from nine. Three boys had succumbed early to disease. Mehmed had been killed by wasps. Mustafa and Bayezid had been strangled with silken bowstrings. And Jihangir, the humpback—poor Jihangir had died of grief. The boy had been present at Mustafa's end, in the corridor off the imperial tent. Suleiman hadn't known Jihangir was there, but he had been, and he saw his half brother's murder, and it finished him. It caused his body, somehow, to double back around the hump and his throat to clack till he choked to death. Jihangir's death affected Suleiman badly. He spoke to no one for days. Jihangir had been his lucky charm.

This left only Selim and his sister, and the change in

Mihrimah after Hurrem's death was something to behold, for once Hurrem was gone, her daughter took shape. She became her father's confidante and counselor. It was hard to comprehend. Did she remind Suleiman of Hurrem? Mihrimah surely did not look like her. As I've said, she looked like *him*. Her eyes were small, her hair thin, and her chin was lost in her neck. She was big, too. Whatever the appeal, with Hurrem gone, Mihrimah rose up out of idleness and demanded a role with consequence. From an invertebrate pest, she became a towering force.

Mihrimah had ideas—two of them. One distressing, the other calamitous.

The distressing idea was a gift for her nephew—the boy who had time after time been such a comfort to her; who'd written to her after the battle with Bayezid because he knew Mihrimah cared for all of her brothers, and he, too, was shaken by his uncle's end.

The gift was accompanied by a very small entourage, led by a pasty white eunuch, who was shown in to my chamber. The Princess Mihrimah hoped the gift would find her nephew well, the weary spokesman reported, and that it would give him cause for happiness. My own eunuch, Sumbul, erect by the door, signaled his concern. The gift was a concubine.

What was Mihrimah thinking? Murad didn't need a concubine. There was plenty of time to make heirs. Selim wasn't yet Sultan himself! And when the time did come, *I* would prepare the girls that *I* would have by then selected. Diligent girls. From Varna, Sulna, Odessa. Black Sea girls. When the time came. But Murad had touched Mihrimah's heart. And Mihrimah, apparently, wanted to touch Murad's.

It was then that the edge around our lives changed. When it thickened and everything seemed to inflate. Something vivid and throbbing attached itself to us. "She is out there," the messenger said, with a gesture to the window that indicated that this gift was not something to be put aside. When she entered I saw that he was right. This girl intended to be installed, like a wall.

She was at ease, lush, filled out. She wore pantaloons the color of smoke and a yellow outer garment, loose and filmy, with ribbons on it, a kind of robe I hadn't seen before. Her veil was well below her shoulders, and she had on a tight-fitting yellow tunic, much of which was concealed by the veil, which was also yellow and which cast an eerie hue across her face. She was even taller than the eunuch, who was tall, and she had no interest in concealing her height. She was self-possessed.

"Lift your veil," I said.

Instead of taking it up from the sides, as is customary, she extended her right arm across her chest, took a handful of the ominous gauze and let it sail up and over her face and head-piece— over smooth black hair, over skin so white it verged on gray, as a baby's does at the moment it's born. She lifted her face slowly, and what revealed itself, feature by feature, top down, was very nearly two faces. Her eyes were huge, wide-set, shadowed above and below. Her nose was straight, mature. Her skin, as I've said, was without blemish and gleaming. Her mouth, however, was mismatched—the bottom being pillowy and wide, the top peaked and narrower than the bottom, and it notched at the edges into a sticky darkness that suggested something beyond experience. There was something well known about this girl. Something reminiscent of food. Something fermented and rising.

She thrust out her chin and shifted her weight—a readying gesture that drew my attention, and Sumbul's, too—to her feet. Wide bands of silvery leather encircled the middle parts and extended on top toward her toes. There they narrowed into thongs that wove under and over and then wove through the wide band to her heels, where they held in place small leather shields that served no purpose that I could see. Embroidered on top of each leather band was a gold star. The bottoms of her feet were bare. "What are you wearing there?" I asked.

"Slippers." Her voice was steady. She admired her feet while patting her hair flat over the sides of her face.

"They don't have soles," I said, fixed on the tangles of leather. They looked like bridles.

"Yes." She looked at me from under her lashes.

"Well, why is that?"

"Well," she drew the sound out so her lips came forward, like a kiss, "it is so I can feel what is under me."

"You will wear normal slippers now."

"I normally do." There was not a trace of color in her voice.

"What is your name?"

"It is—I am Safiye."

"Where are you from?"

"I do not know." She turned to the eunuch.

"It may be true, Khanim," the eunuch supplied. "She says she doesn't remember anything from before she was captured." I had heard of that happening. I asked when that was—her capture. The eunuch looked to her. She shrugged.

"Well, how *old* are you?"

She did not hesitate. "I do not think I know." Her indifference was precocious.

I could have asked what that was supposed to mean—that she didn't think she knew. I could have asked what she'd been doing since whenever it *was* that she'd been brought into the harem—what assignments she'd been given, what promotions. I might have inquired about her education in the Old Palace and before—her knowledge of languages, her ability to compute and read, to sing and embroider. I might have asked what she *did* think she knew or whether or not she'd begun to bleed or how it was that the Sultan's daughter had come to favor her by offering her to my son. But I didn't, because I would get those answers from Mihrimah later, and because I wanted this person out of my sight.

I rose, detached myself from the impertinence of her stare,

and informed her she would be assigned to the Coffee Mistress and reside in the dormitory farthest from the palace, by the river. Without hesitation, Safiye said, "I am not afraid about the water. Many concubines are somewhat afraid—maybe from their capture. I am not one."

Sumbul stood straight as a column. Only his eyes moved, darting like flies. He has always understood everything important. Every part of me that has blood in it was pounding. I wondered if she could see it. That is what unsettled me most— that I wondered.

Tuesday, November 22

The first standards bobbed above the north horizon, and a military band announced the Shadow of God on Earth. Brass, kettle and frame drums. Wood pipes, silver bells, cymbals. The approaching horde was tantalizing and wild. Within an hour it became a city—a large one—on the unassuming plain. Twenty thousand souls gathered for peaceful purposes. The Sultan was paying us a visit. He had decisions to announce.

The imperial pavilion and two hundred tents were pitched in protective arcs across the flatland. The retinue swarmed among the peaks of red silk, their tasks and near-silence producing an unnatural hum. There were divisions of horsemen, scouts, and cooks; there was a contingent of Janissaries nine hundred strong; there were enough doctors to tend an army in battle and enough yeomen to plant a garden, which they did, for Suleiman had brought with him five thousand tulips. Potted, full-grown flowers of every color in the spectrum and some that weren't. Black, for instance. An equator of tulips was planted around the Sultan's silk palace.

Suleiman was there for a week, though the purpose of the visit was achieved in a day. One audience each with Selim, Murad, and me, one right after the next, with mine last. I hadn't seen Suleiman since Kutahya, the icy test on the turret. It had been years. There's a miniature of Suleiman painted around this time. It's flat and static, but it shows true qualities of the Sultan he had become by then. He is thin but upright. His robe is modest—a simple blue, no collar, no trims. He walks slowly before two servants who are colorfully dressed. One of them bears his sword. In front of Suleiman is a tree stump with a few determined leaves on a determined branch. The ground is uninflected by shape or shade, and though the glade he walks in seems arboreal, Suleiman is standing in midair. A man devoid of every humor—blood, phlegm, bile of either color.

I was told to meet him in his garden and found him in the middle of the tulips, bending down. He'd gathered his robe in his hand, and his spidered ankles and chapped heels were revealed. He crouched, grasped a single wilting stem, and pulled. "You can help us."

No glance, no greeting, after all those years. His attention was fixed on the turned-over earth, but his voice was amiable, not like it had ever sounded before. A browned tulip flew overhead. An epicene White Eunuch—still Josag!—had positioned himself to catch it. "We have said you can help. Come here." I went over. "Only the dead ones." They'd just been put in the ground. "This is not a bouquet," he added, in case I was wondering. I threaded into the flower bed and crouched beside him. He had closed an eye and was making an assessment. "You are not well." I was aware my worries had seized up my face and made me a bit gaunt, but I certainly wasn't unwell. I told him I was fine. "We have said you are not well. You will see our physician. You need a Jew here. In Manisa." Suleiman's concern was surprising and welcome. He tossed a tulip backward. He tossed another. He looked nowhere but into the flowers. "What is the matter with our son?"

"You mean Selim?"

All the other sons were dead. "Yes. That is what we mean."

I didn't know the right thing to say. Selim was frighteningly fat. And though only intermittently did he drink too much, the point was that when he did it was way too much. Could Suleiman see that? "Efendimiz . . ."

"He is weak," the Sultan said, getting to his feet. "He always has been." It was a stone-cold statement, especially the second part, and the contrast with Selim's own nature made my head feel heavy, like a head that wasn't mine. Suleiman loomed above me. "Here." He held out his hand. "We are sending him to Kutahya."

"Kutahya?" Kutahya was nowhere. We would die in Kutahya.

"That does not concern you, however. What he has done to himself is sickening." Suleiman inspected his palm and rubbed it on his robe. "Agh," he said, like someone duped. "Manisa"—he waved toward the palace to prove where he was—"will now be for our grandson."

"Murad is fifteen, Padishahim. I am not certain he can manage without his mother."

"We are certain he cannot. That is why his mother will remain here."

"But what about my husband? He should not be alone." Frantically, I was trying to understand the meaning of this rearrangement and the distress it was likely to cause Selim.

"Your son is the one who needs you most. Never forget it." It is worth saying that I did not. As with all Suleiman's commands.

"You will stay with him until his father is Sultan." He started with the tulips again. "And your daughters will be married." The effort of his visit was becoming clear. "Hasan Agha for Shah"—that is, the Chief Falconer, who had murdered Bayezid, for my firstborn; "Piyale Pasha," Admiral of the Fleet, "for Gevherhan, and Sokollu Mehmed Pasha for Ismihan." My youngest daughter. Sixteen. "We like her." Suleiman had seen Ismihan once, when she was one. I was surprised he knew their names.

166

"Is he not very old, Sultanimiz?" I asked. "The last."

Sokollu Mehmed Pasha was Second Vizier. He was over sixty, and I knew it. I also knew he was the most dazzling administrator ever produced by the *devshirme*. He'd been captured as a boy in Bosnia and risen from groom to sword bearer to Chief Taster, Head Doorkeeper, and Vizier—Third and then Second. For his shrewdness and daring Sokollu Mehmed was known as the Falcon. For his stature, he was called the Tall. He was great, he was very old, and before long he was to be Grand Vizier. This would be Ismihan's husband, and there was nothing to say or do about it.

"And our grandson," Suleiman scowled at a blemished bud, "will have a new tutor."

If he'd told me Murad would have a new mother I would not have been more stunned. "*Who?*"

What followed was a concise outpouring—an utterly new expression, and it was about time. *Time* was the key, Suleiman stated—to knowledge and prosperity and to power. Murad should know how to construct a clock, he said, and he *would* construct a clock, and it would be mechanical and excellent. It would measure the positions and speed of the planets. Murad's achievement would be in this domain, Suleiman declared. He could not have been more precise. He laced his fingers in appreciation of the idea, the aspiration, the grandson.

"Murad has pleased us. He sent kind words when his grandmother was ill. He made the journey to her funeral. And he proved himself in that unspeakable encounter with his uncle Bayezid. He proved himself by being there. We know he did not wish to be." All this carried on breaths that whistled between his little teeth. Suleiman brought his templed fingertips to his lips. "He is like his uncle. We did not think there could be another."

I had no way of knowing that Mehmed had remained in the front of Suleiman's heart or that he held Murad alongside him there. I did not know if Suleiman knew Mehmed had been working on a clock for Selim, either. I would have dropped to my knees and asked if he had, had I not thought it would vex him. Spontaneity unnerved Suleiman.

An image flashes before me. The Sultan and his progeny as a clock: Suleiman the escapement, Mehmed the face, Selim and Murad the hands—all of them them affirming order for the ages. The clock Suleiman intended for Murad to make was about more than keeping time. He was ordering the future as he intended it. My children's. Selim's. The Empire's.

"Murad will study now with an assistant of Taqi al-Din. You know who Taqi al-Din is." Suleiman spoke in imperatives—surely the only practice he had in common with my grandfather. "The man is coming from Cairo. He is an astronomer and goldsmith. He is all Murad needs. Matrakci will return with us."

Suleiman had summoned Matrakci occasionally over the years. Every time, I'd dreaded he would keep him. And now it seemed he might. Our life was about to have its keel ripped out. "But he will come back—won't he? Efendimiz?"

Suleiman stopped us in our tracks. He told me to lift my veil. "Matrakci stays with us. I have just said that. He is . . . " I believe he was about to say "mine." "He is old. Do not be selfish. Do you understand?"

No. I did not understand. If I was selfish, wanting Matrakci to stay with us in Manisa was not an example of it. Neither was wanting Selim to be with his family.

I wiped my eyes on my sleeve. "I do not mean to be."

Suleiman smiled. A subtle show of recognition. And then he said, "We know."

There was nothing to do but try to smile back. The only way I could imagine the blow of Matrakci's removal was to believe Suleiman was aware of my sacrifice.

⁂

I have said that Mihrimah had two ideas. The second one was war. It was nearly as invasive as the first, and disastrous.

I can't imagine why Mihrimah's taste for military action surprised me. She had been married to a Grand Vizier for three quarters of her life. Given who her parents were, an interest in combat was probably what she and Rustem Pasha had had in common.

Suleiman, however, had lost *his* appetite for conquest after his last campaign east. "Our borders stay where they are," he'd told Matrakci. He meant all of them. Not only those he had established, on land, in person, but those set at sea by Barbarossa, to whom Suleiman had left naval combat after his victory at Rhodes. Barbarossa had put ports and islands from Gibraltar to Cyprus under the Ottoman flag. What Mihrimah was shrewd enough to train her father's attention on was the meaning of a certain island that had eluded him—Malta: the refuge of the very enemy Suleiman had driven from Rhodes all those years before. The Knights of St. John of Jerusalem.

With the authentic respect that her father prized her for, Mihrimah had waited until what must have seemed the worst of her father's grief over Hurrem was behind him, her own having released her more quickly, and then Mihrimah began her own campaign: to enlist Suleiman's support for war. She opened it with the pledge to underwrite the expedition herself. She'd pay to outfit three hundred galleys and another hundred carracks for the battle and siege. "This is not about money," Suleiman told her. "It is about geography. Malta is more than a thousand miles from our southernmost coast." It aggravated Suleiman that this needed saying. And it concerned him, too. The missed obviousness of it. Still, Mihrimah kept working to wear Suleiman down. That taking Malta was a sacred duty was another tack she tried. This, of course, was a judgment, and it galled Suleiman to have it made by anyone but himself. Suleiman's answer to a Mediterranean venture was no. And stayed no. Mihrimah was losing ground

It was not by accident that I knew the details about Malta. Semiz Ali Pasha, who had succeeded Mihrimah's husband as Grand Vizier, was sending me regular reports, and he'd been doing so—at Suleiman's command—ever since the Sultan's visit to Manisa. It was an unusual honor and one I relished.

As Semiz Ali Pasha's ever more frequent reports came to me, I forwarded them to Selim—except, that is, the ones that detailed the emerging role of Mihrimah. Selim was informed of this by other means, however. As he wrote to me, "the lively Jew" who had accompanied Suleiman in confronting Bayezid had stopped in Kutahya "with an entourage worthy of the Sultan himself" on his way to Konya, site of one of his, Nasi's, carpet export depots. Joseph Nasi stayed with Selim for two weeks en route south and another two on his way back. I didn't suppose it was the first time that two people of consequence with nothing in common found themselves entertained and rewarded by that very fact. That is the most benign comment I can muster about Nasi for the moment. I will come back to him.

Events themselves, then, assisted Mihrimah. Malta's Grand Master nabbed an Ottoman merchant vessel and slaughtered sixty of our men before advancing down the Levantine coast. Barbarossa's successor, Turgud Re'is, failed—with seventeen warships—to even slow the onslaught. The Knights of St. John were out with vengeance.

Here is my grandfather's response to the incident:

My dearest Cecilia,

In greatest haste as the ship that will bear this missive is casting off . . .

The capture of the Ottoman ship does my heart good. Even if it is your navy! You know me. I cannot pretend. Imagine such treasures falling into the hands of those old Knights. Good for them! They deserve it, I say. Especially the diamonds and the quintal of copper and the scientific instruments [unspecified] and the Holbein portrait [subject unknown].

170

In haste, with greatest love,
Your Nonno

Suleiman's argument for not engaging on the Mediterranean unraveled quickly, and Mihrimah picked up every
dropped stitch. The next weeks were spent preparing for the
response. Provisioning the army. Procuring timber, rope,
pitch, and paint. Making fittings and sails for a hundred and
forty galleys and four dozen oared vessels. In command of our
fleet was Piyale Pasha—my daughter Gevherhan's ever-absent
husband.

Eight weeks after it set sail, in the middle of the night, the
fleet reached Mujarro Bay. Our fifty thousand men faced Malta's six thousand. The fighting went on for more than twenty
days. It made a mockery of spring. Everything young and bur-
geoning was cut down, burned or murdered. Six thousand
of our men perished over the next month at the hands of the
Knights Hospitaller.

Reinforcements arrived from the Maghreb, but they might
as well have stayed in Tripoli because the resistance—by five
hundred decrepit and dauntless Knights, many of them older
than Suleiman himself—was supernatural. We took the ravelin, stormed the fort, blackened the air with gunfire. It was
their fire, however, that prevailed: an incendiary mixture that
the old men poured from rooftops, igniting our fighters' tunics and their turbans, making of the men screaming pillars
of flame.

Piyale Pasha was lucky to lose only a hand, though Gevherhan hardly thought so. And the arrival from Sicily of Spain's
nine-thousand-man reinforcement made up his sorry mind
about what to do next. He had lost fifteen thousand men. That
was enough. Piyale sent a messenger to the capital, not only to
inform the Sultan of the outcome, but to give Suleiman time
to accept it. To cool down in advance, you might say. If Piyale
had waited a year, ten years, it would have made no difference.

Suleiman was so incensed—so shamed—he banned the fleet from entering the harbor in daylight. Gevherhan took it especially hard.

Suleiman was upended by Malta. "Only with *us* do our armies triumph," he bayed. It was shattering, Semiz Ali Pasha wrote. And I know why he thought so. Suleiman knew that he was irreplaceable, and he knew what disaster Malta foretold. Let me repeat that. He knew what disaster it foretold.

The loss at Malta aged Suleiman ten years. Rage and shame can do that. Younger hearts than his had stopped beating with far less cause. It made me sick with worry.

෨

I've been giving these pages to Esther. She's the only person I can trust to safeguard all this. Plus, she's the one whose judgment I most care about. My point in mentioning her here is, first, that she was riled by my reference to Nasi—she said it was dismissive. I told her she could expect more and worse, because there is no limit to my hatred of that man, including posthumously. And second, she's talked Hamon into sending to Padua for another physician. There's a new symptom—a taste in my mouth of metal.

෨

Murad had been excited working on the clock. Taqi al-Din's assistant was a demanding and rewarding master, and Murad discovered in himself a gift for mechanical design. He conceived—or contributed to conceiving—a verge-and-foliot escapement of great intricacy and insight, and he sent the design to his grandfather. Suleiman's response came from the capital less than four weeks later: an imperial wagonload of materials: pomegranate crust, horn filings, white lead, and borax.

I watched Murad's face flush as he unwrapped the parcels that day. I stood right there as he lifted out the first brick of gold and sniffed it as though it were a lily. Murad was working on something that promised to give his grandfather a measure of satisfaction after all the grief and disappointment of Malta. More than that, Murad was applying himself to the means to new kinds of advancement and accuracy. Murad had what he needed to make him happy. He had interests, teachers, Suleiman's support.

The day the Superintendent told me Murad had taken Safiye to his bed was the day I made what I believe was my first mistake with my son. I couldn't accept his being trained, and taken, by someone who was heedless of our ways, who did what she wanted when it suited her, who was just like my father, if I may put it that way—the difference being that when my father took my mother he didn't do it slyly, for *he* had been given permission. Which makes me ask, *What are a mother or a father for if not to protect their child from harm?* My point, though, is this: Safiye's sway. And Murad's susceptibility. And my mistake.

Murad himself called on me that same day. His long soggy steps along the terrace took me by surprise. Tap-tap, on the terrace rail. "May I enter?" he said, as though he weren't, as far as I was concerned, a different person from the one he'd been that morning. I asked him where he'd been. I was as cold as a spike. I could look only at his feet. I told him to stay on the stone to protect the rug. But like a large friendly animal he kept coming closer. He must have been told the Superintendent spoke with me, I thought. "I have some news, Valide. Are you ready? I am going to have a son!" He said it as though he'd just discovered fire.

"I knew there was something strange here." I shot a look toward the river where, somewhere, the evidence lurked. "What do you mean you're going to have a son? This is nothing to make light of."

"Valide," he declared, suddenly grave, "of course I would not make light of such a thing. The mountain girl, the Albanian, the one given by my aunt, will have my son. At the end of the year."

Order, custom, calm, everything clattered into the pit of this idea. "What's this about being with an Albanian? The concubine that Mirimah gave you said she didn't know where she was from." The Dukagin highlanders of that region were known to be the most warlike people in Europe. Also the most superstitious. "Besides, how could you know it is a boy? How could you know *anything* so soon?"

"I don't know what you mean—*so soon*. I have had her for months. You surely know that."

I was cold no more. "I do *not* know that. I did not authorize her to visit you. I did not even speak to her. I preside over these matters," I said. "All mothers in my position do. And we do so for a reason. I cannot imagine what you are thinking of or talking about. There are rules for this."

My response to his news repelled Murad, and he stepped back. The mud and water made his boot stick on the floor and made a sucking noise that embarrassed him. "I thought you would be pleased," he said, reddening. Pleased that I had been gone around? That my authority had been flouted? No. I wasn't pleased, and I said so. "Pleased that there is an heir, Valide. Pleased that *I* am pleased." His hands were turned up. He really didn't understand my distress. He was accustomed to my being happy for him.

"Of course I want you to be pleased, Murad. Don't be silly."

"I am not silly," he said just above the deep breath he was drawing in.

"There is something about her," I said unwisely. I was beginning to realize I had gone too far.

"Why do you speak this way? She is just a concubine. The one I happen to have been with. I didn't think there were rules about *this*. Not now anyway." Murad's eyes narrowed in an effort to understand. He needed me to help him do that.

"Murad, listen to me. This is not about you. I'm sorry. You have not done anything wrong. Of course, you haven't. I'm just surprised not to have known . . . something so important—for so long. Aslanim?"

He looked up.

"I regret losing my temper."

"I thought you would be happy."

"I know."

I took a couple of steps, faced the wall, and asked how he knew it would be a son. Heading out of the room all he said was, "She can tell." No three words could have rattled me more. He believed them. And I feared them.

Is the quality of bad so much more powerful than that of good? Murad and I had had years of happiness and calm. Then one sharp—and worrying—exchange, and the air was filled with bitterness for weeks. For every minute of every day of many weeks.

It was only moments later—she must have been waiting in the hall—that Safiye strode in behind the eunuch. Leavened, expressionless, she was dressed in gleaming gold. This was not a girl. There was nothing unformed about her. Nothing tree-like, either, except for the height and the bark and the rings around rings inside. I wished she had never been born. I told her she looked well. "I feel perfect," she answered. I told her she was fortunate. She replied, "I am." I said I'd heard from my son that she recalled where she had been born. "Yes. I have remembered." Then I commented on the gender of Murad's unborn child—that she had told Murad it was a boy. I asked what made her think that. And it was her answer that confirmed she was beyond—or should have been beyond—the pale of our lives. She said, "Everything." It was as though she were her own authority.

I strove for calm. I told her she was dismissed. "I understand," she said, gliding out on the very sandals I'd told her were not suitable. The breathtaking unease this girl set off in me compelled me to sit down and try to reason with myself. I told myself that she really hadn't changed our lives, which was ridiculous. She had. I told myself that human character does not change, which is true. And that Murad's was sound. And that it would see him through whatever one concubine might impose. I told myself that proportion—not perspective—was what leads to proper understanding. And that if Matrakci were to have mapped the matter, Murad's goodness would be very huge and on top and everything else would be small and on the bottom. I told myself that I could navigate this passage on my own. Find proportion on my own. Manage without Matrakci. And I was wrong. Matrakci had died. In his sleep. Not long after Malta. No one was with him.

What did I lose when Matrakci died? This is not a question I asked myself at the time. It was too hard. But I am asking it now—lying here, calm, sicker, clearer. When Matrakci was gone I lost more than closeness—arranged by the Sultan himself—to one of the best minds in the Empire. And I lost more than the artist who'd taught me how to imagine and make a map. I lost the heart that had joined Mehmed's and mine. I lost the very person who could have scaled the threat of Safiye to fact instead of fear. The only person who might have shown me—warned me—because he *knew* him—that my place with Suleiman was in his mind, not his heart.

Wednesday, November 23

The baby came in May, on a comet, at noon. A streaking star invisible against the background light. They said there was hardly a tremble when Safiye gave birth. A new generation of the House of Osman just slipped into our midst. And it was a boy.

I had heard that the extension beyond one's own children into a farther time of one's children's children changes a woman, opens her wider. I didn't notice at first that my grandson's birth didn't have this effect on me. It takes a while to detect not being transported by a joy you've never felt. It also helps if one sees the child. And I had no wish to. To me, the baby seemed less Murad's than Safiye's. Far less.

Then word came from the capital. The Sultan, age seventy-two years and four months, unable to mount a horse, was going to war. Hungary—again. Here had been the site of his first great victory—at Mohacs—when he was thirty. Here, too, over years, over decades, a grueling tug between Suleiman and the Habsburg pretender—that had taken Suleiman all the way to Vienna—but only to its gates: something impossible for him to accept, or forget. Buda was another matter. Suleiman had taken Buda. And later he took other Habsburg strongholds—Szekesfehervar and Siklos and Szeged. He'd taken Habsburg protectorates, too—including Otranto across the strait on the Adriatic. Szigetvar must have haunted him, though. Imagine embarking on a campaign at that age. Imagine the prospect of mobilizing three hundred thousand men and the munitions, animals and gear needed for an eight-hundred-mile march. Not to mention that his feet were mangled with gout. And he intended, before he set out, to see the son of his favorite grandson. The tip of time's arrow. The farthest-reaching point of the order Suleiman had spent his life ensuring.

I realized it was time I saw the baby, too. I called on Murad and found him in the shop he had created, kneeling next to Taqi al-Din's assistant and surrounded by pieces of the striking train they were working on for the clock. His son was by his side, in Murad's own cradle. Murad got up carefully, brushing metal filings from his robe and smoothing his tunic. The little dark-skinned tutor bowed, rolled up his designs, and shuffled backward to the door. Murad held both his arms out to me, a manly gesture of confidence in his confidence.

"I'm so glad you've come," he said genially. He positioned a cushion next to the cradle. "This is my son." I looked at Murad, surprised by the formality and by the suddenness and clarity of what was unfolding. The relations, the roles, the rewards—all there, in a moonstone cradle where I hadn't yet looked.

"Your grandfather is going on campaign in Europe," I said.

Murad's eyes fell to the things on the floor. Brass springs and scoops, slim silver rods, a mound of lead weights. These were the elements of our future, and Murad knew it as well as Suleiman. And yet Suleiman was intent on securing the Empire—one last time—by the old means, bearing the old standards. The incongruity was stark. Murad said, "Won't this be too much for him? I thought he was done with campaigns." I told him we all thought the same thing but that Malta had bowed him low. That he seemed to need a victory. "Of that sort?" Murad asked.

"We return to what we know," I said. "Even Suleiman, it seems. The Sultan wants to see your son, Aslanim, before he leaves. He has sent a summons. This is a great honor."

Murad squinted at the baby, tipped the rocker with his toe, and set the cradle in motion. The baby woke without a start. "This is a great honor," Murad whispered to his son.

I knelt down and peered in. He was loosely wrapped in linen; his tiny star hands framing his face; his eyes calmly closed to the world and its light. Some features of babies are startling—full-grown at birth. This is how this infant's eyelashes were. Thick as grass, and long. They are there to protect him, I thought, and I wondered what those eyes might need protecting from. This child gave rise to many questions of that sort. He was different from any baby I'd ever seen. He was definite, and his skin was so translucent I thought I might see within him the parts that made him whole. Maybe it was this visibleness that made him seem so vulnerable. That, plus having left his mother so recently to come into the world.

Suddenly, journeying to the capital seemed out of the question. It seemed inconceivable. "Now that I see him, though," I said, halting, surprised, "goodness, Murad. I had no idea how fragile he is. Surely the Sultan would understand that the baby is still too young to travel. The last thing your grandfather would want would be to expose your son to any danger . . ."

Gazing at that very boy, Murad said, "It is a mystery. To be both fragile and strong." I had never heard him speak that way. Well, of course he hadn't spoken that way. He'd never been a father before. "Was I not the same age when the Sultan summoned me to the capital from Manisa?" Murad asked mildly, firmly.

"It was summer."

"It is almost summer now."

"He is too young, Aslanim. Really." As though my eyes were the word for *Look!* or *No!* they opened wide and fearful.

"You took me, Valide."

"Yes. I did." I could not take my eyes off Murad's son.

"I will speak to his mother."

Taken aback, yet again, by something entirely reasonable—in this case, Murad's wish to consult Safiye—I had to admit to myself fully that he cared for this distant girl who was now mother of a possible pretender to the throne. I saw that this girl might very well have the same effect on Murad that Hurrem had had on Suleiman—causing him to flout the one-son-per-mother rule. I saw that Safiye might be like Hurrem in many essential ways. That she had a mind of her own, unavailable for shaping. That she did not need to be loved. That her eyes did not need protecting and could accommodate whatever they saw. People for whom these things are true can go places the rest of us can't, or won't. I believe Suleiman thought he had such eyes. But he didn't. If he had he wouldn't have needed Selim as a witness to Mustafa's execution. His own eyes would have been enough. It showed an awful lack of awareness, or courage. I know this only now.

A difficult exchange about this girl lay ahead for Murad and me. But when? Right then? And interrupt that state of enchantment?

"Help me up. Please." Murad took me under the arm as though I were heavy or old. I planted my feet and lifted my chin to show, somehow, that I was neither. "Of course, you will," I said. "You should definitely do that. Speak to her, I mean." The baby was wide-awake then and staring straight up. His lashes were thick on the bottom, too. I know that new babies don't see, not really. But it seemed he could see me, and I wished he could, and I bent closer and beneath my breath I whispered his as-yet undisclosed name. "May I hold him?"

"By all means." Murad signaled to a eunuch for a ewer. I

removed my rings and bracelets, rinsed my hands, patted them approvingly for what they were about to do, slid one hand beneath the tiny back, the other under the tiny head, and lifted Murad's son to my chest—his face to my neck, my nose to his hair. I had not breathed that scent in twenty years. I was suddenly aware of my body, head to toe; an involuntary turning at the waist, some deeper breathing-in of this life in my arms, something simple—from him, in me. It was hope as I had not yet known it. I was his grandmother.

I understood that what I held in my arms was not a part of life but all of life—just as on a boat when I was a young girl I knew I was on all of the water in the world. I understood that these were the first moments of what would shape our lives thereafter, and I believed that Murad recognized the moment, too. We were enchanted together. I would find another time to talk to Murad about his concubine. "Your grandfather has chosen his name," I said. I looked at the baby; drew a breath through my nose down to my feet. "He will be called after Efendimiz's best-loved son who died before his time."

"Mehmed," Murad said clasping his wrists inside his endless sleeves and turning to the Mehmed who was asleep. "The Sultan has favored you greatly," he said, bowing to him. Then he said to me, "I will do as my grandfather wishes, Valide. I hope you will accompany us."

The fountain in the courtyard in Manisa is made of marble from Paros. I learned that only recently. At the base of it are three broad steps. Safiye was sitting on the middle one when Murad went out to tell her we had been summoned by the Sultan. It was noon. The yard was shadowless. No dusky suggestions of columns or overhangs. There was just the octagon of marble, the little jet of water, and Safiye on the steps in the baking sun, determinedly picking at something on her scalp. She was waiting. There was no missing the Sultan's messenger corps.

She wore a lemon-colored tunic over her other garments,

which were all white, as was her veil. Owing to the way vision adjusts, or doesn't, it was difficult to see in the bright light, and I put my hand up to block the sun. Safiye stood up. Her jet eyes and dark-painted mouth were set firm, and she seemed even taller than usual, or was.

Murad signaled to the nurse to bring Mehmed close. As she did, Murad was saying something to Safiye—about Suleiman's summons, probably, or the baby's name. It was apparent that Murad's liveliness aggravated her. She pursed her mouth, laced her fingers around the handiwork on her lap and knelt slightly, laying the thing she had been working on upon the step. Then, by means of a nod and her out-thrust arms, she issued a command that her son be handed over. Safiye took Mehmed expertly, like a practiced nurse, got him into the shade, inspected him as if he'd been exposed to disease. Murad stayed where he was, arrested by I couldn't tell what. Something she had said or asked? I doubted it mattered, or rather, I doubted I could help him with it.

"Of course we go," Safiye was saying. "We go for favor," she said, dropping the article as do so many from her region.

&

We traveled light for speed. Only the essential attendants, except for a medical staff, which I insisted on and which even Murad thought excessive. I won't enumerate them, but there were many. We had an infant with us! Partly from concern for Mehmed's health on the journey, and partly from respect for his parents, I kept my distance. I doubt it was coincidence that it was the first time Safiye evinced—in my presence, anyway— what appeared to be satisfaction. Not happiness. To this day I have never seen her happy. But rather an unfettered pride. It became her.

The route, we were told, was overland from Karesi to Panderma. The rest would be over sea to save time. I hadn't been on a ship since the day I'd staggered off Barbarossa's, and Sumbul hadn't been on one since he'd come, butchered and bound, from Alexandria. Neither of us wanted to board, but the choice was not ours. The day before we reached Panderma, as if by God's hand, the sea opened up. A black corridor rose from the floor of the sea to the sky. Two walls of water pulled east and west. Then they clapped together leaving no wake, and we wondered if we'd dreamed it, but we hadn't. We got to shore and found the landscape in ruins. We passed Gemlik and little Ikizce, most of the way having to make our own road. Houses and lives by the thousands had been destroyed by the earthquake. The place had been silenced.

And then there was the silence of the capital. Not the silence that is former sound but the silence preceded by nothing. Silence itself. It was sickening. I had to get out of the conveyance to release the quiet. It was something like what I feel now, in this bed and empty room. Something oceanic and foreign. When we resumed the approach it was worse—and it was affirmed by the docks and streets, bazaars and shops, tanneries and slaughterhouses. All of them were hushed—not, I reckoned, because the earth *had* quaked but because it was about to. Suleiman was going to war, again.

I called first on the Grand Vizier, as I'd been told to. Sokollu Mehmed Pasha—Ismihan's husband—was alone reading maps in a freezing room near the Treasury. He seemed unconcerned that his fingers were white from the cold, that his turban was back so far his hair showed, that his eyes were gorgeous, blue as sky, or that he looked half his age rather than the forty-five years more than Ismihan that he was. He simply applied a hand to his back, arched, and said Ismihan and I were the image of each other. There was still a thick nap of Serbian on his Turkish, after all those years. I thanked him for the compliment, declined the offer of a seat, and decided to put off telling him how happy Ismihan had become. I'm not sure why. Perhaps out of respect for the pending campaign.

Sokollu Mehmed had little more to say—just that I was to meet that afternoon with the Sultan and that I was to take as little time with him as possible. I decided not to be offended by his haste—he was rolling up the eastern edge of Thrace and pointedly pushing the map into its leather sheath, and I left the room offering him a little nod and smile.

A legend that explains the story of our family is key to the encounter that followed. In the beginning, Osman, the father of the dynasty, had a dream. A moon emerged from the bosom of a holy dervish, wheeled through the heavens, and took up residence in Osman's breast, causing his navel to bring forth a mighty tree. Osman dreamed that the tree gave life to the world with mountains, streams, and arable plains and that it protected the world with its shadow. When Osman awoke, he went to a dervish to learn the meaning of the dream. The holy man told him that God intended that Osman—the tree—and his descendants—the dynasty—be sovereign in the land. He told him that only a contest fought bravely and to death could prove Osman's successor's worthiness in the eyes of God and his legitimacy in the minds of the people. He told him, too, that only one son could succeed the sultan and that the others were destined to accompany their father on his final journey. The dream was a prescription for the order of our dynasty: the will of God—not of man—shall determine succession. Avoid civil war at all cost, for it is poison to the dynasty and to the Empire whose history it shares. The dream, the prescription, and the law to which they gave rise are our story. Like his forebears, Suleiman, in his own way, took their essence to heart.

ॐ

Here is the encounter.

Suleiman was pacing in front of the jeweled facade of the Hall of Petitions in a robe you wouldn't have seen on a page. He'd once said he felt the Empire inside him, and in that very plain garment it showed: the Caucasus and Europe were his shoulders; Anatolia, his heart; Persia and the Mediterranean, his outstretched arms; Algeria and Yemen, the dangling sleeves. It showed on Suleiman's face as well. The minnow eyes sagged. The sinewy neck was rutted as a road. The face of the man to whom I owed my life was all but drained of its own. The last letter I got from Matrakci had been about Suleiman's condition following Malta: the seizures; the not eating or sleeping; the constant shaking of his hands. Why did it take being there, in Suleiman's presence, for me to realize what a new campaign to Europe was going to do to him?

He drew his hand slowly over the row of braided closures on his robe and said, "I am pleased to see you." Not we. I.

"I am pleased to see you, Efendimiz." I did not dare say *Please don't go.*

"I thought we would take a walk, but I no longer wish to do that." He waved off the attendants except for Josag, and he headed toward the Privy Chamber. "I leave soon," he said, as though the mobilization in and around the city of a hundred thousand troops might not have made that clear. In fact, it was in looking out at those thousands of tents that I realized that cloth gives a greater impression of war than iron does. He panted from the exertion of walking and didn't hear me say, out loud this time, that I wished he wouldn't go to war.

We got to his chamber. He stood before the door as one would stand before an opponent. He assessed it, applied his shoulder to the ebony, and pushed with his still great might. The room was full of light. "Sit over there." He nodded to a bench beneath the window overlooking the Golden Horn. He positioned himself beside the fountain on the adjacent wall, protecting himself from betrayal, as he always did, with the sound of coursing water. Josag, inert to his core, remained where he was, by the door. "You have come with my great-grandson."

"Mehmed."

Suleiman slid a finger across his gums. He was raw inside and out. A Black Eunuch appeared with fruits and tea. Suleiman directed him toward me. The eunuch stood before me like a wall and shelf. I knew enough to take what he was offering. Josag handed Suleiman an undecorated box.

"This is yours," Suleiman said, removing what was inside and handing it to me.

It was. Just as he said. The gaudy binding gone, *Elements* as I had first known it. The worn-down red, the elaborate *Es*, the rubbed *uclid*. Suleiman's gesture was laden with meanings. *I love you,* I wished to say. Suleiman had, from the day I first laid my eyes upon him, given me the means to live up to his faith in me. He had put me in the hands of Suna, then of Matrakci; given me to Mehmed; given Selim to me. He'd supplied the most potent ways for me to succeed. I wanted to say *I love you* because the gift he was offering made me love him even more. He knew what *Elements* meant to me. The book was a covenant.

I thanked him. Suleiman pushed out his chest and lifted his chin, and his eyes began to shine. "After Szigetvar the battles will be over." He tipped his head toward Hungary. "*This* is our dominion." He waved toward all the world. "Knowledge," he specified, wheeling like the sun from one order to the next. He was coming to life. He was going to die, and no one was going to stop him. He pressed on. "After this—after me—Selim must not be drawn into military action anywhere, land or sea. Those decisions are for the Grand Vizier. I have told Selim this. I have told Sokollu Mehmed. But you must add your own weight. Selim will be tempted—by his weakness and by those who will prey on it, which is why he will not last long."

"*Sultanimiz.*" It was a rebuke, and I meant it.

Suleiman's arm shot up. He pivoted toward the fountain. "Selim will do what he can. He will supply the protection of more sons, which he has put off for too long."

"You mean take other *women*? At *this* stage?"

He turned back. For just a flash of a moment there was the beginning of a smile. It vanished. "That is what I mean. And when Murad does succeed . . ." Suleiman's voice dropped, "you will do your part to safeguard order."

"I will. Of course. What part?"

"There is a law—the Conqueror's. Its purpose is . . ."

I got to my feet before he said more. "I believe I know its purpose."

"Sit down."

I didn't move. "Sit *down*." I sat. "Its purpose is to avoid civil war. And it has meaning only if it is enforced. My grandson does not have it in him to enforce it. In this as in many other ways he is like my son Mehmed. I am telling you because you are the mother of my grandson, and you have raised him to a different and excellent strength. And I am telling you because you should be proud that Murad will *create* order and expand it, and he will do it in ways that will bring new glory to the Empire, and new sway. And you—*you*—will . . ." I stood and backed away from him. He might as well have been poison or lava. I did not want to be within reach of his words. "Sit *down*. I am telling you because you will enforce the law. You will do what I trust no one else to do."

"But you *cannot* trust me to do this, Efendimiz."

"I have *said* that I do."

"But that is a duty between *brothers*. You have just said so."

"You dare argue. There are exceptions. I enforced it for Selim."

"But Bayezid *challenged* you. And Selim's brothers were *grown*." I was finding excuses for his having done the very thing he was commanding me to do. That, too, I see now.

Slowly, Suleiman lowered his chin to set his sight. It had the effect of hooding his eyes. Not for a moment did he take them off mine. "Children grow. Their mothers champion

them. They arm them. You have armed your son better, differently, rightly." He stressed every word. "You should be
proud."

"I *am* proud," I said, alarmed. I clasped my elbows in
defense.

Suleiman advanced, closing the space between us. He said,
"I know that." It was the closest I'd ever been to him. The
slashes in his cheeks were very deep and still they couldn't
contain the tears of a life that were washing down his face. "I
know *you*," he said. He drew a breath. "A good choice." Then
he uttered my name—which he himself had given me—and he
extended a hand hidden in a sleeve that hung to the ground.
"Here," he said.

It was so simple. *Here* made sense. It joined us—yet again.

Suleiman had long before saved me from oblivion. *Here*
was what he had saved me *for*. For a very long time I believed
here explained more than it did. But it was what he said next,
as I took his hand and he turned us south to west, that mattered most.

Thursday, November 24

There are exceptions—Sumbul being one—but it is fair to say about eunuchs that they are vindictive, babyish, condescending, and easily bored. They also tend to be angry which is hardly surprising. While Josag is their exemplar, I have thought him too aged and limp to make trouble anymore, but he's not. I learned today from Hamon, who learned from Esther, that Josag has had the new dishes from China destroyed. The greenish-gray stoneware—all of it—dust. It has sent Safiye into a rage the like of which no one suspected her capable. Apparently it was she, not Murad, who'd commissioned the extravagant set.

※

"Have you held him yet?" I asked. Murad shook his head. "Well, now you will." Murad made himself taller. "Take your arms out," I said. Murad drew back the lengths of sleeve. For the first time in years I saw those long, bare limbs. They hadn't changed. They were smooth as the silk of his robe. I tapped his forearm. "Make a bend. There. Like this." I slid my hands beneath little Mehmed, drew him toward me, and placed him in the cradle of his father's arms.

Suleiman had gone down to a small and simple kiosk

189

he'd had built not long before. From my terrace I watched Murad walk through Suleiman's hundred thousand hyacinths—it was May. Suleiman heard Murad approach on the pebbled path, and he came out to meet his grandson and his grandson's son. He took the few stairs of the kiosk slowly but steadily, and then he was on the path himself, waiting as Murad and Mehmed approached. They stood together for a moment. Then Murad said something, and Suleiman tipped his forearms up and the sleeves of his green robe slid back, and Murad put Mehmed in Suleiman's arms. Suleiman held out Mehmed for a moment and then drew him to his chest. He closed his eyes, pressed his nose into Mehmed's hair, and kissed the side of his head.

I looked at the three of them and I thought, I wish to close my eyes now. I wish to see nothing else but this, maybe ever.

I withdrew to my chambers and settled myself on the mattress, carefully, as though settling someone else there, and I had almost fallen asleep when a pounding set in, something heavy on wood. Crying. A dispute? It was Mihrimah.

I hadn't seen her since her mother's death—eight years— and Malta had told on her badly. Her face was spudded and gray. She seemed embalmed, except for tearing at her hair with both hands. Her father would not see her. Was I going to see him, she wanted to know. If I was, would I take her with me. She yanked on the string of peridots around her neck. I took her arm—she was even bigger than I realized under all that robe—and I held it the way I thought a friend might hold a friend—a bit harder than necessary. I told her it was the baby the Sultan wished to see. Only the baby. And I acknowledged, without sarcasm, that she had provided the concubine responsible for that very child. Mihrimah shook her head as though she didn't hear me rightly, and the kohl that was supposed to decorate her eyes ran into her mouth and down her neck. I told her it was unthinkable that Suleiman did not wish to see his daughter. It was only that his mind was elsewhere. Mihrimah just cried and shook. I took her face in my hands, and the sadness of what we both knew was coming—plus, I imagine—having just been charged by Suleiman with an unimaginably large dynastic duty—allowed me to put my lips to Mihrimah's eyes, the left, the right, and suggest that she return with us to Manisa. At least for the summer. But she declined.

At noon the next day, as the last note of the muezzin's call burned off the air, a Janissary of awesome proportion sounded the opening note on the Conqueror's own war drum—a leather instrument the size of a cistern. Four hours before, at dawn, immediately following his ablutions and prayer, Suleiman sent a message—about which I would learn several months later—to Mihrimah.

༄

Suleiman reached Edirne in half a day's time. So did his senior party—the Grand, Second, and Third Viziers, the Agha of the Janissaries, Head of the Treasury, Keeper of the Standards, Clerk of Secrets, Chief Falconer, Head Gunner, Master of the Stables and Secretary of the Imperial Council. It took another day for the qadis, tribal chiefs, dervishes, and ulema to pass the same point. By the fifth day the head of the column reached the end of the Maritsa, then cut under Sofia, made Kosovo on the ninth day, headed north for Belgrade and, after Belgrade, made Szigetvar in two days instead of three. Ninety-five thousand men then pitched camp for the battle.

I close my eyes. I feel the Black Sea breeze on my face. I feel it moving my hair around my shoulders. I see Suleiman as the imperial tent itself—stretched to the limit with intention. The fact was, though, that Suleiman hadn't been able to sit upright after Belgrade. The pace of the march had been too much. The seizures were coming daily. His ankles were swollen with edema. He lay on his soaked mattress, lengthened out, rigid. That's what Sokollu Mehmed wrote to Is-mihan. He wrote, too, that the respect with which Suleiman approached his Hungarian foe showed the Sultan at his best. Nicholas Zrinyi was a near match for Suleiman. He, too, was past seventy; he, too, was ready to die for his faith. Inspired by him, his men had resisted ferociously and had been inched back at terrible cost to both sides, until Zrinyi was forced into the city's citadel from whose turret he restated his intention to resist to the end. Suleiman replied that there was no need for that; Zrinyi had just to surrender. He could keep his lands and his title. But Zrinyi spat on Suleiman's offer. Suleiman then sat upright in his sickbed and, calm as the eye of a storm, he ordered our sappers to work. For twelve days and twelve nights the men dug until the fortress was cross-hatched from beneath.

Late the night before the assault, Suleiman summoned Sokollu Mehmed. His voice rattling, Suleiman said something about the drum of conquest: that it would be heard in Vienna and Prague, that it would be heard in Copenhagen. Sokollu Mehmed stayed at the Sultan's side. He watched as Suleiman's eyes, so heavy when open, darted beneath their closing lids, watching something he remembered, maybe, or was about to see. And Sokollu Mehmed watched as they slowed, back, forth, sweeping like a broom, like life. Then a shudder. Suleiman clutched the sides of the mattress and spasmed into a form that must have been something like Jihangir's at the end—something eye-opening—and as he convulsed the tent filled with Suleiman's life as he let it go.

Suleiman, gone from this world.

From an elegy by Baki, favorite poet of Suleiman

At length is struck the parting-drum and thou hast
    journeyed hence;
Lo, thy first halting place is mid the Paradised plain

Praise be to God, for he in either world has blessed thee,
And writ before thine honored name both Martyr and
  Ghazi.

Old Hamon himself, the only other person present at the moment of Suleiman's death, laid open the Sultan's body, removed his entrails, and pickled and interred them near the tent. Then he preserved the rest of the Sultan with balsams, laced him up and chalked his sunken face.

Sokollu Mehmed summoned Feridun Bey, his absolute confidant, dictated the news in a sentence, and had him deliver the letter—plus a *fetihname*, the document announcing conquest—to a certain Hasan Chavush, who'd gained fame for his speed on horseback. He alone would carry the message to Selim in Kutahya. There would be no relief riders on this mission.

Then it was Sokollu Mehmed's duty, and one of his greatest achievements ever, to gather up the Sultan's existence and present it to the people as though it were real and unchanged. The Grand Vizier emerged from the imperial tent with orders from Sultan Suleiman, who could be seen from a certain angle seated on his campaign throne. The bombing should continue, Sokollu Mehmed commanded on Suleiman's behalf, and it did for another five days, until there was no enemy left. With victory ours, the troops were ordered to withdraw to the eastern border.

In those days of breaking camp and the days that followed, there were many other orders from the evidently indisposed Sultan: to fill vacant posts, announce promotions, notify governors of Ottoman victory. All this achieved by Sokollu Mehmed. Finally, twelve days after he died, the Sultan himself quit Szigetvar, borne on a gold-curtained litter, occasionally visible, reclining at a queer angle, eyes downcast, his lap filled with sleeve.

Hasan Chavush made Kutahya in eight days. "The Shadow

of God on Earth is dead," he announced to Selim. "The Empire is without a Sultan until you claim your place." Then Hasan Chavush, or what was left of him, rode on, another three days, to deliver the news to me. Selim had given him an enormous tip, he told me. And the only thing he'd uttered was the command to notify me.

Suleiman, dead.

He once told me that between Islam and Christianity our heavens were different but our hells the same. I hadn't dared ask what he meant. When he was gone, I realized how much it mattered that I know. I could not imagine where Suleiman might be.

Selim was on his way to the capital within the hour and made it there in an unheard-of six days. On the seventh day the Sheikh ul Islam invested him with the Sword of the Prophet at the Eyup Mosque, up the Golden Horn, where the water is still and the cedars are thick. It was urgent that Selim be invested swiftly. The people get refractory when there's time between sultans. They always have. It, too, was something to be avoided.

It was not a joyful occasion for Selim without his family present—we'd all returned to Manisa before Suleiman left for Edirne. There was, however, a self-appointed proxy, a man of many talents. Once again Joseph Nasi was at Selim's side offering support when it mattered. In recognition, Selim—before he had been sultan for half a week—granted Nasi the first of many rewards. I learned of it weeks later from the only person more distressed about it than I; the person who on the very day Selim was dubbing Joseph Nasi Duke of Naxos and Paros was causing a prayer for the dead to swirl up over Suleiman's tent. His Grand Vizier. "In the Name of God the most Compassionate, the most Merciful," the muezzin called out following Sokollu Mehmed's order. "Praise be to God, Lord of the Universe, Sovereign of the Day of Judgment!"

That was when the Sultan's soldiers began to know what

194

had come to pass, and they poured out of their tents, all of them wailing in the same low register, descending upon the Sultan's litter, getting as close as they could to the truth. Then the Grand Vizier bade them honor their departed Sultan with fealty to his son—staunch, timorous Selim—whose single sultanic duty, as prescribed by his dying father, was to do the very thing Selim had refused to do since the day he met and began to love me.

Friday, November 25

Here began the season of children. Purposeful babies as pink as shells. Boys and girls drawing first breaths, taking first steps. Here began the days of renovation, sex, and carnage. The years of couplings and scaffoldings, construction and decline. The days of heads on pales, the years of delirium and shame. Here began the season of children conceived for death.

I had known what was coming. Selim would succeed Suleiman and have more sons. Murad would remain in Manisa, administering, being a father. I would move back to the capital and be a wife again. And yet every step was a jolt—leaving Murad and Little Mehmed; not having an eye on Safiye; Selim being with others.

I had missed Selim. His calm and truthfulness, his clemency. I had missed the weight of his presence. His competence at things he'd learned when he was young. His way with horses and with falcons. His skill with bow and arrow, as goldsmith, as poet. I'd missed Selim's concern for me. Worse, I had not realized I'd missed all these things. It had been time truly and awfully wasted.

By the time I got to the capital, Suleiman had been dead for two months, and still the air remained full of absence and sorrow. It rose up like heat and bent the way things looked, everything death-like in its own way. Rotting lilies lining the banks, household refuse swirling in the Golden Horn, lines of hungry people waiting for their soup and rice, waiting for night to fall. This was a city once enlivened by a vision. Suleiman had secured its life from the inside out. He'd expanded his mosque's hospital into a school of medicine, for example, and created a university in the process. It was a concentrated mirror image of what Suleiman had done for the Empire as a whole, pushing its boundaries as far as they could—and I believe will—go, and expanding our system of justice beautifully, if I may put it that way, by supplementing Shari'ah with *kanun*—religious with sultanic law. It was an achievement I'd heard about from my grandfather when I was a child, and it had conferred on Suleiman the name he goes by here in the Empire. He may be the Magnificent in Europe and Africa. But here he is *Kanuni*. All these years later.

Outside Topkapi, women moved in aimless circles, men stood in clusters, silent children drew idly with sticks in the dirt. Within the walls it was grimmer still; the palace was pervaded by absence. Everyone had withdrawn. The only sound in its neglected courtyards was the clink of a cup chained to a fountain. The only sound until we neared the Privy Chamber.

Suleiman could not have imagined the effect on Selim of the command to have more sons. But that was not Suleiman's strength—imagining in that way. For Suleiman what mattered was the protection of many pretenders. For Selim it was just doing what he'd been told to do.

You'd think Selim would have collected himself when he heard my approach that first day. The entourage was large, even after we'd left the clattering conveyances behind. In the Golden Way, the corridor to the Privy Chamber, there was plenty of commotion, too. But Selim didn't hear a thing—not his own thudding against the bed frame, not the particular sounds of the girl beneath him. He was drunk. So drunk that he wasn't himself. If he had been, he'd have taken care. I knew that for sure. I stood outside the Privy Chamber, stunned and strangely puzzled. I could not make sense of what my senses were telling me. Sumbul touched my shoulder to remind me he was there. Josag stood between me and the door on the other side of which was his charge, the Emperor of the Two Horizons. He had his back to me, and he had it to the door, too. That is Josag, I thought. Two backs. I thought about what Selim was doing, which was following an order, and I thought about what that meant—for him, for Murad, for Little Mehmed, and for the girl in the bed. I do not think I thought about what it meant for me. I think—how can one be sure—but I *think* I saw the task before me—self-imposed—as *not* thinking about what it meant for me. How else could I carry out the duty with which I'd been charged? I stood there a long time. I felt the bones around my eyes get smaller. I'd been traveling for twelve days. I was not going to interrupt the Sultan.

When I returned the next day, an assertively handsome man was leaving the Privy Chamber. Exquisitely clad, purposeful in his stride, he had a vulpine flair that made his surroundings seem like quarry. Only when he saw and faced me was an imperfection revealed: unaligned eyes that gave the impression of seeing this face twice, which was twice as much as I wished for. I had not trusted Joseph Nasi since learning of his visit to Selim in Kutahya, when he had made sure that Selim knew his sister Mihrimah was pushing Suleiman to take Malta.

"You," I said, beneath my breath. Nasi paused and bowed slightly, then proceeded across the Second Courtyard.

I put my shoulder to the Privy Chamber door. The chill walls of the vaulted hall, glorious in their gilt and messages, were dripping from the outdoor heat.

"You took a long time," Selim mumbled as I folded myself down beside his mattress. "But maybe it is better that you did."

I'd forgotten how concise he was. "It is better that we are together, Selim."

"You look different," he stated. We'd been apart for a long time, more than five years. I'd gone to Kutahya twice. Still. Even at that age my looks were changing by the season. I was getting thinner, my features more pronounced. For Selim it was the opposite. His eyes were valanced and watery. A cowl of fat circled his neck. He looked awful, and it didn't bother him. He concerned himself with what mattered: "I have to do this, you know." I told him I did know. He propped himself on an elbow, belched, and waved the air clear. "I don't see them—these girls." His lashes fluttered. I told him it was all right—one of the stupidest things I have ever said. And Selim answered, "No. It is not all right. But I know you understand." He belched again. "You have always had a heart." And handed me a folded parchment. My name was on the outside. Inside:

Shining Arch

Were the eyebrows of Venus painted in gold, they would
not be as brilliant as you.
Were all the light of day poured in the moon's slender
crescent, it would not be as brilliant as you.
Were the jewel on the ear of heaven kissed by the sun, it
would not be as brilliant as you.
Were the bow of the Sultan drawn back to the Empire's
edge, it would not have the curve, the reach, the
brilliance of you.

I was astounded, filled with sad wonder. What other fine ways of being had I missed or overlooked. I asked when he'd written the poem. "It doesn't matter," Selim said.
"It does. It matters very much."
"Awhile ago. Years. There are others. I like this one."
"I like it, too. Very, very much."
"Slender crescent," Selim muttered. He fell asleep.
He'd been in horrible Kutahya all that time, and this was

what he wanted me to know. I bent over him and kissed his puffy eyes. "Selim," I whispered.

"What?" He didn't stir.

"You're the one with the heart. We're going to fix this place. We're going to make it worthy of you." He was gone, though. Fast asleep.

᠀

I gave Selim the wide berth he wanted as he did what he had to do to protect the dynasty. The space did not curb my great unease with what he was doing.

What am I saying? It wasn't unease. It was panic.

I don't know what I had expected of this enforced procreation. An exercise that was spare and contained? Something arithmetic? Did I imagine that Selim would take one woman, have a son; take another, have a second son; do it several times, and that would be that? The throne protected?

In fact Selim was taking not women but girls, and he'd taken not few but many—at least until I arrived and confronted the Superintendent—the same warted crone I'd left behind eight years before—and told her I wanted to see every concubine Selim had been with, which was when I learned that in seventy days he had been with more than twenty, each many times, and that three were known to have conceived. "Bring them to me." The Superintendent took a step back to communicate or remind me of her own authority. "*Now*," I added.

Two were from the north—Circassia, Macedonia; the other was from Rhodes. All were unassuming, unaspiring, confused, and terrified. I knew none of their languages, and I needed no translator to make known to them that they would reside with me in my quarters until the time of their deliveries. All the girls were sixteen. Each carrying the child of a man— an enormous man—three times her age.

"Who chose these girls?" I demanded. It was a very ill-advised question for it allowed the Superintendent to infer there were other important matters I was uninformed about. "*Who?*" The edge of my voice sawed through her gratified silence.

"The Sultan's sister." Her tone was a perfect mix of honey and hemlock.

I know—and I knew then—from long and varied experience that addressing anything important when angry is a mistake. It took huge effort and would have taken more than the one day I was permitted before Mihrimah—alerted by the Superintendent—appeared in my quarters. She'd enlisted the Sultan's own eunuch to gain her entry, and before I could offer her a cushion or refreshment she produced with creepy ease a rolled-up item from her sleeve—exactly the way, as a matter of fact, my father had taken a portolan chart from his. "You will want to read this before you say anything," Mihrimah said. Her voice was marvelously uninflected. I read. "You did well with the concubine for our grandson. She has produced a healthy great-grandson. You will supply your brother with what is necessary to assure the throne is protected. The dangers to princes are many. The protection must be commensurate."

"It was my father's parting command," Mihrimah said. "Before Szigetvar. He had it delivered to me the morning after he received you," she added. Still no inflection. Mihrimah did not know that Suleiman had communicated *anything* of importance to me—let alone that *my* duty was to assure the executions of the children whose existence *she* was charged with ensuring. What she knew and what mattered to her was the sequence. She was the last member of the family he communicated with. She'd been redeemed, her status restored.

Maybe it was because of the consuming effort needed to absorb the news that Suleiman had been responsible for Safiye. Maybe it was something else. Whatever the reason, what followed was, I believe, the only time in my life I was visited by grace. I could tell as it descended: the expansive calm that settled around me, the clarity. I rolled up Suleiman's message, returned it to its tube, and gave it back. "Efendimiz had utmost confidence in you, Mihrimah. And it was unshakeable." I was referring to Malta. "With this directive, he has entrusted you with the future of—much of the future of—the family." Mihirmah said, "Yes, that is true." And her voice *was* inflected then. It went up at the end, like a question. She wished me to repeat what I'd said. "The perpetuation of the dynasty. Its vitality. He knew you understood it."

"Yes."

Her breathing had gotten shallow and quick. I encouraged her to take a seat and, should she feel like it, perhaps to remove her heavy outer garment—a strikingly ugly brown thing. I told a Black Eunuch to bring us drinks. I spoke of the journey from Manisa, a stop in Bursa, the rough crossing of Marmara. I told her things about Murad, whom, to this day, she dotes on. And then I told her I had visited the concubine corps that morning and spent time with the girls and that it appeared some might not have been in perfect health, and, in some cases, might also be—I sought her opinion here—young, too young, to be bearing children, which, conceivably, could result in a royal son who was not robust and fit in all respects. I offered her more tea. Then I asked how she had happened to choose the concubines Selim had been with, noting how very pretty each of them was, and Mihrimah said with no qualm that she had left that to the Superintendent. And still I remained calm. I regarded the two of us as though from another room, and I could hardly believe one of them was me over there. Utterly placid while enraged. I suggested I speak with the Superintendent about the selection process. About steps and precautions that might be taken to assure the intended result of healthy and fit sons. About the frequency of visits. And about Selim's drinking. Yes, that too. Then I thanked her, yet again, for the gift she'd made to Murad—the mother of Suleiman's only great-grandson—and by that time, because there were long stretches of saying nothing during the visit, the sun was going down and the eunuchs were beginning to bob into action, lighting torches and lamps, and Mihrimah, renewed, relieved, thanked me in advance for speaking to the Superintendent on her behalf, and she retired to her quarters, confident of her place in the order of our family.

I wish to underscore something right here. In accordance with Suleiman's command, and abetted by the only daughter he ever had, both my husband *and* my son were conceiving children—as many as possible—whose execution Suleiman had charged *me* with assuring. What did this cause me to think?

I don't know.

Selim was indeed with many other women in the seasons that followed, but never at the rate or even close to the rate he'd achieved in those first months when, as he explained to me, he was trying to get "as much done as possible" before I got to the capital. In fact the women he was with thereafter were chosen according to rules established and enunciated by me: Never would the Sultan be with a woman who was under the age of twenty or who had not been in the harem for three years or who didn't speak Italian or Greek or Turkish so that she could express herself to me. Never again would the Sultan have in his bed a concubine who had no idea what was happening to her or why or to what possible *end*. And that was because I would explain it: that it was a rare privilege to be chosen for the Sultan's bed and rarer still to bear him a son who, like all sons of the Sultan, was not only a pretender *to* but a protector *of* the throne. I said nothing, though, about the other possible end. The prescribed end.

And so I had a great desire not to become close to Selim's concubines. And that desire was very hard to fulfill given my insistence on their care and on overseeing that care during their confinements, and especially at the end of those confinements, and most especially in the case of Astraea, who was from Rhodes and who spoke my mother tongue and had been captured from an island and a girlhood not unlike mine—until I was five, anyway. Astraea was slight but strong, and her face had lost none of its fullness or hopeful beauty, which was unusual and significant, because she'd been in the harem for a year before the Superintendent had brought her to Selim. And when, seven months after I arrived from Manisa, Astraea went into the throes of childbirth, I was at her side, holding her small hands in my own, wiping the wet hair from her forehead, telling her in her own language that she would survive the ordeal, *promising* her that she would. And it was very strange indeed to be suspicious of the relief I felt when the baby Astraea brought forth was a girl—for that suspicion was a stifled revelation. And my sorrow was impossible to hide when, within the hour of that birth, the baby died at the breast of her mother, who was clinging to me like the girl she still was and who kept crying "*Mamma*" in the language of our birth.

ॐ

I cannot swear that this sickness isn't confusing my thoughts. The remedies themselves—the fumiter and horehound—should have killed me. And I *have* had enough of it! I am saying these things not because my inside has become a sulfurous pit or because the palms of my hands are rotting but because that is exactly how I saw them the moment I realized that even having been wife of the Sultan, then mother of a son, then widow of the Sultan and mother of his heir—even *then* it wasn't enough. Even *then* there was another hurdle, another hoop. I had to be the mother of a Sultan *who had no brothers!* And I am saying these things because I must.

I had to create a new arrangement of life. A new structure, within and without. In Manisa there had been few distinctions. The palace was, and is, part of its surroundings; small, ungated, wide-windowed to the plains. The servants moved freely between our quarters and theirs. I knew them all by name. The harem at Topkapi, though, was a decrepit place of prohibition, and the lack of opportunity to shine or rise was a prison of its own, and Hurrem had been its warden. It made no sense. The harem is a sanctuary, after all. Yet the place I found after Suleiman's death was a shame. Listless gazes, gardens gone to seed. The Abode of Felicity had become a wreck. This would change.

I had the sense to consult Sokollu Mehmed on the process. "We need a vizier corps *here*," I told him. "A system that educates these girls." I banged my fist into the opposing palm. "How else can they rise?" Practiced in betraying nothing, Sokollu Mehmed pushed his knuckles into his waxy mustache and let out a snort.

"I see where she comes from," he said of his wife. My daughter.

I told him my own case was a model for no one. I had arrived with a name—my father's—known to the Sultan himself. More important, thanks to my mother, I'd had an education that could not be matched by any female in the harem or one likely ever to be brought in. I'd arrived with more knowledge than I had realized, in fact, and it had given me a confidence I hadn't recognized either. So, after firing Hurrem's handpicked superintendent, I elevated her replacement to a status similar—if not equivalent—to Grand Vizier. I organized a system offering chances for progress, with large stipends at the top levels. And I elevated Sumbul to Chief Black Eunuch—a big step toward a big shift of power—away from the White Eunuch corps, who serve the men in the harem, to the Black Eunuchs who serve the women. This was a change less palatable to the Grand Vizier than the other changes. Finally, I commissioned Sinan to do the harem over, top to bottom, outside and in. And it is something to see. He is the greatest architect anywhere. Better than Palladio, with a better eye, too. He's like Hamon—each is more necessary than ever.

In this matter, too, Selim showed his nature. He didn't care how the harem looked. He cared how it made *me* feel. When I called on him with the plans, I set right in with decorative details, carrying on and on. Selim looked up from the board on which he was playing chess by himself, fixed his netted eyes on mine, and said, not unkindly, "You talk too much. Just show me." I unrolled the parchment. Selim looked at it. "No," he said, pointing to the location of our quarters with a rook. "You should have more space." So that I wouldn't hear. "I want a courtyard between," he said wearily. "And fountains. Two."

⁂

Suleiman's last command to Selim was half of his last command to me. Selim's was about life; mine was not. And whatever I believed or didn't believe I was going to do about that, I needed someone to help me think about it. I am certain I did not admit to myself I needed such help. Even as I sought and found her.

Saturday, November 26

I had seen fires before. There'd been a bad one in the Old Palace in the beginning, and another at the annex in Manisa. The worst, though, occurred not long after Selim became sultan. Half the city went up in flames. A bale of oakum ignited the entire caulking district. Even the first flames were higher than the minarets. They got invested by a wind from the north and consumed the district of Djibali—three thousand houses that might as well have been caulked, they were so tightly together. Down through Vefa the flames went, down through Laleli, through Kumkapi and into Yenikapi, making cinder out of every shelter, family, and hope in its path. Twenty thousand houses were burned to nothing at all. Two thousand shops. Four thousand souls gone before the Janissaries even got their water buckets hoisted.

The great fire leveled many lives. While it was burning, though, it had a way of lifting things up, as calamities can. It provided the occasion for people to save each other—getting each other out, taking each other in—which is how mosques and *kulliyes*, friends and strangers, were able to bring the city alive even as it lay in ruins.

In the Jewish quarter, one woman saved nearly fifty residents. She found them, kept them, gave them the wherewithal to start again. Sokollu Mehmed saw her during the fire. He'd been down there, too, dragging people from their flaming homes. "It happens that she is a *kira*," he said. An agent. "She could be useful to you. To the renovation."

Sokollu Mehmed's suggestion was reasonable and good, and I felt unexplainably resistant to it. I said, "I have an architect."

"With the decoration, perhaps. She is said to have excellent connections."

"I can acquire what I need through the Bailo," I said.

Sokollu Mehmed persisted. "Her language is Portuguese. But she does well in Spanish and Dutch. And French and Italian and Hebrew, of course."

Sokollu Mehmed was a man with the warmth of an anvil. The concern which for a moment softened his caved eyes got my attention. His wife had to have been talking to him. Selim's new way of life did not agree with Ismihan. She worried about me and wanted me fully occupied.

I received the *kira*. This is what was shown in: a tall, slender woman with reddish hair uncontainable by a turban-like headpiece itself at odds with the rest of her appearance—her regal, slightly freckled nose, high-boned cheeks, and wide-set eyes. She wore no jewelry—her clavicles were the adornments between a very long neck and small, high breasts. Her eyes were dark green. As she approached I saw there was a little wetness on her upper lip, and near the bridge of her nose a notch, the vanishing point of overwhelming beauty. This was Esther.

I told her the Grand Vizier had spoken of her. "You are welcome," she said, translating. She said she was pleased to be of service.

I was expecting someone older. I think she knew my surprise. I could feel myself in the company of others—invisible witnesses to her strange strength, and they did nothing to quell the anxiousness she set off in me. I was facing an alertness and capacity, a history. Esther means *star*. It also means *myrtle*, which is a symbol of peace. In the Bible, Esther was a queen, then a liberator, then a leader of exiles. I could say—I am saying—that Esther means everything.

I described the renovation. Her first thought was light. "Many lamps." She named a Venetian glassmaker I'd heard of as a girl. I asked about her relations with the Bailo. "They are alive. Lively, I should say." She was arranging herself on a cushion. Her legs and her toes were exceptionally long. "In view of everything."

"What do you know about Joseph Nasi."

"Ah," she said. Then an assertive sigh. *Ah* stood for her entire experience, versus mine. "You have known him a long time."

"All my life." She took another sip. "My family followed his. He has many gifts, Joseph Nasi. And he is very generous, especially for someone so rich. The money is not all his aunt's, you know." She put her tea down decisively to make the point. "Nasi earned his own. But the *size* of her fortune," Esther gestured to the floor as though it were Dona Gracia Nasi's money, "makes him seek more. The wealth. It makes him sometimes a captive. Sometimes."

She got up. She was making the room familiar to herself. That was when she told me about the levels of misfortune. "It is a terrible fate," she said, out of nowhere. "Captivity." I usually know when a story has been told before. Or if a story is just for me. With that story, with *her*, I couldn't tell. She had her back to the window. I couldn't see her against the sun.

"That is enough," I cut in, aware that my arm was raised and about to slice the air between us. Something had opened inside my head. Not a door. A roof. "Get me the names of the glassmakers," I said, and Sumbul showed her out.

Dear Valide,

The haseki Safiye bore a second son on the tenth of October. I gave him the name of Orhan. The birth was difficult—more than a day and a night, and the child has died, and our sorrow is great.

Work on the clock continues.

Your devoted,

Aslanin

Murad and I had corresponded regularly since he'd gone to Manisa—about his duties as governor, about renovations here, about Tycho Brahe's flabbergasting observations of comets over Denmark, and a lot more. Yet, not only did Murad's letter come more than two months after the second son had died: I hadn't even known Safiye was pregnant. For eleven months they had been joined in happiness, then loss, and I'd known nothing of either.

Retroactive intelligence has always produced in me a combination of very bad feelings. Panic, nausea, and suffocating confusion. Learning about Murad's lost son brought all of that on, and more. It laid bare and confirmed facts I was not prepared to look at. Confusions I was not prepared to unravel. Safiye was causing Murad to flout the one-son corollary to the law of fratricide—just as Hurrem had done with Suleiman. I had a chance and duty to intervene. And I didn't. Not even when I got that letter, which made me sick to read. Why *didn't* I? Did I believe I was trying not to instigate the rage Hurrem had set off in *me* when she descended on Manisa? That kind of anger can, after all, be very motivating. Or was I, perhaps, just trying to spare Murad a hard encounter?

I think—but only now, lying here moulting—that it was something else. I think I didn't intervene because I must have believed there was no need to. Because—and this was the stifled revelation—I believed fratricide was over and that Selim's sons were going to be spared. By me. And that Murad's sons

210

would be spared *after* me. Much as I hated to let Safiye think she could get away with her heedlessness, I think I believed—without admitting it to myself—that there was no need to address the matter.

That didn't mean I didn't talk a lot about going to Manisa. And I told myself that many things delayed the trip—reorganizing the harem, Selim's drinking, managing Esther, my reliance on her, my tolerance of her forwardness. "You might send your son a present" she volunteered, "to console him."

"Any ideas?" I said tartly.

"Yes. Something of your own."

She was right. Of course. And so, I gave Murad my most prized belonging.

My dearest Murad,

My heart is heavy from your news. But it offers its own good command: Look forward. The best of your life is ahead of you. You will have the sons you need—by others, of course. Most important, you have the son you have. He is your bulwark, Aslanim, just as you are your father's. All will be well. I shall visit you soon. In the meantime, here is something special for you. It is a tie to your other family. It was drawn by my mother before I was born. My grandfather sent it to me to celebrate your birth—the happiest day of my life.

Your loving,
Valideh

To this day I don't know what Murad thought about that gift. All he wrote back was that he accepted it reluctantly. Nor have I seen that map ever since. When he's back from Edirne I must ask him about it. I'd like Mehmed to see it.

Sunday, November 27

I turn in earnest now to Joseph Nasi, and I bother with him for three reasons. One, he was the epitome of what is achievable in our Empire by a Jew. Two, he was important to Esther. And three, he was the cause of Selim's demise. No one agrees with me about the third reason, and I don't care.

Like Esther, Nasi had been born and baptized in Lisbon during the Inquisition. He was raised by the aunt Esther had mentioned, the widow of a colossally successful spice dealer, and he was taken by her to Antwerp when Portugal's edict of conversion had become an order of expulsion. Unlike Esther, Nasi was formally and indeed highly educated. And armed with even more languages than Esther had, Nasi helped his aunt establish a banking house that turned *her* financial force into *their* political power.

It did not take long for vying capitals—Antwerp, Ferarra, Venice, here—the Sublime Porte—to compete for the Nasi fortune. The question was, whose desire for the fortune was matched by its tolerance of Jews? It quickly came down to two. And the winner *could* have been Venice had the Nasis been more than a flamboyant exception to Inquisition rules. So important were the aunt's fortune and Nasi's contacts that they alone among "New Christians" were permitted to live in opulence on the Grand Canal even as they practiced their true faith. It took public, insistent betrayal by a jealous Nasi family member to put a halt to the arrangement. Dona Gracia and her nephew were given two months to move all their assets, businesses and belongings, out of the Republic.

Joseph Nasi then staked the Nasi fortune on Ottoman tolerance and Suleiman the Magnificent's own good sense. The reward was great. The Sultan granted the Nasis immediate safe passage and permanent asylum. Six weeks later, Dona Gracia Nasi and her nephew were residing in magnificence on the banks of Galata, directly across the Golden Horn from Topkapi Palace.

Joseph Nasi's greatest talent was knowing how to make the most of what he had and what he faced. It is a talent of Jews generally. Nasi's enterprising spirit didn't fix on a need, however; it attached itself to Selim's weakness. Had Suleiman thought Nasi would get Selim to assign him the proceeds on all wine imported via the Bosporus, he would have changed the tax code. And if he'd known Nasi would subvert our hard-won peace with Venice by the most extreme means imaginable, he'd never have helped Nasi leave the Republic in the first place. When, in the fall of 1569, the worst fire known to Venice broke out in the Arsenal and destroyed the Republic's fleet, Nasi's immediate recommendation was for Selim to seize Cyprus from Venetian control. Malta was a slip, he told him. Cyprus was meant for *this* Sultan because Cyprus had the richest vineyards in the Mediterranean.

Nasi *knew* the lengths we the Ottomans—I—had gone to protect the peace with Venice. I myself had made sure Catherine de Medici's request for favored trade status did not interfere with the Republic's charge of Catholics in the Empire. And I'd make sure that the peace treaty we had in place was formally renewed. But Nasi was content to let all that go. Naxos and Paros weren't enough for him. Nasi wanted a kingdom, whatever that means.

The normally imperturbable Grand Vizier, was more than incensed; he was disconcerted. It was hardly the frame of mind in which to demonstrate the soundness of our position. So I made the first attempt to talk sense into Selim.

He was not alone when I entered the Privy Chamber. The Sultan was on the floor in an embankment of cushions his weight had forced apart. His special agent was looming above him like a grave marker. I went over very close to Nasi, stood right in front of him and told him to leave, and he did.

Selim lay there in three directions, his legs flung out and his head at a bad angle on one of the cushions. His arms and hands, though, wherever they were in those endless sleeves, were crossed on his chest, and it surprised me how much dignity and calm there was in that pose and in his bloated face. It forced me to consider that Selim might, in fact, have thought of Cyprus as an aspiration of his own. I got down and tried to prop him up, but Selim was too big by half for me to move. A eunuch entered with food. "Help me with this," I told him, which made Selim open an eye, blink, and try to lever himself up. The eunuch stood by, uncertain. I waved him away.

"Selim. Can you hear me? Listen to me," I said quietly.

"I am not a child," he said, getting his hind part beneath him.

"This plan about Cyprus is not a good one. It's not in your interest. Believe me. If Nasi's aim is achieved, Venice will be forced to join with Spain and, for that matter, with Rome. It will be a catastrophe." It is exactly what your father warned against, I did not say. Probably I should have. Probably I should have run through the facts and aftermath of Malta, and their effect on Suleiman's spirit and on his reign.

"Calm down," was Selim's reply. He was huffing, his lips pursed.

"Selim. Please. A threat of this sort is about the only thing that could antagonize the Christian powers into an alliance."

"How do you know?" He was waking up.

"I've talked with Barbarigo." In fact, I talked often with Barbarigo. "The Bailo," I added, not sure he knew or remembered Barbarigo.

"Without asking me?" He closed one eye. The other demanded the answer.

"The Republic is committed to our good relations. Barbarigo assures me. My grandfather wrote the same thing a week ago. We mustn't disturb this, Selim."

"You don't like your grandfather," he said simply.

"I'm sorry about not asking you," I replied, jarred. It had been years since I'd spoken about my grandfather to Selim.

"Maybe that's why you look better. Softer."

I had to decide, quickly, whether to indulge the desire to know what he meant—about my grandfather, and looking softer—or to try to stop an invasion of Cyprus. For sure I could not do both.

"I understand Nasi's feeling toward the Republic, Selim. They treated him badly. But he has to contain his anger."

"Hatred."

"Yes. Hatred. I imagine that's true. You understand then. Please, Selim."

"I have plans." He reached for a fig, nipped the end between his teeth, spat it to one side and dropped the fruit, whole, in his mouth.

"That is good, yes—it's good to have plans. But Venice can't defend herself. We mustn't corner her."

"Fine. No corners," he chomped. "Leave me alone now. And stop talking about the place as if it is a woman."

Cyprus had to be stopped, and neither Sokollu Mehmed nor I had the means to stop it. Selim was beyond our reach. Nasi was farther still. Between ambition's pull forward and hatred's pull back, reason had no force with Nasi—not that I could exert. Sokollu Mehmed's animus disqualified him altogether. He himself knew that.

I needed help.

I considered the Admiral of the Fleet—another of my sons-in-law—and I considered the Head of the Treasury. Each had huge influence and a stake to match in anything Nasi did. But that was why each saw Nasi at an angle. I needed someone who would face him squarely, willingly.

Esther did not need to have the realness of the threat explained. She had grown up with hatred and carnage. She knew the metal-on-metal din of ships being armed; the misery it foretold of this man and that man; the suffering of the women left on wharfs and children in fields and in cradles. As an agent she knew, too, the goodwill that can be created out of nothing by a treaty, and how little it takes to return that goodwill to nothing. She would understand the meaning of Cyprus without my explaining.

All of that was true.

Esther had no objection to my argument, and she accepted the assignment to reason with Joseph Nasi, confident that he could and would see the risk of seizing Cyprus in a new light. I watched as she was rowed to Galata and as Nasi's people welcomed her and helped her into the conveyance that bore her up the hill. She was there a long time. When she returned her confidence was intact. "He is known to be excitable," she reported, "but not on this occasion. He listened carefully."

"To what, Esther? Don't be Delphic."

She scowled. She despises pretension. "To the argument for maintaining peace."

Exactly the right answer. This was about far more than an island. "And?"

She paused. "He said he deserved Cyprus."

"Oh God."

"Sumbul," Esther said gravely, "bring tea." Sumbul shot me a look. No one had ever given him an order but me.

I nodded to him. "And? *And?*"

"I told him I agreed that he was deserving . . ."

"*Esther.*"

". . . and that that did not outweigh the importance of honoring our treaties."

I took her arm. "Good! What did he say to *that*?" I could feel the smoothness of her skin through the silk. "He said nothing at first. He was reflecting. Then he said he understood the value of the peace. He, too, began to eat and to drink, and he became more at ease, and then he spoke of times we both recalled in Antwerp and later in France. We both recalled the journey."

"What do you mean he, too?"

"Dona Gracia was there."

"She was? You didn't mention that."

"I am mentioning it," Esther said tartly. "Servants brought her many refreshments. A Nubian brought in apples from Crimea. I know the agent for those fruits. They are as big as melons, come packed in white wool in white boxes. She might as well have eaten pearls, for the cost. She consumed them with great refinement, even though she is fat."

"What did she say?"

"Nothing."

"The whole time?"

Esther nodded. "Her presence was the statement. Nasi does not intend to upend the peace," she said firmly.

"He told you that?"

"He did."

One month later, March of 1570, the Admiral of the Fleet was ordered by the Sultan to impound every Venetian ship in the Golden Horn and to put every Venetian merchant in the capital behind bars. And that was not the worst. Selim had in the meantime sent a message to Doge Loredan:

From Selim, Lord of the Earthly Paradise and of Jerusalem, to the Signory of Venice:

We demand of you Cyprus, which you shall give us willingly or perforce and do not awake our horrible sword for we shall wage most cruel war against you everywhere, neither put your trust in your treasure, for we shall cause it suddenly to run from you like a torrent.

The Chief White Eunuch, Gazanfer, delivered to Sokollu Mehmed a copy of the order after the courier ship had set sail. Revealing more about himself—his fairness—than he ever had or would, Sokollu Mehmed summoned Esther before coming—with her—to show me Selim's demand.

"With all respect," Esther said, her face set with concern, "Do you think Joseph Nasi could force such a momentous move?"

Sokollu Mehmed clenched. "You do not question the wife of the Sultan."

"Do you?" she said, a hand covering her mouth.

Sokollu Mehmed was right. She should not have asked the question. But she really did not know the answer. I was beginning to understand that. For the moment, though, we were at the far end of a long and trembling limb, Esther and I, each of us accusing the other's patron. It is needless to say that her accusation was far graver than mine, but whether or not Nasi—or his aunt—was behind Selim's order was not the point. The point was that the outcome could only be disaster.

Selim was not in the Privy Chamber when I looked for him after hearing of his demands, and Josag, ever lurking, claimed not to know where he was. The sky was turning red when I approached the Throne Room, and the latch was up on the closed door. I kicked it hard and with care, the way I'd been taught to kick a wolf trap. Slumped on the carpeted platform that supports the Imperial Throne, his robes on and off his body, was Selim. Three concubines, not mothers of his children, were sitting upon various parts of him. I backed away like any child who thinks she's done something wrong because she's seen something wrong.

ॐ

Venice responded to Selim's command with a declaration of war. While the great fire had indeed destroyed the fleet, it hadn't destroyed the Arsenal itself, the largest manufacturing site in all of Europe. In fact, the Republic had been able to replace the vessels in seven months by means of a furious building program paid for by the sale of—what else?—noble titles.

I received two letters in the weeks that followed. Important, unwelcome illustrations of resolve. Safiye's. The Republic's.

My Dear Validem,

The haseki S. bore a daughter on the summer solstice. She is healthy and strong and will be called Aysha. Your first granddaughter!

Ismihan has sent word about the Sultan's intentions regarding Cyprus. You will tell me how I may be of help.

Finally, the clock is complete and marvelous, as you would say. It includes an alarm feature and depictions of the phases of the moon. We are embarked now on design for a mechanical pump. Perhaps you will visit when we test it on the Gediz.

Your devoted,

Aslanin

Safiye's determination made me sick.

The second letter was from my grandfather, describing the Republic's celebratory response to Selim's declaration of war—the white peace banners at the back, blue truce banners in the middle, crimson war banners leading the way. Doge Loredan, at eighty-eight, upright on the bow of his *bucin-*

toro as it crossed the lagoon to announce hostilities. Just like Nonno to omit no detail of pageantry.

Europe was not swift in its response to the Republic's call for assistance, every power having her own reason for demurring. The Holy Roman Emperor still had a formal truce with us, Portugal had been decimated by plague, Ivan the Terrible we had our own problems with, Elizabeth of England had, to say the least, issues with the Church, and Catherine de Medici, as I've said, pleaded France's favored trade status. She did, however, volunteer her son, the king—the pitiful Charles IX—as negotiator, which should have alerted me to her own state of mind.

This fractiousness was not lost on Nasi or the Admiral of the Fleet or Selim. It accounted for a certain euphoria when our fleet of eighty galleys and thirty galeots pushed out of the Dardanelles in May. When they joined at Rhodes with the vessels carrying the land forces, spirits rose higher still.

In the first days of July, the Ottoman forces landed more than fifty thousand men at Larnaca. The Venetians of Cyprus were not particularly effective upholders of Venetian law, any more than the Venetians of Paros had been, but they were dogged and proud, and the forces at Nicosia held out for six weeks before all twenty thousand were finished off.

Over the next weeks, the Spanish rolled out an array of excuses for not backing the Venetians on Cyprus, and when the Christians *did* finally come together, at Castellorizo, they decided that Cyprus could not be taken. Nicosia had already fallen. Our numbers and firepower were more than they were willing to take on.

The shameless performance of the Christian fleet convinced the Pope that the allies had to join together formally if they were going to withstand the Ottoman threat. And so they finally did—Rome, Spain, and the Venetian Republic—calling themselves the Holy League and giving new and diminished meaning to the word *holy*. They pledged to join annually to prosecute whatever campaign they deemed necessary to check us, and they were not going to miss the chance for an encounter in 1571.

By August the Holy League's force was assembled at Messina. Two hundred galleys, a hundred round ships, fifty thousand foot soldiers and another five thousand men with mounts. Their commanders were Marcantonio Colonna for Rome; Don Juan, the half-brother of the King for Spain; and, for the Venetian Republic, none other than my father's first cousin, Sebastiano Veniero. This indeed was when my correspondence with him began. It was invaluable—I daresay to both of us—and lasted till his death, which I'll come to. In all events it was thanks to him that I learned the details of what happened on Cyprus. At Famagusta.

The siege had begun after the sack of Nicosia, the year before, when our forces numbered two hundred thousand. The League's were eight thousand, but they had fought all through the fall and winter, and twice they were able to raid our encampments and hold their position. Throughout that time, Marcantonio Bragadin had been able to keep morale up with assurances that the joint fleet would soon arrive with provisions. Month after month Bragadin waited. By spring, the fleet had still not come. Bragadin tried to buoy his men with his own faith in the League's intention. While they waited for relief, fifty thousand of our sappers began their work—circling Bragadin with trench and ravelin. The Holy League might as well have not existed for all the good they were to him. And still Bragadin held on. By summer, his force was down to a few hundred. The heat "settled on the island like a rug," my father's cousin wrote, and there was nothing at all left to eat, not a rat. And the firing continued. By August there was no hope at all of relief or survival. Bragadin let the white banner be hoisted. At least Famagusta would be spared the pillaging of Nicosia, he thought.

Late in September I received the longest letter my grandfather ever wrote me. I copy here the part about what happened next.

Bragadin met with Mustafa Pasha, the Ottoman commander. Terms were arranged. Bragadin and the few remaining of our officers stood before the Sultan's representative. Bragadin himself gave the keys of the city to Mustafa Pasha. Then, for no reason we ever knew, Mustafa Pasha flew into a rage. He unsheathed his dagger and cut off Bragadin's ears, then his nose. He had the Captain's deputy beheaded. Then he did the same to every other Christian within reach and piled them outside the city gates—a pyramid of 350 heads. They kept Bragadin in a dungeon for a fortnight. When they released him, the middle of his face was a brown crater, and still he was not dead. So Mustafa Pasha had weights tied to his limbs and had him dragged behind a starving horse that chased a cart of meat. Then he had him tied naked to a tree in the piazza and had him flogged. By the time the floggers reached his waist, the flesh was hanging from Bragadin's skeleton, but it was not until they reached his chest, that Bragadin died. The Turks cut off his head, stuffed his remaining parts with straw, and rode his separated body around the city for the benefit of victor and vanquished.

My dearest girl, what has come to pass on Cyprus is inhuman and grave. These are your people, Cecilia, both sides. Who but you can redress this atrocity? Tell your grandfather how he can be of assistance.

కఎ

It was reasonable for Selim to believe that with Cyprus he had disarmed the Christian alliance. Since it was an achievement of which no one had thought him capable, it was also understandable that he wanted witnesses for his feat. "Tell my son to come up here," he declared, as though he and Murad were at two ends of a ladder. "The boy, too," as though Mehmed didn't have a name. Not for one moment—not then or ever did Selim feel vulnerable to his son. He had every reason to feel that way. And it says everything one needs to know about the kind of men they were by nature.

For Selim, there was no shame in the events of Famagusta. For me, there was. God, there was—and there is. I will *never* not have a stake in the welfare of Venice. It's why I intervened last summer over Crete. The Admiral of the Fleet had it on his roster of seizable assets—that's what he calls them. Sumbul found this out. I told the Admiral, in writing, that taking Crete, or any other Venetian possession, runs counter to our every interest. And that it would not happen. And it won't. He has assured me. But I'm getting ahead of myself. That the prospect of seeing Murad and Little Mehmed for the first time since Selim had become Sultan could have eclipsed the shame of Famagusta by even a sliver says what I mean to say about how happy it made me.

Twice I'd asked Murad to visit. Twice he'd declined, owing to the births of his daughters, which, I surmised, had somewhat dampened his faith in Safiye's predictions. She was distracted and inconsistent, Murad wrote, noting that her moods sometimes wore on the children. I doubted that Safiye's temperament would cause him to put her aside though. For someone capable of firm if sometimes imperfect judgment, Murad has never been judgmental. He showed this when Suleiman failed to attend his circumcision. He proved it by accepting Safiye as she was. It tied my nerves in knots.

There were two suites in the harem that faced the water, Selim's and mine. Next to each were rooms we'd assigned our Chief White and Black Eunuchs—Gazanfer and Sumbul: fine chambers with long terraces that commanded views of the entire Golden Horn. I would have requisitioned Gazanfer's, but it shared a wall with Selim's. So Sumbul obligingly yielded his quarters for Murad's visit. It would be a good place, I thought, for Mehmed to run around. Also, a boy m the provinces would like watching the ships in the harbor. Any boy would.

I had not seen them since Suleiman went to Szigetvar. I'd missed the first five years of Mehmed's life. All the first expressions and promises of who he was. All the chances to store them in the treasury he'd made out of my heart the moment Murad put him in my arms. And then, one morning, there he was. Mehmed—my every chance. Mehmed holding the hand of his father. My Lion and his Cub. Mehmed was tall for his age. He seemed to have the meekness of an older child, too. My recollection of Murad and the girls—of myself, in fact—was that at the age of five children are headlong. But Mehmed was contained. He wore a blue tunic that was shorter in front than back and blue leggings that tucked into yellow slippers with turned-up toes, not usual garments for a child, especially the slippers. The leggings were big on him and bunched around his knees. He was pulling them up when they entered. His father's arm was around his shoulder.

Mehmed held a small bow in one hand and took his father's hand in the other when he was done with his leggings.

"Valide," Murad said, winded, grinning, kissing me three times. "What a pleasure to see you."

I took Murad's hand. "And what is that you've got?" I said to Mehmed.

He held out the bow.

"It is for you," Murad said.

"Is that so?" I touched Mehmed's flushed cheek. "Is that right?" He nodded. "Well then, let's see what we have here." I took the bow.

"I made it," Mehmed said.

"He did, Valide. It is fine, don't you agree?"

"Why of course you made it," I said inspecting the bow from all sides. "You are a fine craftsman." I slid my thumb up the knotty curve. "I have never had a bow, Mehmed. I am very pleased to have one from you." I was aware of my heart pounding. The onset of a love that has been like no other.

"Yes," he said in his clear small voice.

"I have been instructed to go immediately to the Grand Vizier's quarters," Murad said. "I have been informed he is vexed. He thinks I should have gotten here faster."

"Your father wants you to see the fleet come in. You can understand. He is proud of his victory."

"Of course. I have many things to speak with you about," Murad said.

"I do, too," I said, peering inside a little bag his son was holding open.

"I will come back as soon as I am able. The Grand Vizier will direct me to the Sultan, I suppose. Is that right? And then I shall return. You will be here," he said. "Will you still be here?"

"Whenever you come back, Murad, I will be here. It might be best if you leave Mehmed with me for the time."

"I had planned to have the Sultan see . . ."

"You might want to determine his condition first, Aslanim. Why don't you go to the Sultan yourself. Then, if you like, return for Mehmed."

Murad looked embarrassed and alarmed.

"Don't be concerned. Just go to your father and come back. We will be right here, won't we?" I said, hoisting Mehmed, who was the image of his mother, onto my lap. Mehmed put his arm around my neck, holding the bow he'd made against my back.

꙰

The fleet entered the channel the following morning. From Topkapi's terraces I watched them dock. I then took my position in the Tower of Justice and took Esther with me, for both our sakes. We watched the ranks of the administration assemble around Selim. He wore a robe the color of iron and sat cross-legged on the ceremonial throne staring intently, blankly, at the space before him. Sokollu Mehmed and Joseph Nasi stood on either side. Murad was beside Sokollu Mehmed holding Little Mehmed by the hand. Next to them were the Sheikh ul Islam and the Chief Falconer, the husband of my daughter Shah. Behind them were the eldest of Selim's five other sons. Three little boys—one four- and two three-year-olds—standing still, their arms straight at their sides invisible in their very long sleeves. Murad looked around at the children, all of them younger than Mehmed. His distress was unmistakable.

Outside Topkapi's gate a different assemblage appeared—captains of the galleons leading mates and minions holding loot high for all to see. Enameled reliquaries, gold chalices, jeweled chasubles. The Admiral's prize, though, remained concealed by the crowd assembling in careful formation around the Sultan. Then, like cards, they separated. The Admiral of the Ottoman Fleet was revealed at last—high in his saddle, bearing a pike on which was impaled the head of Captain Marcantonio Bragadin.

Sokollu Mehmed stiffened with a jolt. The little boys, still standing very still, began to cry. Little Mehmed threw up, and Murad clamped a wrist to his own mouth as he clutched Mehmed to his side. Selim, though, rigid as a dead man himself, stared straight ahead at Bragadin's verdigris face.

I rushed to the stairwell. "Get those children away from there," I yelled to the eunuchs patrolling the stairs. "Take them to their mothers!"

I returned to the window as Mustafa Pasha was loudly announcing the booty and then accounting for his troops—the few lost, the many garrisoned. Selim was silencing him with a listless wave. Nasi had edged right up to him, nearly touching the Sultan's person. He was narrating the scene for Selim. He was making sense of things for him. The head on the pike, the glory, the opportunities. Murad, wiping Mehmed's mouth with his sleeve, said something forceful to his father. He shot Nasi a look that would have withered anyone not made of whatever mineral that man was made of, and then he led Mehmed by the hand across the courtyard, scooped him up, and took the six flights to the Tower with Mehmed in his arms.

"Who *is* that?" Murad said, breathless as he put Mehmed down before me. "The one who has the Sultan's ear in such a way? Do you know what he's telling him? That one there," Murad said, pointing at Nasi hovering over Selim. "He's saying that the head of the Venetian, whoever he is, will be displayed for thirty days. In front of the Tower of Justice." Selim's little boys were still behind their father, trying to stand at attention as they'd been told, but they were crying, for Bragadin's eyeless face wasn't ten feet away.

I picked Mehmed up under the arms. He was light and limp, his robe soaked from being sick, his face a terrible grey. I sat him down sideways on my lap and put my arms around him. He let his head rest on my chest. I signaled Sumbul to come close—there'd be no more yelling—and whispered that he bring water, towels, a fresh tunic. Mehmed had closed his eyes. Murad was still at the window, quaking with rage. "Come away from there," I told him gently. "There's nothing more to see." At the other window was Esther, staring, in her own blinded way, at Bragadin's head. "And you come away, too, Esther." I so seldom said her name, I heard my voice in the distance.

"Come away from there," Murad said to her gently. He glanced at me to know what to do. Esther turned, her face full of all she couldn't deny. Disgust, confusion, loss. Except for the last, I imagined that the other feelings were new to her. Esther had believed in Nasi. He had stood for the determining forces in her life—her faith and the will to practice it. He'd also stood for cunning beneficence and probably other things

I didn't know or couldn't understand, so different had Esther's and my journeys been. I imagined that, standing there transfixed, Esther was trying to know what could be salvaged from the illusion she had had of this person. I know how that kind of thinking can make a head crack. I know how awful the end of fantasy is—for it steals into parts of the heart and mind where nothing should be able to go. It is driven by the heat of what we long for, and it melts all that is in its path until it comes out into the open and is exposed for what it is: something that was never true.

"Murad," I said quietly. "Help her away."

Esther turned to me. "It is not for any of us to say what we deserve. We can say what we wish for. Not what we deserve."

Murad took Esther's arm and walked her to a sofa. She slid down onto it. Murad regarded the couch as though it were full of possibility and sat down, too. The two of them so differently gripped and refashioned in those moments.

I kept rocking Mehmed in my lap. When the servant came with fresh clothes I held him tighter, just as he did me. We'd get him cleaned up later.

"What will you do?" Murad said.

"I will speak to the Sultan as soon as he leaves the assembly. He's not in his right mind. You understand that." Murad nodded. "He mustn't be demeaned, Aslanim. Not in public, not anywhere."

"Our enemies will soon know about this," Murad said softly. "They will seek revenge."

I held Mehmed's head close to my chest, covering his ear. "And *we* will show that what has happened here today is an aberration. *We* will remind our detractors how Suleiman was in situations like this. How he was with the Shi'ites when he freed Baghdad, how he was with Zrinyi at Szigetvar. Christendom can claw itself apart with its vanities and heresies. In the House of Islam—this awful spectacle notwithstanding—our finest symbol of victory is mercy. *Mercy.* We will find the means

to make that known, Murad, throughout the House of War."
I said all this as though to a great and restive audience, which
Murad was. Mehmed didn't stir. Esther was back at the window, staring, continuing to undergo the change that would
bind us and cause her to ascend and guide me in ways I am not
done—even alone in this sealed chamber—with discovering.

Monday, November 28

In the last letter I received from Catherine de Medici, she referred to us—herself and me—as a "displaced" Florentine and Venetian! She wrote of how similar our relations to our fathers-in-law—Suleiman and François I—had been. And she addressed me as "fellow" Queen Mother, which meant she either thought Selim was dead or that he might as well have been. On a separate sheet, she catalogued the Catholics murdered by Luther, by Calvin, by Zwingli. She put them in columns and organized them by province and town. "There is no way to stop it. I have done all I can." She wrote it three times in a row—that she'd done all she could.

I expressed my condolences. The paths of duty and order, I wrote to her, are straight, exposed, hard, and right.

Catherine could not have received the letter, dispatched with her own courier, for that same week there was a massacre in Paris—ordered by her son, with her knowledge. On the feast day of St. Bartholomew, Charles IX had ten thousand Protestants slaughtered—out in the open, in churches, in front of their hearths, and in their beds. Children in their mothers' arms, wives in their husbands'. Whole families of them. And in the two days that followed, forty thousand more were murdered all across the country. It shocked even

Sokollu Mehmed Pasha, who was good at putting slaughter in perspective.

I called for Esther when I heard the news. I said it seemed the worst that happens is in the name of God. She said, "You mean in the name of religion. There is a difference." She never missed a chance to correct me. I told her I knew the difference. "In fact," she went on, "the worst that happens is in the name of order."

This riled me. "Certainly not. What fault do you find with order?"

"You can't apply it to everything," was her answer.

"I don't try to."

Esther paused to consider what whe would say next.

"You try to control your son."

"You are not permitted to speak to me this way," I let her know. Esther bowed her head, which I hated. It was as insincere as it was appropriate. "Look at me. There are reasons for what I do, and I don't have to explain them to you."

"But you could." Her head was still down.

"All right. Then listen carefully, because I detest this subject and I won't speak of it again. Murad's favorite is a woman having one son after another, knowing full well that . . ." I stopped. Esther looked up. "There is a law, Esther. You are aware of it. And it is about what matters most. And that *is* order."

"Are you saying you think it is all right to eliminate *half* brothers?" The words floated—binding and irrelevant—in the air. "What is happening to you?"

They were frightening questions. I did not know what I thought was "all right." And I certainly didn't know what was happening to me. I raised my shield. "You don't know me."

"Maybe."

"You will never know me."

Esther knew I feared that was true. I think there was a note in my voice, a crack. It was at that moment that I realized—fully, consciously—that the decision to carry out Suleiman's command *could* be undecided. I wanted to ask her to help me.

"You should trust Murad," she said.

I said, "I don't trust anyone."

"What?" She had me by the arm. I was aware from her grip of how thin I was.

"Why should I?" I pulled away.

"There are a hundred ways I could betray you. A thousand. Do you think I would?" I couldn't answer. "Do you? Would I be here if you thought that?"

"What's happening to me?" I cried.

"I will answer for you." She knelt at my side, those bony knees hard on the stone, and she took my face in her hands. With her littlest finger she pushed off my veil, with another finger she plucked the pins that held up my hair, with a thumb she undid the top of the tunic, the middle, the beneath, so I could breathe, and then she held my face. Held it like a tablet she would write her message on. Held it to give me a chance to say yes.

"All right," I said. "Just this once." She slid me to the floor, softly to the bare, cold stone. Slid a little pillow under my head. Sat back on her heels and looked at her ward. "What's happening?" I whispered.

"Nothing that you cannot manage or contain or change. Nothing greater than you yourself. Do you understand?" I nodded. "Just be yourself. You as you are. That will be enough. Come here," she said sliding her arm under my neck, lifting me just a little. She kissed my forehead. Raked away the wet strands of hair with the backs of her fingers. Kissed where they'd been. She nudged her knees in closer, held me closer to the bumpy rampart, rocked me with her face to my hair. "That's all," she kept saying. I could have gone to sleep then, or died. I was ready. But Esther put her mouth on mine, and I didn't die. I opened my eyes and there were hers. "All the time," she breathed. Deep into me she breathed it as the tip of her tongue went along my lip. I closed my eyes. Her hand was on my cheek, steadying. She lengthened herself beside me. We were two feathers, two fish, two fires side by side. The breathing deepened, her free arm was around my waist, like river grass around a stone, green rooted on rock, swaying, her free hand on my back, a bulwark against the air in the room. Still she didn't take her mouth away. "Here," she said again, putting a pillow beneath my back. "Here." Another. Then with a backward gathering she rolled onto me, and I came to life. She held her head back so I wasn't blurred, and neither was she. She took my hands, held our arms straight out, palm to palm, our fingers laced, my knuckles on the stone, softening, shuddering. She floated into me, gold leaf, gold water, gold night, until we matched, every part, north to south, and everything that was not us slipped away. Then she moved, only she, on the murmuring surge, north, south, north and south, our softest parts lined up, her mouth never leaving mine, nor her arms or middle or thighs; then, fast, our ankles locked, and the surge changed, side to side, east to west, hard, soft, more and more till we went clear through each other, over and over. She slid off me, held me where I'd come from, laid her head in the cove of my neck, her arm across me, her fingers tucked under. And when her fingers loosened and she slept, I slipped into sleep myself and bobbed out on my magic skiff just far enough to see the dreamy shore for the place it was without me, to see my mother standing there, waiting for me. She held a white staff, and I knew it stood for the will that allowed her to vault past my grandfather, to recover from my father, and to raise me to think for myself—or to do my best to.

Tuesday, November 29

The Empire was balancing precariously on points that had thrust up to different heights—a petrified Sultan, a calculating advisor, a righteous Grand Vizier, and me. The order was fragile as a moth. Which of us would influence or save Selim? Who among us could? He was a grave danger to himself.

I couldn't bring myself to be near him until the next day, and when I did find him he was in the company of a pair of buffoons clowning with cucumbers. I approached, shuttered my eyes, breathed deeply, and told him that this was not what he meant to do. This meaning Bragadin's head, meaning falling prey to Nasi, meaning being drunk day and night. Selim picked something from between his teeth to emphasize the quality of his interest in what I had to say and told me to be quiet. I told him that he needed to pay attention, that Murad and Mehmed especially suffered from the display. And Selim, his voice suddenly strong and sensible, said that we all suffered, by which I knew he meant the whole family. He was a man of few words and a sound memory.

Bragadin's head came down soon after. And Selim informed Murad that he expected him to stay on in the capital—to spend time with the Janissaries. He wanted them to get to know him.

It was a worn and agitated Murad who called on me a short time later. He'd looked so fresh and poised just a few days before. Now he looked like someone back from battle, badly enlightened. He had made a decision of his own, to return to Manisa. He had a province to administer, he said. Justice to mete out. His duty was there, not here. "Besides," he added, "I have no wish for my son to be here. Mehmed may be five, but he understands what he saw yesterday. You know how children are at that age, Valide. You remember."

It was a surprising assertion. "Yes. I do."

"Well, then you understand."

It was true. I understood very well that children comprehend a great deal at five. Devotion, deceit, beauty, despair. And depending, perhaps, on how young they are, they can forget—or at least not bury, dangerously, within themselves—what gave rise to those things. If there were a chance of Mehmed forgetting the spectacle of Bragadin's head, it was worth the inexpressible sadness of their leaving. Murad was right. I remembered. "I do understand. The decision is yours. I just wish . . ."

"What do you wish?"

"I was going to say that I wish your grandfather could know you now. But he would not have been surprised. He *did* know you, Murad."

Murad pushed his turban back. He has a high forehead, thank God. Flakes of skin fell on his lashes and made him blink. "You know, Valide, the Sultan was different that last day." The day Murad had handed him Little Mehmed in the field of flowers. "Maybe you saw him. You were on the terrace, I think."

"I'd gone in."

"He was very calm. Not in the way I'd seen him when he was collecting his strength for something terrible. He was calm as though that was the way he was."

The way Suleiman was. The way anyone is. Is there such a

235

thing? I hoped—and I feared—the answer was yes. "You were his favorite, Murad, from the moment you were born."

"He talked about the clock I'd made for him. He was about to go to war, and that's what was on his mind. Time-keeping. And tables. Stars. Maps. He said you would fill me in. It was a fine expression. To fill someone in." Murad had picked up my mother's compass, which, as always, was by my bed. "He said that you would be a great help to me. And that I should prepare my sons as I have been prepared."

"That's exactly right."

"And that I should have many."

A taut wire apparently holding everything together just *went*. Murad was running his finger around the edge of the compass. I took it from him. "Don't."

Murad winced, then stiffened. Immediately I knew I'd made a bad mistake. It wasn't the first time—or the last—that I wondered why, if you can see an error the moment you make it, you can't see it the moment before. "It's barely holding together, Aslanim," I tried to correct. But it was too late. Murad's stung look had not only come, it had gone. What had just passed between us was either going to be all right or it wasn't, and I wasn't going to know which.

He put the compass down, the needle still flicking toward wherever in the world it was pointing. "That is why I wish to bring a new physician back to Manisa," Murad said—exactly as though nothing had just happened. "Mehmed's mother requires it."

I didn't dare hope. "Is she ill?"

"She is expecting another child."

"But," I let out a long breath, "she gave birth only four months ago."

"Five."

I got up. "I see," I mumbled, aware that my face has always betrayed every layer of what I feel. Certainly with Murad it has. "But you told me after the last birth that you found her distant. Isn't that what you said?"

"Distracted."

I dropped onto a hassock. "Distracted—from what?"

But Murad was done. "And it is time for us to leave." He stood. Changed his perspective. "I have been taken astray from the purpose of my visit here. I came to honor my father's wish and to acknowledge the victory of our forces. I have brought my son because the Sultan asked me to. But I am governor of a province. I have duties to fulfill. I should not be detained here, and my son should not be here at all—except to see you—because what is going on inside this palace and inside the Sultan's head is not something Mehmed should be exposed to. I do not blame my father. That is not for me to do. But there is no use for me here. Not now, in any case. If there were, I would be of use. I hope you understand."

He was so lucid. "I do." I believe I was as surprised as he was at how calmly the exchange ended.

⟨⟩

Cyprus, for me—after Bragadin—stood for certain revelations. For Selim, the matter was less complicated. Not complicated at all, in fact. Following his victory, Selim wanted the Christian fleet where he could see it. Right in the Golden Horn. "I beat them," he declared. "I'm entitled." Never have I heard substance so at odds with tone. He could hardly form the words. He was that drunk.

I want to be clear about Selim's demand. It wasn't that victory didn't satisfy him—or that he sought to humiliate anyone. It was that Selim didn't understand that victory *means* humiliation for the vanquished—always—and that therein, always, lies danger. We tried to stop him—the Grand Vizier and I. We explained, slowly, carefully, that the Empire's fortunes had been complicated, not simplified, by its gains; that it was the *quality* of the League's intention that would make the difference. "The response will not come from the Republic alone," Sokollu Mehmed warned Selim. "She has allied herself with Rome and Spain." Selim was on his back, eyes closed, tangled in his robes. By means of a sorry look, Sokollu Mehmed asked if I wished to have a try.

"The consequences will be unimaginable," I whispered, which wasn't true. I could imagine them. Bodies in the Bosporus. Heads on pikes.

"Why are you here, anyway?" Selim mumbled. It wasn't clear that he knew there were two of us by his bed. "Where's Nasi?"

"This is a matter for your admirals," Sokollu Mehmed warned. He was visibly disturbed that it needed saying.

"Get Nasi," Selim said, slipping into nowhereness.

Only overnight, though.

The next day Selim gave the order. One week later, our ships ravaged Corfu. On the first of October, we learned the allied navies had been sighted off Messina. On the fifth, our fleet repaired to the Gulf of Lepanto.

And on October 7, it began. Everything Suleiman had warned against.

The day broke open like an egg and poured thick across the lacquered decks and calm waters. Our fleet was fortunate to have it behind us. The sun blinded the enemy as it cleared the horizon. One of our admirals, Uluch Ali, the one who reported all this, could see them shielding their eyes, trying to get out of the light's way. It was a slight and hopeless gesture surrounded by massive stillness and quiet—if you count as quiet the snapping sails and creaking oarlocks of the Christian navy. Then, out of the silence and all at once, a chant rose up from the enemy fleet. *Kyrie eleison . . . Christe eleison . . . Kyrie . . .* Mass was being said on the decks of five hundred warships.

The enemy fleet was in straight-line formation. Ninety-five vessels on the left, meaning on the north end. Ninety-five in the center. Fifty-five on the right. Facing them we were fifty more—two hundred thirty galleys and another sixty round ships. The lines stretched five miles. They changed the meaning of the horizon.

Slowly, we embraced the enemy line. Then, like blades, the Republic's galleasses sliced out in front. There were six such vessels—the Venetians' astonishing new invention. It was the idea of Giovanni Andrea Doria to move the weight on his ships in order to keep the bows high and make battering rams of the vessels themselves. The shift allowed them to train their cannon directly on our hulls. There was no question what was coming. There was silence again in the Gulf of Lepanto. No motion at all for an hour or more.

Then, from the other end of time, came the dark inside of the Conqueror's drum. The air pitched around the warning. Semiz Ali Pasha raised his arm and dropped it like a bomb. The first cannon fired. The Christians replied. Then cannon fire to numb the brain. The deep forest crack of splitting hulls. The fury of water and men's voices screaming to God and to their mothers. Arms, feet, heads floating in the reddening ocean. Boys dead before they could be brave.

When Andrea Doria saw how far south we reached, panic must have struck him, because he broke entirely with the Christian line. We got close on him, though, and the advantage was ours as we captured the flagship of Malta. But the full weight of the Christian center intervened. The two flagships invaded each other's prows. Their decks became a battlefield, and in no time—an hour, two hours—the center ships had nearly exhausted each other while high above, the enemies' standards affirmed their creeds. The word of the Prophet versus Christ on the Cross.

Don Juan himself boarded the Ottoman admiral's vessel, and Müezzinzade Ali Pasha resisted fiercely. Not for long, though. He took the shot in the face, and they had his head off before his body hit the deck. Just what Don Juan didn't want, but he was powerless to prevent it. The best he could do was refuse the trophy when the head was offered to him. He knew the measure of the man he had faced.

In early November, I received a letter from the commander of the Venetian fleet. As I mentioned, my father's cousin.

To Her Most Serene Highness, Nurbanu,

Today I have sent to the Doge my account of the battle that took place five days ago outside the Gulf of Lepanto. You will have heard about it from your own sources. I wish for you to have my own account, and I enclose it. My wife, may perpetual light shine upon her, kept you in her prayers until the end.

Sebastiano Veniero

The report was identical to Uluch Ali's—the numbers, maneuvers, conduct—every detail the same. I gave it to Selim hoping he might find, as I did, something to be proud of. Instead, he saw nothing but defeat. Defeat rushed into the cavity created by his never having had the respect he deserved. The hour that Selim got word of Lepanto marked the last hour he was not drunk.

The following day, Selim awoke at noon, performed his ablutions, prayed, and announced his intention to have every Venetian and Spaniard in the Empire executed. Aborting that command was the only thing Sokollu Mehmed, Nasi, and I ever agreed on.

Our fleet rowed into the Golden Horn the third week of October. From a navy of two hundred and thirty vessels there remained thirty: twenty-eight galleys and two transports. The city was stunned and angry when those few ships returned. The people bowed their heads in sorrow as they mourned the forty thousand dead.

A week later I received my grandfather's own account of

Lepanto. Attached to his report was a letter that confirmed old age had resolved none of the contradictions of who he was.

My Dearest Nurbanu,

Today, Venice is as I have never seen her—an entirely joyful city. No one misgives anything for once! Victory is ours and everything is ablaze. I wish you were here to see it. Doge Mocinego led the procession from the Palace to Rialto yesterday—the bridge bunted in blue, gold satin puffing up the piers, paintings by Giorgione and Titian hanging from the rails.

Hear what was said at San Marco! "They have taught us by their example that the Turks are not insuperable, as we had previously believed them to be . . . thus it can be said that as the beginning of this war was for us a time of sunset, leaving us in perpetual night, now the courage of these men, like the light-giving sun, has bestowed upon us the most beautiful and most joyful day that this city, in all her history, has ever seen."

I am so proud I had better seek Penance and Reconciliation! And what do you think of Sebastiano Veniero commanding our fleet? Dear Girl, I think of you with concern. I cannot imagine your upset. Send word when you are able to.

Your loving,
Nonno

That he would open a letter with my Ottoman name, and conclude it with an ecstatic celebration of his pride—at the expense of mine—made me absolutely sick. No, he could not imagine my upset. As ever, he could not imagine at all. I cannot say to what extent I've wittingly compared Nonno to Suleiman. Lying here now for however long it has been—eight days? ten? a hundred?—I can see that the comparison dogged me. It directed me toward ends and means I associated with Suleiman's vision and valor—qualities my grandfather spectacularly lacked. That particular letter of Nonno's, though, made it clear to me that while he and Suleiman were both governed by their feelings for the places they were from—a Republic, an Empire—Nonno's aim was always to magnify brilliance. Suleiman's was to assure justice and maintain order. Always. The disorder that was inherent in—and sure to be unleashed by—our defeat at Lepanto made it alarmingly clear that chaos was not an option for the Ottoman Empire.

༚

Bad news. Hamon is confining me—and I don't mean to my bed. He isn't allowing anyone in but Sumbul. I wonder if I am dying.

༚

There is no question that Lepanto changed many things. The greatest naval battle since Actium would. Warships were constructed differently after that. Fighting was no longer hand to hand. The needle on the compass *did* spin west; our reputation was shattered, the Turk proven vincible. But really?

No! We had *not* been shamed. All we'd done was lose. And *that* could be fixed. The people understood that. I saw it for myself. They did not loiter in the streets in grim groups. They did not give way to regret. They thought about who they were—about who we are—and they put their faith in their Sultan, who, thank God, had a Grand Vizier with the will of a warrior. Sokollu Mehmed promised to re-create the navy—on the spot.

Selim was skeptical, especially about paying for a new fleet. But Sokollu Mehmed's response was assured. "The might of our Empire is such that if we wished to equip the entire fleet with silver anchors, silken rigging, and satin sails, we could do it." Sokollu Mehmed made anything seem possible—and, unlike Nasi, who had gone into seclusion, not by making it seem simple.

242

Selim agreed to let him try, and something that could have occurred in only one other place in the world happened in the Imperial Arsenal, on which I look out from this bed. A new fleet—larger, faster, better than anything on the Mediterranean—was built in less than eight months. One hundred and fifty-eight galleasses, modeled on the Venetian creation I've mentioned, impelled by oar and sail.

So, less than a year after the defeat of the millennium, we were set to take the Holy League on. But at that time *they* weren't interested. Not Rome or Spain, anyway. They saw our navy assembling off the Peloponnesus and decided that if Venice still wanted a fight, she could have it on her own, which she declined to do, since it would have been suicide.

One year after the greatest triumph in her history, then, *La Serenissima* was forced to make peace with her nemesis. As Sokollu Mehmed said to the Venetian Bailo, "There is a wide difference between your loss and ours. In capturing Cyprus from you, we have cut off one of your arms; in defeating our fleet you have merely shaved off our beard; the lopped arm will not grow again, but the shorn beard will grow stronger than before."

Little did the world know how strong. We would not only grow stronger, we would move from strength to *new* strength, starting right then. And we would anchor our power not in farther borders but in *knowledge*, just as Suleiman had said. It had been we—in the House of Islam—who had kept alive the essential works of astronomy. We who had translated and preserved them. We who had built the great observatories in Damascus, in Baghdad, in Maragha and Samarkand. And it would be *we* who would do it again—fulfilling Suleiman's vision, honoring his command. There was no time to lose.

I am not sure why I'd never spoken to Esther about an observatory or correcting Ulugh Bey's tables or Suleiman's thoughts about those things or my own dreams or Murad's role. Lying here with nothing to distract me, I'm coming to think it was because Esther was rooted in a realm that was tangent to but not part of any of that. She will read this, of course, and I don't think she will disagree with what I am about to say. Esther and I are defined by our educations, worldly and formal respectively. Each is essential to how we have moved in the world and to how we think—about anything, probably. Our educations were extremely different, and each has served us well. And the extent to which mine was formal is exactly the extent to which I didn't talk to her about things like astronomical tables or instruments or the possibility of an observatory, because that formality has always unnerved me as far as Esther is concerned. It always seemed a possible impediment—I'm not even sure to what—but I am certain of this: that from the start with Esther, I wanted nothing to come between us.

So it was with some trepidation that I went to her with the plan for this very consequential thing about which I'd never uttered a word. I knew her well enough not to be apologetic about not having mentioned it. I just told her that there was no time to lose in constructing an observatory with which to establish the Empire's sway in the realms of exploration, timekeeping, mapmaking, and I asked her for her full participation in procuring the materials our astronomers would describe and catalog for her.

Esther's unhesitating reply illuminates her character and expertness, and exemplifies my ability to—however rarely!—mistake something important for its opposite. "*This* will be a pleasure," she said as though sitting down to a meal of favorite foods. "I have contacts with all the instrument makers in Antwerp. I also know Mercator and Frisius and the people in Frisius's workshop. I can obtain instruments and or the materials for making instruments of every sort. Mathematical, astronomical, astrological. I can reach Mercator readily. Ortelius has published his maps. You would know all about that. It is in one volume."

I was incredulous. The scope of what she knew, and the detail. The novel way she linked *and* and *or*. "An *atlas*?"

"Yes, exactly. When will you have the list ready for me to send?" Esther asked. Then—I am sure without meaning to throw me—she said, "Nasi knew where we would end up. He was helping equip me. To be fortunate." I think the idea that Esther had actually been close to Joseph Nasi must have drained the color from my face. "He was no more important to me than what I have said," she said. "Now enough about that."

I wrote to Murad that plans for an observatory were to be started right away. The design, team, materials. He was surprised and very pleased.

"I think I have never been so excited," he wrote, careful as ever to tell the exact truth.

Then I went to explain to Selim, who—like Esther—though for very different reasons—had never heard a word about an observatory, an astronomical table, a certain aspiration. I found him with his favorite child among the thirteen—five boys, five girls, three stillbirths—he'd produced. In fact he was seldom without that particular boy. Not the boy's mother, just the child. His name was Osman. Little Osman was beginning to talk clearly at that point, and he'd bring whatever was within his reach—a slipper, a bell, an orange—to his father and tell Selim what it was. His mother was Astraea—the girl from Rhodes who'd borne Selim's first "new" child and who had long since become a woman, and a good one. Notwithstanding the distance I kept, tried to keep, I knew the kind of mother Astraea was from the way she was with the boy in the harem, and from the way Osman was without her. Astraea had hope, and she had reason to with the Sultan paying that kind of attention to her son. And with me feeling as I was feeling about the fate of princes. The mothers of the other sons had reason for hope as well, for the same reasons. If they were not aware of it, *I* was—and I had been since Astraea had given birth the first time. Their sons were going to be spared.

Selim slowed the swollen ankle on which he was bouncing his son. He let go of Osman's hands, little reins, and Osman dismounted. Selim noticed me in the doorway. "What are you doing here?" he asked, not unkindly. Osman, sidled up, was pressing against him.

"Just watching. You're a good father, Selim."

"Maybe. Maybe now."

"No. Always. And you're a fine Sultan. A fine commander. This fleet and this treaty are great achievements."

Gazanfer himself—Chief White Eunuch—was there with food. He held out a bowl of something. Selim put one arm around Osman, made a ladle of his free hand and dipped in.

"Why don't you just say what's on your mind. I'm busy."

"Yes. I see you are, and I'm glad." I brightened my face with what I hoped looked like a smile. "I thought I might talk to you about the Tables of Ulugh Bey."

"Oh, God," he said wearily.

"Astronomical tables, Selim. Correcting them." Selim offered Osman a nut. "He shouldn't have those," I said. "He's too little."

"He is? Why didn't someone say so." Selim signaled to Gazanfer. "Bring some . . . Can he have bananas?" I nodded. "Bring bananas!"

Gazanfer exited backwards into a corridor crammed with buffoons and dwarves.

"This will be a great contribution," I went on. "Charting the movement of the stars." I spoke slowly, hoping to make him care.

Selim's attention drifted from little Osman to me as, up and down, his fist dispensed nuts into the woolly O of his mouth. I reached out to remove a small husk clinging to his beard. Gazanfer, back already, removed another.

"You know, Selim, it is said that knowledge of the stars

actually calms the soul. And it prepares the soul to greet . . ."
Selim was peeling Osman's banana ". . . to greet with steadiness whatever comes."

"Who said?"

"Ptolemy."

"Ptolemy," he said to Osman. He pushed a pair of fingers under his sweaty turban. He took a large bite of Osman's snack and made a show of liking it. Osman laughed at his father's antics.

"You are tiring," he said to me. It wasn't an insult, or so I hoped. Just a matter of fact.

"I know. I've been told. I don't wish to be."

"Good," Selim said, tugging his son's earlobes one after the other. I sat still through their little game. Then I asked if we could be alone. Selim shrugged and signaled to Gazanfer, who, not glowering or moist as he usually was, bent over, took Osman under the arms and swung him up. The littlest flank in the Empire's armor. Osman locked his ankles around Gazanfer's waist and his arms around his neck, and out they went. Osman didn't complain about anything. He was an exceptional child.

Selim took a long drink of wine, then another. I got down beside him. "Selim." He looked at me, muddled. "Selim?" He closed his eyes. I reached behind his bristly neck, felt the full force of his monkey breath on my face, drew my finger along the edge of his turban. Then I traced the emerald that secured a modest aigrette. "Selim . . ."

"*Stop* it. You've said it three times."

"I wanted to say that it will be a great thing. Correcting the Tables."

"Murad should come, then. He should be part of it."

"Yes. He should."

I put my hand to Selim's reddening face, and I closed my eyes. I believe he knew what the alcohol was doing to him. It was why he'd wanted Murad to spend time with the Janissaries after Famagusta—because Selim knew about the long gestation of loyalty. And the longer one of trust. Selim was trying to ready Murad, to protect us—all of us. He had been all along. I should have told him more often how good he was.

I craned over and kissed his forehead. He let go of the edge of the cushion and brought his hand around my waist. His head wobbled, but his hand pressed firmly on the small of my back. His fingers were walking. A little march across my tunic. His eyes closed, and the walking slowed, then stopped, and I put my lips to the lid of his eye and made a kiss there, a butterfly, and his fingers took another step or two. "I am here, Selim." He was nodding, trying to find me. I brought my face close to his. "You have a wonderful son," I whispered. "You can be very proud."

"I am," he whispered back.

Wednesday, November 30

What holds anything—a tree, a hair, an intention—in place? A tangle of roots? The underside of the flesh? A law?

If I fell the tree, if I tear my hair against the force of nature's will to cloak me, if I subvert my own intention with someone else's, then what?

I will tell you. I bring what was beneath the crumbly mool into the light of day. I destroy one order with another.

It is dawn. I have not slept. Across the Bosporus the sun looks like a red dome atop the mosque of Asia. In an instant, it has lifted itself above the hills and sucked itself into something smaller and less red.

Gazanfer enters my room without a sound. He has made his way past Sumbul, who is a black outline behind him. Gazanfer is almost upon me before I see him. He looks discharged. He has no color, and his hands are dangling, the backs of them against his thighs, in an unnatural way.

I sit up, and I say, "It is the Sultan." Gazanfer stands there. "Is it? What happened? Where is he?"

Gazanfer says, "In his . . ." He is barely able to stand.

"In his bath."

"*Alone?* Oh God. Who is with him?"

Gazanfer is banging a fist on his chest. "No one, Valide. I had to come for you."

"Esther, where is she, bring Esther here." But she is there already, in the doorway. She has heard water.

"I will go with you," she says coming in.

"No." I press the sides of my head. "Yes." I stop. "No."

Sumbul is by my bed now, taking my elbow. He will come.

I put on slippers and a second robe, I look for the comb to hold back my hair; I go into the hall without it. Then I hear the water—a sheet of it sliding across the marble. It is already moving into the Golden Way. Sumbul has my arm and he lets it go. He knows. There is light in the corridor, but I go forward like someone in the dark who is heading toward life's never being the same. You can do this, I say to myself. You can do this.

Selim is on the floor. He is splayed: his limbs are out at angles they never would be at in life. He is puckered and huge, and his head and neck are propped at a broken angle against the overflowing tub. Water is washing over his eyes, which are half-closed. Water is washing down the bridge of the family nose, washing into and out of the man I belong to. He is naked. He is larger than ever. He is huge-boned except for his little feet, but even they already have become big, his toes melded. His knees, his sex, everything is bluish-white and withered from the water and everything else that has happened to him since I last laid eyes on his body, before Murad was born. My balance is gone. I kick off my slippers, reach to close the spigot, and my back foot slips out from under me, and I am on top of him, across him like an X, and it is not fearsome or awful. It is normal and warm, and I think, *I have missed you, Selim.* I stay that way, and when I sit up I do not take my eyes off him. If I keep my eyes right where they are, I think I believe he will still be there. Not alive. But not any more gone than he is at that moment. *Selim, where are you?* I am saying. *Can you hear me from there? Hear me. Help me, Selim. You are what has saved me from what is com-*

ing. I should have said that to you. You would have stayed longer, if you had known.

Let me see, indeed.

I see this: Selim was my protection. Not from deciding about Suleiman's command. I *had* decided—when Astraea was about to give birth and in agony called for her own mother, and I held her in my arms until she delivered the child who had been conceived to protect the dynasty, the empire, and the order of things, and that child was a girl, and she was dead. I did not know I decided then, but I know it now: Suleiman's command is the law and it was right for him, and let us say that it was even right for the empire, but it it was not right for me, and that decision was made firmer with the birth of every one of Selim's children. Boys, girls, born alive or dead.

I asked to see. I am seeing.

Selim protected me not from what I would decide, but from what I might do. He did this by being alive.

Gazanfer, fly-eyed, is behind Esther, who is beside Sumbul. She whispers my name, inches her fingers under my arms. I tell them to leave me alone—all of them. Selim's skin is sliding closer to his bones now. He is departing. I want no one there but me while this is happening. Except there is someone else, and it is Suleiman, and he is being carried toward me by the very tide that is taking Selim away. I stay there a long time.

Sokollu Mehmed enters my quarters and appears rested. He is unannounced. He says he will summon the messenger who, with no relays, will take six days to reach Manisa to notify Murad that the Sultan is dead; the throne empty. I tell him we will send word by carrier bird. Time is a greater risk than interception. Sokollu Mehmed then says, "The mute is alerted. I will see to the mothers." He observes that I am assembling the parts of what he is saying and not saying. "Their welfare," he says. And then he adds, "Suleiman Sultan knew you well. Certainly better than I. When the time comes all will be ready." That is all he says, and he leaves, before I can think what to say, such as *What do you mean, "all will be ready"*? or *Where will that mute be "when the time comes"*? or *"I decided not to do this seven years ago."*

So, Sokollu Mehmed has known all along what Suleiman commanded me to do.

I tell Sumbul to leave my meals outside the door. Because she knows me, Esther is not surprised when I don't receive her the next day or any of the other days in between, which are a single, endless day in which there is nothing rooted or unthreatened. And when Sokollu Mehmed brings the word that Murad is a day from the capital I am ready for nothing. I retreat. And when night falls, leafless trees make their lugging sound against the Black Sea gusts, and the wind dies, and there is only one thing left to hear: drops of water from the basin in my bath. Drops I never would hear in daylight. Why is it only in the dead of night that water reckons itself out loud? Seven, six, six, four, three. I am saying the boys' ages. Then I whisper their names. Osman. Mustafa. Jihangir. Suleiman. Abdullah. Can I hear the sleeping breaths of those children? Can I hear the reasonable hopes of their mothers? Can I hear Astraea's words of thanks when I tell her that her son is Selim's favorite?

The next day of the dynasty depends on me. The decision I've long since reached versus the dead weight of order. *Suleiman's* order. I owe my life to Suleiman. He *honors* me with his command. Do I not owe him the honor of obeying?

I stand on the black headland of morning. From there "right" and "good" are as indistinguishable as "right" and "wrong." Trust, order, God, hope, birth, murder—*everything* merges. As happens to the horizon on a sweltering day, the line between earth and sky vanishes.

I step back into my room. There is a wall that's dividing my mind. I am on one side of the wall. Suleiman is on the other. Murad and the boys are inside of the wall. I can hear them breathe. "It is murder," I tell Suleiman over the wall.

Suleiman says, *Nothing is more important than order.* "They are children," I say. *I have chosen my successors with care,* Suleiman says back. *You have armed your son well,* he says. *You have raised him to achieve power differently.* I wonder if Murad can hear from inside the wall what his grandfather and I are saying. I wonder if Mehmed, at whatever distance death has put him, can hear. I hope he can hear. I want him to understand. Suleiman says, *You will protect your son as necessary.* I say, "I cannot, Efendimiz." Suleiman says, *You will not waver.* Then we are not in the wall. We are in the Privy Chamber, in front of the fountain. Suleiman's army is assembling to go to Szivetgar. He says in a voice I have never heard, *I know you. A good choice.* He says my name, and then he says, *You are as good as my own.* There they are—the words I've needed from the beginning. And hearing them I am his. I do not know how much I have needed those words until he speaks them. Perhaps I have thought that, over the years, the need has diminished, or been satisfied—by being married to his son, by bearing his grandson. But I have needed to hear the words from Suleiman himself. A man not perfect but great. A man most excellent, most original, most daring and just.

I open the door to the corridor. In front of me is a small and stocky male. Not a dwarf but not a usual-size person either. He is wearing blue breeches and a red cap that comes down like a Janissary's but not exactly like it, and his shirt is tight and cut in a way that shows his chest, which is hard from work and which has no hair. Never have I seen a shirt like this one. The mute stares hard at what's before him. He has no doubt. He himself is order. And so am I. A sharp unearthly light. He is the instrument, I am the word. I say to him "Let it be . . ." And he is gone. Gone like a hard-shelled insect, at an angle down the hall. Gone before I say *done* or hear my heart crack. Gone because my word is kept, and order kept as well.

An uncelestial calm descends. From that moment on, I do not think. I remove my headpiece and combs, bend over and shake out my hair. I stand up, gather my hair, secure it with the combs, and leave the veil behind. I set out for the terrace reserved for the rite. I've known of its existence since I first came here as a girl. Everyone has always known. In fact, I go not to the terrace but to a room that looks upon it. I do not think about where the boys are while I am waiting. I do not think about where their mothers are or what is happening to them as their sons are pried from their arms or their fingers unlaced from theirs. I do not wonder where Sokollu Mehmed or Esther are, and I do not think about what my mother or Sylvana might be saying to me from their graves. I even do not think about Mehmed—when he still had a chance in life— saying that were it to fall to him, he would not carry out the law. I think of Suleiman and about armies of warriors from the same family, the travesty and madness of that. I think of all of the sultans who have come before Murad, and I say their names out loud, and I think of the battles they have fought not with each other but with Persia and Mesopotamia, with Arabia and across North Africa, and the victories that have made our empire vast and varied. I think about the name that is mine thanks to Murad. I think about the Conqueror and his might and about what made him promulgate the law that binds us, and about the tree that is our family and that it must not be split or cut or allowed to rot, not even its extremities.

When I get to the terrace there is no one and nothing there. Then I see that I am wrong. There is something there. Blue bowstrings are laid out on a ledge. Even from my prospect above I can see that there are knots at the ends of the strings to assure a firm purchase. Then nothing. And then the mute appears against the blackness of the entrance to the terrace. He's not even half the height of the doorway. Behind him is Selim's oldest boy, Jihangir. The mute has him by the hand. They come into the sunlight. I squint trying to make out details, and swiftly six more mutes, built and clad like their leader, appear, one after the other, and each has one of Selim's boys by the hand. That's fourteen people, albeit small, on that narrow terrace, and there is not a sound except for everyone's slippers scuffing on the stone, and that is because the boys are gagged, and their eyes are covered too, which I imagine makes them quieter still because they don't know what is happening or because they think they are safe or because they are sons of the Sultan and have mothers who love them and until that moment because they had lives that were happy and full of promise. They may even be quiet because they think the small men who came for them are buffoons of their father's. That they're playing a game. Children that age would think such a thing. Everything the mutes do is in unison—placing the boys' hands on the terrace wall so that their own hands are freed, getting behind the boys, taking up the cords and, as though those five, razor-slim, silken strings are one instrument, swooping them around the boys' necks, crossing their wrists one over the other and—their muscles distending their tight shirts—pulling. The boys' legs buckle all the same way, and though they don't go down all at once, they go down fast, and for that I thank God—out loud I thank Him, and I think I might have made the sign of the cross, but I cannot be sure.

Then I hear an unheard-of sound, an airless purple gargle. Four of the five mothers have been spirited elsewhere, but Astraea has somehow broken free and caught sight from wherever she was of what has come to pass. She doesn't need to confirm Osman's condition—she doesn't need to get close to his body. She knows. And she tears down the stairs through the harem gate, flies across the Meeting Place of the Jinns, the Courtyard of the Favorites, the Garden of the Elephants, and the Fig Grove. Barefoot across the frozen earth she sails, the frosted grass speeding her flight. The Black Eunuch crying after her catches her hem as she hurtles herself toward the Golden Horn, but the arc of her dive frees her from his grasp and releases her to the harbor's depth. This is when I hear the earth howl from its core.

Murad had set out with a party of fewer than a dozen. He'd taken only four days to reach Panderma, where the Admiral of the Fleet was waiting for him. By oar and sail, hard against the freezing wind they had hauled themselves across and reached the capital not very long after Osman's mother had sunk to the bottom of the Golden Horn.

He came to me directly, stood in the doorway nearly invisible, his presence making the darkness deepen. The attendants shuffled out as he came toward me. He was soaked, and when he dropped to his knees by my side, I felt the freezing journey on his coat. Then he was in my arms, and all the distance he'd traveled shuddered out of him. I held him close, then back, to have a look. He was a ruin. He'd become a little fat in the long time since I'd seen him; his breathing was effortful, and his eyes were red and swollen—from thinking about his father's being dead? or that the fate of the Empire and its peoples was in his hands? or that the fate of his brothers was, too? *Had* Murad had a plan? An intention? Maybe Murad did have it in him. Maybe Suleiman was wrong. Maybe I should have given Murad the chance to carry out the law himself. Then I thought *No.* No. Of course Suleiman was right. Murad was—Murad *is*—incapable of killing his brothers. And he would have kept me from killing them, too, if I'd let him have the chance.

I *had* done the right thing. That is what I said to myself. That is what I believe I believed. And so, with a calm that was both real and not natural, I raised my hand to Murad's bearded cheek and did what I would never do again—reaching to the top of his turban, unraveling the enormous length of muslin, removing the scarlet cap covering his skull, and putting my lips to his forehead. "Oh, Valide," he murmured. "Oh God."

Indeed.

It had been seven days since Selim died. Only six of us knew what had happened—concerning Selim, I mean. Sokollu Mehmed Pasha. The Admiral of the Fleet. The messenger, Esther, and Gazanfer, who had packed him in ice. We alone knew that the Empire was without a sultan. The mutes and I alone knew the rest. And Sokollu Mehmed—yes, I assumed he did as well, though I did not seek him out, nor did he come to me. But he knew. After all.

Take them, I indicated to Sumbul as I walked Murad around the ill-smelling heap of pelts. He collapsed on the window seat and buried his face in his hands. "Where is he?" Murad said.

"In the Privy Chamber. You should take some rest first, though. You are dead tired, Aslanim."

Murad didn't answer. He held out his hand. I took it, closed my eyes, and I thought I might never let it go. Murad saw that. "Are you all right?" I nodded. "Was it you who found him?" I shook my head. Told him what had happened. Murad raised his hands, spread his fingers and drove them into his hair. "Oh, Valide," he said, raking, then digging. "I am so sorry."

Until that moment, I had never considered that Murad had precisely the same force of concentration that Mehmed—his uncle Mehmed—had had. They both paid attention to what was before them. They both saw things clearly. And what Murad saw at that moment was his mother, whom he loved, and whose husband was packed in ice in a nearby room. What mattered to Murad at that moment was my grief. And I wondered—since he did see clearly—if he could tell I was dreading what he would think—what he would feel—when I told him what had been done. "I know," I said over and over, trying to be capable of his own sympathy; trying, somehow, to join him. "We will manage. We will." And then we went to see his father.

Selim was out of the ice and on a bier. The mutes had husked his frozen head and shoulders—everything the color of a bruise. His beard glimmered with stars of frost, and his sealed eyes bulged as though they still held an image. Murad let out a high-pitched groan, dark and womanly. I thought it might have been a recognition. Selim's face *did* look like Bragadin's on the pike.

"Leave me to this," Murad said quietly. His tongue was flicking about catching tears. He put his hand on his father's. The cold of it. "Please," Murad said.

I returned to my chamber. The call to prayer warbled over the city. Midday. I had heard no prayer at dawn. I had heard nothing.

Murad was gone a long time. When he came back he was different. He had been not with Selim but with his death. I understood. He said, "Dear Valide, I wish to see my brothers."

"You will," I said. "Tomorrow. There is time."

"Now," he said. He wasn't perturbed. "I wish to see them now."

"Murad, you are tired and . . ."

"Valide, *you* are tired. And *I* understand. Gazanfer will take me."

"Gazanfer?" Murad nodded toward the dark of the doorway. "We will be alone now," I said to Gazanfer fairly steadily. "I will take you, Murad—but not yet. You need to rest, and— you are right—so do I. Then we will talk. I will take you to them. But not now."

Murad struggled with what to say next. I handed him a cup of water. Pushed a little pine bowl of dates closer to him. "We can talk now." There was a sudden heaviness. Of the present being attached to the down-pulling past. Of the future having the same force and weight. "Or." He paused. "Or, at least for now, I wish you to know my intention. I intend to spare my brothers."

There it was—the line. Everything was about to be after whatever was said next. I heard myself say, "I understand, Aslanim."

I heard Murad say, "I knew you would."

"Do not worry, Murad."

"I am not worried."

"Murad." The tone. He stiffened. "The decision . . . Murad, you understand . . . in this matter . . . about your brothers . . . there is no choice. The decision can only be one way."

Stiffer still. "That is not so."

"Aslanim, please. Have some tea. Sleep. We'll see each other in the morning."

"Why do you talk this way? You speak to me as though I am a child. What do you mean *There is no choice?*" The cords in his neck were hard, straight up and down.

"It is the law, Murad. You know that. It is not up to any of us."

"It surely is. I am Sultan."

Quietly, very calmly, I said, "In fact, you are not yet—not until you are invested with the Sword of the Prophet. And I do not exaggerate when I say that you may *not* be Sultan for long if one of the pretenders lives." *Had* lived.

In a voice darker than Bragadin's livered lips, Murad said, "They are children, Valide."

"And you will not concern yourself with this matter," I continued. "You do not need to. It is why I'm here, Murad."

He let out a choked groan and turned away.

"Aslanim." He said nothing. "Murad. Please. Look at me."

"Do . . . not . . . say . . . it."

I stood up. "Look at me." He wouldn't. "It is done."

In one ropelike move, Murad rose. The heat coming off him made the walls heave. He was not enraged, as far as I could see, nor was he shamed either. Those things would come later. Right then, he was simply altered. He was molten. Molten the way the roof above the terrace had been when the boys were strangled and when the lead would have become liquid and coursed down the walls and onto the tiles and risen around the mutes like a full-moon tide about to drown everything in roof. Murad was able to say only this: "Who *are* you?" And though I wished to remind him that order does and must exist in this world and that the heavens prove it and that we on earth can emulate it, his question was so chilling and reasonable that I could not say a word.

࿐

At dawn the next day, cannons that exist only for the purpose announced that the throne had been claimed. Murad III, successor to beleaguered Selim II, who had succeeded the Magnificent, who had succeeded the Grim, was invested with the Sword of the Prophet.

> Oath of allegiance taken by Murad III upon acceding to the throne:
> *With God's help, I have gained the sultanate. On this date, with the perfect concurrence of the viziers, ulema, and people of all stations, high and low, I have ascended the throne of the sultanate that has come down to me from my forefathers. The hutbe has been recited and coins struck in my name. As soon as you receive this decree, proclaim my enthronement to the people in all cities and towns, have my name mentioned in the hutbes in the mosques, have cannon salutes fired from the citadels. . . .*

Save for the muffled clop of hooves wrapped in velvet, all was silent as the Sultan advanced from one courtyard to the next, from innermost to outer, the new hope of his people.

At the Bab-iHumayun he paused, took in the crowd, and, with the slightest rowel of his rubied spur, Murad set the cortege in motion. "May the Sultan and His realms endure a thousand years," called out the Keeper of the Gate.

"Ten thousand," I whispered, alone, at the top of the

260

Tower of Justice. "This is *your* turn, Murad. *Your* reign. It is deserved. You are secure. Believe me."

The highest-ranking officers of state, the chief administrators of the Palace, the avant-garde of the Janissaries, platoons of eunuchs, and residents, thousands of them from every district, were all there, waiting in silence for what they had come to see, and when it came—Selim's coffin, draped in the Prophet's green, topped with Selim's turban—the quiet crowd became quieter still, out of respect for Selim and for the throne and for death.

It was Sokollu Mehmed's idea to have Selim's sons follow at a distance. That, too, out of respect, but also with an eye to the unknown, for what the people were about to see was something they'd never witnessed before, did not expect, and might not be able to comprehend—for the lawful execution of brothers had, until the day before, taken place outside the capital—usually far outside—and one by one.

Crossing over the sill of Bab-iHumayun from inside Topkapi to where the people were—tens of thousands of them—a small green-draped box came into view. Then another one. Then another after that. When the fourth appeared the crowd's quiet, already dense, became solid. Silent for sure, but deafening. And before the fifth cleared the gate the people were not silent, were speaking—their lips were moving—and I imagined they were counting out loud. Women drew their veils across their faces. Men put their hands to their mouths. Many had to turn away altogether for the knowledge of what was in those boxes all borne by Janissaries was too much. Do you know what a six-year-old weighs? A three-year-old? I could have carried Osman's box myself. But there were four soldiers for each boy, and I imagine that it was the knowledge of the insufficient weight on their shoulders and of death's being light that pushed the bearers' eyes identically outside their heads, like scarabs' eyes. I thanked God that Little Mehmed had not yet arrived from Manisa.

You can do this, I whispered again to Murad far, far below. *You can lead this terrible parade. It won't last long. Then it begins. Everything. The worst is done, Aslanim. For you. You can do the rest—convey power, assure order. You can. You will.*

Murad in his mourning purples, pulled back his chin and curled his lower lip into his mouth. It was an expression I'd seen a hundred times during his lessons as a boy, when he was concentrating, when one thing was leading to another. *Don't stop, Aslanim. Don't mind the way they look. Don't waver, and your people will know this is right.* He didn't stop or falter, and when the procession advanced the silence resumed. A blind man would not have known there was a person in those streets, let alone a parade, because there wasn't a sound—not from the fur-soled pall-bearers and not from the army or the navy either. From the Tower of Justice I looked out in four directions upon streets filled with a grieving people who had the merged intensity of larvae, and they gave to the streets themselves a soft-bodied motion of sorrow and disbelief.

Thursday, December 1

I do not sew. I hate to sew. It was still the same day and I was slumped on a window seat poking with a long needle at a torn veil. It was something to do. Esther strode in. I had not seen her since Selim died. Nor had I wished to. But there she was. I put the mending aside, asked why she was there, and she, too, was clipped. Sumbul had admitted her, she said, because he was as concerned about me as she was. I looked to the Golden Horn, black with caiques bearing hunched mourners, and at that moment it would not have surprised me if their oars had become wings and the barques had taken to the sky. Anything could happen. Life had become that extreme. What I faced, though, was a question. The one Esther had come with: "How could Murad have done such a thing?"

I was surprisingly ready with the answer, meaning I was indignant at the question. I did not wish to discuss the matter, I told her; her question was forward and impertinent; and she was excused. Esther stood close, her citrus scent right beneath my nose. She put her hands on my shoulders, and she said no, she wouldn't go. I thought, *Can she tell I have no bones?* Esther persisted. She told me that what had occurred was not my fault. That she knew I had tried. That our children are not

263

us. That my son had a mind of his own, and that I should not be ashamed.

For her to think that I was ashamed of Murad, that I needed to be told how to think about him, and that, indeed, I was not capable myself of giving an order as crucial as any the Sultan ever gives allowed me to collect myself and, rather than upbraiding her for talking about what she was ignorant of, I disabused her. "Murad did not give the order."

She looked hard into my eyes to remind me that there is such a thing as trust, and she said, "Of course he didn't. That's what executioners are for. To absolve the commander."

"I did."

Esther did not believe me. She pushed me away and said that lying on Murad's behalf was almost as bad as what he had done. Her voice was sharp as an awl. I could not assume Murad's guilt, she informed me, and I shouldn't try. And the fact is I was both shocked and flattered that Esther didn't believe me, and for a moment I thought about letting her believe the best—her inclination. But just as there was no *yes* and no *no* anymore, so there was no best and no worst. Nothing meant what it once meant, and I felt the floor falling from under me. The before about to be gone forever. I had to hold on to what was there. And that was Esther herself. I thought: *I need her. Maybe I should explain everything. That I struggled for years with the decision. That an insuperable force prevailed.*

But I didn't explain everything. Instead I invoked the essentialness of order. I told Esther about the law—that it was Mehmed the Conqueror's idea. That it had proven right, civil war averted, and that I believed and feared Murad did not have it in him to discharge his greatest duty, and that I didn't fault him for that and she shouldn't either. And Esther did not understand. She got up, went to a wall and pressed her forehead to it. I knew the feeling. "You mean it," she said. When she finally looked at me, her beautiful green eyes were shot with red, and wet strands of hair stuck to her cheek and neck and chest and looked like script. "They were children," she said. It wasn't a protest but a plea. A statement of the obvious intended to make the impossible true. "*You* are the captive," she said. The pity in her voice had turned to dread. There was no mistaking it.

Esther didn't come back the next day or for a very long time. Not even when I asked her to. She explained why not so long ago—when I got back from my trip with Ismihan—now that she thinks I can bear to hear. She thought I would be coated with the smell of what I had done, and that she might stop loving me if she breathed it.

ॐ

Dear Nonno,

You will have heard that the Sultan, my husband, has died, and that my son has succeeded him. The transfer of power is complete and secure. Order is preserved. It is a time of surpassing sorrow.

I usually sign the copies of the letters I write. This copy is unsigned.

I stood alone, with Murad's and Esther's revulsion. To Murad, I was a usurping stranger; to Esther, a self-appointed function of a monstrous decree. I was in an infernal position, and, because I could make myself believe, most of the time, that I had done the right thing, their horror made me furious. I knew better than to show it, though. I have never seen anger in action lead to anything good. The best it can do is rearrange what's wrong, which makes things worse because it lasts longer. So I consoled myself with the belief—it was surely more than hope—that in time, the answer to Murad's *Who are you?* would spark at least some awareness that order had been kept and that what I had done was not the same as who I was. And that Esther's estimation of my captivity would correct itself when she saw the benefit to the Empire and people of a secure transition of power. It would be all right, I told myself, if I could just manage the sorrow and the torment of justification, and the solitude.

I knew that the benefit to the Empire would be known only over time. I thought, though, that the benefit to the people would be more readily felt. But I was wrong. While the new Sultan had proven himself decisive, in the people's minds he seemed to them alarmingly so. Something was needed to mitigate, even slightly, what they had witnessed. No one was more alert to this need than the Grand Vizier, who had eight years before, in the name of order and in the interest of the people, made a dead Suleiman seem alive in far-away Hungary. Sokollu Mehmed Pasha excelled at obfuscating gestures when needed. He also approved of what I had done. He called on the Sultan with a proposal.

Sokollu Mehmed's suggestion that Murad associate himself with me, and in particular with "the good works for which the Sultan's mother is known and the goodwill she has engendered overall," drove benign, measured Murad into a scathing rage. "Associate myself with the person who has established me in the minds and hearts of the people as a leader of so little imagination and courage that he could not find a way to maintain order without murdering children? Celebrate the very person who has usurped my authority before I was even invested with it? Are you *mad*?"

Sokollu Mehmed thought but did not hesitate. "Exactly what I have said, Efendim. The people know they have a Sultan who is resolute. They need assurance only that he is concerned for their needs—as his mother has shown herself to be. Honoring her publicly—and soon—will establish you rightly."

Murad stormed and brooded, and when night fell he recalled Sokollu Mehmed and made an announcement: that goodness had no meaning to him anymore, that calming an offended people was essential, and that if having a parade to honor his mother was the only way to calm them, he would swallow that bitter pill. Those were his words.

A celebration without a precedent in our history was planned in short order by the Grand Vizier himself. It was difficult to contain or express my gratitude to Sokollu Mehmed. Emotion, I was sure, was something to husband. Still, I did not keep myself from bowing gently when he came to call. "You deserve this," he said with only a little warmth. "Yours is a great force. I would not have thought that—" He bowed. He believed what everyone but Suleiman believed. That I hadn't had it in me.

The morning of the procession I woke before dawn—my hands off the mattress, my nails chalky on the freezing floor. I've always liked moving my mattress around the room so I can wake to different views. That day there was nothing but sky. It was still night at seven. I looked toward the closed door beneath which I could glimpse the heels of Sumbul and other Black Eunuchs standing at attention. Then I turned toward the passageway between Murad's chambers and my own. Safiye had arrived the day before with Little Mehmed and his sisters. I had not seen them, but I knew from the Superintendent that she had appeared that same night in Murad's chamber, not only unbidden but accompanied by Mehmed. She'd used him as a passkey to gain access to his father. She'd been in a hurry to prepare herself for the visit, the Superintendent said—bathing, steaming the garments she wished Murad to see her in, because they were crushed from the journey. The smoky-yellow silks, the fetching cinched tunic. The rest I know from Sumbul, who watched from the corridor. When Safiye and little Mehmed entered Murad's chamber, Mehmed ran to his father, and Murad held him firmly against him, then picked Mehmed up, but Mehmed was too big—he was seven—for such an embrace, and he pulled away. Murad said nothing to Safiye, but he did order a meal and watched as Mehmed poked at the meats and rice and then sought with a glance his father's permission to eat only the sweet, and Murad gave it, of course, and asked Mehmed about the journey—the conditions, relays—and Mehmed answered between bites. Still no conversation with Safiye. Murad stared at Mehmed—I imagine to protect him with his love—while Safiye watched in silence from a cushion. Finally Murad kissed his son on the forehead and asked him to return in the morning. Then he dismissed the attendants—the eunuchs in the chamber and corridor and the Superintendent, too. The night passed in silence, and then it was dawn. I stared at the door to Murad's chamber with a notion that my attention would somehow yield information, and it did. First words—disconnected, quiet, and near. Then a window opening, though no steps to the window. Then a humming—haunting and rhythmic. Then more words, his voice, hers, then nothing, and then a sound I had never heard before—of the most infinitesimal blade slicing a balloon filled with mercury and stars that had been heated and cooled and heated again and now poured from the tiniest slit ever made or imagined. It was Safiye.

I called for the Superintendent. Dispatched her to the hammam to have it readied immediately. But I couldn't wait. What filled the room next to mine was more than I could stand and more than I could understand or wanted to. The Mistress of the Baths found me in the corridor, guided me to the bath, hissing and fogged. She undressed me—robe, nightdress, undernightdress—turned me toward the marble slab and eased me down onto the slick stone. She got astride me, the barely clad crux of her hovering over me, and with the strength of a man and grace of a girl she washed my back— long strokes from waist to neck, her own weight never coming down on me, her knees bearing it all on the marble as she pressed and withdrew, pressed and withdrew until the sensation on the underside of me produced by this rhythm and care overtook all other thoughts. She sat me up and, holding a clay pot containing mud made from arsenic and unslaked lime, lifted my arms, painted the mud under them. She rinsed her hands, scraped a line of the mud with the one long fingernail she had on her smallest finger, and then, with a golden spade, she scraped the rest and handed the spade to an assistant in return for a pail of water and then another. "Valide Sultan," she said once again, and I sat up and rested my forehead between her breasts as she curved over to reach the small of my back and then, without the brush, she washed my neck, pushing into and shaping it. Finally, she held the pail of rose water high above my head, and let it pour gently over every indentation, and she gathered the lengths of my hair, kneaded my scalp and rinsed me once again, missing nothing. She had done this a thousand times, and every time I was surprised.

Sokollu Mehmed himself came for me. Beyond the walls of Topkapi were the people of the city, thousands of men and women dressed not for the freezing cold but for festivity. They were people who felt they knew me and who wished me well. Glowing in the gray air was a gold-lacquered palanquin inscribed—in pearls—on its side with Murad's tughra. "Your conveyance," Sokollu Mehmed said. I peered inside. "Please." He offered his hand. Black Eunuchs appeared and were strained by the jeweled box they deposited at my feet.

"What's this?" I pointed a toe at the coffer.

Sokollu Mehmed leaned inside. His face was close. "Donatives. For the people." The eunuchs pushed in an iron box. "And these are for the troops."

"Is this the custom?"

"It begins with you, Valide Sultan."

Sokollu Mehmed backed away so an attendant could cover me—first with sable, then lynx. The tantara sounded, the door was latched. Casting coins to our people and protectors, I led the procession forth. Grand, Second, and Third Viziers, Agha of the Janissaries, Head of the Treasury, Clerk of the Secrets, and a long parade of thoughts: Of Murad, his anger and the bed he shared. Of Selim, so barely departed.

Of my mother, Sylvana, and Mehmed and where they were and the awful uncertainty of what they might be seeing. Of Suleiman. Of civil war. Of the judgment of Esther. Of myself, before and after.

Inside Hagia Sophia, I read aloud the Word of God inscribed on medallions the size of the moon. I thought about the Conqueror's entering that church, mounted, and making it a mosque with his presence. I thought about the sorrow of conquerors everywhere. About the vagaries of faith. Standing before the vitrified Infant on the lap of His Mother—herself floating above the blessed mihrab, I still could not think about the boys and their mothers and the perpetual light and darkness they would cast on everything. I could not bear to. There were many things I could not think about at that time.

When, at the procession's end, my palanquin was set upon its marble plinth, the face that met me was a stranger's. Murad's eyes were as hard as the grip with which he assisted me, though not as hard as the glare of his favorite, who stood at his side. Despite those icy looks—and because of them—I made a fast and sound decision. My grandson, whom I had not seen for three years, was standing between them, obedient as a Janissary, looking right at me and smiling like a little camel, and I decided not to take his hand or kiss his forehead or express my nearly unbearable happiness at seeing him. I just said his name. And he said mine back. *Nonna.*

꩜

Hamon is vexed. It is worry, I can see. He still can't name the ailment. And I'm having trouble seeing now. And the nature of the pain is changing. It feels as though it has a force, and that it's heading to my extremities with urgency.

I will put it differently, since I seem to be thinking very clearly this morning. The force of this pain makes me wonder if it is precisely for me.

I don't remember very well the months after the procession in my honor. Days shed their distinctions, weeks edged imperceptibly into seasons. There was the sorrow and solitude and the unvoiced anger, but there was also the reviewing of what had happened and the never getting to the end of it or getting to the end and feeling I'd left something out in order to get there, and I'd begin the review again, which, in fact, was an attempt at an explanation—to myself, of course. Only to myself. I was fording a fast-moving stream, stepping on rocks I couldn't see and couldn't feel—meaning I could not understand what I had done. I wrestled guilt to the ground and slid into oblivion, excited and grateful there was such a place, for this is when I began to drink.

When I was little and wished to hide, I would make myself invisible by closing my eyes. Forty-five years later it was no different. I drank and believed no one could see me. Not Murad, who was no longer looking, and not Esther and Sokollu Mehmed, who were. Of the three, only one was speaking to me. After months of numbing myself had passed, Sokollu Mehmed called on me. He left quickly without saying what he'd come for but he came back the next morning, before I'd had a sip of anything, for he wanted me to hear clearly what he had to say: that if I didn't stop what I was doing, it would be the end of everything I cared about and had ever strived or prayed for. He said it would nullify the sacrifice I had made. Those were his exact words.

I had taken up wine so that I wouldn't feel, and the prospect of feeling again was terrible. But worse was Sokollu Mehmed's warning—which, thank God, I could recognize as true. And I stopped. I haven't had a drop to drink since. Given what happened after, this surprises even me.

I took my place on the threshold of the Observatory. Of all it meant and would mean.

Suleiman had illuminated the gate of that undertaking, and Selim, distracted as he had been, had helped push that gate open. As I began the hard march out of my haze, the Observatory alone loomed as hope. It presented itself as fully possible, fully great. It would change everything—for the Empire, for Murad and me. All I had to do was see that it be built.

"Murad should be part of it," Selim had said. Whatever else Selim understood or didn't, that much was clear to him. Selim impeded nothing that was good, ever.

I turned to Sokollu Mehmed in the hope of gaining Murad's approval. Murad assuredly would not give it to me. I hoped the talent that had twice equipped Sokollu Mehmed to make the impossible *seem* true might allow him to make the impossible *be* true—that is, getting Murad to believe the Observatory was his own idea. Overtures—mine, Sokollu Mehmed's—to astronomers in Cairo, Damascus, and Baghdad had, while Selim was still alive, yielded designs of instruments large and small. There were drawings of dripping clepsydras, of devices to measure azimuths and altitudes and diameters and eclipses, of a mural quadrant the height of an oak. Sokollu Mehmed presented these to Murad as elements of a legacy that would be like no other. Each instrument would be a vital sign of *this* Sultan's vision, Sokollu Mehmed assured Murad. The Observatory—its inventions, corrections, and particularly its vision, would then and forevermore set Murad apart from every Sultan who had preceded him. Owing to the extreme legacies of his immediate predecessors as well as to his own spirit, teachers, appreciation of scientific knowledge, and talent for mechanical design, this appealed to Murad. He gave the order to proceed. I did not construe this as forgiveness. But it was a gesture in my direction. Of that there could be no doubt—or lack of appreciation.

It is a measure of the force that had separated me from myself in Murad's first seasons as Sultan that I failed to see there was another hope looming beside the Observatory. It is unthinkable to me now that Little Mehmed could have been in Topkapi for half a year before I spent even an hour with him. I don't know what he was told about my condition in those months. He must have wondered. We had had a bond, after all. He'd carved me a bow. I believe he was waiting for me to reappear, because the first day I ventured into the garden of the Third Courtyard he was there. He did not ask what I'd been doing all those weeks. Instead he told me—that day and for many days after—what he had been doing. Hunting with his father, working with the Chief Fletcher on a new set of arrows, studying geometry with a tutor I hadn't heard of and who, he said, had a lip that was "broken." When the opening report of Observatory construction rang across the harbor, Mehmed and I were on the shore to hear it. A startling clatter of iron against rock announced the future, and over the thunder of debris Mehmed's voice rang out, "Shall we go across, Nonna?"

Yes. We would go across. Mehmed and I would start where we were. A boy on the shore with his grandmother. I put my arm around his back. "As long as they know where you are," I said with a nod toward the harem. What I meant was, *Is your father allowing you to be with me?*

Mehmed and I boarded a caique and crossed the Golden Horn to where sturdy men stood rooted in the arcs of their instruments, swinging ax and maul to open the earth so the heavens might be known. It was the first breath of Suleiman's dream, and Mehmed and I were taking it in together. I was a grandmother again, once and for all—and Mehmed's well-being was—and is—my highest aspiration.

Friday, December 2

Dear Nonno,

I wonder if there has ever been a time like this time in which we are living. Every season a device is created to newly gauge something essential: time, space, the speed of things on the earth and above. Does this mean that the distance between what is known and what there is to know has shrunk, even a bit? I say it does not. The ratio of what we know to what we can know is constant. That is imagination's beating heart. And if that constant were to change, it would not be gradual, believe me. The heavens and their light, and the earth and its waters, would contract in a spark that would leap from mountaintop to mountaintop, from mast to mast in an instant, and the spark would end everything including the desire to know about it. Not even that would survive. I have learned this from none of my wonderful teachers. I have learned this from no one.

In the weeks before I slipped into the oblivion of alcohol, I had imagined the ways Esther would soften her heart and let me reenter her trust. I'd imagined they would be the ways I wished and needed her to return: When she learned Murad was refusing to see me, she would seek and embrace me, panicked that she had known too little to judge me so harshly. I would accept her change of heart, show no rancor. She would admire me for that; we would resume. Or, as more weeks went by and still she didn't come, I imagined that she would decide, finally, to write. She would express her revulsion but her understanding, too, because, with time, she would have accepted the need for order—however horribly enforced—in a world such as ours. To that rapprochement, I knew I would take longer to warm. The hurt would have gone deeper with all the months of being shunned. But I, too, would relent. I would let her forgive me, meaningless as that might be, for by that time, I'd have needed her shelter more than water or air.

But Esther did not come, and she did not write. So it was I, finally, who went to her. It was simpler than I imagined and probably would have been all along. She was unruffled when I called. For seven months I hadn't seen her. She was standing at a window, leaning out—bracing herself like a sailor. It was freezing. Even through my slippers, my feet were getting numb on the stone floor. "You should cover yourself," I said. She turned her top half. Her wild hair was all around her shoulders, copper coils down her back. She looped it into itself, tugged it back, pulled the shawl she wore around her shoulders. She didn't answer. "You have no idea," I said.

She'd turned back. "Yes I do."

She took the fur she'd slept under and threw it around herself. She looked like a king. "I hate what has happened," I said.

Esther said, "I am not done sleeping. You should sleep too." I lined myself up alongside her, close enough that I could hear her breathe. Our rhythms were not matched but regular—the way the ocean is, every wave different in the same way, and I did sleep.

It had been a steady bond Esther and I had forged before Selim died and the boys died. She thought it would end because I was covered in a horrible deed. That I had chosen the cage of alcohol, though, over the freedom of pain made her believe that she didn't know all there was to know about why

I had given the command—which was true. She didn't. To this day I've said nothing of Suleiman's command. But that is exactly what allowed her to keep loving me: her belief I had not acted alone. That I had indeed made a promise that I had to obey.

༄

From *Brightest Stars for the Construction of the Mechanical Clocks* by Taqi al-Din
With the name of God.

The one who created the motion and the rest, and made the sciences of full moons emerge from the hidden horizon. He set these circles and the spheres in motions as the essence of truth and the minutes of signs. He smoothed the way to the noble intelligences to receive his abundant generosity and to enjoy the manifestation of truth. You granted to bless and obey the one who acquired Your qualities and declared Your signs, Your servant and Your Prophet, distinguished Muhammad and his relatives and his friends are strengthened by the magnificence of the ascertained news. O! my God our expectations are in you. Finish our work so that it will be good, convenient and worthy.

It had taken just one visit to Galata to know I shouldn't go again until the Observatory was finished, and not being there was like missing seasons with Mehmed or summer forever because what was going on at the Observatory had never gone on anywhere, and my imagination was not up to the massive, intricate novelty of it. But Murad had to know and believe that the Observatory was his and that the policy and goal of expanding Ottoman power through knowledge were his. Yes, it was Suleiman's aspiration, as well. And mine. But first and most it was Murad's. So as the woodworkers were hauled in

276

from Russia and the masons from Crete, as architects came from Baghdad and glass cutters from Bruges—all of them arranged for by Esther—I stayed away from Galata. I stood on the shore, and I watched and hoped.

My restraint did not cause Murad to call for me, however. And for months he communicated with me only through the Grand Vizier. "I believe the Sultan would have a different view, Valide Sultan—he would act differently if he knew the truth," Sokollu said finally of Murad's silence.

"About?"

"About not having acted on your own."

"You are impertinent, Sokollu Mehmed."

"I am not," he said. "The Chief Astronomer is to submit his report on the first of the new instruments, and the Sultan is inviting you to the audience as a courtesy. If he knew the truth he would not seek justification for entertaining the Valide Sultan."

I said, "The Sultan knows enough of the truth. The answer to *that* question is no."

Murad received us, significantly, in the Privy Chamber. He was seated on the floor facing Little Mehmed over a chipped chessboard, Selim's favorite, jade with tourmaline pieces. Another possession of Selim's, the mechanical clock Murad had made and given Suleiman, stood on a porphyry pedestal made for the purpose. Mehmed sprang up and hugged me. I whispered that he should finish his game. Murad didn't look up from the board. The raised pattern of his robe did not conceal the sag of his back and shoulders any more than his beard hid the caving in of his face. More than ever he looked like me. He made his move on the board. Then Mehmed made his. Back, forth. It went very fast. "I won," Mehmed said slyly, peeking up at me from under his giant eyelids. He knew I didn't know the game, despite my grandfather's efforts to teach me. I congratulated Mehmed on his victory.

Murad stood, brushed bits of food from his robe and,

without any preface, after all those months, said that Taqi al-Din would begin his report. The Imperial Astronomer was admitted dragging sheets of parchment across the room. He arranged them before us, put his hands above his hindquarters, and bent backward. "The Sultan brings great imagination to this work," he said as he bowed the top of his little frame to the Sultan. Murad wrung his forearms—something he'd often done when faced with a compliment. Then he signaled to Little Mehmed to come near. He placed a hand on Mehmed's back. And, before my eyes, Murad began to revive. He expanded visibly, like a plant, watered.

"Of course he does," I said.

As Taqi al-Din described the depth and dimensions of the well and produced designs for the huge mural quadrant and the instrument whose name I can't recall that he invented according to Ptolemy's description in *Almagest*, Murad's shape and color became more defined and vivid. And when Taqi al-Din said to Murad that this was just the beginning, Murad half-closed an eye—a substitute smile invented by me—and he answered, "I know." Then he said to me, "It is excellent." And he added, "Isn't it?"

It was the sort of question I had thought I would never again hear from him. A question seeking my judgment. A question rewarding me for leaving to him—actually and honestly—something important. "It is. It surely is."

Murad picked up a drawing of the Observatory's well. "Europeans were hugging the coasts for five thousand years," he declared, "while we were navigating with magnets. Our astronomers made the most potent instrument we have today"—the marvelous flat astrolabe with which they can both compute and observe—"and they did it seven hundred years ago. Ulugh Bey at *his* observatory reckoned the tilt of Earth's axis with an accuracy still unsurpassed. We will regain our lead. And we will never lose it again."

To all of this I said only, "You are right, Murad." And

I only said it once. I wanted nothing to alter the aspiration that filled the room. It seemed to have happened with so few words. I feared it could be undone with fewer still.

It was that very fear that made me not wholly surprised when Safiye appeared the next day. It was with apologies that Sumbul announced her, for she had managed, with the Chief White Eunuch in tow, to push past him. It was her first call on me ever. Safiye has always gone to extremes.

"I have accompanied her by order of the Sultan," Gazanfer said, with a distaste that interested me. Sumbul tried to stay in front of her in order to be between us, but his determination was no match for hers. She approached, drew back her veil, and leveled on him a freezing glare. From her sizable ears hung pear-shaped rubies that nearly touched her shoulders. I told her to come in.

"Sit down, Safiye." Unnerved attendants scurried near with cushions. "It has been a long time." I counted the months as I said it.

Without effort and like a snake she lowered herself. Five births in seven years. Her body didn't show a sign of them. "We are glad to be here," Safiye said. She sat, as did I, with legs crossed in front. She placed her hands, which were stippled with gray, on her knees. "Glad," she added crisply, "except for my quarters. I request to face the water with a balcony." Quarters like—and adjacent to—the Sultan's. And mine. "My son had such a quarters when he came here with his father many years ago. His mother should have the same," Safiye said. "Near the Sultan. Who takes no others." As though I didn't know. As though I were standing beneath something heavy and about to fall. I told her I would speak to our architect. She ran a finger around the rim of the glass of tea she'd been offered, took a sip, kept her lips on the glass. I told her how wonderful her son was. She narrowed an eye, appearing to calculate, but said nothing. And then, too quickly for sure, I told her she was excused.

"How are your daughters?" I said before she was to the door.

Safiye turned—head, shoulders, arms—one part swirling after the other, and said, "They are perfect," and the swirl didn't entirely stop before she was out of the room.

Considering it in a certain way, I could understand Safiye's frustration. In spite of being the favorite of the Sultan and the mother of his only son, she was left out of certain matters. Why? Because Safiye wasn't educated. No one had enticed *her* as a girl—as I had been enticed—with Homer or Ptolemy. No one had suggested to *her* that there were different ways of knowing and prizing the mystery of what surrounds us. That is a lot to lack. And it is clear to me only now the resentment that would encase such incompleteness. I disliked Safiye. I found her aloof, intrusive, controlling, and rude. Nevertheless, she had reason to be unhappy. I knew then as I know now that *that* was good for no one, especially my grandson, because a bitter mother is a bad thing.

❧

Dearest Cecilia,

My respects to your son for moving ahead with an Observatory. You had better tell him—and tell his Astronomer—there is no time to lose! The King of Denmark is besotted with the young man I have told you about. The King has given this fellow Tycho Brahe an island of his own from which to record his observations! He intends for this place to be unsurpassed and unsurpassable.

I have your list of books and manuscripts before me. I shall send what I can. It looks like something Egnatius would have planned. And an Observatory library—what a good idea! I have sent notice to Aldus's son who now presides over the printing press. I urge you to reconsider having the bindings undeco-

280

rated. *These are valuable works of art, after all. They should be
known as such from the outside! Did I tell you about the Duke
of Mantua's portrait of your departed husband? I will soon!*
  Your devoted,
  Nonno

One after the other, my grandfather's letters came. About
the catalogs of the instruments Tycho Brahe was creating, the
long-lived comet he was studying, the axioms he was disprov-
ing, the supremacy at stake. He had no idea, nor did I, how
far ahead of the Danes Taqi al-Din was—even *without* the Observatory. I wrote to my grandfather. I told him that unlike
the King of Denmark, Suleiman had needed no scientist to
spur him. That he had had his own standard in mind, his own
idea of excellence and invention. Suleiman had had a new way
of thinking about power and progress, and it had to do with
knowledge not war, life not death. Murad had inherited that
same turn of mind, I wrote to Nonno, and, unencumbered by
challenges to the throne, he was free to pursue a *new* order.
And the glory would be his. *Nurbanu*, I signed the letter, and
below that I wrote *Valide Sultan*.
  On a cold sunny noon in November of 1577, one year, ten
months, and three weeks after the dredgers had set to work,
the last instrument, an armillary sphere six fathoms across, was
riveted in a limestone well twenty-five meters into the earth.
The greatest observatory ever conceived was about to be inau-
gurated. There were so many of us crossing to Galata the day
that we could have strolled across the Golden Horn from the
deck of one vessel to the next. Murad, cloaked in marten, led
the way. Mehmed, like a regnant mink in his sleek wrap, rode
with him. My caique followed, then my daughters' and Mihrimah's, then the Agha of the Janissaries', the chief administrators', and Safiye's. It was like any dynastic ceremony—the
procession told our story with elegant compression.
  Taqi al-Din and Sokollu Mehmed awaited us on the sunny

far shore. Standing beneath a paneled baldachino, they glowed like embers under the red silk—Taqi al-Din's turban wound especially wide; Sokollu Mehmed's mustache waxed into a commanding bar. They had given thought to their appearance. So had Esther, who was standing with them. She was dressed in bright violet and wore no jewelry.

In order, we disembarked beneath the canopy. Murad, for the first time since he was Sultan—nearly three years—gave me his hand, and we stood together in the stripes of sunshine as the others followed, and it was with neither balance nor grace that Safiye put her foot on the gold runner, for, as any woman could have told you from the shape of the breasts and general look of being inhabited and triumphant, she was pregnant again. This was a woman who had her own way. I had known that for a long time. But only then, at that moment, in fact, did it occur to me she got her own way by extraordinary means. A spell, say.

Murad went to assist her. I gave Mehmed's paw a squeeze and let go so as not to transmit the enmity pressing out of my every pore. Taqi al-Din led the way, and slowly, as we marched up the hill, the Observatory revealed itself: the sparkling glass cupola, the curve of the brass dome, the unadorned stone facade of the library containing all our books—Suleiman's, Selim's, Murad's, and mine. Waiting there was the Sheikh ul Islam. Behind him, the holy men and men of science and men of law. Scores of them. One by one, they kissed the hem of Murad's garment. Then the Sheikh ul Islam stepped forth, and he—he alone—kissed Murad's hand. Murad proclaimed, "It is said that whosoever is assiduous in his reflections on celestial marvels and stellar motions"—he lifted his arms, his chin, his voice—"will find in this a conclusive proof of the existence . . . of its creator." He stared at the earth that had yielded up this gift, then showed his face to heaven. "And this will make manifest . . . the unity and magnificence of God." Murad understood what he had created.

"Long live the Sultan," Sokollu Mehmed called out.

"It is superb, Murad," his aunt exclaimed. "From Topkapi one has no idea."

But the Sheikh ul Islam's head was shaking with consternation. "It is stated in the Qur'an that nobody but God can know the future."

Little Mehmed came up from behind and slipped himself under his father's arm, and Murad positioned his son directly in front of him. Murad smiled at Mihrimah and answered the holy man. "That is correct, Efendi," he said. "Stars and planets give us no knowledge of our future. But their arrangement tells us much about what exists. And it suggests possibilities. My interest, Efendi, is the possibilities."

"Knowledge of the heavens acquaints us, Efendi, with God," I added.

Sokollu Mehmed stepped forth. "It is part of God's purpose for us to know what we can, Efendi. God gives us what we need in order to glorify Him. We ignore or conceal it at terrible cost." What a bold one that Sokollu Mehmed was.

The Sheikh ul Islam's eyes and nose flared. Murad, aware that his favorite had made her way to his side, cleared a bigger space for her in the cluster. Then he waved and bade us enter the most perfect astronomical observatory ever built. My grandson was the first one inside, and because he was so delighted by what he saw—that huge well, paneled in teak and amaranth, amboina and brass—and because he didn't know how upsetting it would be to his mother, he called out to me, "Oh *Nonna!*"

OhNonnaOhNonnaOhNonna. His voice twirled up to the top of the cupola.

From the center of the strand, Safiye then broke apart. There was no commotion, no dashing off or screaming. Just a lengthening of neck. With a neat, whip motion she snapped off her veil. Pinned between her ballooning breasts was a ruby the size and shape of a nose. Safiye looked down appraisingly at the jewel. Mehmed turned around and squinted toward his mother in the light of the doorway. She was unfastening the jewel from her bodice, illustrating what she was—and was not—attached to. Then she assumed precisely the stance my grandfather used to affect when he'd hold a book to assess its value, and she smiled at Little Mehmed, turned toward Murad, and smiled at him faintly. She was tired—that was clear from her eyes. She entered the Observatory, walked past her son without a glance and went to the edge of the well—to the topmost of the thirteen ladders that led to the well's floor. "An offering," she said, "to commemorate the occasion." Then she held the ruby over the edge and let it go. Quiet, quiet, quiet. No one breathed. It fell not like a stone but like a feather. It took forever. And when forever came and the offering hit the stone floor there was nothing too surprising. Just the scattering of a million pieces of ruby. Nothing more or less than what Safiye had intended—a shattering emblem of her will.

Saturday, December 3

Jean-Baptiste Egnatius, my beloved tutor, died in 1553. I think—because I never heard from him—that he never received my letter inviting him to visit Selim and me in Kutahya. I had sent it to my grandfather and asked him to forward it. My father's envy could explain an undelivered letter. Egnatius's abrupt departure from Venice following my mother's death drew a dark line under why he had come to 'Ca Baffo at all.

Twenty-four years later—in the very month the Observatory opened—the Egnatius estate was probated in Verona. My grandfather was notified, and he traveled there to represent me. The will had been contested bitterly by two of Egnatius's sons. The contest had been prolonged and, for them, fruitless. In the end, the deceased won. Egnatius had left the entire contents of his library to me.

My grandather was permitted to visit the Egnatius villa outside Padua for an afternoon. He said all of Venice was buzzing over the oddness of the bequest, the particulars of which were the subject of another epic letter.

My dearest Cecilia-Nurbanu,
   I have just returned from Verona—via Padua. My head is filled with the effects of your Egnatius, and yours will be too. You

will soon receive a complete accounting of the contents of the library. There are thought to be over three thousand volumes, as I told you in an earlier letter, but in the meantime you may wish to know what I have seen this very afternoon.

On Egnatius's desk were two things—a small brass astrolabe, and a copy of the tract on the circulation of blood, which got Servetus burned at the stake. And on the large table in the middle of the principal room of the library—there are five rooms all together—were a large volume, bound in red leather deep-stamped with gold: "On the Revolutions of the Celestial Orbs," and next to it, Pacioli's "About the Divine Proportions." The illustrations of the regular solids are by Leonardo himself. Fra Pacioli dedicated the book to Egnatius. And Egnatius has inscribed it to you:

To Valide Sultan Nurbanu, née Cecilia Baffo Veniero
With admiration and affection
JBE

There were many drawers beneath the bookshelves; they are shallow and long and I was told they contain maps. I was being hurried, so I was not shown them.

Now, before I close, let me tell you what was on the great table in the room at the back. On each end of the table were brass globes—two on one end, one on the other—which record early voyages of Magellan. In the middle of the table was an object that will interest you even more. The superintendent called it an astrarium. He said it was built by a Giovanni Dondi of Chioggia and completed in 1364. It took him sixteen years! It is badly corroded, but I am told it was among the most valuable of Egnatius's possessions. I remember you like clocks.

Below, verbatim, is Professor Egnatius's reference to your portion of the estate. I hope it will please you even half as much as it pleases
Your devoted
Nonno

"I give, devise and bequeath to Cecilia Baffo Veniero, also known as Nurbanu, wife of Selim II, sultan of the Ottoman Empire, the contents of my library in its entirety, including, without limitation, all books, codices, maps, parchments, and instruments (astronomical, cartographic, and navigational), with the confidence that she shall make good use of them to further scientific knowledge and the advancement of man."

There was no mention of my mother in the will, but I believe that all of us—Egnatius, my grandfather, I—knew the library was meant for her.

I called on Murad with Nonno's letter. The work of the Observatory had released an energy in him that seemed to deflect his anger—though that softening could have been due to the music, too. The ruby travesty—about which Murad had never said a word—convinced me Safiye *had* cast a spell on him, and Esther had found a Balkan pythoness to break it by means of music. The dulcimer players stationed along the Golden Way and the young men strumming *ud*s at sunset in the Third Courtyard cost me a fortune and seemed worth every ducat. Murad actually acted warmly toward me. "You deserve this," he said, glancing up from my grandfather's letter. He didn't say it the way Sokollu Mehmed had said something similar when Murad was acceding to the throne. He said it as a good parent would to a good child. He said it as though it were true.

In the months before Egnatius's library arrived, Murad had visited the Observatory nearly every day. He'd always gone unattended. True to himself, his interest was learning, not ceremony. He wanted answers not to the questions he had but to those he didn't know enough to ask. Taqi al-Din and his men were supplying them abundantly by means of instruments ancient, improved, and new: a quadrant of wood for gauging azimuths; a mechanical clock with three dials—for hours, minutes, *and* seconds; a framed sextant with chords for figuring the equinox. Tycho Brahe himself copied that sextant, and no wonder. Taqi al-Din's inspiration was Islamic science—the achievements of Ulugh Bey, of Al-Uqlidis before him and Al-Kashi before *him*. With their work in mind, Taqi al-Din abandoned fractions for decimals in recording his observations. Building on their achievement he created a terrestrial globe.

Murad immersed himself in all of this, and it gave him much pleasure that his son was with him at the Observatory being educated, formally, by the intense and slow-to-warm Taqi al-Din, who had become devoted to Little Mehmed. Taqi al-Din said he had never had a student like him. "Disciplined and imaginative in equal parts," were his words. And one had only to see Mehmed's progress to know its larger importance: that he would be a champion of astronomy, mapmaking, time-keeping. Like his forebears. Like Suleiman and my mother and Murad. Murad endorsed the bond between Taqi al-Din and Mehmed. And, unlike his favorite, he did not object to my being at the Observatory often, and I was—watching, listening, being in the company of the Imperial Astronomer and his best student, the Prince Mehmed.

Then Egnatius's bequest arrived. The wing of the Observatory built for books became the repository of not just his marvelous volumes and maps but his collection of instruments, automata, and timepieces, the most glorious of which was the Dondi clock. There is nothing in the world like it. It shows solar time and sidereal time, tells the motion of the planets, the date of Easter, the phases of the moon. No, nothing like it anywhere. And I gave it to Little Mehmed.

I gave the Dondi clock to my grandson because—I don't know—because he was young, I suppose, and because it would teach him. But it was Murad who had always loved clocks. Murad whom Suleiman had enlisted to build one. I should have given that clock to *him*. It would have connected—perfectly—the meaning of time and space and the marvelous instruments that measure them. And it would have restored—or added to—Murad's faith in what he means to me.

But I didn't. I gave the Dondi clock to Mehmed because it made me happy and hopeful to do so. It was a grave and selfish error. That gesture cut Murad to the quick—again. He stopped visiting the library, and within a few weeks he stopped going to the Observatory at all. I would say that this reaction hugely exceeded its cause—especially (I told myself) since I'd given him the Piri Re'is and since Mehmed insisted that the clock be kept with the rest of Ignatius's treasure, in the library—but that would suggest I comprehended the hurts that, over the years, Murad had managed and kept within. Until the sum of them forced their full effect.

❧

The air is visible with the fragrance of jasmine. It is December. Maybe I am dreaming the scent, or willing it. I have noticed a high alertness to beauty since this illness began. Sinan has made a world of it for me: the walls around me are my garden; the baldachino above is my sky; the light well in the vault of this ceiling is my prospect to the heavens. I note these surroundings because they constitute my life now, as I lie here, and they are calming and magnificent, and I do not wish to write only about the difficulties that have seized us over the years.

Still . . . I have had regrets. I regret for all of France that Catherine de Medici believed there was no way to stop the killing of fifty thousand Protestants on St. Bartholomew's feast day. That massacre shocked even Sokollu Mehmed Pasha, who was good at putting slaughter in perspective. I regret that a yet another fire in the Doge's Palace took Bellinis, Carpaccios, Titians by the scores, and I regret even more that it took the Doge—who died from grief—for he was Sebastiano Veniero. And I trusted him. I regret 1578, the year of plague and Persia and losing Sokollu Mehmed and more. I regret every season and week of that year, for each was another blow to Murad. And they added up to more than he could stand.

First, plague. Sly, unruly, it settled on the capital and sifted like pollen into every pore. People stumbled in the streets bloated from the infection and the black mood and purple swellings that announced it. Everywhere you turned, hearts were heavy with death, the fear of death, and death's details. It took a hundred thousand people in eight weeks. From the Tower of Justice, I looked out over the city and watched the narrative of plague inscribe itself in the air. Entire families exhaling their names and lives. The sickness bubbled up between slabs of pavement, enveloped babies and mothers, merchants and soldiers, men of science. People who had survived many other horrors succumbed to that one as it nestled in the private coves of bodies both weak and strong. The steaming scordium did nothing but foul the air.

Among the dead were Piyale Pasha, Joseph Nasi, and Mihrimah. For Piyale, I have to say, I had no pity at all. The Admiral of the Fleet was conceited, remorseless, and the reason my daughter Gevherhan drank. I'm sure of this, because the day he died was the day she stopped. She didn't need to heal. She just needed him to be gone.

Joseph Nasi's death taught me that my imagination, about which I have been most unhumble in these pages—I know from rereading—was very much smaller than Nasi's effect on the lives of Jews everywhere in the Empire and Europe. Here in the capital they poured into the streets around his residence and around the library he had endowed and opened to the people—all people. *Glory of Israel*, Nasi was termed in eulogies around the capital. His star had fallen with Lepanto, as it should have. But he spent the rest of his life sharing his wealth and privilege. He was a freed man with a memory. Once again, Esther was right.

The death of Mihrimah enlightened me more, for, as specified in her father's will, she was laid beside him. Mihrimah alone and forever—next to Suleiman. I, who believed myself alone to be as good as his own, stood shaken, if not corrected. I thought I couldn't see what Suleiman or Murad cared for in Mihrimah. But I could have seen it—the force of her loyalty and unbartered affection—had I not been blind with jealousy. There. I have put it on the page. Murad was crushed by his aunt's death. I hope he did not take note of my relief.

In November of that year—still 1578—beyond the frontier that Suleiman had warned never again to breach—the Shah was poisoned by his wife. *Deadly nightshade,* the bane was called. The throne of the Persian Empire was vacant. On the far side of the Black Sea, waiting out winter, was our army. Word reached Murad from across the swallowing waters: the commander in chief, stationed auspiciously in the Crimea, was seeking permission to cross into Georgia. To take Azerbaijan. To invade Persia.

Now *here* was a mistake that had *not* been made yet—and one that *had* to be avoided.

Sokollu Mehmed, who had campaigned in Persia with Suleiman forty-three years before and who had gone with him a second time many years after, needed no reminder of the perils of that place and of that distance. He called on Murad in a hurry. He told him an invasion was not a sound idea. Murad was indignant. He yelled at Sokollu Mehmed about being intruded upon, and I'm afraid that Sokollu Mehmed might have yelled back to make the point that a campaign at that distance was doomed, that it took four months to get to the border, that he knew from experience with Murad's grandfather.

It was the reference to Suleiman that set Murad off—like a grenade, Sokollu Mehmed said. It brought the Sultan to his feet and senses. "I have heard enough about the experience of my . . . " he started to say grandfather, but he said forebears instead. They were in the Privy Chamber, and Murad relocated himself under one of the gilt baldachinos—huge and garish things recently installed—near a brazier. He extended a leg to the lip of the brazier and began to rock it, and Sokollu Mehmed, thinking the Sultan was simmering down, began again. "It will be a pity," he said. Murad continued rocking the brazier back and forth. It tipped and spilled embers on the hem of his robe and many more around the floor. Fixed on the smoldering fabric but doing nothing about it, Murad told Sokollu Mehmed not to speak to him of pity.

This was when Safiye stepped forth into the acrid air. She'd been there all along. Sokollu Mehmed was shocked, and he looked shocked when he reported to me what followed. Without troubling about the Grand Vizier or the attendants, Safiye knelt beside Murad and wrapping the hem of his garment in that of her own, extinguishing completely any spark that might have remained, she said, "Is it not you who determines the fate of this Empire, my Fortune-Favored Sultan?" She put her head in the Sultan's lap. "Is that not so?" Murad put his hand on her shoulder and told her yes, that was so.

Distant the way the arrow is from the string.

I doubled the musicians' wage. Harpists and fiddle players were added to the intervention.

And so, with the added impetus of a certain comet—described in 'Ala al Din al Mansur's verse, which I will copy below—Murad decided, God help him, to let his commander wage war on Persia. In winter.

*From "Concerning the Appearance
of a Fiery Stellar Body"*

*A still more remarkable thing is that through the
    ignition of vapor,
And as an occurrence pertaining to the fiery
    phenomena of the high regions,
A strong flame, one of those stellar bodies referred to as
    the seven sinister objects*

Which is quick in vengeance and is called the one with
  the forelock
Suddenly appeared, on the first night of Ramadan
And shone with a strong and clear light.
Passing through the nine sections of the ephemeral
  world,
in the year nine hundred and eighty five of Hegira,
Like a turban sash over the Ursa Minor stars,
It soared like the sun for many nights.
Through it the night of the Moslems became blessed,
And its light was world-pervading like that of the
  full-moon.
In the apogee of the firmament it remained for forty
  days,
And sent a gush of light from the east to the west.
As its appearance was in the house of Sagittarius,
Its arrow promptly fell upon the enemies of the
  Religion.
At the end its longitude and latitude were in
  Aquarius,
And its descent and disappearance coincided with that
  watery sign.
And as its tail extended in the direction of the east,
It discharged its inauspiciousness like a scorpion upon
  the enemies.

Prepared and excellent, our troops finished the Persian battalions one after the other, taking Georgia and pressing on to the Caspian Sea—an additionally bad turn of events for Sokollu Mehmed because the last time our armies had tried to reach that Caspian coast, it had been *his* idea and it had failed. "The Grand Vizier wants *no* one to succeed where he himself has blundered," the commander in chief told the Sultan. "The Grand Vizier's failure brings out the coward in him now. The least trustworthy of men is the coward."

It was Ismihan who called my attention to the change in Sokollu Mehmed—for what had seemed gradual to me, to her felt sudden. Accustomed as she was to the umbrage of her husband's advanced age and waning power, she was startled by his withdrawal. Sokollu Mehmed had seen it all when it came to expanding the Empire, and yet Murad's indifference to his counsel on Persia seemed to crush him. Our victories were begetting more victories. Our generals were daily vindicated. The long wait for Sokollu Mehmed to be proved right about the perils of Persia was bringing the Grand Vizier down.

I called on Murad. I informed him that his commander in chief was wrong. That on the matter of Persia, patience was essential and so was imagination. I assured him that Sokollu Mehmed's experience was vast and invaluable and that his valor was unassailable, not to say demonstrable. "My Grand Vizier is failing," he said before I was fully in the room. "The Agha of the Janissaries has told me that he is completely discredited among his men. This puts him—and all of us—in danger. What is happening? You know him. Sokollu Mehmed is wrong about Persia. He should admit it."

"He will not admit to what he is not wrong about," I answered. And Murad's reply was, "He is also too caught up in your Observatory."

"*My* observatory?" I thrust an arm toward the window. "That is *your* Observatory, Murad. Your legacy."

"I am not dead," Murad said.

I was not going to let him turn everything upside down like that. I told him that the observations, projections, and tables coming out of *his* Observatory had vaulted us—dynasty and Empire—past Tycho Brahe; that the radius of Taqi al-Din's newest quadrant was a third larger than Tycho's; that our observations were accurate to within a half a minute; that all this was *his* achievement. But Murad's eyes were wide with uninterest. His breath all at once got heavy, and he said that he knew "all that", and it didn't matter. And then he said this:

"As Mehmed's mother has observed, you are too close to see things as they are."

I leaned close to him, too close for sure, and said, "You should wish she did not say such a thing to you, Murad. Or you to me."

And then this. Sokollu Mehmed, grizzled and drawn, emerges from the Hall of the Divan. The ambassador of France and his flamboyant suite are filing out behind him. Janissary guards line the Second Courtyard in ribbons of rank. And Mehmed, from a corner of the Courtyard near the kitchens, is coming in from hunting. Sokollu Mehmed nears the Gate of Felicity. A dervish, or someone dressed as a dervish—someone in white with a tall, stiff, firmly fixed hat—streaks across the grass to where Sokollu Mehmed has paused to greet his nephew. A sharp cry cuts the air. Inside the harem, Murad and I both hear it. Everyone hears it. The corridors fill with attendants; they flatten against the walls when the Sultan appears, and when I appear. We are running. Together Murad and I burst outside. Across the court a circle of Janissaries and eunuchs is forming around a blue and gold mound. The sash of blood across Sokollu Mehmed's chest is taking over his robe. Mehmed is on the ground huddled beside his uncle. His quiver is on his back, his bow is thrown down and his hands are one on top of the other on Sokollu Mehmed's chest. Murad falls to his knees beside Mehmed, and I drop down beside Murad, and Murad calls Sokollu Mehmed's name, reaches in front of Mehmed and slaps Sokollu Mehmed's cheek and spreads open his eyes. It is done. The knife has gone into and out of Sokollu Mehmed's heart. Murad's chin drops to his chest and he holds Mehmed, and makes that slight boy shake with his own shaking.

So died another bearer of Suleiman's hope that the Empire be thought about differently—through knowledge. And let us place the responsibility for this devilish act exactly where it belongs: on the heads of those few who are *threatened* by progress. Murad was angry with Sokollu Mehmed, but he feared for him even more, and he reviled this act. He knew why his sister loved her husband. He knew it was for good reason. And, oh, how this death ripped her apart. So, let us point directly to the fanatics in high places who do not represent their holy ilk. Indeed who betray the right-thinking among them, for the upright among religious authorities are many. They are fine, disciplined holy men who teach our sons, interpret our laws, call us to prayer. They are many, and they are good.

⁂

Now, imagine this. One month afterward. I was at the Observatory. It was midday, and the bar of sunlight was plumb to the bottom of the well where the Imperial Astronomer and scientists of many kinds were shattering old notions and rendering fresh ideas. From a platform at the edge of the well I watched. Taqi al-Din was so far away he looked like a beetle, a determined dot. Plague had found him, too—found his groin where the sticky buboes are so fond of forming. But it hadn't stopped him. Taqi had achieved his task—he had "completely measured the latitudes and longitudes of all parts of the earth" just as the poet had written. The muezzin called out, and, for a moment, an idea far greater than the Observatory filled the well, and all the astronomers and mathematicians and builders of instruments faced Mecca and went to their knees. When the prayer was over, Taqi noticed me high up on the rim, and he waved. He climbed the first ladder. Climbed the second. The third and fourth. The thirteenth. Sweating, wheezing, he bowed, mopped his forehead, and bid me follow him. On a hassock in his study was the report I'd requested. The list of every instrument soldered or lathed. Every element of work completed, started, or conceived. Every detail of Mehmed's achievement. Arrayed on a bench behind Taqi were Ulugh Bey's Tables corrected so that, henceforth, the stars could be read rightly. Also a loosely bound sheaf bearing the Sultan's tughra and the year on the Islamic calendar—987. I reached for it. Taqi reached too and, catching my hand in midair, brought it down under his own on the title page. He told me the Sultan had ordered their work to stop. I lifted my veil to better understand. He told me that by the order of the Sultan, all observations, measurements, research, and manufacture of instruments were to cease immediately and until further notice; that all documents were to be gathered and made ready for delivery to the Sultan the next morning. I did not understand. Not at all.

"And Mehmed—what about his studies?"

Taqi handed me a folio. Mehmed's work was collected inside. "You will be pleased."

"Has the Sultan summoned you?"

"You will be pleased with the Prince's work," was all Taqi would say.

Then it was the next day. Murad had just come in from hunting. I did not greet him. I asked what the order was that had been issued to Taqi al-Din. Murad freed himself from his quiver and girdle, dismissed the Chief Falconer and the others. I asked Murad why he had hidden himself since the Grand Vizier's murder, and he answered my question by saying that his own grief over his Grand Vizier was more than enough for him. He did not want to share or manage mine. I asked him what was wrong. "What is happening, Murad?" I asked very gently. "What can I do to help?" And he said to me, "Nothing." And I said, "Surely there is something. Tell me. Talk to me," and I asked him if this news from Taqi al-Din—the suspending of work—concerned the correction of Ulugh Bey's Tables. And if it did, then perhaps certain authorities would benefit from having more thoroughly explained to them the *need* for corrections. Murad didn't answer, but shook his head back and forth to indicate how far I was from the mark. "What's the matter?" I asked.

He told me. "The need for a correction is great," he said. "It is overwhelming and will not be ignored. The Tables of Ulugh Bey, however, will wait. They can stand uncorrected for another generation. The correction in this dynasty cannot. The correction needed here is to power—judgment—usurped. It could happen again. I will not allow it."

A huge maw opened around my head and clamped through it. I could see but I could not know.

Here is what happened next. The end of that same day. The beginning of the next.

It is a black but moonlit night. From my chamber I look out on the Observatory, shining like Venus against the blue-black sky. I wonder what Taqi al-Din and his people are doing up there with their observations called off and their subject—the heavens themselves—spread so clearly and unreachably overhead. I lie down, and I sleep. Sometime before dawn, I have a dream of thunder; wrought-iron rumblings barreling down the Bosporus. I rise and move toward the window as though I am outside my body. Directly across the Golden Horn, on the highest point in Galata, encircling the Observatory, I see a mangled metal hedge—an encampment of siege engines. I see giant trebuchets, incendiary missiles in tidy heaps, rows of stout cannon, naft pots stacked high. The iron engines start to move. The Observatory is being invested from all sides. This is not a dream.

It is daybreak. A human chain rings the artillery. The Janissaries form a bulwark, their arms confirm their purpose— to demolish the enemy.

Esther has heard the appalling noise and has appeared. So has Sumbul. "They're going to destroy the Observatory," I say to them. "There will be nothing after this."

Esther says we have to go to Galata. I cannot move, though. Esther goes alone.

The firing begins before she is in the boat. Iron balls streak the space as one after another they bomb the Observatory's roof, its stone walls, its copper panels and iron ribs. An oared barge slips in and out of view. Another barge in its wake. Clay missiles filled with pitch rip through what's left of the roof. Flaming pots of ruin hurtle inside. And still the Observatory stands! Still the Janissaries are at attention. There is an eerie pause. Then from across the dell comes more thunder. Esther, floating in the middle of the Golden Horn, stands up to look. On the hill facing Galata is the largest gun on earth—the width of its bore is the length of an arm. It is Mehmed the Conqueror's cannon, last used in 1453. The siege master on this occasion will use no less. A thick orange flame shoots from the bore, emitting a ball the size of a dome. Over the arsenal and docks it flies, hitting its mark dead on. And finally there is no hesitation left in those beautifully joined materials. The Observatory simply falls into itself. The main tower first, then the smaller tower, Taqi al-Din's quarters and his men's quarters, the library, our prospect to the heavens and to everywhere else.

The next day broke with the stench of sulfur. Directly across the Golden Horn, on the highest point in Galata, where five years before there had been no observatory, there once again was no observatory. Just a smoldering foundation with a few demonic spars against the morning sky.

The Sultan was alone when I found him—attired, turbaned. Gazanfer announced me and disappeared. Murad invited me with my title. "Valide Sultan." Murad stood there clad in the Observatory's destruction. The deed was his. I did not think a spell could cause such alteration. He let me take his hands between my own, palm to palm. Night had collected on his cracked lips. His eyes were vacant. "You have lost your mind," I said gently, the way I would have if he'd lost a book.

He said, "Yes. I have. Or I did." He drew his tongue across his lip. "I lost it when you lost yours." I was still holding his hands.

"You mean . . ."

"I mean when you killed my brothers."

He did not twitch. I did not dare let his hands go. "I see. But that *had* to be done. This, here . . ." I said keeping my eyes on his, not looking to where the hideous smell of destruction was coming from, "this did not. This . . . here . . . should . . . need not have been done." I was learning the language as I went along. And I was absorbing confirmation that Sokollu Mehmed had not revealed the secret of Suleiman's command.

"This . . . too . . ." he said with a mocking cadence, "was necessary. Because it has taken *this* for you to know what *you* did."

I let go of him. "But you have destroyed the greatest chance for the Empire's advancement, Murad."

"You think there can be such a thing as advancement as long as brothers have to be killed to preserve order?" He did not raise his voice. "I don't know what happened to you. It is grotesque."

I knew what had happened to me—the captivity, the command—and it was grotesque, and I was not going to explain it. And I knew what had happened to Murad. He, too, had been pushed by someone to do the unthinkable, and *he* wasn't going to explain it to *me*. Our loyalty to the people who had caused us . . . No . . . our loyalty to the people we'd chosen to obey was symmetrical to an extent that bound us.

I said, "Nothing can justify this . . ." My arms stretched out to encompass the awfulness of the Observatory. Then I faced him and stretched them wider still. ". . . or the act—my own—that caused it." What happened was whole, and I saw it. I said, "Please forgive me."

Murad was drinking something, and a trickle had gone into his beard and onto his neck, and it startled him. He swatted at his collar and said, "You told me a long time ago that forgiveness is a feint. You were talking about your father." I thought I had said that only to Esther. "Does it matter if I forgive you? Or you me?"

"I don't know."

"It doesn't. What matters is where we are."

"You mean that we are even."

"I mean that we are aware. Of what our actions mean to the other." Murad extended his hand to help me up.

"I am glad I knew enough to come."

"You have always known enough, Valide," Murad said without emphasis.

I started to leave. Again, Murad said my name. "That it was you who gave the order to execute the boys was worse than the order itself."

"I know," I told him, though I hadn't until that moment.

⁊ఎ

I thought I could never visit Galata again. Mehmed asked me to go with him, though, so I went. Standing by the still-smoldering ruins, I asked if he had spoken to his father about what had happened, and he said he had not. I asked if he understood what had come to pass there, and he told me, with respect, that he did not think it was important for him to understand.

Mehmed is tolerant by nature. Just as his father had been before his authority was interfered with. Mehmed would preside over a new kind of order. I was sure of it. I believe that was when I began to feel the possibility of being whole again.

When I finally wrote to my grandfather after the Observatory was gone I didn't tell him my heart was breaking, because I didn't want him to know, and I didn't tell him why it was breaking because I knew he would have heard. News has always traveled fast between the Sublime Porte and the Venetian Republic. This news would have traveled faster still. Even faster than the order Esther had the Chief Taster put in for a new set of celadon dishes.

I told him instead about the mosque and *kulliye* Murad

has built for me. About the dervish convent and hammam, the soup kitchen and hospice, the quince orchard and sycamore grove. What I told my grandfather was how, on the route between Topkapi and my mosque, people call their petitions out to me as though they can see me in my palanquin and as though they know me. I told him how many of their requests are for justice—settling deserts, figuring what is right and good and maintaining it. I told Nonno about the plans I've made for my slaves to be freed when I die, which, given the way I feel today, might be any hour. I told him about Esther's husband's son wanting permission to sell gems in a lottery on Rialto; about the heinous pair of dogs sent to me as a gift by the Doge; about how I was continuing to change the harem from a jail to an institution that allows advancement for girls and women so that now, when they crawl into each other's arms, it's not out of despair but because they wish to, because now there are other ways for them to feel safe. I told Nonno about the renovations of the Privy Chamber and of my quarters and of the quarters I've arranged for Safiye, too. She is the favorite of the Sultan, after all, and mother of his heir. It is fitting. I told Nonno about the marquetry walls and ebony window casings. About the sound of porphyry being chipped into glistening plinths, of gold being hammered into latches, of fountains jetting higher than the Tower of Justice and anointing the peacocks who, decked in pearl anklets and ruby diadems, are roaming the geometric void. I told him that above the gate connecting the harem to the Second Courtyard are inscribed these words: "Thus the pavilion of paradise became an excellent palace." It is a chronogram that yields the date on the Muslim calendar, 986.

Sunday, December 4

It is three years since the destruction of the Observatory.

Meanwhile, Persia mounted a counterattack.

Mehmed passed to manhood.

My daughter Shah died in childbirth.

And Safiye gave birth to a son. The delivery nearly killed her, and it brought Murad to a brink of his own—another one—half a year after the Observatory came down. It convinced him that Safiye would, in his words, "spare nothing, including her own life," for his sake. With this in mind, I paid her—and my new grandson—a visit.

The baby was in Murad's own cradle—the ugly one with the moonstones that had been his birthday present from Hurrem. He was swaddled, but his arms were free and bent upward around his tiny face. I picked him up and took him closer to the light. He looked as though he'd been underwater. There'd been no mention that the physician suspected that he, too, was near the end, but you could see it. He was only faintly alive. I cupped his head in my hand, kicked off my shoes and walked him around, whispering to him through his sleep. My fleeting grandson. Safiye was two rooms away, stretched out on an immense yellow mattress—it looked more like a pool than a bed. She herself was in yellow. Her hair, black as sable, was loose about her shoulders. Her eyes were closed. She was beautiful, even in extremis. When I went close to see her better, though, I saw that she was empty. Not just her middle, but everywhere—neck, wrists, ankles. Emptied. I stood there staring at her as I swayed Murad's son in my arms, just as I'd swayed Murad himself and Gevherhan and Shah and Ismihan, and whispering to him that I loved him, saying it over and over, so that he'd know. Suddenly Safiye's eyes were the barrels of a gun—open, black, aimed. "*No.*"

Murad's third son died the next morning. If there ever was a spell it was broken then. A horrified surprise filled the Palace, and before nightfall, Murad's new son was laid to rest with Selim and the boys. Never has the line between life and death been so invisible to me. Murad said he didn't have it in him to attend the burial. I told him he was wrong, but he wasn't.

In preparation for the rite that I could not, by tradition, attend, I asked Safiye to join me in cleansing the tiny corpse with rose water and binding its tiny limbs with linen from Egypt and setting him on a cushion before us as though perhaps he were not dead. She declined.

Very soon after, Murad began to take other women.

Early the following year Mehmed was circumcised.

Lie down and look up at the night sky, and you will see that heaven is no guess. It is there, figuring in a hundred million stars, five planets, and a sun in hiding. It is an incalculable measurement of marvels. *That* was how Mehmed's celebration was. Something so marvelous that—notwithstanding the destruction of the Observatory, which had meant as much to him as to anyone—he would never doubt how greatly he was prized.

The planning went on for months, and the construction itself took all spring. Craftsmen created theaters, banquet enclosures, mock holds for mock battles. They invented an impression of the Empire for our guests—a spectacle to be carried out by every artisan and guild: furriers, curriers, victuallers, spurriers, glassmakers, net makers, and feather makers.

Then the world began to appear on the hills of Thrace. The representatives of two empires, nineteen nations, and the Holy See were en route, to bear witness to Mehmed's coming of age. From the Tower of Justice, Mehmed and I watched the approaching force. Through the valley north of the Golden Horn they came from Europe; on the sea they arrived from Cairo and Mecca. And from down and up the curve of the earth, they came from Venice, just as I had a lifetime ago.

Ismihan and I thought up most of the festivities. Her best was a pantomime—an allegory about protection. It featured a winged boy, Cupid, wandering the created night of the stage unafraid of the uncertainty hinted at by lutists. A glamorous youth swung in on a rope. He beckoned Cupid with compliments and promises. Cupid resisted, though, and it enraged the villain, who seized him and shook him, causing the people in the stands to caw with disapproval. That was when a big girl with a javelin, a minion of Diana's, slid down on a wire, freed Cupid from that murderous grip, and drove the fiendish faker from the world. I loved it.

At nine in the evening on the eighth of May of last year, Safiye and I again found ourselves side by side. In a room built by Suleiman for the purpose, Mehmed was purified. Restored to health, his mother held the ceremonial tray while I proffered the implement for the unthinkable exercise.

Two days later Mehmed took his leave from his still-grieving father in the Hall of the Divan. From the Conqueror's ceremonial stepping-stone, Mehmed mounted his beloved Barbary, given him on a birthday by his uncle Sokollu Mehmed. Nilufer was dressed for the occasion, bearing on her forehead a medallion with rubies in the shape of a star—a gift from Charles V to Suleiman. The Holy Roman Emperor's motto was engraved above the star. *Plus Ultra* it said. Indeed.

When Mehmed was secure and Nilufer adjusted, Mehmed put his lips to her jowl, as he always did before they set out, and told her where they were going: the Hippodrome, where his aunts and I awaited him.

They came into view at the end of the vast oblong course and weaved their way through fire-eaters brought from Rhodes by Ismihan and a spun-sugar menagerie dreamed up by me. Wearing Suleiman's own Circumcision Day robe, Mehmed trotted among the sticky beasts, waved to well-wishers, then clambered up the stairs to our gallery and knelt before me. I wished more than anything to kiss the top of his head, but I put my hand on his shoulder instead and withdrew it before Mehmed rose, thrust his arms up like victory poles, and declared, "Here I am!"

"Indeed you are," I cheered, "and the better for all of us. Congratulations, Mehmed. Come sit." I tapped the seat beside me. "How is your father?"

"He said to me that he hoped I would build an observatory of my own someday." That was Mehmed's idea of how his father was.

"Of your own." Mehmed nodded. "Well, I am glad to hear it."

"I told him I hoped the same thing." Mehmed pointed slyly to the little sapphire that decorated his ear—a gift from his grandmother, who could barely blink back the cresting tears. He took my hand. "You will visit me in Manisa, won't you?"

"I will."

"If you came now it would be fine."

"I'll visit when you're settled." I smiled down at my knee. "What is that paw doing there?" I said to a hand the color of saracen wheat.

"It's saying thank you, Nonna."

❧

I append to this entry the most recent letter from my grandfather:

My Dearest Cecilia,

What a celebration you have put on for your grandson! And what a letter you have written your Nonno. It is very full of color and of life. You cannot imagine how much I wish to have been there.

Regarding the jewel merchant you have written about—I will look into the auction, but the gentleman should write to me himself. I will arrange to have him taken to Marco Caorlini. He is the grandson of the goldsmith who made that awful helmet for The Magnificent a very long time ago when you lived here. Do you remember? I wager it is in your own Treasury.

As for the dogs—since I am an old crow, I will say that this does not sound like you. You should have kept them. They were a gift after all. And they are dogs. I think your life is not easy, my dearest girl. I wonder if it will help if I tell you what our Nonna used to tell me. Be kinder to yourself.

Please write when you can to your old Nonno who loves you more than anything.

తు

Esther said—and I know Sumbul agreed—that I became churlish after Mehmed left for his post in Manisa. I complained about everything, apparently—Persia, Crete, the Doge's defective dogs. Well, I stand as accused. Thanks to Murad's generals and the dullard who succeeded Sokollu Mehmed, we are now mired in Persia. Our thousand-mile supply lines are cut, and we *are* losing. Crete? We have no business being in Crete! It's a Venetian possession, and our policy is peace, not expansion. And as for the animals sent by the Doge—with amends to my grandfather—I sent them back. I requested hounds, not a pair of masquerading rodents.

My temper did improve once Murad began taking fewer women. The number of concubines who passed through his chambers after the death of the baby shocked everyone. Yes, it was necessary for Murad to protect the throne with more sons. The way he has gone about it, though, is not something I would have imagined. For nearly twenty years, he was with no one but Safiye, and then suddenly he was with a new concubine—sometimes two—nearly every night. At least he followed the rules I established for his father. No one new to the harem and no one under twenty.

Safiye seemed to be able to turn a blind eye to this, or at least she didn't complain about it. Such was and is the certainty of her own son's succession. Such is Safiye's own place next to Murad—spell or no spell. She also had the sense to be absent from the capital—she went to Manisa—for the recent births of Murad's children: three boys and four girls—one of them stillborn. Had she been present, though, she would have seen Murad's lack of joy in those events. That would have been good for Safiye—seeing that.

I waited to pay my own visit to Mehmed until Safiye was back. This pleased Murad—he said so—not to have both of us away at the same time. "Who will accompany you?" he asked

"The usual entourage," I answered inanely, since I hadn't traveled in more than fifteen years.

"You shouldn't go alone," he insisted. "Take Ismihan. It will do her good."

You would think I'd invited Ismihan to heaven without dying. It reminded me that my youngest daughter is, at heart, an enthusiast. "I wonder if it will be as we remember it," she said, apparently unconcerned that it might not be. "I wonder if Paros is as *you* remembered," she added.

"No, Ismihan."

"Please?"

"It's too far. And an awful journey. No."

"It's not far from where we will be, Valide." She took my hand. "We can decide when we are in Manisa."

"I can decide," I said, giving her hand a kiss and letting it go.

As her husband used to say, she's equal parts jinn and general.

We traveled light, and not only for speed. I have tired of belongings—and not a moment too soon. Unburdened, we took the journey at a pace that made the landscape look streaked and luminous. The palisades of Bursa looked silver not black, the groves of Karesi were golden, not gray. The land before the Gediz looked like a velvet cloth that had been shaken out on the alluvial plain. A welcoming mantle, Ismihan called it.

Mehmed, a cub no more, was waiting for us. He's grown so much since he left that my cheek comes only to his shoulder, and I am tall. He carries himself as he always has, with a certain pensive energy. Ever since he was a little boy—ever since he was a baby—Mehmed has seemed on the verge of something good that was new. "I have surprises for you," he said before Ismihan and I had our feet on the ground. I thought of the bow he'd made me. I think it has never occurred to Mehmed that the ability to delight the people he loves is a gift.

The first surprise came the next morning. "It's down by the river," Mehmed explained. It is a place I had never allowed myself to go. There was no need for Mehmed to know that. And at last—this was nine weeks ago—it was time for me to do so. Mehmed put a walking staff in my hand, Ismihan took my elbow, and we set out. The bank on which the surprise was installed has a mild slope, nothing steep anywhere in view. This bend in the Gediz was safe—for me and for the pump Mehmed had had constructed and installed. His father had designed it, Mehmed explained. Yes, I remembered hearing about such a project. A letter long ago. "And he left it unfinished because he became Sultan so suddenly," Mehmed added.

Mehmed had earlier in the year sent his father drawings of the machine. I had no idea.

The second, third, and fourth surprises were saved for the following day when, walking backward in order to address us, Mehmed led his aunt and me to the far end of the palace, where suddenly he became shy. Ismihan, the most intuitive of my children, said she would see the surprises later and went off to rediscover the rooms she had grown up in. Mehmed led me down the arcade. Something made me skirt the diving dolphins that decorate the floors there. All the years I had lived in that place, I had walked heedlessly on those mosaics—they're ancient, from Smyrna. Now my alertness was heightened, and my respect. There was a vivacity to the floor and to the walls and in where they were leading.

On the west side of the palace is a new room—the second surprise. It was completed shortly before Mehmed took up his post, he told me. It had been commissioned by his father.

"Look what's here," Mehmed directed, pushing on the door.

I couldn't see anything at all. It was like emerging from a cave into the full sun. It was blinding. All I could see was the outline of the entrance. Mehmed took my arm and steered me in.

The room has eight sides, each with a tall mullioned window and a cushioned seat beneath. There is no tile work. It's all teak and brass. On each side of each window are shelves, filled with books. In the middle of the room is a large round table. I stood still, letting my eyes get used to the light. It is a library.

"It's yours," Mehmed said, bequeathing it.

"I have what I need," I said slowly, disingenuously. I was, maybe, just beginning to understand what I was looking at.

"No, Nonna. It *is*. It is *yours*. Come see."

I got limp, then taut—winded and poised. On the credenza near the door was a distinct and familiar outline. "The Dondi clock," I said.

"And everything else. The small instruments. Everything," Mehmed added. "There were so many crates, Nonna. You cannot imagine."

"No. I can't."

"And a special corps of White Eunuchs for guarding them. They had been here all that time. Since . . ."

"Yes. There was a message with the shipment. From the Sultan."

". . . two years."

"More."

He handed me the message.

My Dear Mehmed,

You are reading this. That is good. That means you are in Manisa and you are governor. You will find in these boxes the contents of the library in Galata. They were important to you, I know. Now they are yours.

There was Murad's name in purple ink.

"I think I will sit."

In fact, I wanted to lie down somewhere that wasn't in that room. I wanted to close my eyes and just think about Murad and the meanings of what he had done, and it was fortunate that I couldn't do that because it forced me to know that all that mattered was that the library exists. That the past was more behind than around us. So I sat for a while, and the roots of me reached through the cushions and floor and into the earth beneath the palace where things are held steady even as they grow. Mehmed kept a hand on my shoulder. His robe was the color of the ink, and for a moment he made me think of an iris. Mehmed walked me around the room, naming the treasures in that magic grove, as though I had never heard of them or might have forgotten.

Egnatius's library stood for my mother's plight and her teacher's acceptance. And just as bequeathing the library to me had been Egnatius's final way of honoring my mother, Murad's saving the libary for me extended that honor farther still. The shockingly sudden urge to get to Murad so I could tell him about the facts of my birth made it difficult to think or breathe. I *must* tell Murad this, I thought anxiously. As soon as Ismihan and I are back.

"I have another surprise for you, dear Valide," Mehmed said. "Are you ready?" He was walking me outside toward what to him was the best news of all. Seated on a small carpet on the flowering ground was a girl of about Mehmed's age and an older woman, a teacher. The girl appeared ready to give birth. She was learning to read, Mehmed explained. "If the baby is a boy, we should be on our way to the capital next month," he said with a wink. He knew about Suleiman having summoned him—and his father—as infants. He knew my views on the matter. I told him he should make the journey when the baby was strong and eating on his own, not before. And that whenever that happened to be, it would give great pleasure to his father and his mother. I did not need to say—and to no one more than this grandmother.

"It would please my mother if Leila stays here," Mehmed said with a nod to the beautiful girl.

"I understand. She is lovely, Mehmed. I would like to meet her. After her lesson." My thoughts turned for a moment to Safiye, to her demands and trials; then to my mother, who would have stood in relation to Safiye as I did to Leila. I knew that my mother would have seen Safiye in her entirety. My mother would have guided me, and I could not bear to think that I might not be able to guide myself the same way.

Ismihan and I stayed a week. Mehmed asked if I would stay—really stay—and manage the Palace for him. He said it would help him, and I had no doubt that it would have. But I'm too old to manage a household such as his in Manisa. It doesn't matter that Topkapi is a hundred times larger, or that its staff is five hundred times more, and I'm not exaggerating.

I can manage Topkapi in a way I could never manage Manisa because a real system is at work here now. It puts my mind at rest just to walk through the place. Or it did. When I could still walk.

Ismihan and I took our leave quickly. I embraced Mehmed. Then I embraced Leila—as much as her body would allow. No, more than that. And I felt through our fabrics the shape of the dynasty to come. There was no time for silence. No time for not knowing what was right and necessary. I kissed Leila's cheek, hardly a customary gesture, and I told Mehmed I wished him to walk me to my conveyance. I did not make a speech. I just said that it was important to understand that as the Sultan's designated heir his brothers' lives—not their deaths but their lives—were his responsibility. Mehmed took my hand, put it nearly to his lips, and said that he understood.

I did not look back as Manisa dwindled and the road blew up around us in a scarf of dust. "It's not going to be what we think," Ismihan said of where we were headed. I told her that nothing was. We were both wrong.

☙

I'd argued with Ismihan in Manisa about going to Paros. "It's where you're from," she said. "You have to go."

And so we set sail from Eski Focha. It's the closest harbor to Manisa by a hundred miles or I wouldn't have gone there. A galleon was anchored at the mouth of a harbor, famous for its depth, prosperity, and alum. It had been my father's first anchorage in the Empire. I had no wish to linger there—accepting of him as I strive—or think I strive—to be. The library had nearly done me in. I could not cast off quickly enough. With the whinny of shrouds, the flapping of linen, then the snap of sails getting full and taut, we were on our way.

How different it felt to be moved once again by wind on water, instead of by muscle on land. I had forgotten so much of what I had known about the sea, that it looks like mica, smells young, and can feel murderous. An hour out of Eski Focha, I was on it once again, riding my childhood dream-monster back home.

I meant to be on deck when we made landfall, but I didn't wake up till a sudden thrust of jibing. There was Paros before me. Its name one minute and itself the next. Approaching no more. Real at last. Vigla peninsula, whipped up and fair. Agios Ionnis chalky lee of its curve. There was the wharf and gantry, the merchants' berths, the steps to nowhere slick with seaweed. Iron cleats big as bales, ropes around them thick as arms. The castle. The fanning sky, the nets and bait, the industry. Everything the same. The things, their size and meaning. Not as I might have recalled them, but as they were, and are. All protected from the scrape of memory. Like the child I'd been, I thought God had, after all, stopped time to avenge my being taken away.

Ismihan thought I possessed some special strength. I let her go ahead of me so she wouldn't see how wrong she was. The knees that could barely bend. The feet that didn't feel the plank.

The Duke of Naxos was waiting for us with an embarassing retinue. Freeing myself of it as best I could, I pointed Ismihan toward the castle that had been my home. The wharf side of the structure was locked and sound, but through the small, unboarded window of the entrance I could see that the harbor side was gone. Water was smashing against the foundation in layers of foam that swept across the terrace, into the building and back out.

"Vacant for forty-five years," the Duke let us know, "since Barbarossa himself liberated the island from Venice—along with . . ." and he listed the islands and ports Barbarossa had taken before "liberating" ours.

I requested donkeys, drivers, and provisions for the day. Then I asked the Duke to leave us on our own. "Kefalos,"

Ismihan commanded the driver in her soft, strong voice, and soon I was on the plain I'd last crossed bound and blindfolded. As Kefalos grew from a spot on a hilltop to a fortress in the distance I got knotted inside. I looked to the west toward the quarry, then south to Lefkes, where Sylvana had built her little house, and I was alarmed to find myself where I was. For a moment, I didn't know how I'd gotten there. Ismihan was watching all this. "Perhaps we will skip Kefalos," she said. "I'd rather not climb. Let's go to the Church with All the Doors. Then tomorrow, the quarry." These were not suggestions. "*Parikia*," she called out to the driver. "Is that how you say it?"

I nodded.

"Parikia," she called out again, settling herself onto blankets embroidered with fish.

In the narthex of the Church of the Hundred Doors is a shocking depiction of the sin of Envy. It was one of the few things about Paros I had told Ismihan—and very long ago. "Where's the frieze," she whispered, gawking at the structure, the Crucifix, the effigies and altar. She'd never been inside a church.

I took her to the ghoulish wall. Ismihan stared at the two men falling through frieze space. It was the architect of that very church, Isidorus of Miletus, and his teacher, Anthemios of Tralles, the architect of Hagia Sophia. Anthemios had come all the way from Byzantium to Paros more than a thousand years ago to see his pupil's work, and the boy's talent was more than he could bear. So the master had lured him to that very gallery in the Church of the Hundred Doors and pushed his student over the railing—sixty feet above the place where Ismihan and I stood—but the boy held on to his teacher for his dear life, and the two had gone down in a killing embrace. Ismihan knew the tale by heart.

"But it's a picture of *here*,'" she said peering.

"Indeed it is," I said, taking its awfulness in as though for the first time. "You remember everything," I added, hoping that wasn't true.

"No, I don't," she said and wandered toward the altar.

"Ismihan," I whispered, "It's time we leave."

"I'm coming," she said over her shoulder.

I faced the open entry, squinted, felt the cold of the inside on my cheeks and the heat from outside on my forehead, and I stepped into the sunlight . . . onto the bright white marble steps . . . into the garden where there would be a well, if I recalled correctly—yes, there it was . . . and an olive tree from ancient times, yes . . . and a low wall. Sylvana used to sit me down on that wall before mass—to prepare me with prayers of her own. She did not believe in penance for children, but she wanted to make sure I loved God. She had no difficulty bending rules—penance is a sacrament, after all—as long as it was good for me.

Ismihan's hand was on my shoulder. I said, "I'd like to leave here now," and she took my arm without a word. "Lefkes," I told the driver. "I want to see what became of her house."

Ismihan said, "I know you do."

The scent of statice was thick on the plains, and so was the scent of kalathropos—Good Man. I've never seen it anywhere else. It's a simple stalk with furry buds that Sylvana used to dry and soak in oil. They were flower wicks. Good Man burned every night at my bedside beneath the Virgin's gaze. The last sound I heard before Sylvana's kiss and my mother's was the striking match, and in the morning the flame was always there.

Sylvana's was one of only a few houses left on Lefkes. It was still surrounded by bougainvillea and still well kept, for which I thanked God. "I'll stay here," Ismihan said. "You go."

The windows were open, the front door ajar, and once inside, I saw the back door was open to the garden behind. Hibiscus everywhere. A hundred shades of pink and red. On a stool, shelling beans, an old woman in a purple wool skirt.

Old, straight toes peeking from under its folds. Old, strong hands folded in a lap that once was mine.

"It is you," I said.

Sylvana squinted.

"Can you see me?" I said.

She tilted her head.

I came close. "You are Sylvana."

"I am." I knelt down by her. Her hands shook in fast, tiny trembles. She held them out. I put my face between them.

"How are you here?"

"How are *you* here?" she said in her old voice.

"You didn't die."

"You didn't. You are the same." Her thumb, rough as a road, swept under my eye collecting tears that were heavy and joined, no space between them.

"Do you know . . ."

"Shhh."

". . . where I've been . . ."

"Shhh."

With my head on Sylvana's shoulder and her hand on my cheek, my mind was quiet. I was nowhere else but there, and I had no questions.

We stayed for nearly a week. Ismihan took boat rides with fishermen and marble rides with quarrymen. She went out on her own up and down and across the island. "She is an explorer," Sylvana said. I had been merely surefooted.

Sylvana and I stayed at home. We sat beneath the arbor and spoke of many things. Over the days I told her about Ismihan's and my family, about Mehmed, Matrakci, Esther. About the people who had helped and taught me. About Safiye, about the Observatory and that it had come down. Some of these were long talks. Some were brief. The day Sylvana asked me to hitch a cart and take us to Kefalos I declined. "I understand," she said. "That is why we are going." She and Ismihan could have been mother and daughter.

At Kefalos, we didn't make the climb to the castle. Instead, we descended to the shore. Sylvana steered us toward a whale-like rock. She got herself down on its big, smooth back and made her skirt a tent over her knees. Naxos was visible. I told her about Nasi, its onetime Duke. The advantage he'd taken of Selim. About how good Selim was; how very good.

"You are the image of your mother," Sylvana said, as though in reply. "Old as you are."

"I thought I did not look like her."

"You do. Tell me why the observatory was destroyed."

I had not said that it had been. A swath of stones was rattling with the outgoing tide. "I know why we're here," I said. "You want me to see where I was taken from. To end the memory."

"Why was it destroyed?"

"Why?" I didn't know what to say. "To hurt me." Then I said, "It is not frightening to be here, Sylvana, or to remember. They took me, and I became one of them. Now I am with you, and I am still the person I have become. Look how clear Naxos is."

"Why? Look at me."

I moved only my eyes. "I ordered the death of my son's half brothers."

Sylvana did not flinch or stir, and I think that took great effort. "Why?"

Why.

"There is a law." I cited it swiftly. Emphasized order, preservation of the dynasty, prevention of civil war.

"I asked you why."

"To protect Murad. To spare him. To *free* him."

Sylvana said—and not warmly, "You had a choice."

Yes. I did.

All I could get out was, "Suleiman."

"What about him?"

"It was his command."

"I said, What about him?"

"He saved my life, Sylvana. He gave me everything. Teachers, Selim, everything. He was good to me." I put my hand up to block the light. There she was as she'd been a thousand times before. Never has the truth seemed so meager. "It was the only thing he asked of me."

"It was *everything*, Cecilia. A terrible thing."

"Is it always like this?" I could barely breathe. "Do you always have to *do* the worst thing to know it is the worst?"

"No. But this time, it is like this. And you understand why."

This did not mean, *Do you understand why?* It did not mean, *I command you to understand why.* It meant, *I know you understand why.* With great effort, Sylvana got up from the rock.

"This stops with you, Cecilia."

"Yes."

"You reverse that law." Sylvana took my hand; pulled me up. She is nearly ninety. "You make a new law."

"I will."

She would not let go. "And you must think for yourself. *Always.* When you were twelve and came back here you thought for yourself."

"What do you mean?"

"You chose not to speak about what your grandfather told you before you left."

"What do you *mean*?"

"You said you had something to tell me. But you didn't tell it."

"Why do you remember that?"

"Because it was important. What were you going to tell me?"

"You mean about my parents?"

"Yes."

"That they weren't married to each other."

319

"Is that all?" She hesitated. "Capritta. Did your grandfather tell you that your father was married to someone else?"

"How did you know that?"

I felt the world stop against the force of all the minutes of my life, from the moment I had been delivered from the womb of my mother into the hands of my father's wife, to the moment in which she and I were facing each other, knowing everything there was to know.

"It's all right, Capritta."

"So that means when my father came that time—with the invitation—he was *your* husband." Sylvana nodded. "And the son—the boy that died—was *yours*. And you never told me? *You* were the one my father was always leaving. Did my mother know who you were? Who you *are*?"

"No. She did not."

Now here is something very strange. I felt no panic, no nausea, no confusion. I felt only one thing and it was complete emptiness—the only time I have ever felt it.

"I was saving something to tell you as well. When you came back. A birthday present. When you were twelve. The two of us keeping important things in abeyance." Such a strange word for her to have known. Sylvana did not know how to read. Have I said that? Sylvana did not know how to read.

The purple skirt had a pocket. She held out a little scroll. No tube. No parchment. Something made of paper that was old. "What is it?" As if I couldn't see. Or read.

It was a single sheet. On top, as I unrolled it, was the deeply embossed and elaborately illuminated Great Seal of the Venetian Republic. "Read it. Out loud."

By the powers vested in me by the Republic of Venice, and for good cause shown, the undersigned, lawful Governor of the Island of Paros, hereby grants the verified application of Sylvana Zantani Veniero to adopt Cecilia Baffo Veniero as her child with the same mutual rights and privileges between them as would prevail were Cecilia the natural child of Sylvana including, without any limitation, Cecilia's right of inheritance from Sylvana and to Sylvana's obligation to provide Cecilia with a reasonable and adequate dowry. May the Lord's blessing shine upon them.

Signed and Sealed this eleventh day of August, 1537

Francesco Sommaripa Veniero, Governor

_____x_____for Sylvana Zantani Veniero

Sylvana said, "I know laws matter."

"What is this?"

"You are the one who can read!" she said with a big, true, and unsettling laugh.

"You adopted me."

"I was going to tell you—with a celebration."

"I don't understand."

"You don't understand what?"

"How you could have been as you were—with Mamma and me."

"We had a great deal in common," she said.

"And you adopted me." I squeezed her hand. In that slight exertion there was a return to myself. A bringing into the present of what had been let go. "I was yours."

"Yes. You were. You have many years ahead of you," Sylvana said. "And you are free." She offered her elbow. I replied with mine. She took it, and we headed to the cart and back across the plains.

Monday, December 5

Dearest Nonno,

I have news to make you happy. There is a new generation of our family. My grandson Mehmed is a father. I never thought I would live so long. I never thought I would wish to.

I await your own news, and I send love,

As always,

Cecilia–Nurbanu

My dearest Cecilia–Nurbanu,

It is not bad to be old! (only hard to hold this pen!)

96 for me and 58 for you!

Such wonderful news!

Tell your grandson he will receive a parcel via Baffo shipment to Eski Focha.

Your mother's maps. In celebration!

That and more from

Your Nonno who loves you more than anything.

NB What is my great-great-grandson's name?

❧

Do not ever think you've seen the end of human kindness. People will surprise you till the very last. The least likely will step forth and hold out a hand.

Look at Safiye. I had her visit shortly after I returned, and I found a changed woman. There was an aura of acceptance about her, and it was no illusion.

I invited her to join me over a meal. I had inquired about her preferences and was told she disliked lamb, vegetables, fish, and foods derived from milk. That left raisins, pudding, and cake, and so on many gold trays were arrayed baked and boiled sweets. Safiye reviewed the choices, pointed to the pumpkin in syrup, then knelt down in a way that reminded me of Matrakci—bone by bone. I congratulated her on the birth of her grandson, born while Ismihan and I were on Paros. She said nothing. I extended my hand. "How are Ayshe and Fatma." Her daughters.

"Thank you." Words I'd never heard her utter. "They are well." Carefully she drew back her veil. "The older one misses the Sultan—who is in Edirne."

"Yes. So I am told." I had sought to see him the day I returned.

I said, "Ismihan and I had a fine visit with Mehmed. He is an admirable governor."

Nothing.

"And the palace is well changed. The library."

Nothing.

"We were happy to meet Mehmed's favorite."

"I am pleased," Safiye answered finally. "I chose her." Something I had not known. She moved her spoon in circles through the pudding.

I reached behind the hassock and produced a small but heavy leather parcel. "I want to give you this. It is from Mehmed. To celebrate your becoming a grandmother."

She put the bowl down on the patch of floor inside where

323

her legs were crossed, took the bag, and opened it. She held up the little armillary sphere. It was made of gold. Perfectly conceived, joined, engraved.

"He made it," I said. "Your son descends from a long line of very fine goldsmiths." I had Suleiman in mind.

"I do not think my son's talent has to do with that," Safiye said with her calm, familiar awkwardness. "It is very good," she added, looking up from the instrument—not at me but directly past me, where a mirror hung.

"You know, Safiye, your son is a great credit to the dynasty."

"Ah." Her jaw went out to one side. She placed a hand on her neck, holding it in place.

"You must be very proud."

"I am. I would like like some juice. Apricot."

"Of course." I waved to a eunuch. "I have just had a remarkable journey. After Manisa, I visited my birthplace." I paused. "I saw places and people I hadn't seen for a very long time."

"They have changed," Safiye said. There was no indication whether this was a question or claim.

"In fact, they haven't. It is calm there. It allowed me to reflect. I have thought especially about something that concerns you."

"Ah."

"As you know there is a law."

"Of fratricide." She missed nothing.

"Yes. That is right. Promulgated by Mehmed the Conqueror. You know why—of course."

"Yes."

"Yes, well, we see now that its purpose—that order—can be achieved by other means. There is no call for killing brothers. Anymore." Every word and element the opposite of Suleiman's command.

"We see?"

"Do not misunderstand me, Safiye. Mehmed will succeed

his father. You have raised a wonderful son. But that law is not necessary. It is not a credit to the dynasty."

"What other means?"

"That has not been determined. But it will be. You will be of help with this. You can help Mehmed very much."

"Yes," she said, looking down at what Mehmed had fashioned for her.

"So," I paused, thinking that might be enough for the time being, "I would like to show you my mosque in Scutari one day soon. I understand you have never been there."

"That is right."

"Well then, you will see what a special place it is. Sinan could design something similar for you." Safiye looked at me quizzically. "It would be another way of making your mark."

"Another?"

"You have made a great one already with Mehmed."

"Ah," Safiye said once more, that time as though she'd not received the answer she expected. She pulled her knees up to her chest, and rocked gently. She sipped her juice, rose and asked to be excused. Then, cupping Mehmed's present as though it were something that might fly away, she left.

Three days later she was back. Unbidden, unannounced, radiant. "I have something for you, as well," she said, waiting in the doorway for permission to advance.

I invited her in. Waved away a roomful of attendants. "Have a seat." I patted the cushion next to me. "You look wonderful." I was noting the gleam and color in her cheeks. An unusual brocade sack hung from her shoulder.

Safiye reached into the bag and withdrew a bulky pouch. She held it out as though her hands were a tray. "Please." She smiled, extending her arms farther. I took the pouch. It was made of ribbed yellow silk. "A way to thank you—for everything."

"How very kind, Safiye."

"For bringing to me the present from my son Mehmed.

Also for being present when my son Ismail was born. And for helping prepare him."

Prepare. "Ismail?" I said, taking the offering. "You named him."

"Ismail. Yes," she said, sliding her palms down the sides of her robe as if to cleanse them. "I did not know that anyone held a baby the way that you did," she said.

"You mean . . ."

". . . bouncing . . . the hip . . ."

"Yes, well . . ." I wondered why she was recalling this now. "Holding a new baby can lead you to do things you've forgotten, or don't quite expect."

"You took your slippers off, I remember."

"Yes. I suppose I did. My feet often hurt." I lifted the hem of my robe. There they were, ten bony outposts pointing in ten directions. I was entrusting Safiye with the knowledge of the deformity. "I've gotten used to it—the discomfort," I said redistributing my robe, then untying the cord, "but not to the way they look." I reached into the pouch. "It's of no importance, though." I withdrew the oblong object—a gold case, with a pearl latch. Inside the case, the item was wrapped again—in silk decorated with five astonishing circles of different sizes, outlined in rubies, sapphires, emeralds, diamonds, and turquoise. "Gracious."

"The planets," Safiye explained. She'd lifted one foot to scratch her ankle beneath her robe.

I held the thing closer to better see the jewels. "It is extraordinary." My fingers noticed a pattern on the other side—a circle the size of a baby's fist sewn in yellow diamonds. "Heavens. The sun."

"That's right. But the gift is inside."

"Well, shall I open this now?"

A coiled intensity caused her to sit unnaturally straight. "You are welcome," Safiye said.

The bag was cinched with a gold cord. I worked my fingers

into the puckered closure, wiggled the cord loose, and looked inside. There was a pair of slippers such as I've never seen. No rungs, no heels. Just pillowed soles and three silk straps. The long ones wrap around my ankles for balance. They're the first shoes I've ever had that didn't hurt.

"They are delightful, Safiye," I said, fitting one of my new slippers over my hand and admiring its inventiveness.

"I had a pair made for myself. My feet also hurt," she said, lifting the hem of her own robe to reveal not the young feet I'd seen in those first soleless shoes, but a set of imperfect toes vying for space in her own slippers, just as she said, identical to mine.

"So they do," I said, captivated by the display. I leaned back into the cushions, holding my slippers in my lap, staring at her feet. "This is very kind of you."

"You are welcome," she said again.

Seated, Safiye held her toes as though to warm them and said that she had spoken to Sinan about a mosque and would speak to the Sultan about it when he returns, but in the meantime had chosen a site, a prominent one, on the Golden Horn shore of Seraglio Point. She told me, too, that she was planning to visit Mehmed again—to see his new son. She asked about the different ways of getting to Manisa, and just before she left she asked if perhaps I'd like to make the journey with her, an invitation I surprised myself by accepting.

More surprising—and touching—was the attention Safiye showed me in the days that followed, bringing me trinkets and a fur blanket and another pair of padded slippers in another silver case, but this time, thank goodness, with fewer jewels on the silk pouch. I think Esther was even more surprised by these gestures than I. But then I have just had my heart forcibly extended by Murad's gift—and I do believe that whatever I have yet to know or learn in this life it will be in light of what I have learned about my family.

And then, shortly after—what was it? two days? three?—

the fever began and the bleeding under the nails and all the rest of it, and Hamon confined me to my bed, and Esther instructed me to to make sense of what has happened in my life and what I have done. "Understand it." Esther's command: Write it down. See it.

And so I have. I believe I have written the map of my life.

Tuesday, December 6

Hamon has ended my confinement—and not because I am better. I'm down to blood and bone. He has simply—finally—ruled out plague. In other words, my illness is not contagious.

I can have visitors!

The first, thank God, was Murad. How I have been longing to see him—to tell him how my mind has cleared. To tell him what saving the library means to me. And I have a present for him. The little map on goatskin I did with Matrakci. I will have Esther find it for me. I think it will please him. But he is a wreck himself. I barely recognized him. He's become so drawn and rutted and stooped. He was frantic, and he, too, seemed half-dead from waiting. I couldn't bear to see him that way—especially on my account. He got back from Edirne days ago, and Hamon wouldn't let him near me. After all the seasons of anger and absence have finally led us to such good ground, and here I am sick, and Murad's been barred from visiting. Well, that is over now. We are close again, and that is how it will stay.

We had trouble speaking—both of us. I held his hands very tight and kissed them. All I said was *the library.* He understands. For three years he understood what it would mean—when I finally found out. A magnificent reserve.

He told me he had heard from Mehmed already about

Ismihan's and my visit, and how happy Mehmed is—about everything, which is the way Mehmed is. And Murad knew from Ismihan that we went to Paros. He knew about Sylvana—that we had found each other by chance and spent days together. I hesitated to bring up the law then—everything was so calm, at last, and I thought of waiting till he comes to see me again tomorrow, but then I thought, no. Better to say it today. The law must be changed. I tried to say it in a way that didn't sound like a command, but Murad was receptive. More than receptive. He said, "That is *right*." And when I said *right away*, he said "Yes, right away." Given Safiye's commitment to keeping the law, this is quite a surprise—and relief.

But then he began tugging at what is left of his eyebrows, and he seemed confused, and he said "Where did this come from?" He was talking about my sickness, and he was waving to the room as though it contained the answer or the cause. He noticed my pens—the ones he made me—by my bed here, and if it is possible to smile with just one's eyes, that's what he did, and then he wound the point of his sleeve around his fingers and tapped at the edge of my mouth and at the blood going down my chin. It is coming from far back in my throat now, and from the cracks in the soles of my feet. I took his hand, drifted to sleep, and when I woke he told me Mehmed is on his way from Manisa—he is only a day away—and that he is bringing his son so that I may meet him. The baby's name is Mahmud.

There were things I was going to mention to him—things that have come up these past days, but I think I didn't have the energy. I tried to sit up, but I couldn't, and Murad put his hand under my head, and he kissed the eye I can't keep open, and I guess I went to sleep again because I've just waked up and he is gone.

Wednesday, December 7

Hamon has just come. It was a short visit. He had to collect himself before he left.

He was accompanied by a medicine man from Cairo. Also old, also a Jew. He said he sent for him when my feet turned black. The expert examined my soles, my nails, then he widened my bloody eyes with his little fingers, and he put his long nose to the nape of my neck in order to smell it. He said something in Hebrew that caused Hamon's chin to drop to his chest. "Where are your shoes?" was all he said. I pointed to the cupboard.

And so it is poison after all. The slippers. The ones in the sun-and-moon pouch—and the other slippers that came later. All of them soaked in arsenic.

And now Safiye has come, and she has gone. She, too, looked different. All her youth is gone. Such old eyes that gazed at my feet. Safiye's face is to beauty as a corpse is to life. And there was a sour smell on her, vomit.

I told her Hamon has found poison in my slippers. That an expert from Egypt has confirmed it. And here is what she said: "*I* confirm it. And I will have another child before leaves are on the trees, and it will be a son. And you will not hold *him*. You will not *live* to hold him. Or to harm him." Such an outpouring.

Should I have protested? I didn't. Safiye will believe what she wishes. But her sons keep dying because she long ago bore all the healthy children she can. Hamon told me that many years ago. It is no wonder Safiye looks as she does—she is carrying another baby's death within her.

So Safiye believes Murad's sons—born and unborn—won't be safe until *I* am gone. She thinks the law will protect whatever sons she bears. She is wrong about that. None of Murad's sons—not by her or anyone else—will be safe until fratricide is over. The safeguard of our dynasty is life, not death. Invention, not war. Murad will change the law. He promised. He will imagine a new way to keep order. That is Murad's strength.

✦

I hoped to see, and I have. It does not surprise me that it would happen just as my vision is going. Bloodshot in my eyes. It's a world gone red, then black, then white. I accept this. I do. Less world, more light. I'm released by truth that has pushed past memory to the present. I can see. I can say what I see. I know doom. This is not it. I'm doing nothing more than die. I will save Murad's sons. And if I don't live to see those yet to come, I'll see the one who is the world to me and who is only a day away.

HISTORICAL AFTERWORD

SOURCES

ACKNOWLEDGMENTS

Historical Afterword

Valide Sultan Nurbanu died on December 7, 1583. In her will, she specified that all her slaves be freed. Sultan Murad III ordered that his mother be buried next to his father, Selim II, in his tomb within the walls of Hagia Sophia—the first time a manumitted slave was laid to rest beside a sultan. The practice of fratricide did not end with Nurbanu. Nineteen small coffins followed that of Murad III, when his son, Mehmed III, took the throne in 1595. Nor was the law abolished, ever. The executions of Mehmed's half brothers were, however, the last case of mass fratricide in the House of Osman. Mehmed was known as Adli, the Just.

It is not known who gave the order to kill Mehmed's many half brothers, but a reasonable inference that it was not Mehmed himself can be drawn from his decision to protect his own sons—at least from one another—by keeping them inside Topkapi Palace for his entire reign.

This sequestration was formalized into a system called *Kafes*, or "the cage," and it marked the beginning of lasting changes in Ottoman succession, in the quality of princely pretenders, and in the might of the Ottoman Empire. That it coincided with the rise in female dynastic power should not be misconstrued. Nurbanu had transformed the harem not into a "sultanate of women" intended to undermine male rule, as often alleged, but into a political institution designed to uphold and shield that rule—especially as the sultans after Suleiman succumbed one after the other to apathy and fear. Like the system that preceded it, the cage aimed to contain rivalries among princes and it succeeded in perpetuating the dynasty. It did this at the expense, though, of princes whose lives were drastically contained and of royal mothers whose chances to improve anything at all shrank from a spectrum to a point. The specific misery of the next twenty generations suggests that the highest level of misfortune may indeed not have been death.

Sources

BOOKS

Neal Acherson, *Black Sea* (New York: Farrar Straus & Giroux, 1995).

A. D. Alderson, *The Structure of the Ottoman Dynasty* (Oxford: Clarendon Press, 1950).

Metin And, *Istanbul in the Sixteenth Century: The City, the Palace, Daily Life* (Istanbul: Akbank, 1994).

———, *Turkish Miniature Painting: The Ottoman Period* (Istanbul: Dost Publications, 1974).

R. C. Anderson, *Naval Wars in the Levant* (Princeton: Princeton University Press, 1952).

Francis Bacon, *The Essays* (London: Penguin Classics, 1985).

Fernand Braudel, *The Mediterranean and the Mediterranean World in the Age of Philip II*, vol. II (New York: Harper & Row, 1973).

L. W. B. Brockliss and J. H. Elliott, eds., *The World of the Favourite* (New Haven: Yale University Press, 1999).

Patricia Fortini Brown, *The Renaissance in Venice* (London: Everyman Art Library, 1997).

David Buisseret, ed., *Monarchs, Ministers and Maps: The Emergence of Cartography as a Tool of Government in Early Modern Europe* (Chicago: University of Chicago Press, 1987).

Filiz Cagman and Engin Yenal, eds. Topkapi: *The Palace of Felicity* (Istanbul, Ertug and Koluk).

Carla Coco and Flora Manzonetto, *Gli ambasciatori veneti:*
Storia e caratteristiche dell'ambasciata veneta a Constantinopoli (Venezia: Stamperia di Venezia, 1985).

Dizionario Biographico degli Italiani, vol. 5 (Treccani), pages 161–63.

Kate Fleet, *European and Islamic Trade in the Early Ottoman State: The Merchants of Genoa and Turkey* (Cambridge: Cambridge University Press, 1999).

Edward Seymour Forster, *The Turkish Letters of Ogier Ghislelin de Busbecq: Imperial Ambassador at Constantinople* 1554–1562, trans. from the Latin of the Exzevir Edition of 1633 (Oxford: Clarendon Press, 1968).

Charles Frazee, *Catholics & Sultans: The Church and the Ottoman Empire* (New York: Cambridge University Press, 1983).

E. J. W. Gibb, *A History of Ottoman Poetry*, vol. 3, ed. Edward G. Browne (London: Luzac & Co., 1904).

Daniel Goffman, *Izmir and the Levantine World 1550–1650.* Publications on the Near East (Seattle: University of Washington Press, 1990).

Anthony Grafton, *Cardano's Cosmos: The Worlds and Works of a Renaissance Astrologer* (Cambridge, MA: Harvard University Press, 1999).

Alain Grosrichard, *The Sultan's Court* (London: Verso, 1990).

Talat S. Halman, *Soliman le magnifique poete* (Istanbul: Dost Yayinlari, 1989).

P. D. A. Harvey, *Medieval Maps* (London: The British Library, 1991).

Ahmad Y. al-Hassan and Donald R. Hill, *Islamic Technology: An Illustrated History* (Cambridge: Cambridge University Press, 1986).

Halil Inalcik, *An Economic and Social History of the Ottoman Empire*, vol. 1, 1300–1600 (Cambridge: Cambridge University Press, 1994).

———, *The Ottoman Empire* (London: Weidenfeld & Nicolson, 1994).

Peter Kemp, ed., The Oxford Companion to Ships and the Sea (London: Oxford University Press, 1988).

Lord Kinross, *The Ottoman Centuries: The Rise and Fall of the Turkish Empire* (New York: Morrow Quill, 1977).

O. Kurz, *European Clocks and Watches in the Near East* (London: The Warburg Institute, University of London, 1975).

Vladimir Lamansky, *Secrets d'Etat de Venise,* vol. 2 (New York: Burt Franklin, 1968).

Harold Lamb, *Suleiman the Magnificent: Sultan of the East* (New York: Bantam Books, 1954).

Bernard Lewis, *The Arabs in History* (New York: Harper Torchbooks, 1966).

———, *Cultures in Conflict: Christians, Muslims and Jews in the Age of Discovery* (Oxford: Oxford University Press, 1995).

———, *Islam and the West* (Oxford: Oxford University Press, 1993).

———, *Islam in History* (Chicago: Open Court Publishing Company, 1993).

———, *Istanbul and the Civilization of the Ottoman Empire* (Norman and London: University of Oklahoma Press, 1963).

———, *The Middle East: A Brief History of the Last 2000 Years* (New York: Scribner, 1996).

———, *A Middle East Mosaic* (New York: Random House, 2000).

———, *The Multiple Identities of the Middle East* (New York: Schocken Book, 1998).

———, *The Political Language of Islam* (Chicago: University of Chicago Press, 1988).

———, *Semites and Anti-Semites* (New York: W. W. Norton, 1986).

Bernard Lewis, ed., *The World of Islam: Faith, People, Culture* (London: Thames and Hudson, 1992).

Giulio Lorenzetti, *Venice and Its Lagoon* (Trieste; Edizioni Lint, 1994).

William Manchester, *A World Lit Only by Fire: The Medieval Mind and the Renaissance* (New York: Little, Brown and Company, 1992).

Robert Mantran, *La vie quotidienne a Constantionople au temps de soliman le magnifique* (Paris: Hachette, 1965).

Philip Mansel, *Constantinople: City of the World's Desire 1453–1924* (London: Penguin Books, 1997).

Rhoads Murphey, *Ottoman Warfare 1500–1700* (New Brunswick, NJ: Rutgers University Press, 1999).

Gulru Necipoglu, *Architecture, Ceremonial, and Power: The Topkapi Palace in the Fifteenth and Sixteenth Centuries* (Cambridge, MA: MIT Press, 1991).

Nicolas de Nicolay, *Dans l'Empire de Soliman le Magnifique* (Paris: Presses du CNRS, 1989).

John Julius Norwich, *A History of Venice* (New York: Vintage Books, 1989).

John P. O'Neill, ed., *The Islamic World* (New York: The Metropolitan Museum of Art, 1987).

Arnold Pacey, *Technology in World Civilization* (Cambridge, MA: MIT Press, 1996).

Leslie P. Peirce, *The Imperial Harem: Women and Sovereignty in the Ottoman Empire* (Oxford: Oxford University Press, 1993).

N. M. Penzer, *The Harem* (London: Spring Books, 1965).

Ptolemy, *Tetrabiblos,* transl. F. E. Robbins (Cambridge, MA: Loeb Classical Library, Harvard University Press, 1990).

E. G. Richards, *Mapping Time: The Calendar and Its History* (Oxford; Oxford University Press, 1998).

Piri Re'is, *Kitab—I Bahriye,* vols. 1–4 (Ankara: Ministry of Culture and Tourism of Turkish Republic, The Historical Research Foundation, Istanbul Research Center, 1988).

J. M. Roberts, *The Penguin History of the World* (London: Penguin, 1992).

Cecil Roth, *The House of Nasi: Dona Gracia* (Philadelphia: The Jewish Publication Society of America, 1947).

Aydin Sayili, *The Observatory in Islam and Its Place in the General History of the Observatory* (Ankara: Turk Tarkh Kurumu Basimevi, 1960).

Rebecca Steffoff, *The British Library Companion to Maps and Mapmaking* (London: The British Library, 1995).

Henri Stierlin, *Turkey: From the Selcuks to the Ottomans* (New York: Taschen World Architecture, 1998).

Barbara Freyer Stowasser, *Women in the Qur'an, Traditions, and Interpretation* (Oxford: Oxford University Press, 1994).

Sevim Tekeli, *The Clocks in Ottoman Empire in 16th Century and Taqi al Din's "The Brightest Stars for the Construction of the Mechanical Clocks"* (Ankara: Ankara University Press, 1966).

Mustafa Sevim, *Turkiye in Gravures,* vols. 1, 2, 3 (Ankara: Istanbul Republic of Turkiye Ministry of Culture Directorate of Publications, 1996).

Kemal Silay, ed., *An Anthology of Turkish Literature* (Bloomington, IN: Indiana Turkish Studies and Turkish Ministry of Culture Joint Series 15, 1996).

Dava Sobel, *Longitude: The True Story of a Lone Genius Who Solved the Greatest Scientific Problem of His Time* (London: Penguin Books, 199).

Dominique du Tanney, *Istanbul Seen by Nasuh and the Miniatures of the Sixteenth Century* (Istanbul: Halbout Dost, Yyinlari, no date).

Norman J. W. Thrower, *Maps & Civilization: Cartography in Culture and Society* (Chicago: University of Chicago Press, 1999).

Gerard L'E Turner, *Scientific Instruments 1500–1900: An Introduction* (Berkeley: University of California Press, 1998).

Lucette Valensi, *The Birth of the Despot: Venice and the Sublime Porte* (Ithaca, NY: Cornell University Press, 1993).

EXHIBITION CATALOGS & GUIDEBOOKS

Accademia Galleries in Venice, ed. Giovanna Nepi Scire (Electa, 1998).

Correr Museum, ed. Giandomenico Romanelli (Electa, 1995).

Palace of Gold and Light: Treasures from the Topkapi (Istanbul: Palace Arts Foundation, 2001).

Paros and Antiparos (Athens: Toubi's Editions, 1998).

Portolani e carte nautiche XIV—XVIII secolo dalle Collezioni del Museo Correr Venezia (Istanbul: Museo del Topkapi, Guzel Sanatlar Matbaasi, A.S., 1994).

The Sultan's Portrait: Picturing the House of Osman, ed. Kangal, Selmin (Istanbul: Isbank, 2000).

Acknowledgments

This book, embarked on in the last century, was the idea of Bernard Lewis. His confidence that I would find Nurbanu's story between the lines of her life was a life-changing surprise and goad. To Bernard, now one hundred years old—as teacher, author, advisor and friend—go my first and enduring thanks.

Jean-Claude Vatin and Lowell Milken have also been completely present throughout the creation of this book. Each has improved the story—many times over—with perceptions I could not have imagined, and both have sustained me—truly—with their friendship.

Only imagination and kindness could have gotten Arnold Rampersad, my first reader, through that embryonic slog. For taking the book seriously at that early stage, I am deeply grateful. As the book took first shape, Richard Ford and Jeremy Treglown answered and anticipated questions as only friends as trusted as they could have done. To other early commenters—Sandy Climan, Amanda Urban, Lisa Chase, John Eastman, Lynne Fagles and Robert Loomis—also go my thanks.

While researching this book went on nearly as long as writing it, one work laid out the circumstances surrounding Nurbanu's experience with magnificent precision and clarity. Without Leslie Pierce's *The Imperial Harem* I could not have imagined

The Mapmaker's Daughter. Lisa Jardine's *Wordly Goods,* Gulru Necipoglu's *Architecture, Ceremonial and Power* and Aydin Sayili's *The Observatory in Islam* were also indispensable to my understanding of the years Nurbanu lived, places she roamed, disciplines she mastered and ground she broke.

Off-springing from this book is a true family of friends in Turkey—always there—taking me in, getting me around, over the course of years of research. Suna Aksu became the sister who, all my life, I didn't dare wish for. The Kirdars—Berna, Uner and Nezir drew me into the bosom of their huge clan—orienting and buoying me. Maureen Freeley was indispensible to the beautiful translation into Turkish by Ozge Spike. And the Honorable Ekmeleddin Ihsanoğlu—who knows as much as anyone, anywhere, about the mystery of the Istanbul Observatory, spent hours helping me understand and imagine what happened to it.

Bill vanden Heuvel, a champion in every sense, showed me where the courage is in encouragement, and he lead me to Joan Bingham who with memorable care helped me see a better shape lurking in the narrative. She, in turn, lead me to the Gernert Company where Rebecca Gardner has unfailingly championed the book, and to Martine Bellen—whiz, gem and saint rolled into one—who helped me reconstruct and rethink it—twice. In the last stages, the breath-taking faith and finesse of Lori Milken and Joseph Olshan helped turn a draft into a book, and, in this, they were perfectly complemented by designer Jonathan Lippincott and copyeditors Nancy Green and Ruth Mandel. Also, in the last phase, Stacy Schiff, Edmond White and, yet again, Arnold Rampersad, gave the great gift of their time and eagle eyes, and Princeton's Sukru Hanioglu, with supreme generosity, corrected and improved two drafts. Whatever inaccuracies or anachronisms may remain, are my responsibility alone.

C. S. Lewis says that friendship gives "value to survival". In the long seasons when I wondered if this book would see the light of day, "mere" survival was my goal, and it was true and trusted friends who made it attainable. For this I cannot sufficiently thank Catharine Buttinger, Stanley Weiss, Wendy Gimbel, Betsy and Davis Weinstock, Angelica and Neil Rudenstine, Henry Finder, Anthony Appiah, Daryll Pinkney, Dan Kurtzer, Inger Eliott, Peter Duchin, Elisabeth Sifton, Mariana Cook, Melinda Blinken, Richard Sloan, David Lilly, Susan Glimcher, Alexander Nehamas, Jean Carter, Dan Halpern, Debbie and Alan Poritz, Judy and Ed Stier, Anne Thompson, Miriam Lowi, Connie Steensma, Liz Newman, Kim Bleiman, Mitch Draizin, Phillipe de Brugere, Farhad Kazemi, Jane Opper, Lisa Rosenblum and, in a category of his own, my brother Michael Nouri. Every one of them—each in a different way—has helped me hang on over a very long time. Three particularly dear friends—Peter Benchley, Ted Sorensen and Fritz Stern—whose combined command of language and history could and will not be matched—enlivened draft after draft with their insights and steadfastness—each till the end of his life.

The presence in my life and heart of my daughters, Caitlin and Johanna, and of my grandchildren, Oliver and Audrey, has permitted me to write about the love of children and grandchildren without having to imagine it. Each of them in an essential way has been a corroborator of what has mattered most.

At the center of everything every step of the way was my husband, Robert Del Tufo. He knew each character by heart, imagined each circumstance with fidelity and with flair. Over the many years this book was in the making, he considered my every question wisely and seriously, handled my every insecurity with patience, humor and love. I do not know by what magic one person could both shield and liberate another, but in doing that for me Robert made this book possible. Wherever this story reflects love, it is mine for him, and the memory of him.